Praise for the Authors

Eden Bradley

"This riveting tale of complex relationships... Bradley's well-crafted descriptions help you to visualize the edgy and erotic scenes.... Strong characters surround the main couple, and a deftly handled subplot rounds out this amazing novel." —*Romantic Times* on *The Dark Garden*

"There are two things you can count on when you pick up a book by Eden Bradley, that you are embarking on a journey of sensuality, and that your emotions will be fully engaged." —Eva Gale, Romance Divas.com

Sydney Croft

"*Unleashing the Storm* is one of those rare reads where the characters linger long after the story ends. Intense intrigue, action, eroticism, and a fascinating world combine to create an enthralling winner. Sydney Croft is a fabulous new talent." —Cheyenne McCray

"In this action-packed, inventive tale, each character's strengths and weaknesses are more fantastic than the next. Croft redefines sizzle and spark." —*Romantic Times* on *Riding the Storm*

Stephanie Tyler

"Stephanie Tyler is a writer whose name you'd do well to remember as she writes sexy tales about sassy women and gorgeous men which hook you from the very first page and which keep you engrossed until the final full stop." —Julie Bonnello, CataNetwork

"[Tyler's] straight forward, dead-on writing style invites us to get hot and happy and bowled over by love." —Michelle Buonfiglio, Romance: Buy the Book.com

Also from the authors of

HOT NIGHTS, DARK DESIRES . . .

BOOKS BY EDEN BRADLEY

The Dark Garden

The Darker Side of Pleasure

Exotica

Forbidden Fruit (November 2008)

BOOKS BY SYDNEY CROFT

Riding the Storm

Unleashing the Storm

Seduced by the Storm (August 2008)

BOOKS BY STEPHANIE TYLER

A new trilogy coming in 2009:

Hard to Hold

Too Hot to Hold

Hold On Tight

HOT NIGHTS, DARK *Desires*

EDEN BRADLEY

SYDNEY CROFT

STEPHANIE TYLER

BANTAM BOOKS

HOT NIGHTS, DARK DESIRES
A Bantam Book/June 2008

Published by
Bantam Dell
A Division of Random House, Inc.
New York, New York

This is a work of fiction. Names, characters, places, and incidents either are the product of the author's imagination or are used fictitiously. Any resemblance to actual persons, living or dead, events, or locales is entirely coincidental.

Book design by Sarah Smith

Library of Congress Cataloging-in-Publication Data
Bradley, Eden.
Hot nights, dark desires / Eden Bradley, Sydney Croft, Stephanie Tyler.
p. cm.
ISBN 978-0-553-38517-5 (trade pbk.)
1. Erotic stories, American. 2. New Orleans (La.)—Fiction.
I. Croft, Sydney. II. Tyler, Stephanie. III. Title.

PS648.E7B73 2008
813.60803538—dc22
2008006140

Printed in the United States of America
Published simultaneously in Canada

www.bantamdell.com

BVG 10 9 8 7 6 5 4 3 2 1

ACKNOWLEDGMENTS

We would like to thank our wonderful agent, Roberta Brown—we're lucky that the three of us share her as an agent, and it's impossible to thank her enough for being the impetus behind this anthology.

We would also like to thank our brilliant editor, Shauna Summers, for believing in us and making this project happen. This was a fabulous opportunity to work together.

HOT NIGHTS, DARK DESIRES

THE ART *of* DESIRE

EDEN BRADLEY

CHAPTER *One*

"Did you hear me, Sophie? I'm getting my new tattoo today and I want you to come with me."

Sophie pulled in a breath, trying to concentrate on her friend's words over the sharp buzz of desire running through her system. *Tattoo*. That word, the mere idea, had always had this effect on her. And once more, she hated that she wasn't ever brave enough to indulge her secret yearning.

She shifted her weight, the old wood floor of Crystal's apartment creaking beneath her. "Sorry, Crystal. I was . . . thinking about something. Why isn't Boone going with you?"

"He had a last-minute gig come up, a studio job, so he packed his drumsticks and took off. Anyway, he spent the night last night, and if he came with me he'd want to stay again. If I let him stay too often, he'll begin to think he owns me. You know how I hate that."

Sophie rolled her eyes and laughed.

"I don't want to go alone, Sophie; say you'll come with me." Crystal turned around on the old, wobbly piano bench that sat in front of her baby grand, where she'd been playing and singing when Sophie had knocked on her door. "Hey, you're not afraid, are you? I know the whole tattoo thing freaks some people out."

"No, I'm not afraid. I mean, I guess I am, but it's because . . ."

Sophie stopped herself. How much to tell? She'd only known Crystal for three months, since she'd moved into the apartment upstairs. She certainly couldn't tell her new friend that she had such an intense attraction to the idea of tattoos, of being tattooed, that it bordered on obsession. That even thinking about it caused her entire body to surge with an unexplainable, searing lust.

She looked out through the French doors behind Crystal's piano, through the paned glass with its peeling white paint, to the small enclosed courtyard with its overgrown greenery, the profusion of flowers whose perfume fought against the smell of mold and decaying plaster in the air.

This place was like something out of a dingy, perverse dream: old pink stucco that was literally falling down at the corners, every window graced with the intricate black ironwork New Orleans French Quarter architecture was famous for, the wide-plank wood floors countless generations had walked over before her. Sophie had loved the place immediately. And she and Crystal had taken to each other right away, too. But she had to pay attention to what Crystal was saying.

"Because why, Sophie?" Her friend's exotic, turquoise eyes were trained on her.

Sophie shrugged, trying to dispel the knot forming in her

stomach. Trying to make this all less important. "I've always had a sort of fascination with tattoos," she admitted. "I've always wanted to get one. You have no idea how badly."

"Then why don't you? I don't get it."

"God, Crystal, I can't!"

"Why not? You're a writer, Sophie. It's not like you have to clock in at an office, wear a suit every day. Or, God forbid, panty hose. And with the stuff you write, all those ghosts and vampires, people probably expect you to be a little eccentric anyway. So, why not?"

Yes, why not, indeed? She tugged on her dark, waist-length brown hair, twisting a strand around her fingers. Maybe because the rules her strict Italian-Catholic parents had ingrained into her ran far too deep for her to ever completely escape? Maybe because, despite the fact that she'd escaped their house, she could never quite get away from what they'd taught her about who she was, and what she should be.

She hated that no matter how far she'd run—and she'd spent most of her life since the age of eighteen running, all over the country—they still had a hold on her. She'd never managed to shake the sound of their voices in her head.

Why can't you be more like your brother?

Maybe because her brother, that uptight, sanctimonious snob, was a priest.

Crystal snapped her fingers in front of Sophie's face. "Hey, where are you?"

"Sorry." Sophie shook her head. "This tattoo thing is . . . an issue for me. A huge issue, if you want to know the truth."

"Yeah, I can see that." Crystal flipped one of her thick, dark braids over her shoulder and leaned back, resting her elbow on the keys of the piano, and a small clash of chords sounded. "I think you should do it. You obviously want to. And if something is holding you back, then maybe the only way to ever face down that issue is just to go for it."

"You're probably right."

Just the idea was sending tremors over her skin, making her warm all over. She could never tell Crystal the real reason why she was so afraid of being tattooed: She was afraid she would love it too much.

Crystal leaned forward and put a hand on Sophie's arm. "Look, why don't you just come with me and see? This artist is a friend of Boone's. I've seen some of his work and he's really good. It can't hurt to sit and watch me, right?"

"I suppose not." She took in another breath as her pulse fluttered with excitement. Crystal was right; there was no harm in watching. And to be that close to the process, to see it happen . . . irresistible. "When is your appointment?"

Crystal glanced at her watch. "In about twenty minutes. The shop is just down on Canal Street, but we should get going. I let Boone take my car, so we'll have to walk."

Her heart skittered in her chest. "Now?"

"Yes, now." Crystal laughed as she stood up. "Come on, Sophie. I don't want to be late."

They walked down their little street that was really nothing more than a cobblestone alley, onto Dauphine and turned right, headed toward Canal Street. The air was damp and close around them, but Sophie liked it, enjoyed the feel of it soft on her skin.

They passed the crumbling buildings, the lovely old architecture a beautiful combination of French, Spanish and Caribbean influences. Sophie loved the look of the French Quarter: the colors, even the decay caused by the constant heaviness of the tropical air. Many of these places were literally falling apart at the seams. Small piles of plaster lay at the corners of the buildings, the red brick underneath showing through. No one bothered to clean it up. And everywhere vines clung to the walls, climbed the iron balconies, trailed across the tiled roofs, in brilliant shades of green in between the flowers. New Orleans was pure magic to her. Dark magic, to be sure. The first place she'd found that felt like home.

Crystal took her hand as they walked, humming a tune.

"Is that a new song?" Sophie asked her.

"Yeah, Boone and I were working on it late last night. Sex always inspires me."

"Crystal!"

"What?" Crystal turned to her, smiling, a wicked gleam in the tilt of her blue eyes. The sooty black eyeliner she always wore made them stand out against her pale complexion. "What could possibly be more inspirational than sex? That feel of skin against skin, that buildup, and then—"

"Okay! That's more than I need to know about your sex life." Sophie shook her head. "Tell me about the tattoo you want to get."

"Well, you've seen the little Cheshire cat on my ankle. He's cute, and I love him, but I wanted something more meaningful this time. So I went to talk to Tristan Batiste—he's the artist—and he helped me figure out the design. It'll be two koi fish, arched around each other like a yin-yang symbol, with their fins sort of fanning out. And they'll be in black and white, which is Tristan's specialty. I love the idea of the image being all about contrast. It seems symbolic of the yin yang. Opposites, you know?"

"Yes, light and dark. Balance."

"Exactly."

Crystal swung their clasped hands as they walked, turning left down Canal Street. They passed colorful cafés, funky used-clothing stores, antiques shops. And everywhere, people lined the sidewalks. It was mostly locals here, the wealthy old New Orleans gentry as well as the more bohemian younger crowd.

"Here it is." Crystal stopped in front of a storefront with a blue neon sign in the window that spelled out "Beneath the Skin." The glass was painted in classic Japanese style: tsunami waves; cranes flying against a backdrop of snow-capped mountains; warrior gods with frightening faces, brandishing swords.

"Wow. This is beautiful." Sophie reached out to lay her fingertips against the cool glass. "Did he do all this?"

"Tristan? Yeah. He owns the shop. Come on, wait until you see what he can do on skin."

On skin. Yes...

Just thinking about it made her shiver with anticipation. She followed Crystal into the shop.

Inside, the cool air washed over her, raising goose flesh on her skin for a moment before her body adjusted. Music played, a hard-driving rock song. Godsmack, she thought. She looked around curiously. She'd never actually been inside a tattoo parlor before. The first thing she noticed was the enormous carved desk to her right, a beautiful Asian piece. A tall, skinny man with fully tattooed arms stood behind it, bent over an appointment book.

Crystal approached him. "Hi. I'm here to see Tristan."

"Sure. I'll get him."

He came around the desk and disappeared behind a heavy gold velvet curtain. Sophie and Crystal sat on a wooden bench against one wall to wait.

Sophie's heart was pounding as though she were the one about to be tattooed. She glanced at Crystal, who was humming her new song again, as calm as though she were there to get a massage.

"Aren't you nervous, Crys?"

"Why should I be? I've done this before. It doesn't really hurt much, you know. God, you're pale, Sophie." Crystal laughed, taking her hand and giving it a squeeze. "Maybe you'll relax when you see how hot Tristan is."

"Hey, Crystal."

Sophie looked up to find a man coming through the curtain. He was tall and broad; a football player's physique outlined by his fitted black T-shirt and worn jeans. His head was nearly shaved, just a layer of dark stubble showing against his skin. Square features, partially covered by a dark, close-cut goatee. But the most striking thing about him was his eyes. They were a dark shade of gray, like smoke. Striking. Intense.

Sophie blinked, letting her gaze fall to the dragons tattooed in coils of black, red and gold around both arms. The work was exquisite, she saw right away. But that wasn't the only reason why her entire body was lighting up with need.

Calm down.

She had to tear her gaze away, to look instead at the samurai swords that decorated the wall behind the desk. To catch her thready breath.

But then Crystal was standing up, pulling Sophie with her. "Hi, Tristan. This is my friend Sophie Fiore. She's going to sit with me today."

"No problem. Hey there, Sophie."

Deep voice, with a beautiful accent; a little of the South mixed in with that exotic European inflection so many people in New Orleans spoke with. And oh, God, he was holding his hand out to her. She couldn't very well refuse to take it. His fingers wrapped around hers, warm and strong. Her knees went weak.

Pull yourself together!

But he was still hanging on to her hand, making it hard to think. And he was looking at her, a small smile on his strong mouth. Too beautiful, this man. She tried to smile back, to behave normally.

"It's nice to meet you, Tristan."

"Very," he murmured, staring at her a moment too long. Then, "Let's get started."

He released her hand and she had to pull in a deep breath of the air-conditioned air to cool her system, to clear her head. She felt as though she'd just been slammed in the chest by a wall of heat.

And pure desire.

Was it this man? Was it being here, in this place? Was it the sheer ecstasy and fright of being so close to her most secret and powerful fantasy?

But she had to follow Crystal through the curtain, which Tristan held aside for them. As she passed, she caught a faint whiff of his scent, something dark and fresh at the same time. Like the deepest part of a forest.

God, she must be losing her mind.

Behind the curtain were six workstations; some with leather chairs, some with long padded tables, all of the furniture covered in black, making a strong contrast to the red-painted walls. Two of the stations were in use. To her left, a short, stocky woman with a shock of spiky white-blond hair was bent over a man lying on one of the tables, a humming tattoo gun in one gloved hand, a white cloth in the other. To her right, the tall man they'd first seen out front was talking with a female client, showing her drawings of what Sophie assumed were tattoo designs.

Her pulse was racing.

Tristan led them to the largest workstation, one that spanned the width of the back of the room. There was another padded table, and one of the big chairs. It reminded her of a dentist's chair, everything adjustable. And, she noticed, everything was spotlessly clean.

"Climb on up, Crystal." Tristan patted the table and Crystal sat down on the edge while he pulled out a drawer in a metal cabinet built into one wall. "I have your design here. Take one last look and make sure it's right."

Crystal took a translucent piece of paper from him, smiled, then passed it to Sophie. "It's perfect. What do you think?"

Sophie nodded, and handed the paper back to her friend. "Yes, it's beautiful." But she'd hardly glanced at it. She was too shaken up inside. Trying too hard not to look at Tristan.

"Sophie, why don't you take a seat here?" Tristan laid a hand on the back of the big chair.

Too good, to sit in that chair. Too close to her fantasy. She trembled a little as she slipped into the seat.

Crystal was unbuttoning her army green cargo pants and pulling her white tank top up around her waist, settling onto her stomach on the table. Tristan leaned over her, wiped the skin at the small of her back with a white cloth. Sophie watched as he took the transfer paper and laid it at the base of Crystal's spine, then smoothed his hand over it. Then he carefully pulled the paper away, leaving an imprint of the design on Crystal's skin.

All Sophie could think was, *It's going to start now.*

Her heart was hammering harder and harder as she watched Tristan pull on a pair of latex gloves, check his equipment. The intensity of his expression as he bent over her friend, the tattoo gun buzzing in his big hand, was almost too much for her, but she couldn't look away. And when he touched the needle to Crystal's skin, Sophie jumped inside as though it were her own. Shock filtered through her in waves. And lust stabbed through her like a lovely, hot knife.

God.

She never knew she would respond this way to simply watching this. She shifted in her seat, trying to ease the ache that had started between her thighs.

It only got worse—or better, depending on how one looked at it—as she watched Tristan work. The muscles in his forearms flexed as he worked the ink into Crystal's flesh, and Sophie saw the dusky golden tone of his skin beneath his tattoos.

She took the opportunity to really look at him, letting her gaze wander over his features. He truly did have an incredible face. Beautiful, yet thoroughly male at the same time. An aquiline nose, a strong jaw. And his voice was deep and husky, rolling over her like whiskey each time he spoke.

"I'm done with the outline, Crystal. Now for the shading. How are you doing?"

"I'm a little sore, but it's fine."

"We'll take a break for a minute." Tristan looked at Sophie, his gun poised. "And what about you?"

His dark gray gaze on her was too intense, too piercing. She didn't know what to say.

Crystal spoke up. "Sophie's always wanted to get a tattoo."

"Really?" His brows raised a fraction of an inch, making his eyes seem even more penetrating.

"Yes." Her voice was barely a whisper. She swallowed, hard.

"Do you know what you'd want, Sophie? What sort of design?"

She nodded. This was something she'd thought about for years. "I like . . . the Kanji symbol for *create*."

"She's a writer," Crystal interjected. "She's just sold her first book. She'll be published soon."

"An artist, then." Tristan nodded. "What do you write?"

"Paranormal. Ghost stories, vampires. Dark stuff."

"Ah, you're in the perfect place, then, New Orleans."

"Yes, it is. I've been going to the old cemeteries. They're so beautiful." She let out a nervous laugh. "That must sound strange to you."

"Not at all." He smiled, his teeth a strong flash of white that sent a warm chill down her spine. "A true artist can find beauty in anything. Everything. But some things are, by nature, more beautiful than others."

He paused, his eyes locked on hers. What was he saying, implying? She was going hot all over.

He went on. "I've done a lot of sketches at the cemeteries myself, the Cities of the Dead, we call them. Some headstone tracings. Saint Roch is my favorite. I love the starkness there, the statuary, the gray-and-white stones. It's a shadow place."

"I haven't been there yet. I've only been in New Orleans for a few months."

"Ah, well, it's not to be missed."

Still hard to talk, with him looking at her like that, with her pulse racing at a thousand miles an hour. Why did his gaze on her feel like a caress? And that he understood her fascination with the graveyards! Was she imagining this sense of connection?

He glanced back at Crystal, lying quietly on the table still. "Are you ready to begin again?"

"Yep. Let's finish it. I can't wait to see how it looks."

He dipped his tattoo gun in a small pot of ink, leaned over Crystal and began once more. The electric hum of the equipment seemed to resonate deep in Sophie's body, in her breasts, between her thighs. She couldn't look away as he moved over Crystal's skin, the needle pushing the ink into her flesh.

She wanted to do it. She'd wanted to for as long as she

could remember. And to have Tristan be the one to do this to her for the first time . . . the idea of it was too good. But could she really do it?

Hell, she was never going to be what her family wanted her to be. That had been perfectly clear for a long time. She hadn't even talked to any of them in months. She'd gotten tired of the constant recriminations. Why did she still allow herself to be manipulated by them? This was her body, her life. They didn't like that she was a common fiction writer either. Useless, they called her career. And her mother was convinced she'd been influenced by the devil, simply because of her subject matter.

Sophie knew it was ridiculous. So why did she let what they wanted hold her back from what she wanted for herself?

As she watched Tristan fill in the shading on the gorgeously drawn koi fish, she became more and more convinced that if she were ever going to do it, to get tattooed, he *must* be the one. And frankly, the idea of this man putting his hands on her was irresistible. Almost frightening how overwhelming her attraction to him was.

"Okay, you're all done," Tristan announced, giving Crystal's skin one final wipe with his white cloth. "Go take a look in the mirror."

He helped Crystal to sit up, steadied her with a hand on her arm as she stood. A gentleman, Sophie thought vaguely. Nice.

Crystal stood before the full-length mirror on one wall, looking over her shoulder. "Oh, I love it. It's exactly what I wanted! Sophie, you really should get one."

Tristan turned his penetrating gaze on her once more. Yes, exactly like smoke, those eyes. "Well? What do you think, Sophie? Are you ready?"

"What? Now?"

"I have an open schedule today. It could be now. Or

another day. It's up to you. But I'd be honored to work on you. To be your first."

He grinned at her and she felt her cheeks go hot. The question was not whether she wanted to do this, but could she? She wanted to, with her entire being. All but that censorious voice in her head that was becoming more and more faint by the minute.

Crystal was still admiring her new tattoo in front of the mirror. "You should go for it, Sophie. You know you want to. And Tristan's the best."

Oh, she wanted to. Her heart skipped a beat as certainty washed through her, making her go weak all over. Yet strong on the inside somehow. There was strength in choosing her own path. She'd come to understand that in the last few years. Or, she'd thought she had. Maybe this was that last step she had to take before she was truly free?

She looked at Tristan, right into those impossibly dark eyes of his that seemed to see through her.

She nodded her head, beginning to shake inside with nerves and heat and yearning. "I'm ready."

CHAPTER Two

What was wrong with him? Tristan nodded to her, this ethereal creature, whose delicate features made him want to touch her face, just to lay his fingertips against her smooth skin.

Sophie.

He wanted to tattoo her. So badly he could hardly trust his own judgment.

Had he pushed her too hard? But no, he could tell by the flush on her skin, by the excited glimmer in her eyes, that she wanted to do this.

Such beautiful eyes. They were gold and green all at once. Innocent eyes, yet there was something of shadow in their depths. He was a man with shadows too. He could understand that hint of the dark in her.

You are too much the artist. Calm down. She's just a pretty girl.

But he'd known the moment he laid eyes on her she was more than that.

He pulled in a deep breath and picked up a roll of paper towels, the spray bottle of alcohol, and began to wipe down his workstation.

"Why don't we talk about the tattoo you want," he suggested. Yes, talk business. Get his head straightened out. But it was his business to touch her skin, to mark her.

"Well, I've always thought it would look good on the back of my shoulder."

He nodded. He couldn't have done it if she'd wanted it on her belly, the small of her back, someplace more intimate. "And do you have any ideas about size? Color?"

"I'm not sure. Something small, but not too small. I want it to... to mean something, to have some significance. Do you know what I mean?"

"Yes." He did, he knew exactly. Nothing too small, nothing to be entirely hidden. That would defeat the purpose. He loved the way her mind worked. "And color?"

She shook her head, that silky dark hair swinging. Christ, it nearly reached her waist. What would she look like naked, with only that hair against her pale, translucent skin?

Get ahold of yourself, man.

"I don't think I want any color in it," she said. "What do you think?"

"I prefer to work in black and white, in grayscale. I like to use light and shadow, rather than color. There's something more stark about it to me. More spiritual. More true."

Her eyes met his. They were absolutely glittering. He knew she understood exactly what he was trying to say. "Yes, that's just what I want."

"Give me a minute to draw up the design, then."

He turned to the light box behind him, pulled a piece of the opaque transfer paper they used at the shop to draw their designs on, and went to work. It took only a few moments. He cut the paper down and turned back to Sophie and Crystal. He'd nearly forgotten Crystal was there.

He really had to pull himself together.

He held the paper out to Sophie. "Here, what do you think?"

She smiled, nodded. "Yes. It's perfect."

"We'll start, then."

He stood and pulled a Japanese shoji screen around his work area for privacy, then turned to Sophie once more. "You'll have to take your shirt off."

Why did that feel dirty coming out of his mouth? He worked on half-nude women all the time. But there was definitely something sexual about it now, with her. He expected her to blush, to stammer, but she simply nodded and pulled her T-shirt over her head. Beneath was a white cotton bra. Nothing overtly sexy, nothing over the top, yet seeing the rounded swell of her breasts beneath the plain cotton went through him like a shock. Arousal, keen and raw, vibrated in his veins.

Calm down.

"I need you to turn and sit sideways in the chair. Yes, that's it. And lean forward a little. Good. Perfect."

Yes, perfect, her naked back.

He sat on the stool, commanded his body to calm while he pulled on a fresh pair of gloves and set up his tray: checked his tattoo gun, changed needles, filled the small ink pot with black ink.

He wiped her skin with alcohol, then laid the transfer paper on the right spot, at the top of her left shoulder blade, trying to ignore the fact that he was touching her. Skin like fucking silk. He pulled the paper off.

"Do you want to take a look before I begin?" he asked her.

"No. Just do it."

There was a tremor in her voice, but it wasn't fear, he could tell. She was excited. He could feel it coming off her in waves, like heat. Like scent. Like some chemical in the air.

He leaned in and held the needle over her skin. "I'm going to begin now."

She could barely believe she was there, that she was about to get her first tattoo. That it was this man, Tristan, who was going to do it.

Her entire body was flooded with heat. With lust. There was no denying it. It had been hard to take her shirt off only because she wanted to take everything off, to lay naked on Tristan's table, to have him use his tattoo gun all over her body. To have him touch her.

She was soaking wet, trembling with desire, and he hadn't even begun yet.

When he started the gun, the tiny engine whirring to life, a stab of need went through her in a blazing rush. She closed her eyes, pulled in a deep breath.

She'd always known she would love this, being tattooed. But her imagination had never brought her here, to this level of exquisite anticipation as she waited for the first touch of the needle.

She had never dreamed of a man like Tristan Batiste.

She'd never bothered to wonder who would tattoo her; for her it was all about simply getting the tattoo. This was a thousand times better.

"It might hurt a little, but not too much." His voice was deep, smooth, like the Southern Comfort Crystal had taught her to drink. That little bit of fragrant sweetness along with the edge.

She knew she would welcome the pain. But as he touched her skin with the tattoo gun for the first time, there was no pain. Rather, a heavy buzzing sensation that quivered into her skin, down through the layers. Deeper, and deeper still, invading her body. Goose bumps raised on her flesh, her nipples went hard beneath the soft cotton of her bra, and the sensation ended in an ache between her thighs. She almost moaned aloud.

The ache grew as the needle moved over her skin, and time faded away. She closed her eyes, breathed it in: the faint scent of ink in the air, the male scent of him. She breathed in the sensation itself.

"How are you, Sophie?" he asked after a few minutes. "Are you okay?"

She nodded. "Yes. Fine. I'm fine."

"Hey, since you're handling, Sophie, I'm just going out to get a Coke from the liquor store a few doors down," Crystal said. "I'll bring one for each of you, too. Be right back."

Tristan really went to work then, the needle gliding over her flesh, every stroke spearing into her body, making her hotter and hotter. Her sex gave a squeeze, and she shifted forward just a little, so that the seam of her jeans rubbed against her mound. And had to bite back a moan once more. And at every moment she was keenly aware that it was *him* sitting only inches behind her, that he was doing this to her.

It took everything she had not to arch her back, to squirm, to pant. And when he laid a few fingertips against her skin as he worked, another jolt of pleasure rocketed through her.

"It might hurt now, as I fill it in and do the shading. I'll need to trace over a few times in some areas. Okay?"

"Yes." The word came out on a soft hiss.

She felt the needle bite a little deeper as her sensitized skin grew sore. But she loved it, loved the sensation. She drew in a deep breath, and could swear she smelled the heat of Tristan's body behind her: dark, like New Orleans itself, and all male.

The gun buzzed on her flesh, pleasure washing over her skin, arrowing deep inside her. Her sex was on fire, aching with need. She shifted, the seam of her jeans pressing against her swollen clit. And each moment she grew wetter, hardly believing her own response. Desire rose in her, crested, as he traced the lines over and over, the ink pushing into her skin. Her sex throbbed, harder and harder.

"I'm almost done."

No!

But he kept working. She could sense the heat of him, could almost feel that heat invade her body as the needle hummed through her. Her sex squeezed.

Yes, don't stop now. Don't stop.

"Nearly there," he said, his voice deep, full of smoke.

Oh, yes. Nearly there . . .

His voice, the nearness of him, the buzzing thrum of the needle on her skin, it was all too good. Pleasure built, her sex filled, swelled, until she couldn't hold back any longer. She came, hard jolts of pleasure shafting through her sex, through her body. Her fingers dug into the arm of the chair as she tried to control her shaking. She bit her lip, but a small sigh escaped her. And the warm wave of pleasure quivered deep inside. Finally, it eased, and she pulled in a steadying breath.

God, had he known what had just happened to her? Did she even know what had just happened to her?

"It's finished."

She could swear she heard the raw edge of desire in his voice. Or was it only her overheated imagination?

He wiped down her skin with a wet cloth, and she pulled in a deep breath, smelled the sharp, acrid scent of rubbing alcohol. If only it was his bare hand on her flesh.

He stopped and she turned to him. His gray eyes were dark, hazy. His mouth was soft. Yes, desire on his face. He caught her gaze and held it, and there seemed to pass between them some silent communication. The message was simple, clear: *I want you.*

"Hey, are you all done?"

Crystal came back into the screened-off work area and handed Sophie a can of Coke, then set another on a table for Tristan. Sophie bent her head to open it, needing the time to cool down. "Thanks," she murmured.

"Let's see." Crystal moved around behind her. "Wow, it looks awesome."

Tristan put a small hand mirror in Sophie's hand. "Here, go take a look."

She moved to where a long mirror was mounted on the wall, held the smaller mirror up so she could see behind her.

"Oh." Her breath came out of her in a rush. She was tingling all over. "It's beautiful. Perfect."

When she looked up Tristan had a smile on his face, a small, crooked smile. There was an unexpected dimple in his right cheek. She shivered inside, her legs weak.

"Yes. Beautiful." He paused a moment, locking gazes with her once more, and again she felt that shocking jolt of chemistry, of connectedness.

Impossible.

Or was it? She was feeling these things, this intensity.

Could he feel some of it too? But she was too shaken to know. All she knew was that she wanted to do it again. To see him again. But Tristan and the tattoo and the shocking orgasm were all jumbled together in her head. Desire and guilt, over the tattoo, over coming like that. Desire won.

Yes, see him again. Yes, yes.

"Come back in a week so I can check it and see how it's healing. Both you girls."

Sophie nodded. "I will. We will." She glanced at Crystal, who cocked an eyebrow at her, before turning back to Tristan. "Thank you."

If only he had any idea of the gratitude flooding her body, absolutely flooding her, like a warm tide. She almost wanted to sink to her knees, kiss his clever hands.

Oh, yes, on my knees . . .

That didn't even begin to describe the things she wanted to do with this man. God, she'd better get out of there before she did something really foolish.

More foolish than quietly coming in the man's chair?

She started to shake her head, caught herself and stopped. She had to get a grip. Had to think.

"You ready to go, Sophie?" Crystal turned expectant blue eyes on her. They really were turquoise, like the Caribbean Ocean.

"Sure. Yeah."

"You might want to put your T-shirt back on." Crystal gave her a grin as she tossed Sophie's shirt at her. Sophie pulled it over her head, smoothed her hair.

Tristan was already beginning to clean up his work area. But he'd never taken his eyes off her.

"Come back," he said, his voice quiet.

"I will. In a week, as you said."

He nodded. Crystal pulled on her arm. "Come on. I paid for both of us when I went to get our drinks, so we're all done. And I got the instruction sheet so you'll know how to take care of your tattoo while it's healing."

Sophie nodded once more. She knew she wasn't yet capable of putting an entire sentence together. Luckily Crystal could usually keep up enough conversation for two.

"Bye." She gave Tristan a small, ineffectual wave, let Crystal half drag her out of there.

Outside, the heat and the humidity curled around her skin like a caress. Lovely.

The door to the shop closed behind them with a small rattle. As soon as it did Crystal turned to her.

"Jesus, Sophie, what was that all about?"

"What was... what?"

"That was crazy in there! The way you two looked at each other. And when he was working on you... shit. I've seen Boone get a bunch of his tattoos. Other people. But I've never seen anything like that."

"Like what?"

She wasn't just playing innocent. She really wanted to know. She'd been too much in her own head, her own body, to know what had really happened.

"It was like you two were in your own universe. When he was tattooing you, it was like he was... like he was making love to your skin. Jesus!"

Sophie smiled, turned her head a bit to hide it. She was quiet as they walked, back past the shops and cafés, the small galleries. The scent of New Orleans was all around her, that scent of decay and flowers, garlic and strong chicory coffee.

"So?" Crystal prompted, more quietly this time. "What was that? What happened to you back there?"

"I don't know. It was... it was amazing." Sophie stopped, pulled on her friend's arm. "I want to do it again."

Crystal looked at her, her dark brows drawn together.

"Getting this tattoo really affected you, didn't it? I mean, you weren't kidding when you told me how big a deal it was going to be for you. Should I be sorry I pushed you into this?"

"What? No. And you didn't push. Well, maybe a little nudge. But I'm fine. It's fine. I'm glad I did it." Her blood was pumping through her veins, fast and hot. "Except, how do you know how to stop?"

Crystal shook her head and grinned. "You are in deep, girlfriend. One tattoo and you're obsessed."

"Oh, I was obsessed long before now," Sophie muttered as they began to walk again.

Crystal was quiet for another two blocks. Then, "So, what is it? What about it made you so . . . whatever you were? Hot. Right? Because you looked pretty damn heated up to me."

"Yeah . . ."

What was it? Had she ever really questioned it before? She'd simply accepted this strange fascination. But she'd never understood how far that fascination went until today. Not until that climax had rocked her body, her mind.

"I think it started when I was a kid. And I mean ten or eleven. I had this neighbor, Jenna, and she had an older brother. He was maybe five, six years older than we were. He rode a motorcycle, had this long, dark hair. A real bad boy. I remember when he got his first tattoo. He couldn't have been any older than sixteen. My parents used to say he was no good, that kid. But I thought he was beautiful. My first sexual fantasies were about him. Rory."

"He sounds hot."

"He was. One of those tall guys, kind of thin and wiry. I used to watch him when he worked on his bike in the driveway. Every summer he'd get more tattoos. He had full sleeves by the time he turned eighteen and left home. The artwork wasn't even very good, looking back. Biker stuff. Skulls, daggers and roses, that kind of thing. But it didn't matter. He was exotic to me. And the more my parents and my brother put him down, the more attractive he became."

"So that was it? Your first crush was an older guy with tattoos?"

Sophie shrugged, walked a little faster.

Crystal caught up with her. "Hey. What else?"

She took a minute before answering. "I lost my virginity to him."

"Wow. How old were you?"

"Fifteen."

That old mixture of lust and shame rushed through her, making her hot all over. So good. So bad. Irresistible. And yet she still paid for it.

Getting the tattoo today had been even better.

And even worse.

She had a sudden urge to go to confession. And just as strong was the urge to go back to Tristan, to have him tattoo her again. To fuck him.

God, she was messed up.

"So what happened?" Crystal asked.

"He must have been twenty, twenty-one by then. It only happened once, which was okay. He'd been my fantasy for so long."

"And how was it?"

Sophie turned to her friend and smiled. "To this day, it was the best sex I've ever had."

Crystal grinned. "You slut!"

Sophie laughed. "Yeah."

They linked arms and walked the last block laughing together.

But the image of Tristan, the burn of the new tattoo on her skin, didn't leave Sophie's mind for a moment.

Oh, yes, she was going back. She would get more tattoos. She'd meant what she'd said. No matter what it meant for her to do it. It was too late now, anyway. She already knew she'd burn in hell. She may as well make it a roaring bonfire.

CHAPTER Three

She was on her knees, the stone floor biting into her bones, hard and cold. Hands on her shoulders, raising her to her feet. The rough fabric of her tunic rubbed harshly against her skin, her bare feet numb as she followed a long line of girls. All she could see was their feet, row upon row of bare legs, numbed toes. She knew she was meant to keep her head bowed, an act of respect, of contrition, of humility.

Into a large room, the floors and walls all the same gray stone. She was told to stand still while they raised an enormous pair of gleaming scissors and cut off her hair. It fell in soft hanks to the floor; she heard the whisper of it as it hit the stone.

Yes, the necessary sacrifice, washing me clean.

Her head felt cold and bare. Vulnerable. Empty. But she would be pure, finally.

Moving down the long hall again, and into the chapel itself, row upon row, down between the long wooden pews. The scent of incense in the air. She glanced to the right, and they were there, smiling at her. Her parents, her brother. Proud, finally.

Yes, wash me clean.

She followed the others and knelt before the altar. Hard, icy stone beneath her knees once more.

Pray for redemption.

Pressing her hands together, she asked for mercy, asked to believe. Her tunic shifted, slipped off her shoulder.

"Whore!"

Shame washed over her, hot and seething. She lifted a hand to cover the tattoo, felt the ink-raised skin beneath her fingers, but it was too late.

"Yes," she whispered.

Lust surged through her body. Lust and shame and fear.

Then, turning to look behind her, she saw her brother, wearing a self-satisfied smirk. Her parents were next to him, expressions of absolute horror on their faces.

She wanted to get up, to run, but the cold stone beneath her knees kept her frozen there. Trapped. Until she began to sink right into it, through it. Down and down and down . . .

Sophie bolted upright, the dark night like a blanket around her, smothering and hot. She reached to turn on the bedside lamp, her fingers slippery on the tiny knob. Finally, it worked. A dim amber glow illuminated her small bedroom.

"Just a dream," she murmured. But her hand went to the raised skin on the back of her shoulder.

Desire pulsed in her body simply from the light touch of her own fingertips. Simply knowing it was there. That she had done it. That Tristan had done this to her. Too good, yes. And so bad.

Why was she so fucked up?

She got up and went to the paned windows overlooking the tiny courtyard, moved the old lace curtains aside. Two stories below her, she could see by the blue-washed moonlight the small stone fountain burbling, the ancient, worn angel in the center covered with dark moss. That angel had always looked to her like the angels on headstones in a graveyard. The tiny, overgrown courtyard was what she'd first fallen in love with about this place, why she'd decided immediately to live here.

The fountain, the angel, were shadowed now, only that faint glow from the moon and the stars overhead making them visible. She loved the way it looked; that mysterious play of light and dark.

What had Tristan said about that? Something about light and shadow. About the old graveyards being a shadow place.

She shivered, remembering his smoky voice. Remembering his touch. Between her thighs a low pulsing began, fevered, insistent. She touched her fingertips to the smooth glass of the window. So cool beneath her heated skin.

She peered down into the garden, into the darkness, the shadows. If she tried hard enough, she could imagine him standing there, on the uneven paving stones, the fallen petals of the crepe myrtle crushed beneath his heavy black boots. Oh, yes, he'd worn those black boots she loved so much. Those boots alone were enough to draw her to him. But it only started there.

Tristan had one of those faces that spoke of absolute masculinity. That strong jaw, carved features, those dark gray eyes, like two pieces of smoky quartz. And that impossibly lush mouth set against his evil-looking goatee. What would it be like to kiss a man like him? To kiss that lovely mouth?

Her own lips twitched, and she bit down, hard, onto her lower lip, needing that little bit of pain somehow.

He was enormous, well over six feet tall, and built like a solid wall of muscle, dwarfing her. And yet his touch was gentle, delicate, even.

A hot shiver ran through her, and she squeezed her thighs together at the ache that lay heavy between them. She let out a sigh, spread her palm against the cool glass, needing to draw it in, to calm the lust raging in her system. It didn't help.

All she could see was his face, those incredible eyes, the way he'd looked at her, *into* her. She couldn't get the scent of him, of the ink, out of her mind. When she let her eyes flutter closed, she could feel again the buzz of the tattoo gun on her skin.

Yes, so good...

Her hand went to the hem of the cotton tank top she slept in, her fingers creeping under the edge, smoothing over her naked skin to cup her breast. She brushed her nipple, and it came up hard beneath her touch.

Yes.

She slipped her hand down, lower, beneath the band of the cotton panties she wore. She brushed at her curls, slid two fingers over her damp cleft. Hot and slippery and aching with need. Her own hand working between her legs became his hand in her mind as she pressed against her clit, circled it, then paused to dip inside.

She leaned into the window, her legs growing weak. Moving faster, rubbing, pinching, plunging, she opened her eyes, looked out into the garden of shadows below her, and came. Shuddering with the pleasure that shafted deep inside her, curling and twisting through her system.

The window glass was cold now against her skin, cold yet lovely. The heat in her body was retreating finally as the last trembling surges moved through her. She took a step back, her gaze still on the darkness below.

"Who are you, Tristan Batiste?" she whispered. "And what have you done to me?"

The next few days went by in a blur. She tried to write, but was constantly distracted by small noises outside, by the muffled sounds of other people in the building, by her own wandering thoughts.

She sat at the tiny wrought-iron table in her kitchen, her laptop open and waiting. She'd been working on this story since she'd first arrived in New Orleans, a dark story of haunted houses, of old mysteries, of sensuality. She'd come to this city, inspired by the lush and decadent beauty of the place, knowing she could write here. And she had. She'd written like mad every day. Until she met Tristan. Until she'd gotten the tattoo that burned on her shoulder in a way that was somehow different from any mere physical sensation. There was no actual pain, and yet she was acutely aware of it every waking moment.

She wanted to do it again, as she'd told Crystal. She wanted to be tattooed everywhere. Always. Strange and ridiculous thoughts, but she could barely think about anything else. Just the tattoos, and *him*. Tristan.

She got up and opened her refrigerator, poured herself a glass of the sweet Southern tea she'd come to love. She drank it quickly, the cold tea giving her a rush of pain in her head as she sat down in front of her computer again. Setting her fingers on the keyboard, she tried to clear her mind, to concentrate on the task before her. But her characters seemed vague to her, the story meandering and dull. Only a few days ago she'd loved this story, been excited about it. But now, nothing.

She couldn't stand to be there any longer, to sit in her apartment, alone in the serene, sunlit kitchen she normally loved. The old white tiles, her refrigerator covered in art she'd cut from magazines and band posters, postcards she'd collected in her travels, everything warm and familiar, and yet suddenly she couldn't bear it.

Standing, she went into the bedroom and slipped off the loose cotton pajamas she always wore when she was writing, and exchanged them for a pair of jeans that sat low on her hips and a tight vintage T-shirt in black, the Ramones logo in white lettering across the front. She added a small pair of silver hoop earrings, picked up the ornate silver cross she always wore in some perverse act of contrition, and slipped the long chain over her head. Grabbing her purse, she slid her feet into her favorite sandals, then pulled on the rickety front door. It stuck, as usual, and she had to lift it a little and pull hard before it swung open.

Down the stairs, through the papery scent of damp plaster and the countless people who had passed by these walls that lingered there: someone's perfume, stale cigarette smoke. Then she was out on the sidewalk. She didn't want to think too much about where she was going, or why, as she made her way down Dauphine and headed toward Canal Street.

It was a quiet day. The sky was gray with clouds, even though the air was warm and damp, as always, and soft on her skin. The walking itself felt good, helped to clear her head a little.

Soon she stood before the door of Beneath the Skin. She paused for a moment on the sidewalk, unsure of herself now that she was there. What, really, was she doing there? What did she want from him?

Instead of allowing herself to linger on that thought,

she pulled a breath in, swung the door open and stepped through.

A cool blast from the air-conditioning as she walked into the front room. The same tall guy was behind the carved desk.

"Hi. Um, is Tristan here?"

He looked up, nodded at her. "Yeah. You have an appointment?"

"Well, no, but I—"

"It's okay, Henry. I'll see her."

God that deep voice, like wood smoke, like sex. She looked up, and Tristan stood framed in the curtained doorway as he had the first time she'd seen him. All dressed in black again, and as powerfully attractive as before. But now she knew what he could do to her. She shivered. When he smiled at her, that shiver drove deep into her body, lit her up with need inside, and a strange craving she couldn't describe even to herself.

"Sophie. You're back so soon. Is there a problem with your tattoo?"

"What? No, it's fine. It's perfect. I just . . ."

She shook her head, unable to finish the sentence. She didn't know what to say.

"I'm glad you came." Tristan's smile widened, and she saw again that flickering dimple in his cheek.

Relief washed over her, along with another surge of desire. She smiled back.

He took a step toward her. "Do you want to go get some coffee?"

"Yes, I'd like that." Her heart beat a little faster.

"Café du Monde isn't far from here. You've been there?"

"Oh, yes. It was one of my first stops when I came to New Orleans."

"Good. Let's go, then." Tristan turned to the man behind

the counter, gestured with a tilt of his chin. "I'll be back, Henry."

Tristan moved closer, laid a hand at the small of her back. His hand was warm and so big it spanned her entire waist. He guided her through the door as her mind emptied out and sensation moved through her body. A small part of her wondered how this man could have such an effect on her. But it didn't matter really, did it? It was happening, and she had no control over it, didn't even want to.

She was a little better outside as they walked down Canal Street and made their way to Decatur. They walked in silence. There was tension between them, but it was purely sexual, and the silence was lovely and excruciating all at the same time.

They were still a block away when she caught the first scent of hot pastry in the air, then the coffee itself as they drew closer to the green-and-white-striped awnings that spread over the crowd of tables on the terrace. All around the café, powdered sugar was scattered on the sidewalk, like a faint drift of snow.

Tristan turned to her. "When I was a kid growing up here, I always thought the sugar was something magical. Like Christmas."

"It seems that way to me now. Like fairy dust on the sidewalks. Like something that could only happen in this city."

"Yes, exactly." He smiled a little, curled her fingers in his, and his gaze caught hers. "You understand me, Sophie."

She nodded, stunned, yet she knew just what he meant.

He led her under the awning and they found a table right away, facing Jackson Square across the street. Immediately, a wizened old waiter approached, and Tristan told him, "Two café au laits and an order of beignets." He turned to Sophie, leaned in and took her hand in his once more. "You do like chicory coffee and beignets?"

"Better than almost anything."

Except, perhaps, his large, warm hand holding on to hers.

The waiter returned in moments, setting two steaming mugs before them, along with a plate of the delicate, hot pastries Café du Monde was famous for, covered in fine, white powdered sugar.

Tristan let her hand go to pick one up. "Damn, it's hot. Why are they better when they burn your fingers?"

Sophie laughed. "I don't know why, but they are." She picked one up herself, let her teeth sink in. The sugar melted on her lips, on her tongue.

When she looked up Tristan was watching her closely. A shiver ran over her skin.

"What?" she asked him.

"You eat that beignet like it's . . . a small treasure."

"It is, don't you think?" She took another lovely bite.

He smiled, then reached out and used his thumb to wipe some sugar from her lip. She wanted to let her tongue dart out, to taste the sweetness of his skin. But she didn't do it.

"Who are you, Sophie?" he asked, his voice low.

"What do you mean?"

He was quiet a moment. "You're very beautiful."

Her cheeks heated. She didn't know what to say. She only knew that she was pleased he thought so. Hell, she was thrilled.

"You're blushing," he said. "But you are beautiful, you know. I want to draw you, all those delicate bones. Like a bird, you are." He reached out again, and this time his fingertips grazed her cheek. Her skin was immediately on fire. "Tell me something about you."

Yes, touch me.

"What . . . what do you want to know?"

"Anything. Everything. Where do you come from? How did you end up here, in my city, in my shop?"

"I come from . . . everywhere, I guess. I've traveled a lot." She took a sip of the strong, rich coffee, buying time. She wasn't sure what to tell him. Did he really want to hear this? But he watched her so intently, she realized he did, or he wouldn't have asked. He was that kind of man. "I grew up in Barstow, a small town in Southern California."

"Yes, I know it."

"What? You're kidding. Barstow is a nowhere town. How have you heard of it?"

"Fort Irwin Army Base is just north . . . shit."

"You were in the army?"

His face went dark, his eyes shuttering. "No."

She didn't understand what had just happened, but she knew better than to pursue the subject. A mystery about this man. That was fine with her; everyone had their secrets. Maybe he'd tell her more someday. Maybe she'd tell him hers.

"Well," she went on, talking over the momentary discomfort, "I always wanted to get out. Needed to get out. I left when I turned eighteen, put myself through college at UCLA waiting tables."

"Ah, I can see you as a student." That small dimpling smile again, just one side of his mouth, she realized. "What did you study there? What was it like?"

"I was an English major. I loved it, going to school. But I left before I got my degree. After a while it got to be . . . too much. Too structured. And I wanted to travel. I felt like . . . like time was running out. I mean, I was twenty years old, but I needed to just *go*." She sipped her chicory-laced coffee, the brew deliciously bitter. "Have you ever felt that way?"

"I've felt that same need most of my life."

"And where have you gone, Tristan?"

He shrugged, his broad shoulders moving beneath the tight black T-shirt, the dragons tattooed on his arms coiling, writhing. "Everywhere, as you said. I left home when I was young too. I traveled. Europe, mostly." He stopped, his eyes staring into the distance over her shoulder, and once more something dark passed through them. The muscles in his jaw worked, clenched. Then he seemed to shake it off. "I studied art over the years. Not formally. I went to the museums, to galleries. I hung out on the streets of Montmartre, talking to other artists, learning to really draw. Several of them were kind enough to mentor me. And then I went to Japan and learned the art of tattoo."

Another delicious shiver, just hearing that word on his lips. "But you came back."

He nodded. "I always come back. When you're born in New Orleans, it's in your blood. This city is always a part of you."

"And are you here to stay?"

He picked up his mug of fragrant coffee and sipped, taking his time. "Yes. This time, I am. That's why I opened the shop."

"What's different this time? What made you decide to do something as permanent as opening a business?"

She watched his fingers tighten on the worn white mug. She was immediately sorry she'd asked. But whatever it was, he recovered quickly enough. "My mother died. She was the last of my family. It was time to come home. Her death made me realize the impermanence of things. And I wanted some permanence, for the first time. I was tired of running from it."

"I've never wanted that. Not yet anyway. Maybe someday I will. Although I love this city so much, I don't know that I'll ever want to leave. I'm in love with New Orleans really, in a way I've never been before anywhere else. But to see some of those places you've been to, I'd love to do that. I've lived all over the United States—in Arizona, in Washington, Colorado, Florida. But the only times I've left the country were to go to Canada and Mexico."

He took her hand in his once more, and heat flashed up her arm, came to settle in the center of her body.

"I'd love to show you Paris, Sophie. Paris is the perfect place for you."

She laughed. "How can you say that? You've just met me. You don't even know me."

"Ah, but I do."

That smoky gray gaze caught hers again, and she saw something in his eyes. Something dark and intense. And she knew immediately that he did know her, in some unfathomable way. She had always wanted to see Paris. Her entire body gave a long shudder, and she drew in a shaky breath.

What was this man doing to her?

Whatever it was, she wanted more. Craved it, needed it. Needed him.

"Tell me about the tattoos," he said quietly.

"Wh-what do you mean?"

"It's more to you than it is for most people, isn't it?"

Her cheeks went hot. She looked away. A group of teenagers were hanging out across the street at the entrance to Jackson Square, smoking, punching one another as teenage boys often do. She couldn't remember being young. Not in that way.

"Sophie?"

"It's . . . the tattoo thing is . . . important." She looked back to him. His dark gaze was on her, steady, unwavering. "Do you know what I mean?"

"I know it's important to me. The art of it. The symbolism of decorating the human body that way."

"Yes."

"But I think it's even more for you."

"Yes." The word came out on a whisper. She could not tell this man what the tattoos truly meant for her!

Too much, too much.

She wanted to run away. She wanted to stay there with him even more.

They sat quietly for a few minutes.

"Sophie, I have to get back to work. But I want to see you. Will you come to the shop on Monday?"

"Yes. I'll come." Her stomach fluttered.

"I want to show you the graveyards. To show you Saint Roch."

"Saint Roch. Yes, I'd love to see it."

"Good. I have to go, but you should stay and finish these beignets. They're too good to waste."

"I'll do that."

He lifted her hand to his lips and laid a soft kiss there. Heat surged in her system once more, traveling to the vee between her legs. She grew damp, shaky. From his touch, from the mere sight of the ink on his skin, covering his forearms.

"I'll see you Monday. Come in the afternoon. We close early on Mondays." He smiled, tossed some bills on the table and left.

She watched as he moved through the crowded patio, in between the tables. Incredibly graceful for a man of his size. He moved like an artist, with an awareness of everything around him.

Monday. Two more days. They would drag interminably. But perhaps she could use that time to get her head sorted out, to get her feet back on the ground. Because this man made her float, as though she were ten feet in the air. The only thing that brought her back to earth was the pervading sense of guilt she normally lived with every day. It was absent whenever she was with him, which scared the hell out of her. And more powerful than ever when she was alone.

She knew it was the tattoo.

She'd done it, and she was glad. She loved it. Yet at the same time, that sense of having sinned weighed her down. How was it that she gloried in the sin, even as she regretted it? It was a puzzle she might never figure out, a dichotomy she struggled with every day of her life, that keen awareness of good and evil. Crystal had talked to her about balance, something Sophie had been searching for but never found. Some way to rectify the good and the evil within herself. And it was all worse now, since she'd gotten the tattoo. So much worse. Tristan made it worse. Because every thought she had about him reeked of the very sin she'd spent her life trying to cleanse herself of.

But if Tristan was all about sin for her, then she was happy to be a sinner. No matter how heavy a price she had to pay.

For two days Tristan had forced himself to focus on his work. Two of the longest days of his life. What the hell had gotten into him? And here it was, Monday afternoon, and his gut was knotted up and all he could think about was *her*.

He could not get the image of that long, dark hair out of his mind, and in every picture he was running his hands through it as it slipped between his fingers like strands of silk. He could get hard just thinking of her hair. What was that about?

He realized with a jolt that if she decided not to come into the shop today, he didn't even know how to reach her. He'd gone against policy and had tattooed her the other day without having her fill out a form first, without her having signed a release. She'd really twisted up his head.

They hadn't set a time and he jumped a little whenever the bell on the front door rang. And he'd had too few clients today, not enough to keep him busy. He'd already cleaned his station, restocked his cabinets, ordered supplies he didn't really need. Now he was hanging around the front desk, rearranging pens, looking at the appointment book over and over, as though it held some kind of answer. Pathetic, that a woman could do this to him. It had never happened before. He'd never allowed it to happen. Never let anyone get too close.

Something about Sophie made him all soft and loose inside. And he wanted her in there with him. Except that inside was a very dark place he couldn't share with anyone. No, that was his burden to carry alone.

A pang of guilt that he hadn't gone to Sainte Benedictine's this month. Or last month. The one cemetery in the city he avoided. There were some days when he could not do it. Couldn't face it. But Sainte Benedictine's wasn't going anywhere. Nor was Phillipe or Maman. He would go next week, he promised himself. And knew it was a lie.

Bastard.

Yes, he was. But there was only so much one man could do. At least, that was how he justified things to himself on days like this, when he found himself incapable of facing his past.

The door jangled and brought him out of his moody reverie. His pulse skittered.

Don't be a fool, Batiste. She's just a girl.

Then she walked in, and he knew that was a lie, too.

Yes, that long dark hair that hung to her waist, her eyes a mysterious blend of green and gold, like a dragonfly. And her mouth too lush and red to really look at. He glanced anyway, going hard beneath his black jeans. How much longer could he resist before he kissed her?

But it would never be enough. He wanted to get her naked, to touch her all over . . .

"Hi, Tristan." She smiled, her face lighting up. Christ, she was fucking beautiful.

"Hey. You came."

"I told you I would."

"Do you always do everything you say you will?"

He meant it to tease her, but she took her time, thinking about it. "Usually. Not always. Some things that come out of my mouth are more wishes than reality."

He loved her answer. He didn't even know why. Maybe because it was so honest.

"Did you come to go to the graveyard with me?"

"Yes. I brought a notebook. Will you think I'm foolish if I take some notes? Is that too . . . bourgeois?" she asked with a small laugh.

"Not at all. I always take my sketch pad. Give me a minute and we'll go."

Sophie waited while Tristan disappeared into the back room. He was only gone a moment, but it was enough for her to let her lashes flutter closed, to draw in a deep breath of his scent lingering in the air. Male and ink and sex. He came back quickly, and she had to open her eyes, trying to appear normal even though her heart was hammering, the blood running hot and fast through her veins. And between her legs was an insistent, throbbing ache.

"Let's go." Tristan moved past her to hold the door open, and they went out to the street.

Outside, Tristan swung his leg over a large black BMW motorcycle Sophie had noticed on the way in.

"This is yours?"

He grinned and patted the tank. "One advantage of settling

here. Do you mind riding on the back of a bike?" Tristan handed her a black helmet.

"No, I love it, actually." A small shiver inside as her mind played back the old images of Rory on his bike. "I've always wanted to learn to drive one myself." She put the helmet on and buckled the strap beneath her chin.

"You should do it. There's nothing like it, that sense of freedom. When I feel too closed in from staying in one place, I go for a long ride and work it out of my system."

"You really are a wanderer."

He smiled, held out a hand to help her onto the seat behind him. She slid into him, her thighs on either side of his. This close, she really got an idea of how enormous a man he was. She could feel every solid ridge and plane of his back hard up against the front of her body.

He started the engine. "Hold on."

He reached for her hands and slid them around his waist, held them tight over a stomach taut with muscle, her breasts crushed against his back. She nearly groaned.

And then they were off, weaving in and out of traffic, in between the sleek Cadillacs and Mercedes the old-guard New Orleans crowd loved so much, the more modern compact cars and the old streetcars on St. Charles Avenue.

They got onto the highway, the speed of it giving her a small thrill, pressed up against Tristan's body, the heat of him coming through their clothes. And the vibration of the powerful engine beneath her, thrumming between her thighs. Her sex went damp, swelled, while she tried to concentrate on the view flashing past on either side. Impossible.

Too soon they were exiting, turning onto a wide street that led to a smaller one, until they approached the high walls of St. Roch. The stone was almost white, bleached with age and the sun, the years of New Orleans heat and humidity. But even here, the bougainvillea and vining lantana grew in a profusion of color, a stark contrast against the old white walls.

Tristan parked the motorcycle at the curb. They both got off it, pulling their helmets off. Tristan took hers and hung both helmets from a bolt under the seat, locking it.

"This place isn't safe, Sophie. Don't ever come here by yourself. Promise me."

"I promise." She felt ready to do anything he asked. But there was also a warm, lovely surge that he was so sincerely protective of her. Odd, after her years of independence. But she couldn't help herself.

They walked up the sidewalk to the entrance, an arch of black ironwork between two enormous stone pillars, topped by a pair of praying angels.

"Saint Roch, Campo Santo," Tristan said, reading the words worked into the scrolling iron. "This place is dedicated to Saint Roch. They say the saint's divine intervention saved the people of New Orleans from a yellow fever plague in the eighteenth century. It's one of the few cemeteries honoring the living as well as the dead. In the chapel there's a room full of relics: crutches and leg braces, plaster castings of hands and feet. It's bizarre. The strangest sort of altar. They say voodoo rituals were practiced in that chapel, that it's haunted. We can see it later, if you like."

"Yes, I'd like to see it. I've heard about it. I think it's fascinating, these sorts of rituals people go through. I think all of us can relate, on some level. That we all have our rituals. I'm not even certain there's that much difference between the Catholic rituals and the voodoo rituals, in the end."

"I agree." He paused. "You're a very interesting person, Sophie. I like the way you think about things."

He smiled at her, and she had the oddest sensation of... she wasn't sure what. Connection? So strange that they were having this conversation about the cemetery, about old saints and voodoo, and she felt they understood each other on this weird level. Maybe it was something about being artists, about being creative people?

They walked beneath the archway and down the wide main aisle of the graveyard. On either side stood rows of the old aboveground graves, stone and marble blocks with gorgeously inscribed gravestones topped by crosses and angels. Some had small iron gates around them; some had stone pillars, short staircases and marble urns, like the entryways to miniature mansions. It was a little spooky, which she liked. But it was also a little romantic.

God, she must be losing her mind.

When she turned to glance at Tristan she found his gaze on her.

"What?" She was self-conscious suddenly, that he'd found her daydreaming over the graves.

"They're beautiful, aren't they?"

She relaxed inside. "Yes. Beautiful and fascinating. Doesn't it make you wonder who all these people were? How they lived? How they died?"

"Yes, that's exactly it, the sense of history in this place. And the colorlessness of the stone, the starkness of it. It's lonely."

"Yes, but the stone is gorgeous, and not really colorless, if you look closely."

He laughed. "Don't ruin my illusions about the lack of color. That's what I love about it."

"Ah, yes, I almost forgot. You like to work without color. Black and white."

"And shades of gray, yes. Sort of a statement about life."

"Maybe. About parts of life, anyway. I like to think there are moments of color, though, don't you?"

He was quiet a moment. "Not nearly enough of those."

She saw again those shadows passing over his face, and

wondered once more what his secrets were. Something he held close. None of her business, really, but she wanted to know about Tristan—who he was, what had made him into the man who intrigued her so.

They moved down the aisle toward the small chapel at the end. The sky was gray overhead, adding to the sense of quiet isolation, to the monochrome color scheme of the day. Yet the warm humidity of New Orleans was still there, sultry and damp. Sophie could feel the slightest veil of moisture on her skin.

"Do you want to explore the chapel now?" Tristan asked her. "Or look at the graves?"

"Is it okay if we just look at the graves today? I want to sort of absorb the atmosphere."

Tristan nodded. "We can come back again. Come on, let me show you one of the mausoleums here. The stonework is incredible."

He took her hand, and suddenly she could barely focus on anything around her as he led her down the long aisles. The gray and white of the stone moved past in a chiaroscuro blur as heat radiated through her fingers, up her arm, making her body ache with need.

They stopped in front of an old mausoleum. Dark gray and white marble created a texture on the smooth walls; in front, a pair of carved pillars flanked a heavy door. Tristan sat on the marble stairs, pulling her down beside him. But she was too distracted to take it all in.

"You can feel the history of the place, right here, where you can touch the stones," he said quietly. "I don't go to church. I don't get that. But this feels sacred to me. This is some sort of divine beauty." He reached out to stroke the underside of her chin with his fingertips, cradled it in his hand. "And so is this."

His gaze was hot on hers, the gray smoke of his eyes

penetrating. She swallowed, trying to breathe past the hard knot of hunger in her chest, in her body.

When he leaned in and brushed his mouth over hers, the sensation roared through her like fire; that hot, that electric. His hand went around the back of her head, pulling her closer, and he pressed his lips to hers, so soft and lush. She moaned against his mouth; she couldn't help it. And when he parted her lips, slipped his tongue inside, she just came apart, her limbs going liquid and weak.

His mouth was hot, wet, his tongue sweet as it explored, thrust, swept over her teeth. She found her arms going around his neck, his skin warm beneath her grasping fingertips.

He pulled her in hard, one arm around her waist, until she was nearly in his lap. His body against hers was all hard muscle. She breathed in his scent, that dark, masculine scent becoming a part of the kiss, a part of the physical sensation.

She was going hot all over, hot and damp and weak with surging desire. Her fingers bit into his shoulders, his hands on her hard and hurting, he held her so tight. She didn't care. All that mattered was his mouth on hers, their panting breath, the pure need swarming her body.

Bells went off in her head, a metallic clanging, growing louder...

He pulled back.

"Christ, Sophie," he muttered.

It was then she realized the bells were coming from the chapel. Her head was reeling.

Tristan smoothed her hair from her face. He was still holding her. She didn't care that they were in a cemetery, that making out on the steps of the mausoleum was probably some sort of desecration. All that mattered was that he was touching her.

His gaze was on hers. "I shouldn't have done that. Not here."

She understood what he meant. But even though the inevitable good girl in her knew it was wrong, it felt right. That she should be here with him, his hands still hot on her, the taste of him lingering on her lips.

"Tristan, don't say that. It doesn't matter. I mean, that we're here. It made it..."

She stopped, shook her head. She couldn't say it aloud.

"It made it better," he murmured, finishing her thought.

She nodded, unable to speak as the intensity built between them once more. Simply sitting there, their minds working in sync. God, his eyes were the darkest shade of gray. Like burning charcoal.

"Tristan, I want you to tattoo me again."

"What? When?"

"Now."

"It's too soon, Sophie. You need time to get used to the first one before you go any further."

"I know what I want."

He stared at her a moment. "Alright. Do you want to go now? Right now?"

"Yes. Please. Can we just do it?"

He stood up, pulled her with him and kept her hand in his as they silently walked back to the gates of St. Roch. It didn't even matter that they weren't looking at each other, the electricity was still there, arcing between them.

They got on his motorcycle and she wrapped her arms around his waist, loving the heat of his body pressed against her breasts, between her thighs. She ached all over, her body hungry for him. She needed him to touch her. To tattoo her.

Yes.

The ride back seemed to take forever. But finally they pulled up in front of Beneath the Skin. The sign was turned off, the shop closed. Tristan got off the bike, helped Sophie off. Even with his back to her as he unlocked the front door, she could feel the energy between them.

Inside, it was quiet and dark. Tristan stood at the doorway to the back room, held the curtain open for her. She moved past him, remembered the first time she'd done this same thing, breathed in his scent as she passed him, just as she'd done before. She felt an odd sense of isolation moving through the empty shop, a heavy sense of them being alone together. Her pulse was hot, racing.

Tristan turned on a light over his chair. "Come and sit down, Sophie."

She did, watched as he sat on a swiveling stool and prepared his equipment. Just watching him move, hearing the buzz of the tattoo gun as he tested it, made her heart beat harder in her chest, made her legs go warm and weak.

Finally, he turned to her. "I have a feeling you know exactly what you want. Don't you?"

Oh, if he had any idea...

"Yes."

His eyes on hers were dark, glittering. "Tell me."

"Cherry blossoms. A scattering of them across my back, from my left shoulder, starting just under the Kanji symbol, then kind of blowing in an undulating curve, over to the right side, then down to the left hip. And I want you to do them mostly in black and white, but with a few touches of pink. Is that alright? To add some color?"

"I'll do it however you want me to. But you're sure? That you want to be tattooed again? That you want your body marked in this way?"

"Yes. I'm sure."

Yes. Oh, yes...

"I'm going to free-hand it, rather than using a transfer, alright?"

"Yes. I trust you. I know it'll be beautiful."

He nodded. "I'll need you to take off your shirt. Probably your bra, too. Here's a towel; you can hold it over the front of your body."

She took the towel, even though she hardly cared about covering herself. Her system was still thrumming with need; being naked in front of him would be perfect.

Such a sinner. Your mother is right.

She would worry about that later. Feel the guilt, which she was almost coming to enjoy.

God, you really are a mess!

She pulled her shirt over her head. Tristan turned away as she unsnapped her bra and laid it on the counter, held the towel over her breasts.

"Turn sideways in the chair, as you did the first time. It works better than laying you flat on the table."

She nodded, swung her legs to the side, resting the front of her body on the arm of the vinyl chair.

He began with some sort of marking pen, sketching onto her skin. It tickled a little. Not as good as the tattoo gun, but she closed her eyes, let herself sink into the sensation.

He finished quickly.

"I'll add more as I go. Do you want to look at it in the mirror before I start?"

"No. Just do it."

He started the tattoo gun, the buzzing of it trembling through her body: pleasure, anticipation.

When he touched the gun to her skin, the anticipation turned to liquid lust. Her sex went damp, her nipples came up hard against the arm of the chair, the rough towel abrading the sensitive flesh. She pulled in a deep breath, blew it out, trying to get herself under control.

The tracing of the needle, a humming on her skin as he began to work, made her quiver inside. She flexed her toes, trying hard not to move. And every touch of the needle went through her as though he had his hand between her thighs.

"Are you alright, Sophie? Not too much pain? Your breath is coming fast."

"No. No pain at all."

No pain, just pleasure. Exhilarating. Ecstasy.

She had no idea how long she sat there in a state of exquisite arousal. All she knew was the touch of the needle, his gloved hands on her, smoothing over her skin as he wiped off excess ink. And his presence behind her: so strong, so purely male. And again that dark scent of him mixed with the ink.

He had completed work on her shoulder and moved across her mid-back, down to her lower back.

"I need you to roll down the top of your jeans so I can work on your hip, Sophie. Alright?"

"Yes. Of course." She dropped the towel to do as he asked. She didn't bother to pick it up. It was too good to be half-naked in the chair, with Tristan behind her. Her breasts ached, her nipples were painfully hard as she leaned into the arm of the chair, the vinyl warm against her skin. Almost impossible not to rub her thighs together to ease the tension there.

He was working again, drawing the needle over her needy flesh. The buzz of it drove into her, as it had before, deep inside her body.

If only it were him inside my body.

Surge after surge of pleasure as he moved the needle across her skin, pushing the ink in, beneath the surface. She could imagine his big hands, the intent expression on his face. She had never needed a man to touch her so badly in her life. And she swore she heard his breath hitching behind her, felt his warm exhalation on her bare back.

"Tristan..."

"Yes, I'm almost done."

That wasn't what she was going to say. What was she going to say? That she wanted him? Needed him to strip her bare and fuck her every bit as much as she needed him to tattoo her? Her mind was spinning.

His hand smoothed over her back in long, gentle strokes. She shivered.

"I'm done."

She nodded, pulled in a breath and turned around in the chair.

His eyes went for a moment to her naked breasts, then back to her face, focusing on her mouth. He licked his lips. When his gaze met hers, his was dark, glossy.

"Christ, Sophie."

CHAPTER Five

He stripped his gloves off and went for her, pulling her face to his in a rough kiss. So hard, his mouth on hers, crushing her lips, bruising them. But it was exactly what she wanted.

He opened her lips with his tongue, thrust inside. And she pushed into him, pressed her breasts against his chest. He let her face go long enough to mutter, "Fuck, Sophie . . ." Then he pulled his shirt over his head and she had a moment to glimpse the red, thornbound heart pierced by a knife blade tattooed on his chest, before Tristan pulled her back in. The sight of it, the bloodred heart, the way the ink rode his flesh, made her sex flood with heat.

He kissed her again, harder this time, his hands buried in her hair. He was all wet heat. Lips, teeth and tongues, clashing, twining. Her body was on fire, the need for him melting her.

When he pulled his mouth from hers and moved his

hands down to cover her breasts, she gasped, arced into his touch. Almost shocking, how soft his hands were; she could hardly stand it. Then he began to knead the soft, aching flesh. Pleasure moved through her, thick and slow, like honey in her veins. Her hands went to his wide shoulders; she loved the ripple and bunching of muscle there as he moved, loved seeing the dragons writhing on his arms. His skin was unbelievable, smooth, silky. She leaned in and ran her tongue over the lines of the tattoo on his biceps. The flesh was raised the slightest bit, but she could feel it, how the design was worked into his skin. She shivered, lust stabbing deep inside her. The ink, the taste of him, the texture on her tongue. She moaned softly.

When she looked up and caught his gaze, his smoky gray eyes were as intense as ever, his lids heavy. He bent and pressed his lips to her throat, his tongue swirling there, sending shivers of heat through her system. She let her head fall back, let him feast there, sucking, biting. Even better when he moved lower and took her nipple into his mouth.

She gasped, the wet heat driving through her, into her. Her sex was soaking wet, aching and full.

Touch me. God, please touch me...

As though hearing her need, he slid his hands over her thighs and in between them, pressing against her mound through the denim of her jeans. So close. Not nearly enough. Unbearable.

"Tristan..."

He pulled back, helped her squirm out of her jeans. Her cotton panties went next, and she was naked in the chair, acutely aware of her wet cleft against the black vinyl.

He went down on his knees then, and she saw the black bat wings tattooed across his shoulders. Gorgeous work, she thought vaguely. She loved the look of it, the dense blackness of ink on his skin. Exactly what she'd craved her whole life. Her whole body surged with lust.

Yes.

Tristan spread her thighs, and dove in. His mouth went right to that wet and hungry place. Using his hands, he spread her pussy lips, used his tongue to delve in between. He found the hard nub of her clit, licked it, the soft texture of his tongue making her crazy.

"More, Tristan, more . . . please . . ."

She bucked her hips, pushing against his searching tongue.

Oh, yes . . .

He thrust his fingers inside her, and pleasure shot through her like an electric shock; hard, intense. She was trembling on the edge of orgasm already. She wanted to hold back, tried to. But his hot, sucking mouth, his plunging fingers, were too much for her. Her climax slammed into her, a solid wall of pleasure, crushing her completely. She shook with the force of it, her thighs clenching, the walls of her sex grasping at his driving fingers.

"Oh . . ."

And before it was over, he stood and kicked off his boots, his jeans. He bent over her and whispered, "Your skin is too raw, Sophie. I have to turn you around."

"Yes. Do it. Please."

He grabbed her around the waist, turned her over until she was kneeling on the chair, her elbows resting on the back of it.

"Fuck. Hold on," he muttered.

He walked away, and she heard him fumbling in a cabinet. She could barely hold still, waiting for him.

"Thank God Henry keeps these on hand."

She glanced over her shoulder and watched, fascinated,

as Tristan rolled a condom over his cock. A beautiful cock, hard and as big as the rest of him was. She licked her lips, trembled in anticipation.

His hand went around her waist again and he pulled her to him, used the other hand to spread her pussy lips. He pressed the head of his cock to her opening and pleasure rippled through her.

"Just do it, Tristan. I need it. Please."

He slid in. Right into her wet heat. He'd never felt anything so damn good in his life as this girl beneath him. And to see his work on her back, the pale skin still pink and tender, went through him like a shock, a jolt of unbelievable pleasure. And something about the way she yielded her body to him, just gave herself over, was thrilling as hell.

He pulled back, and as he thrust into her, her hips moved back to meet him. She was too perfect, this girl.

Still holding her body close to his, he slipped a hand around, filled his palm with her breast. So firm, so soft. One of her hands came up to cover his, and she guided him to take her nipple between his fingers, to pinch it, hard.

Oh, yes. Fucking perfect.

He slid out, let his cock rest just inside that hot, wet opening, waited while she squirmed beneath him.

"Tristan," she gasped. "Please."

"Please what?" Too good, to make her beg for it. Sick bastard. He didn't care.

"Please fuck me. I need it hard. Please."

He smiled to himself, then plunged, sinking into her hot, grasping pussy. He pulled back, drove in once more, until his balls were tight up against her. He started to pump then, faster and faster. And he moved his hand down from her swollen nipple to that hard nub between her thighs, rubbing, pinching, loving the feel of her slippery flesh under his fingertips.

"Oh! Yes, Tristan!"

He felt that first tremor deep inside her body. And when her pussy started to clench around his cock, his own climax came thundering down on him, roaring through his system. Pleasure shook him to the core, his body trembling. And still he drove into her, reveled in her cries.

"Christ, Sophie..."

More, and more; he kept driving into her silken flesh, felt her shiver beneath him. Watched her skin go pink from where he'd gripped her hip too hard. Watched her tattooed flesh, knowing he had done that to her. Decorated her. Marked her.

Don't think about it.

But he couldn't help it. On some level, in some strange way, Sophie was already his.

You're not built for that shit.

No. He knew damn well he wasn't. He was going to have to stop. Stop thinking that way about her. Stop seeing her, if he had to.

But right now, he was still buried inside her body, pleasure shifting through him like sunlight through the cloudy New Orleans sky.

Fuck it. He would deal with it all later.

He bent over her, swept the long fall of dark hair from the back of her neck and bit her there, tasting her skin. His cock twitched at her low moan. Almost wanted to get hard once more already. Just the taste of her skin, that small sound of pleasure.

"Tristan." Her voice was a sultry, breathless whisper.

"What is it, Sophie?"

"I need to do it again."

He smiled to himself, pulled out of her and turned her around so that she was sitting in the chair. He left her there for a moment while he disposed of the condom.

"I'm sadly unprepared, Sophie. As much as I'd like to pretend otherwise, I need a few minutes to recover."

He looked at her then, at the flush on her breasts, her cheeks. The heavy-lidded eyes, just a glimmer of color from beneath her long, dark lashes. So fucking beautiful. And that pouting mouth of hers . . .

He leaned in and kissed her. Her delicate arms went around his neck. She was hot and panting in moments, kissing him hard. He wanted to fuck her again.

Instead, he pulled her to the edge of the chair, spread her thighs wide. Loved that she just let him do it. No questions, no resistance. Just her damp, pink cleft opening like a flower for him.

He reached out and stroked that wet slit with one finger. She tensed, moaned softly. He couldn't believe how beautiful she was, open, wanton.

Wanton. An old-fashioned word. But that's exactly what she was. And so unexpected, from a girl like her. Such a sweet face, and that silver cross around her neck, hanging between her breasts.

He stroked her again, using his fingers to delve in between those swollen lips. She arced into his touch. He glanced up, found her eyes tightly closed. She looked . . . lost. Lost and lovely and all his, in this moment.

His cock stirred, needy already. But he wanted to watch her come. Wanted to see his fingers plunge into her body.

He used one hand to spread those pink lips wide, and touched his fingertips to her opening, then slipped inside.

"Ah . . . Tristan . . ."

He spread her wider, fascinated by the sight of her, open and pink and raw. By the feel of her, all wet silk inside. And her hard little clit, begging for attention.

He pressed on it with his thumb, circling, his fingers still moving inside her.

"More," she begged, her voice a husky whisper.

He drove deeper, harder, his thumb rubbing hard on her clit. His cock was absolutely bursting with need.

He glanced at her face again, was shocked to find her gaze on him. Her eyes were all glittering green and gold, like sea glass lit with fire. She bit her lip. Those lush red lips. He wanted to fuck her mouth. To slip his cock in between those lips. He wanted to come in her mouth, into that heat. He wanted to feel her come into his hands. He wanted all of it.

"Sophie. Come for me."

"Yes . . ."

She arched, her whole body moving, clenching, that lush mouth opening in a long, keening moan. She bore down on his hand, her insides clutching, hot and so damn tight. He could barely stand that it wasn't his cock inside her.

She sighed, held on to his arms and slipped down to the floor in front of him. He didn't have time to think before her lips touched the tip of his cock.

"Jesus fucking Christ, Sophie. You are too perfect." He watched as she wrapped those red lips around his cock, and groaned as she pulled him into her mouth.

The floor was hard beneath her knees. But she didn't care. It felt like doing penance. She loved the sensation, the idea of it. She drew him in, that hard flesh, all silk over steel against her tongue. He buried his hands in her hair as she began to move, sliding her mouth up and down that rigid shaft.

"Fuck, Sophie, yes!"

His hips were pumping now, but gently, as though he was afraid to hurt her. But she wanted it. She pulled him in, her hands around his strong thighs, which were covered in heavy black Maori tribal work, down her throat until it choked her. Tears filled her eyes; it was hard to breathe. He pulled back, long enough for her to catch her breath before she grabbed his hips, her fingers digging into his skin, and she swallowed his cock once more.

Yes, just like praying. Painful. Lovely. She was shivering all over, with his groans of pleasure, with her own. He was hitting the back of her throat, over and over, sliding over her tongue. She sucked harder, dug into his hips until she felt his flesh break under her nails.

Yes . . .

He drove into her mouth, feeding his cock to her. The tears ran down her cheeks as she pulled him deeper. She wanted to please him, needed to. She was weak with that aching need. To be good for him. To be good. To be bad.

"Ah, God, Sophie!"

He tensed, shuddered, and come shot down her throat. That thick liquid, sweet as honey. She tried to swallow it all, but she couldn't do it. He was too big. She wiped the corner of her mouth with one hand as he slipped from between her lips, cradled her head in his hands.

He was panting, shaking a little. She was filled with a sense of pride. And a sense of power.

She rested her cheek against his thigh, breathed in the musky scent of sex.

"Sophie, Sophie . . ." he murmured.

The salty-sweet taste of his come lingering in her mouth felt sacred to her somehow. Sacred and dirty.

God, she was fucked up.

He pulled her to her feet, held her close to his body. She leaned her head into the hard wall of his chest, over the designs traced into his skin. His heart beat against her ear, a staccato tempo. Her pulse thrummed with that same beat, lust still singing in her veins.

"God, I love your hair, Sophie," he muttered as he buried his fingers in it. "Like fucking silk."

She didn't answer. There was nothing to say. She'd never

been so sated, yet still so needy, in her life. The need itself was intimidating as hell, but she couldn't escape it.

They stood there together for a while. The strange dynamic between them resonated between their bodies, like some invisible cord. She pressed her cheek into his skin, trying to figure out how she could feel so good and so scared at the same time. This was all too much, wasn't it? She'd just met him!

Finally, she stepped back, and there was an odd sense of being released, like a rubber band snapping; sharp and a little painful.

"Are you getting cold? Let's get you dressed. Don't put your bra on; your tattoo is too new. In fact, you should go a few days at least without it."

Her stomach dropped. She'd hoped there would be more. That he'd invite her upstairs, where Crystal had told her he had an apartment, to stay the night with him. Why hadn't he?

He was picking up her clothes and handing them to her. She stood there stupidly for a moment before she stepped into her panties. They were still damp with her earlier arousal.

She watched him as he got back into his clothes, as she put on her jeans, her T-shirt, slipped into her sandals. Was this it? Was he going to simply send her home? But maybe it was for the best. Her head was spinning.

He ran a hand over his short thatch of hair, left his hand on his head as he stood, staring at her. She knew her emotions were all over her face, and hated herself a little for it.

He's a guy. They're like this.

Not Tristan. No, he'd led her to believe there was more to him. That he had more depth. But was she even ready for that?

"So," she said.

"So..."

"I guess . . . I guess I'll go home."

"Yeah." His eyes were dark, completely shuttered.

She felt absolutely crushed, even though she wanted to run, even as doubt flooded her mind. And dammit, she still wanted him!

"Be sure you take care of your tattoo."

"I will. Um . . ." She wasn't going to be the one to say it, to ask when she would see him again, hear from him.

"Alright. Well. I have a nine A.M. client tomorrow. Early for me."

"Right. Okay. Good night, then."

She turned and walked out, without waiting for his reply. She knew she didn't want to hear it.

Outside, fog hung heavy in the air, making it a little chilly. But the coolness felt good on her heated cheeks.

She couldn't believe what had just happened! The sex had been unbelievable. And she'd never felt so connected with another human being in her life. And then—nothing.

This was her penance. She knew in the back of her mind it was coming. It always did. Her mother, her brother were right about that.

Still, she couldn't believe it was ending this way. So fucking classic.

At least, for a little while, she'd been able to push her own fears away and believe in that magic. She needed to. Needed to know that life wasn't all about sin and repression and guilt that never went away, even when she truly hadn't done anything wrong.

A wind came up, blowing through her hair, where Tristan's fingers had woven only minutes earlier. If she inhaled deeply, she could still smell him on her skin. She could still taste him in her mouth.

She wound up Dauphine and into the narrow alleylike street to her apartment building. On the first floor, she saw lights on in Crystal's apartment, heard the soft strains of the piano. She bypassed the stairs and went instead to her friend's door.

She knocked, heard Crystal singing: some old Billie Holiday, she thought. She knocked again, louder this time. A moment later Crystal opened the door, wearing nothing but a short, red vintage silk kimono, her dark hair touseled.

"Oh, shit. I'm sorry, Crystal. Boone's here. I can come back tomorrow."

"No, don't worry about him. Come on in."

Crystal took her arm and pulled her into the apartment. Boone sat on the old overstuffed damask sofa in a pair of black boxer shorts.

"Hey." He gestured with his goateed chin.

Boone's dirty-blond hair curled around his shoulders. He had the hair of an angel, Sophie had always thought, with those gold-tipped ringlets. And he was a nice guy. But Crystal treated him like a dog.

"Boone, we need some girl time. Go get us some ice cream, will you?"

"Yeah, sure, baby." He got up and went into the bedroom, appeared a moment later in his torn jeans and a sweatshirt. He started to kiss Crystal on the mouth as he passed her, but she pulled back, rolling her eyes.

"Jesus, Boone, you'll only be gone twenty minutes." She turned to Sophie. "Come on, sit down."

Crystal pulled her onto the couch as Boone shut the door behind him.

"I don't mean to interrupt."

"Not a problem. Now, if you'd come half an hour ago..."

"Yeah, well..."

"Hey." Crystal grabbed Sophie's hand. "You're all flushed and...glazed over. What's going on?"

"Tristan took me to the cemetery today. And then he tattooed me."

"Oh, my God. Let me see."

Sophie turned around and pulled her shirt up.

"Wow. That's gorgeous."

She turned back around, pulled her shirt into place. "Yeah."

"So why do you look so glum?"

"I did something really stupid, Crystal. I had sex with him."

"Tristan? Why is that stupid? He's hot. And the way you two were looking at each other that day we were in the shop, I'm surprised it didn't happen sooner."

Sophie shook her head. "No, it's not the sex that was stupid. It's me." She wrapped the ends of her hair around her fingers, twisting it tight. "I . . . you should hear the way he talks to me. The things we talk about. He wasn't like some guy out to get laid. We really *talked*. God, I sound like some fifteen-year-old with a crush!"

"No you don't. Go on."

"He . . . he talked to me about things that mean something. Art, life, death. And I felt this intense connection. I thought I did. It scared the shit out of me, if you want to know the truth. That it was happening so damn fast. That just talking with him made me feel so . . . close to him. Like it's too good to be real." She shook her head. "But it was there, I swear it was."

"I believe you, sweetie." Crystal rubbed her arm.

"Then why, when it was over, did he just send me home? Like I was . . . like I was some whore?"

"No, Sophie, I'm sure he didn't mean it like that. Look, some guys just get weird about sex. Maybe it got too close for comfort, you know? Maybe it did mean as much to him, and he couldn't handle it. It sounds like it was almost too much for you. I'm sure he'll call you. I'm sure he'll want to see you again. He'd be crazy not to."

"I don't know."

All she knew was that she was miserable.

Whore.

Yes, maybe she was a whore. Maybe she was getting what she deserved. Paying her penance. But part of her didn't quite believe it. How could it be a sin when she wanted him so much? When being with him felt . . . important?

She didn't understand it. Wasn't sure she ever would. The one thing she did understand was that there was something special between her and Tristan. She was sure of it. She'd seen it in his eyes, in the way he touched her.

But she wouldn't go to him and grovel at his feet, either. Which left her with nothing. Exactly where she'd started, so she was no worse off, right?

But that was a lie. She was much worse off. Because she'd had that taste of what she and Tristan could have together. And as frightening as the idea of having something that special was, the idea of giving it up was impossible.

CHAPTER Six

He felt like an asshole.

He *was* an asshole.

Tristan paced the wood floors of his apartment above the shop, his hand wrapped around a double shot of Jack Daniel's. He'd poured it, meant to drink it. But he didn't really deserve that relief, did he? He yanked on a cord and drew the wood slat blinds up, looked down at Canal Street below. Even this late at night, light shone from the shops and restaurants, people still wandered the sidewalks. The partying crowd, ever-present in New Orleans, regardless of the time of day or night, the time of year. He loved and hated that about this city.

He was such a cold bastard. He knew it was wrong, even while he was doing it: shutting down. Making her leave like that. And God, her face . . .

But he'd never been any good at this stuff. Never got emotionally involved with a woman. He wasn't responsible enough to handle it. And tonight proved that point. He couldn't be trusted with anyone's feelings, anyone's well-being. Hell, look what had happened to Phillipe.

And now Sophie. He'd known from the moment she'd walked into his shop that he wanted more than just to fuck her. Oh, he'd wanted that too. Hell, he still wanted to fuck her. But he wanted to talk to her too. To *be* with her. That was the dangerous part. Dangerous to her. Dangerous to him. Better to back off now, before anyone really got hurt.

Too late, asshole.

He could not get the image of her stricken face out of his mind.

He lifted the heavy glass to his lips and tossed the shot down his throat. The fragrant liquid burned, warmed him. He didn't feel any better.

He took the empty glass into the kitchen. The open bottle of Jack sat on the counter. He stared at it for a moment before pouring another shot into the glass. Lifting it to his mouth, he drank it down so fast his eyes watered. Then he did it again.

It wasn't working. He set the glass down on the old black-and-white-tiled counter and stalked back into the living room, settled on the big brown leather couch to sulk. He knew he was doing it. He didn't care.

He'd completely fucked up with Phillipe, the one person he'd ever really cared about. The one person he was supposed to protect. No, he didn't deserve to care about anyone. And no one deserved what happened to them when he *did* care. He was bad news. Always had been, always would be, no matter that he'd cleaned up his life, settled down, started a business. That didn't change who he was on the inside. That didn't redeem him.

What the fuck was he going to do now? If he called her, apologized, he would only lead her on. If he just let her be, didn't see her again, she'd be hurt, but she'd get over it.

He wasn't so sure he would.

Fuck.

He ran a hand over his hair, scrubbed at his head. She was so damn beautiful, this girl. Just thinking about fucking her in his chair after he'd tattooed her... that was the hottest experience of his life. He'd had sex with a lot of women—too many, probably—but he'd never felt anything like he had with Sophie tonight.

He would not call her.

But he could sit here and picture her face, that full, red mouth, that long hair, like Lady Godiva. And the tattoo on her pale skin...

His cock was getting hard again. He could see in his head her naked body, kneeling on the floor. Remembered her hot little mouth on him.

He pressed down on his swelling cock, but that only made it worse.

He really was an asshole. He'd hurt the girl, and right now all he could think of was fucking her, her sucking him off.

Jesus.

He pulled his cock from his jeans and grasped the shaft, hard. Then he started to stroke, her perfect face in his mind's eye. All that smooth flesh, the mounds of her breasts, the dark, hardened nipples. God, her mouth on him, sucking and wet.

He stroked harder, until it hurt. He deserved the pain. But it felt good too.

He pumped his cock in his fist, remembered her legs spread wide. The sight of her pussy, all hot and pink, wet and waiting for him. Then pushing into her. Into that tight sheath.

Sophie...

His come shot out, flowed over the leg of his jeans. He sat a moment, trying to catch his breath.

Yeah, he was a bastard, drinking and jerking off so he'd feel better. Except that he didn't.

Fuck. He knew he wouldn't feel any better until he talked to her. Saw her.

Bad idea.

Yeah, it was. For her. For him. He didn't fucking deserve her, and he knew it. But he was going to do it anyway.

He got up, stripped down to his gray boxer briefs, tossed his jeans on the floor. And picked up the phone.

The ringing seemed to go on forever, but she never picked up. Where was she? Finally her answering machine kicked in, and he hung up. He didn't know what to say, didn't want to talk to the machine. He wanted to talk to her. But what was he going to say? That he was an asshole, that he didn't do relationships, so even though there was some weird, intense, beautiful thing between them, he was walking away? He sure as hell wasn't going to tell her why. He didn't tell anyone about Phillipe. No, that was his private burden.

Phillipe. He really had to get out to St. Benedictine's. The idea twisted into his gut like a knife. How long had it been since the last time he'd gone? Months? Too long, he knew that. Too long since he'd had the guts to face his shame. His guilt. His brother.

He went back into the kitchen and poured himself another shot. He drank it down fast, and then another. But there wasn't enough booze in the city to chase away the demons of his past. Or the problem he'd just created with Sophie.

He took the bottle and went back to the sofa to brood. He flipped the TV on, hoping for some momentary distraction. The bottle was nearly empty by the time the remote slipped from his fingers, and he slept.

A week had gone by. Sophie's tattoo was healing well, the skin only a little itchy now. As she stepped from the shower, she turned to admire it in the misty bathroom mirror, as she did every day. And every day she thought of the man who had put it there.

Tristan.

She couldn't believe that just his name running through her mind still hurt so much. She barely knew him! And yet she felt as though she'd known him forever. That he really *knew* her, inside.

She ran the towel over her body, drying herself. As she rubbed the nubby fabric over her breasts, her nipples went hard, peaked.

Tristan.

God, she couldn't get her body, her emotions, under control. She'd barely been able to write all week.

Dropping the towel, she stared at her image in the mirror. Her dark hair hung in wet, twisting strands against her pale skin. Her breasts were full, swollen, the nipples dark and needy. She angled so she could see part of her back in the mirror, the tattooed cherry blossoms scattered across her skin. God, the sight of her own tattooed body was a turn-on!

She swept her hand down the front of her body, over her belly, brushing the curls between her thighs, and sighed. She couldn't seem to forget that night with him, his touch, his cock inside her. And even though she was physically obsessed with him, just as strong in her mind were her conversations with him: at his shop, at Café du Monde, at St. Roch. It took every ounce of strength she had not to go see him, to make him tell her why he'd had sex with her, then chased her away.

She knew she hadn't imagined that intensity, that level of connection. Had she?

Maybe she was finally losing her mind, as her mother had always promised she would if she didn't change her depraved ways.

She really had to stop thinking about her mother. Her family was toxic for her, she knew that. But no matter how many times she thought she'd put them and all their head trips behind her, she couldn't seem to let them go.

Maybe the key was not to let them go, but to find a way to sort of coexist with them? Even if she didn't see them, speak to them.

She shook her head, started to comb her hair out. Almost impossible to think of Tristan and her family in the same breath. Strangely impossible not to. Why was it all mixed up together?

God, she was a mess. Even worse since Tristan. But she still felt so damn drawn to him. *Needed* him.

Damn it.

She yanked the comb through her tangled hair, pulling until her scalp burned. Punishment, yes. But never, never enough to chase away the thoughts she was having night and day about Tristan. Never enough to ease that hovering sensation of guilt.

And yet, she realized with a shock, the guilt had not been there while she was with him, while they were having sex. She'd loved what he'd done to her, what they'd done together. And while she'd had some fleeting thoughts about that whole idea of pleasure as sin, she hadn't really felt at all bad, for the first time. No, it only made it hotter. What did that mean, if anything?

God, what a fool she was.

And even now, she burned for him.

She stroked her fingertips over her hardened nipples, felt them swell even more. And the vee between her thighs filled with need, until she had to press the flat of her hand against the hungry flesh.

Yes...

She slipped her fingers into that damp cleft, thought of the humming touch of the needle on her skin, of Tristan's hands on her, shivered with pleasure. She paused to draw in a breath. The telephone rang.

Shit.

She was not the kind of person who could ignore a ringing phone. She ran into the bedroom and grabbed her cell off the nightstand.

"Yes, hello?"

"Sophie."

Her mother. She hadn't talked to her in months. Ironic that she was calling now. If she only knew that her sinful daughter was standing there entirely naked, her flesh aching with desire, the juices of her own arousal on her fingers. She took some perverse pleasure in that.

"Hello, Mother. How are you?"

"I'm fine. Which you would know if you ever bothered to call home."

That is not my home. Hasn't been for years. Maybe it never was.

But she couldn't say these things. And she knew better than to get started. "How is Dad?"

"He's fine."

Ah, just the quarterly check-in, then. Excruciating, but she could get through it.

"I'm fine too, Mother." Not that she'd asked. Of course, her mother really didn't want to know how she was, what she was doing. "My writing is going well. I sold another book this year."

"Well, I'm glad to know you're not starving in that place. That awful city."

"I love it here, Mother."

"Yes, of course you do. It's a place of depravity, Sophie. Not the kind of place for a proper young woman."

"Have I ever really been 'proper,' Mother?"

She'd have a fucking heart attack if she saw the tattoos.

There was perverse pleasure in that idea too.

"When did you become so disrespectful? It's all that traveling. That trash you write. Your whole life is a disgrace, Sophie. When was the last time you went to church?"

"I was at a chapel here a week ago."

A small lie. One that made her smile. She really was going to hell.

"Well, it hasn't done you much good, I can see. You need guidance. Your brother could help you—"

"My brother doesn't give a damn about me, Mother."

"How dare you use that foul language? You're talking about a priest!"

"Yes. But he's not God, no matter how much you'd all like to think so."

Her mother gave a heavy sigh. "I don't know why I bother."

"I don't know why you do either, Mother," she said quietly.

"If you would just start—"

"Come on, Mother. We both know I'll never be what you want me to be. I'll never do what you want me to do.

It's sad, but that's just the way it is. Why do we even do this? Why do we have these shallow conversations four times a year, when we both know we have nothing to talk about?"

"You're still my daughter," her mother said through clenched teeth.

"Am I? Not in the way Anthony is your son. I'm beginning to accept that." She realized suddenly that it was true. That part of her was shifting, growing. And she was learning to live without her family's approval. It didn't hurt quite as much anymore. She wouldn't have been tattooed otherwise. She couldn't have done it.

And she was back to thinking about Tristan again. Her body heated, remembering the state she'd been in when the phone rang.

"I have to go, Mother. Say hello to Dad for me. We'll talk . . . eventually."

She hung up without waiting for a reply. More condemnation she didn't want to hear, she was sure. What was the point?

She went to the old armoire in the corner of her room, an enormous piece with faded and chipping white and blue paint. She wondered vaguely how anyone had ever gotten it up the narrow stairs, as she pulled out her one G-string, a tiny scrap of black lace, added a black lace bra she'd bought on a whim and had never worn. She pulled on a simple black tank top and a pair of jeans. Her silver cross, hanging from the glass knob of the armoire, caught the morning light coming through the sheer curtains at the window, and she almost didn't put it on, for once. But fuck it. It was hers and she loved it. Maybe it meant something different to her than it did to her mother, her brother, but that was her business. She slipped it over her head, let it hang heavy between her breasts.

She was going to him. Whether he wanted her there or

not. She was not just going to lie down and take his dismissal of her. If Tristan Batiste thought he was going to get off that easily, he had better think again. He was going to have to deal with her. *Now.*

She looked for her sandals, realized she must have left them in the living room. As she went to find them, there was a sharp knock at the door. Probably Crystal. She'd have to tell her she was going to see him.

Tristan.

She swung the door open, and there he was, as if by magic. As though she had manifested him somehow. Her breath hitched. A shiver passed over her skin, almost as though he had touched her.

"Jesus, Tristan. What are you doing here? I was just..."

"Just what?" His eyes were that dark, smoky gray. He looked wary. He looked determined. "Are you going to let me in?"

"God. Yes. Sure, come in."

She stepped back and let him pass by her. She caught his scent, couldn't help but pull it into her lungs whenever he was near. So earthy, so elemental. So *him.*

She'd missed him. But he'd hurt her.

"Why are you here, Tristan?"

He stood in her tiny living room, dwarfing the place. The morning sun poured in through the windows, washing everything in pale golden light, making everything appear pure, clean; the old plaster in dire need of paint, the small, antique sofa with its decaying dark red velvet. Even the battered leather motorcycle jacket he wore.

He didn't answer, he simply stared at her, his gaze roving her face: her eyes, her mouth. He moved in, slowly, and her legs went weak. She was paralyzed. And then he was on her, his mouth crushing hers, his tongue sliding between her lips.

She opened for him, melted into him. He dragged her in closer, his hands gripping her shoulders, biting into her skin.

She pulled her mouth away. "Tristan... you're hurting me."

"Fuck, sorry."

Then he pulled her in again, as hard as ever.

Doesn't matter. All that matters is that he's here.

Her hands went to grasp his face, the stubble on his cheeks scratching her palms. But the sensation grounded her in the moment as much as his fingers bruising her shoulders did, the hard, hurting press of his mouth on hers.

Her clothes came off quickly, then his. She wasn't sure how it happened. As soon as they were naked he was pushing her to the floor, onto the ancient Persian rug she'd found at a Sunday flea market. It smelled of mold, mothballs, years of footsteps and history. But it was worn and soft against her back as he covered her body with his.

Skin to skin. *Yes.* Ink to ink would be even better. An image flashed in her mind, of her entire body covered in tattoos. Her stomach, her breasts.

Yes!

Her sex clenched hard. She spread her thighs for him, felt his cock pressing hard against her belly, and ran her hands over his tattooed shoulders, over the serpentine swirl of the dragons on his arms. And his greedy mouth on hers didn't stop. His thrusting tongue, his sharp teeth, bruising her, drawing a little blood from her lip. And all she could think was, *More...*

Her legs wrapped around his waist, spreading her body wide for him, but he slid down, dragging his open mouth over her breasts, her belly. He paused, bit into the soft flesh there, and she cried out. In pain. In pleasure. In the purest driving need she'd ever felt. He moved lower, spread her pussy lips wide with his hands and dove right in.

His mouth was all wet heat, sucking, licking. He flicked his tongue at her clit and she shivered all over. His fingers plunged inside her and she arced her hips, wanting more. He drove deeper, hurting her, but she needed it.

Penance, yes.

She gasped when he drew her clit into his mouth and sucked. And when he bit down on that hard nub of flesh she came, long undulating currents of pleasure rolling over her, crushing her. She was coming apart under him, her mind gone.

He left her shuddering in the aftermath, but only long enough to find a condom in his jacket pocket, to sheath his beautifully erect cock. He knelt on the floor, pulled her up and draped her legs over his strong thighs so that she straddled him. With one thrust, he stabbed into her body, impaling her.

Her arms wound around his neck. She watched him for a moment, panting with need, her sex clenching around his cock deep inside her. He was so deep it hurt. But she wanted it to hurt, wanted that primal sensation of his command over her body.

His flesh rippled beneath the dark ink on his arms, inviting her, and she bent her head, sucking his skin into her mouth. The texture from the ink beneath her tongue sent a jolt of sensation through her. She spread her lips wider, wanting to take in his tattooed flesh, to swallow it, to make it a part of her.

Yes!

This was the fulfillment of her darkest fantasies, the tattooed man, the ultimate bad boy, fucking her on the floor like an animal.

Pleasure shot through her as she writhed, his cock pulsing against her womb. She could almost come again just thinking about the ink on his skin, on her own, from his cock heavy inside her.

"Tristan," she panted, "promise me you'll tattoo me again."

"Yes, the ink all over your skin. I want to do it. I'd fuck you and tattoo you at the same time if I could."

He snaked a hand down beneath her bottom, holding her body over his, and drove into her, his hips pistoning.

"Jesus, Sophie. Jesus, Jesus . . . I need to fuck you. I need to fuck you so hard."

"Yes . . . Tristan . . ."

The tension built in her body once more, his cock slamming into her. He moved one hand up and slid it around the back of her head. His fingers gripped her hair, pulling her head back hard, and the look on his face was so open, so torn with pleasure, she could hardly stand to see it, to see him so vulnerable. But soon the lovely friction of his cock moving inside her, right up against her G-spot, was too much. She felt the first waves of climax, surges of heat burning through her veins. She shook as she came, cried out his name over and over. And when he tensed, a new wash of pleasure moved through her, driving her orgasm on, further, deeper. She felt him shiver, felt somehow the heat of him coming inside her body.

"Damn it, Sophie," he muttered, his breath hot on her cheek. "I couldn't stay away."

"Good."

He was quiet for several long moments, the only sound his panting breath, the slight creaking of the old floor beneath them.

"No, it's not good. You don't understand."

"Then tell me, Tristan. Tell me why being with me is bad. How can you say that? Especially right now?"

"I'm sorry. Fuck, I'm sorry, Sophie."

"Tell me what you're sorry for." She took his face in her hands, forced his head up, forced him to look at her. "Because you are here with me. And you're still inside my body. And it's all good, as far as I can see."

He shook his head. "No. You don't know me."

"Do you remember what you said to me that day at Café du Monde? I *do* know you, and you know me. Don't tell me I'm wrong, that I'm . . . delusional. I get enough of that shit from my family. This is true, you and me!"

He paused. "It is. It's why I had to see you. But I shouldn't be here."

"Why do you have to be so mysterious, so vague, Tristan? Tell me what this is all about. Because I really don't understand."

He dropped his head onto her breasts, the weight of him heavy on her sensitive flesh. She could not believe they were having this conversation, with his softening cock still inside her, their breath still ragged with pleasure.

He lifted her from him, his cock slipping out of her, then sat back on the floor, looking a little dazed. Well, so was she. The rug was scratchy beneath her bottom, and it was only then she realized he'd left marks from his nails digging into her.

His voice was rough. "I think I'll need a drink for this. What do you have?"

"There's some vodka in the freezer."

"That'll do."

He got up, naked, wandered into her tiny kitchen. God, he was something. All muscular male beauty. Like some sort of ancient god, and covered in the most exquisite artwork.

His tattoos alone made her sex give a hard squeeze of longing. He pulled the condom off with a paper towel and dropped it into the trash, opened the freezer and pulled out the bottle of Stolichnaya that had been there since the last time she and Crystal had had a girls' movie night: chocolate and martinis and a good cry.

She felt like having a good cry now.

Instead, she got up and pulled her G-string back on, her T-shirt, and sat cross-legged on the sofa, trying to hide her shaking hands beneath a pillow in her lap. Tristan came back with vodka in two glasses, handed her one. She wasn't sure she wanted it, but he threw his back in one swallow before bending over to retrieve his discarded gray boxer briefs. He pulled them on, then joined her on the old sofa, the weight of him making it creak as he settled in beside her.

She waited, cradling the glass in her hand. A series of emotions passed over his features. She couldn't figure it out, but she was certain he was going to tell her something important. Her stomach was one hard knot, her palms slippery, and it was all she could do not to allow the tears burning her eyes to spill over. Because she didn't know if this conversation would end with them being together, or if this would be the last time she saw Tristan Batiste.

CHAPTER *Seven*

Tristan ran a hand over his stubbly hair, as though it might help him think. Damn hard to think with Sophie sitting half-naked in front of him. Even harder after what they'd just done. But she deserved some answers. And he knew that right now, while he was still loosened up from the sex, the shot of vodka, might be the only time he'd be willing to tell her. Things he hadn't spoken to anyone about since his mother died four years ago.

"Sophie," he started, "there are some things you should know about me." He paused, looked at her. Her eyes were dark, somber, full of emotion. Better not to look her in the eye right now. Instead, his gaze wandered to the window behind her. The blue and gray New Orleans sky was hazy through the sheer fabric of the curtains. That's how he felt now, hazy, dim. His pulse was racing. "Are you going to drink that?"

"What? No. Here."

She handed him her glass and he downed the vodka; it burned sliding down his throat. Pathetic that he needed to be half-buzzed to tell this story. Pathetic that this story was his.

Fuck it. Spit it out.

He wiped his mouth with the back of his hand. "I told you I came back to New Orleans because this place is home for me. That it's in my blood. But that was only part of the story."

"So tell me the rest," she said quietly.

He drew in a deep breath, looked down at the empty glass in his hand. His fingers tightened around it. "My brother's name is Phillipe. And I want you to know, I do not talk to anyone about him. And I mean no one. Not even my staff at the shop know about him." He could feel his face heating up.

"Why not?"

"Because he's always been my responsibility."

"Why is he your responsibility, Tristan? Is he a minor?"

"He's dead."

She was looking at him now, her gaze unavoidable. "Tristan, you're not making sense."

He was quiet for several long moments, trying to get his thoughts together.

"My father was in the Marines. We lived all over the place when I was growing up. We didn't have anyone but each other, my brother and me. I was older and he looked up to me. And I'll tell you, I loved it. Loved being the big brother, loved the blind admiration.

"My father always wanted me to follow in his footsteps. He didn't even want to hear me talk about being an artist. Art was pansy shit to him. And Phillipe was into music, which my father blamed me for. I was a huge disappointment."

"I'm a disappointment to my family too," Sophie said, her voice soft. "But I'm beginning to realize that I can't take responsibility for that. They can accept me as I am, take it or leave it."

"Yes. But in my case, that's not the part that matters." He stopped, looked down at the empty glass in his hand, wished for more vodka. "I was in Europe, studying art. My father was still holding out this dream that I'd do the military career, like he had. That I'd be a good influence on my brother. But I wasn't about to give up my life. Certainly not for him. I was doing what I'd always wanted. Learning to paint, fucking too many women, drinking, doing some drugs. Living the bohemian life. And I have to tell you, it was a blast. And Phillipe, he was a teenager and he was a brilliant guitarist. I always told him how good he was, how he could be a rock star. And he . . . he sort of worshipped me, in the way younger siblings do sometimes. I played it up, sent him postcards from all over Europe, telling him what a wild time I was having over there. He came to visit me in London once he turned eighteen. I took him everywhere for about a month. We went to Berlin. We went to fucking Amsterdam, and I bought him a whore in the Red Light District. We smoked hash. It was insane.

"Dad was pissed. And he was devastated that neither of us was willing to go to war for our country. He blamed me for Phillipe, for him being into music. Said he always followed me blindly. That he could have made a good military man out of him if it wasn't for my influence. Maybe it was true. I don't fucking know anymore."

His gaze was on the window again, but he wasn't really seeing it. In his head, like a movie playing, was his apartment in Paris, the old-fashioned black telephone buzzing, the glass of French table wine in his hand dropping to the floor, shattering, staining the rug like a pool of blood. The girl he'd just fucked staring at him, openmouthed. He still couldn't remember her name.

He went tight all over, cold. He didn't want to talk about this.

"Tristan?" Sophie's voice was soft, urging him on.

"I didn't know that after he came back to the States things got so out of control. I didn't know until after he'd OD'd that he'd been using coke, speed. Heroin." He stopped, ran a hand over the stubble of his hair, grinding his fingers into his scalp. His head felt like it was going to explode. "If I hadn't been so fucking selfish, so self-indulgent, such an asshole, Phillipe would still be here. Would have a life."

"God, Tristan, surely you don't believe it's your fault?"

"Damn right I do."

"But he chose to do what he did, to use drugs. To take it too far. He followed his own destiny, regardless of whatever bad example you may have set. Do you believe that? That we each have a certain destiny?"

He shook his head. He was absolutely twisted up inside. "I don't know. I don't know what I believe. All I know is that *I* led him down that path. That my father was right; I was a bad influence."

Sophie was quiet, chewing on her lower lip. "I'm sorry about your brother."

"Don't pity me. I can't fucking take it."

"It's not pity, Tristan. I'm just sad. Tell me what happened to your parents."

"My father died a few months after Phillipe did. Heart failure. The doctor said he had a heart defect no one had found before. But I think it was the stress. My mother died four years ago. Just went to sleep and didn't wake up. An aneurysm. It was sudden. But at least it was peaceful. Being the last one in our family left on this earth, it made me wake up, finally, and realize that what I was doing was not a life. Not one that meant anything. Even after my self-indulgence ended Phillipe's life, I was still traveling, partying, refusing to come home and face up to what I'd done. It was time for me to grow up."

Not that he was really facing anything. How long had it been since he'd visited his brother's grave?

"You didn't do anything, Tristan!"

"I did."

"Well, I'm still not getting it. What has all this got to do with . . . us?"

He really wanted more of the vodka now. Wanted to make the anger and the shame blur around the edges. But it was sharp and clean inside. He said carefully, "I'm not a good person, Sophie. I am not the kind of person who is capable of caring for another person in the way they deserve."

"Why not? Because you think you failed once? God, Tristan, you don't have to give up your life because of what happened to your brother. You don't have to give up loving people!"

Love? Was that what this was? This sensation of being punched in the gut every moment he'd been apart from her? How was that even possible? "I don't expect you to understand."

"Oh, I understand better than you might think. I live with my own guilt every day. With shame."

He glanced at her then. Her eyes were glittering. Was it anger he saw there?

"Shame and guilt for what?"

"For being... who I am. For not being the good girl my family needs me to be. For fighting against the mold they want to fit me into. And for knowing I will never, ever fit."

"Jesus, we are one fucked-up pair."

She nodded. "That's part of why we understand each other. I always wanted to be a little bad, but I couldn't really do it. Couldn't let the guilt go long enough to be... to be myself, really. It's only those tapes playing in my head, from my parents, from the church, that tell me what I want is bad. And you... you just want to be good, and you feel like you can't. But it all comes down to the same thing. We both pay and pay for this twisted sense of who we are. A lifetime of penance."

He had to admit it made a sick sort of sense. And she did seem to understand him, in a way no one had before. Maybe because he'd never let anyone close enough to try. So why now? Why her?

"There is some weird thing happening between us. I can't stay away from you, Sophie. I don't know what it is. And it's not just the sex. Not just the tattoos. Although, that's really... Fuck, I don't understand that part of it, either. You get the tattoo thing on some very deep level, in a way other people just don't. It's more than art to me. It's sex. It's the primal permanence of it. It's... *more.* And you feel it too. I don't want to let you in. But you're getting in anyway."

"Maybe that's not a bad thing."

"Maybe."

He'd told her about Phillipe, and she was still there. She hadn't condemned him for it. Maybe it was time for him to stop condemning himself?

"I want you, Sophie. I don't know what else I want right now. I don't know what I'm capable of."

"Neither do I. But it all feels so right, being with you. Being tattooed by you. As though no one else could have done it. Yet at the same time, I can't quite seem to justify it to myself. I still have to work that out. All that old Catholic guilt."

"Is that what this is about?" He reached out and took in his fingers the big silver cross that hung between her breasts.

"No. That's my own thing, my own beliefs. It has nothing to do with my family. Really nothing to do with the Church, even."

He dropped the cross, stroked the back of his fingers over her heated cheek. "I like that about you. Your independence. Your strength. Even your anger. You look so fragile. But you're not."

She was quiet, watching him. "I think we're both angry."

"Yes. But it's just one more thing we understand about each other."

"Tristan..."

Her gaze on him was intense, gold and green and silver all at the same time, those dragonfly eyes. Her brows were drawn together, her lush little mouth set. There was so much in her face, in her eyes. Yet all he could focus on suddenly was her mouth. Had a flash of her on her knees in front of him, sucking him deep into her throat. He shivered.

Fuck. Not the time for this.

No, this was a serious moment. He'd just bared his soul to her, for God's sake! It was insane, how he bounced back and forth between wanting to virtually open a vein for her and then in the next moment fuck her. The real beauty of it was that he knew she'd let him do it. Talk to her. Tattoo her. Fuck her. She seemed to be willing to do whatever he wanted. Seemed to want it too.

He drew her to him, quickly stripped her little T-shirt off. The cross swung between her breasts. Her nipples were dark, swollen. Like overripe fruit waiting to be picked.

He leaned in and took one nipple in his mouth, sucked

hard. She moaned, just a soft sigh of air, and his cock hardened. Too good. But he wanted to kiss her, wanted to feel her mouth. He raised his head and pressed his lips to hers. Almost romantic, how soft she was, how yielding, if he was a romantic kind of guy.

And then he stopped thinking as she opened his lips with her wet little tongue. She drew his tongue into her mouth, sucked on it. And he remembered again that hot mouth of hers on his cock.

He pulled back. “Sophie.”

“What is it, Tristan?”

“Suck me.”

She slipped down to her knees in front of the old sofa while he slid his briefs off. So gorgeous, all that dark hair falling over her shoulders, over his thighs. Her skin was so pale, delicate next to his. But there was nothing delicate about her mouth as she slid it over his cock. He groaned at the heat of her, her swirling tongue. And then as she drew the sharp edges of her teeth over his swollen flesh.

“Christ, Sophie... yes, bite it, bite it hard.”

He buried his hands in her hair, all that dark silk sliding between his fingers as her teeth sank into him, the pain and the pleasure shooting from his groin deep into his belly. He pumped into her mouth, and she took him in, sucking, sucking, until he thought he’d explode. She paused, bit into the tender flesh at the head of his cock. It fucking hurt. He deserved it. Needed it. Needed her. He pulled back.

When she looked up at him her mouth was soft and red, bruised almost. Her eyes were enormous. He pulled her to her feet, stood with her tight in his arms. Her breasts were crushed against his chest; he could feel the hard peaks of her nipples on his skin.

Have to fuck her... just fuck her...

He tore her little G-string down her legs, cradled her ass

in his hands and lifted her, took a few steps until he had her up against the wall, right next to the window overlooking the courtyard below. The curtains were sheer, filmy. He didn't give a shit if anyone could see them. He had to be inside her.

"Spread, Sophie. Just do it."

Her legs went around his waist and he pushed into her. Hot and wet and milking his cock right away as he drove into her body. She was panting, gasping. He bent and bit into the tender flesh of her shoulder, his teeth sinking in. What was it about the pain for them? Didn't matter. Just taste her flesh. Just fuck her.

"Harder, Tristan!"

He rammed into her, using the wall behind her for leverage. And still, he couldn't seem to get deep enough. Pleasure rippled through him: his cock, his belly, his arms and legs.

"I'm gonna hurt you, Sophie."

"Yes. Do it."

"Christ..."

Harder and harder, his hips slamming her up against the wall. And when he felt the first tremors of her orgasm gripping his cock, she caught his gaze, held him there, biting her lip and whimpering as she came. His orgasm stabbed through him, pleasure shafting deep into his body. And her eyes were like two glittering jewels, searching his face, seeing inside him as though his skin were invisible, a needless barrier. They didn't need it anymore.

He almost fell, staggering back to the sofa with her warm body still coiled around him. He collapsed there, his legs shaking, his mind whirling.

Something had just happened. It was more of what had happened between them before. But more important this time.

Jesus. He had to stop this. Before... What? He didn't

know anymore. Every argument for staying away from her had suddenly disappeared. He wanted this. To be with her. To talk with her. Fuck her. Tattoo her.

Yes, he wanted to tattoo her. There was something about that, about marking her, he'd never felt before.

Mine.

He didn't understand what was happening to him. But it felt too good to fight it. She felt too good. For now.

Sophie watched him, emotion shifting across his features. His eyes were dark, distant. And just as she was beginning to worry, he focused on her. She felt it, knew he was really seeing her, no longer lost in his own head. And it warmed her all over, in a way the heat of sex couldn't quite do.

"What are you smiling about, Sophie?" Tristan stroked her cheek, the edge of her lips.

"I'm just . . . happy. Strange, that this feels so . . . alien to me, being happy."

"I understand what you mean. It's unfamiliar. As though I don't deserve it."

"Yes, that's it exactly."

She thought for a moment about how everything between them was all tied together: their guilt, their need to be redeemed. And how these things connected them every bit as much as their mutual love for tattoos and rough sex.

"Tristan, I need to tell you about the tattoos."

"Tell me."

"It's more than that I love them. That I think they're beautiful." She ran a finger down his arms, over the dragon inked into his smooth skin. "I didn't really understand until the first time you touched me with that needle." One long, lovely shiver at the thought. "I understand now that it's a true fetish for me. That I need it. I have for a long time. And finally having that is such a . . . relief. But my need for it is also endless."

"I'll tattoo you again."

"Yes. I need you to. It can only be you."

"Good." He squeezed her tight, and she loved that he felt proprietary about her. That he understood exactly what she was saying.

It came to her once more how they could just be together, at any moment, with his body still joined to hers, and talk, *really* talk. Amazing.

They lay together on the scratchy old velvet of the sofa for a long time, every bit as content to be silent and still together, while the muffled sounds of traffic, other tenants in the building, came up from the street, the courtyard.

She had never felt contentment with anyone else. It was a strange and wondrous thing, something she didn't want to question right now. They'd had some pretty heavy conversation today. There would be more to come, she was sure. But this was enough for now. Far more than she'd ever hoped to have.

"Tristan, let's not talk about anything else right now. Nothing of consequence. Alright?"

"Yes, alright."

His arms tightened around her. She inhaled, breathing in the scent of him, dark, earthy, sexy. Yes, this was all she needed, right now, right here. They would figure out the rest later.

They spent nearly a month together, every moment that Tristan wasn't working. They went back to Café du Monde, their favorite haunt, eating the steaming hot, sweet beignets, watching the people on the street, in Jackson Square across the way. They loved to sit there in the warm Louisiana rain, protected beneath the green-and-white-striped awnings, while the tourists ran for cover in the shops. They often went late at night, at midnight, at three o'clock in the morning, after their rumbling stomachs forced them out of bed.

On Tristan's days off they explored the city. Sophie loved the funky little shops, selling everything from Mardi Gras beads and Caribbean handcrafts to leather goods and vintage clothes. They went to the Museum of Art, spent hours wandering the long halls, the sculpture gardens, debating the purity of abstract art, of the Surrealist painters. They went to the funny little Musée Conti, the wax museum with scenarios depicting the history of New Orleans.

In the evenings they sometimes went to a small, smoky bar close to Tristan's shop, where they served Spanish wine and hearty food, listened to the Flamenco guitarists, watched the dancers with their colorful costumes, their sensual, flashing hands and dark eyes.

He tattooed her. First a string of tiny black stars around her right ankle, then a Sanskrit "om," the symbol of the essence of the universe, on the inside of her left wrist. And each time he took the needle to her skin, it was an intense erotic experience for them both.

And they talked, about everything, anything, except for those dark secrets each of them had and neither wanted to explore any further just yet. This was their Neverland time. Sophie knew it would end eventually, that they would have to really open up to each other, figure out their individual issues before they could have anything more than the dream time they currently shared. But she could wait.

For now, they talked, ate, fucked, in a sort of exquisite dream state. They had sex on Tristan's chair again, on the tables in his shop. They had sex with her bent over the seat of his motorcycle after a long ride out to the bayous. Sophie had loved it, that thrill at the possibility of being caught.

She loved the sense of danger just being with Tristan brought.

She sat now at her kitchen table. Tristan had just left for work. She'd hardly been able to let him go. He'd been sleepy still, his hair wet from the shower, the clean scent of soap all over him. He'd kissed her good-bye in a way that told her she would have more of him later, after he was done with work tonight. Or maybe on his break he'd sneak back to her apartment, strip her down and fuck her on her bed, on the sofa, on the floor, as he often did when the shop was slow.

She shivered just thinking about it.

She felt them moving closer and closer all the time. Physically, mentally. Emotionally. She knew they still had issues to work out. But right now it was hard to care about anything but being with him.

She wanted him to tattoo her again, a large piece this time. She knew he would do it, as soon as she found a design she wanted. God, to feel the needle on her skin again…

She shifted in her chair, crossed her legs against the ache that started there. She sighed, sipped her tea and opened her laptop. She needed to get some work done today, so she would be free to be with Tristan tonight. He'd definitely edged into her writing time, but Sophie found she was more disciplined about it now, using her daytime hours more efficiently.

She opened her document, tried to focus on the words on the screen, forcing her mind away from thoughts of Tristan. She knew she would see him tonight. She saw him every night. Still, she could hardly wait.

A knock at her door made her jump, wondering if it could be him coming back already. She got up and opened the door.

"Hey there." Crystal stood in the hall, her dark hair twisted up into a series of small, spiky ponytails all over her head.

"Hi. Come on in."

Crystal moved past her, went into the kitchen and put the kettle on the stove, pulled a mug and the box of tea from the cupboard. "So Sophie, things must be getting pretty serious with you and Tristan. I've hardly seen you in weeks."

Sophie smiled. She couldn't help it. "Yeah, well, we see each other a lot."

Crystal flopped into the other chair at the small kitchen table. "No kidding." She reached over and grabbed the half-eaten toast left on Sophie's plate and took a bite. "So. You gonna tell me about it?"

"What do you want to know?"

Crystal grinned at her. "Everything. Well, except that I *am* your downstairs neighbor, so I already know you two fuck at all hours of the day and night."

"There is no such thing as privacy with you, is there?"

"Nope."

Sophie sighed and took a bite of toast. It was cold. She dropped it back onto her plate.

"So?" Crystal prompted.

"What?"

"You seem pretty casual for a girl in love."

"I am not..."

Was she?

It hadn't even occurred to her to label what she was feeling. All she knew was that she loved being with him, could hardly stand to be apart from him.

"I don't know, Crystal. He makes me feel... different than I ever have before. With him I don't feel like what I'm doing is wrong, not in the way I usually do. Like this is good, us being together. That *I'm* good. I don't know how to explain it."

"That Catholic-girl shit."

"Yes, I suppose. It's more complicated than that. But love?"

"Why are you so resistant to the idea, Sophie?"

"For different reasons than you are," she said quietly.

Crystal laughed. "Alright, I know. But you . . . you have this amazing guy. And you're totally glazed. Why not just admit it?"

Why not? She wasn't sure. She knew it had something to do with all that twisted shame she was still trying to work out of her system. But she'd never felt better than she did being with Tristan. It was right. *He* was right.

"God, Crystal . . ."

The teapot sang and Crystal got up, made her tea, brought it back to the table and sat down. "It's okay that you love him," she said.

Sophie nodded, her throat tight. She felt like crying suddenly. Crystal reached out and put a hand on her arm.

"It really is okay, Sophie. In fact, it's pretty awesome."

It was awesome. Awesome and terrifying and beautiful. She loved him. She did.

Relief washed over her, warm and soothing. And as entirely unexpected as falling in love with Tristan Batiste.

Her heart gave a hard thump in her chest. What would happen now? She didn't know. She wanted to tell him. She *would* tell him, the next time she saw him. Tonight, she would tell Tristan she had fallen in love with him.

Chapter Eight

Tristan leaned over the appointment book, looking at his schedule. Only one more client and he'd be done for the day. Maybe another hour, then he'd be with her again.

Sophie.

He'd been distracted today, thinking of her. Not even the sex, necessarily, which was always on his mind, present in his body. Just *her*.

Maybe he'd take her out to dinner tonight. There was a real hole-in-the-wall Cajun place he'd been meaning to show her. Food hot enough to burn your head off, but he loved it. The home-brewed beer there was some of the best to be had anywhere. And they had live music—real, old-fashioned Cajun music. Funky stuff, but he loved that too. Then he'd take her home and . . .

Fuck it. He had to see her.

"Henry," he called out.

His manager appeared from behind the curtain leading to the back room. "Yeah?"

"Take my last client today, will you?"

"Sure. Everything okay?"

"Yeah. I just have to get out of here."

Tristan grabbed his keys and his helmet from behind the counter, paused, then stalked back to his workstation and put his tattoo gun, the small, airtight containers of ink, the sterile wipes and some gloves into a small metal travel case. He walked back out and swung through the door. He'd take his bike; he couldn't wait long enough for the ten-minute walk over there. His heart was pounding in his chest.

In minutes he was there, running up the old creaking stairs. She opened the door the moment he knocked, her green-and-gold eyes wide with surprise.

"Tristan, hi."

That beautiful smile lit her face. Only a moment, and then he was on her, crushing her mouth beneath his. He stripped her bare while he kissed her, just swallowed her sweet mouth, pushing her into the apartment as he went. Then they were in the kitchen, somehow, and he lifted her onto the counter, shoving a plate onto the floor with a crash. He pulled back.

"I have to tattoo you, Sophie, alright?"

Her eyes were glowing, on fire. "Yes. Anything. Whatever you want to do."

He spread her thighs wide. "Wait here."

He got his kit out of his jacket, snapped open the case, filled the gun, pulled the gloves on. Sophie sat on the edge of her kitchen counter, naked, her nipples hard and dark, her lovely thighs spread, the pink lips of her pussy plump and open.

Fucking beautiful.

He yanked one of the small iron chairs over and set it

between her legs, sat down. He touched her left thigh, and she spread farther for him without protest. When he pressed two fingers at that spot just below the crease of her inner thigh, only inches from her damp slit, she shivered.

"Right here. Okay?"

"Yes. Yes..."

He leaned in and touched the needle to her flesh, and she moaned softly. His cock was rock-hard. He could smell her arousal, could sense the damp heat of her.

Focus.

He began to draw the outline, a small dragonfly. It seemed to represent Sophie to him. Delicate, beautiful. It made him think of her eyes. *Dragonfly eyes.* He was done with the outline almost too quickly. He glanced up at her. Her gaze was on him. Her lips were parted, red and lush. She was panting. He couldn't help himself. He pushed two fingers into her, watched her bite her lip, her eyes narrow, heard her gasping breath. His cock twitched.

"I'm going to tattoo you, Sophie. Then I'm going to fuck you right here on the counter."

"Yes, please, Tristan."

He smiled, pulled his fingers from her, went back to work. He used green and a little gold, dragonfly colors, and highlighted with some white, listening to her panting breath, feeling her shiver in pleasure. He knew what tattooing did to her. What it did to him. His cock was going to fucking explode if he wasn't inside her soon. But this was too good.

He paused, used his left hand to press her clit, while he finished coloring the tattoo with his right. Just a few moments, but she was groaning, trembling all over.

The second the tattoo was finished he stood, set his tattoo gun down on the seat of the chair and pushed it aside. Then he was back between her thighs.

He unzipped, pulled his swollen cock from his jeans and stabbed into her.

"God, Tristan . . ."

She began to whimper as he drove into her, pleasure coursing through his veins as her legs wrapped around his waist. He ran his hands over her body, that pale, cool flesh. He couldn't get enough of her. When his fingers skimmed the raised skin of her back, the cherry blossoms he'd tattooed there, a shock of lust and a deep satisfaction went through him.

"Fuck, Sophie," he muttered. "Need to go deeper."

"Yes, please . . ."

He was hurting her again. Had to be, he was fucking her so damn hard. But he couldn't stop. Couldn't get enough. Never enough. He had to have her, all of her, inside and out.

That idea filtered through the back of his mind, the small part that wasn't in full-blown animal mode. That thought he'd had before.

Mine.

What the hell?

No, he'd think later. Now he just had to fuck the girl.

He rammed into her, felt the first tremors of her orgasm as her tight pussy gripped his cock.

"Oh, oh . . ."

Her cries drove him over the edge, hurtling him into darkness as his orgasm slammed into him, pleasure driving deep into his body, his mind. He was stunned, blank. All he knew was her body warm against him, around him, as she whispered, "God, Tristan. I love you."

His breath froze in his lungs.

"No, Sophie."

He pulled back to look at her face. Her eyes were enormous. Her breath was coming in short, sharp pants.

"Tristan—"

"No. Don't say it."

"But why . . . ?"

She looked dazed. Shocked. Hell, so was he. He pulled out of her, shoved his still-hard cock back into his pants and zipped up as she slid her feet to the floor, leaning against the counter. He didn't want to believe she'd said that to him. He felt as though he'd just been condemned.

Fuck.

He could not handle this. He could not love her. He couldn't love anyone. He'd fucked up. Again. He'd let it go on too damn long. Selfish bastard.

Again.

"Tristan." She was pulling on his arm now, trying to get him to look at her.

Don't do it.

"I have to go, Sophie."

"What? Why? Please just talk to me."

He took a step back.

"Tristan, don't do this," she pleaded.

He couldn't look at her. She was naked, beautiful, in pain.

"I have to go."

He turned and headed for the door, nearly ran down the stairs he'd so eagerly run up only a little while earlier, and out into the sultry New Orleans heat.

A week had gone by. Sophie remembered that other week of waiting for Tristan. He'd come to her eventually. She'd been surviving on the hope that he would do it again.

She'd called him, a dozen times or more. He'd never called her back. She felt like a fool for not having given up. But no matter that she understood, logically, that she should move on with her life and leave him behind, she just couldn't do it. Their connection was too strong.

She thought it had been anyway.

She pulled the old woven blanket tighter around herself, curled farther into the sofa cushions. Outside was another gray Louisiana day, warm and damp with an impending storm. How many days like this had she and Tristan spent together, at Café du Monde? In her bed? She'd loved the gloomy weather then, safe and warm with him beside her. It had felt womblike to her. But now the weather only depressed her. It seemed to be a manifestation of how she felt on the inside, gray and . . . dead somehow. Lifeless without him.

Crystal had been up to see her every day, tried to tempt her to go out, to leave the apartment. She'd finally brought her a small bag of groceries yesterday. But Sophie didn't feel like eating. She was too torn up inside, too pathetically desperate to talk to him.

Tristan.

God, she was a mess. The man had left, there was no arguing that. And he didn't want to talk to her, or he would have called. But she could not give up on him. Would not give up. Why should she have to, just because he had?

Anger burning through her, she threw the blanket off. Fuck it. She refused to be a victim. She wasn't going to let him walk away without explanation. If nothing else, he would have to face her, would have to come up with some excuse. She had faced down her demons to be with him. She still had work to do, she knew that. But he was going to have to either do the same or tell her why the hell he couldn't.

The rain was coming down in a light drizzle as she pushed through the door of Beneath the Skin. It was warm and dry inside. She could swear she smelled the ink. Always pure sex to her. Just being there made her breasts ache, her sex swell with need. How screwed up was that? But now it only made her lonely.

Henry was behind the desk, leaning over the appointment book, as he had been the first time she'd walked into the shop.

"Henry, I need to talk to Tristan."

The man looked up. "He's not here. Hasn't been all week."

"What do you mean? Has something happened to him?"

"I don't know and he's not talking. He sleeps here. I saw him leave this morning. But he hasn't taken any clients. I've been holding down the fort and, I dunno . . . waiting."

Sophie nodded, said quietly, "I've been waiting, too." Tears stung behind her eyes. "Thanks anyway, Henry. I guess . . . if you see him, just tell him I stopped by, okay?"

"Yeah, sure."

Back on the sidewalk, the rain came down a little harder. She didn't know where to go, what to do. She felt empty, hopeless. She didn't want to go home, couldn't face sitting alone in her apartment anymore. She didn't even care that she'd forgotten an umbrella. It didn't matter.

But she couldn't just stand there, outside his shop, wishing he would come. It was too sad, too awful. He wasn't coming. He couldn't love her. Why couldn't she just accept that?

Tristan . . .

She stepped into the street, crossing to the other side, walked along the edge of the small park there, past the lush lantana, the twisted branches of the crepe myrtle, the pink blossoms sodden with rain. All around her was the scent of wet pavement, the perfume of flowers, the dark green scent of decay.

Her hair was soaking wet, plastered to her forehead. She pushed it away from her face with an impatient hand. And then the tears came, mixing with the raindrops on her cold cheeks.

The tears turned into long, wracking sobs, and she couldn't walk any farther. Grief poured through her, paralyzing her. She staggered a few more steps through the downpour, sat down on a wooden bench, not caring that she was soaked through. The grief came like a series of blows to her chest. Old grief, and new. She cried for everything she'd never had, for everything she'd never hoped to dream of, and had somehow found with Tristan. She cried because that was all gone, and now she was left with nothing.

Sophie had no idea how long she sat there, on the bench in the rain. She was too filled with misery to care. She was cold, right down to her bones. But nothing seemed to matter.

"Sophie? Jesus, Sophie."

She looked up, through her wet hair, through the rain, and there he was, like some sort of wraith in the rain and the mist.

She couldn't speak. Emotion flooded her mind, her body. She started to shake.

He stepped closer. "Christ, you're soaked to the skin. What are you doing out here? It's pouring. I saw you from across the street and—"

"What? You came to say good-bye finally? Don't bother. I get it, okay?"

Heat worked its way into her system, the heat of anger, a pure fury burning bright.

"I don't know. I don't know what I was going to say." He dropped his head, staring at the ground.

"Do you want to tell me where the hell you've been?"

He shook his head. She could see, even through the rain, even through the tears stinging in her eyes, the clenching and unclenching of his jaw muscles.

"I've thought about you every day. Every fucking minute of every day. But I had to stay away from you, Sophie. It wasn't fair of me to stick around, to lead you on."

"Is that what you were doing? Because you did a damn good job of it. I know we're both completely fucked up, Tristan. I'll admit to that. I'm just as fucked up as you are. But why did you have to do it this way? Why did you have to hurt me?" A sob welled in her throat and she fought it back.

"Sophie, I'm sorry. I am so damn sorry. I *am* screwed up. I'm a fucking mess, if you want to know the truth."

She stood up, got right in his face. "Yes, I want to know the truth. So tell me, Tristan. Stand here and tell me to my face that you don't love me!"

He looked at her, his eyes dark, blazing. But he didn't say a word.

"You can't do it, can you?" she asked quietly.

"Fuck, Sophie—"

"Just tell me. Tell me you love me, or tell me you don't. But don't stand here and say nothing, like that's some sort of viable alternative, because it's not."

His eyes went a shade darker, bore into her. Through gritted teeth he said, "I love you, Sophie."

"God." The tears came, hot on her cheeks. "Then why did you leave?"

"Because I don't know how to love anyone. Because I'm not . . . not fucking good enough."

"Don't give me that crap. We've already talked about it. No one is irredeemable, Tristan. Not even you."

He shook his head. "I'm beginning to understand that. But I'll hurt you."

"You already have."

"That's exactly what I'm saying." He ran a hand over the short thatch of dark hair on his head.

She said very quietly, "I still love you, Tristan. Even though you hurt me. You can hurt someone without killing them, you know."

He looked as though she'd hit him. "You don't know what you're talking about."

"I'm still here, aren't I? I'm hurt, but I'm alive. And you really need to stop talking as though I'm some sort of angel. As though I'm so much better than you. We are both totally messed up, Tristan. I can deal with it."

"Why do you want to?"

"Because I love you. I love you enough to stay and do the hard stuff. That's what you do when you love someone. Don't you see, Tristan? Love is what makes us good finally. Love is what redeems us."

He felt like he'd been sucker-punched. She was right. Maybe the mere fact that she loved him, that he loved her back, was the only good thing about him. Maybe it was enough to make up for everything else. Maybe it was the only chance he had at making something meaningful out of his life.

He was behaving like a coward, afraid to love her. But he did. And he could hardly bear to see her like this, so torn, shaking in the rain.

He pulled her into his arms. Burying his face in her wet hair, he breathed in the scent of her, while something inside him broke apart, opened up. "I love you, Sophie."

Her arms tightened around his neck. "I love you too. Don't ever do this to me again."

"I'll do my best, I swear. But I'll be honest, this scares the shit out of me. And I'm going to fuck up."

"It's okay. I don't expect either of us to be perfect."

He pulled back, his hands on her cheeks, gazed into her

eyes. “You are perfect, Sophie. Perfect for me. I know we have a lot to work out. But I’m finally getting that we can do it better together. That maybe part of the reason why I’m still so messed up is that I’ve always tried to do it on my own. And for the first time in my life, I need someone. I need you.”

He kissed her then, hard and bruising. She trembled in his arms, and he loved it. Loved knowing he could do that to her, by kissing her, touching her. Tattooing her. That was part of it. The pain, the tattoos. How fucked up was that? But it didn’t matter anymore. All that mattered was that they understood each other. They loved each other.

When he pulled away he realized the rain had stopped. Sophie’s eyes were enormous, glistening. Too beautiful to be believed.

“You’re what makes me good, Sophie,” he told her. “You’re what redeems me.”

She smiled. “And you’re what allows me to be bad. To accept that part of myself.” She was quiet a moment, blinking tears from her eyes. “We are one fucked-up pair. You were right about that. But together, I think each of us is more whole.”

He nodded. “So what now?”

“Now we just love each other. And maybe we learn to forgive ourselves along the way.” She was quiet a moment. “And you tattoo me again.”

“Every beautiful inch of you, if you want me to.”

She smiled, brilliantly. “You understand me like no one else, Tristan.”

And she understood him. Loved him. Regardless of how twisted up he was inside. How twisted up they both were. They would love each other anyway. That was more than enough.

SHADOW PLAY

SYDNEY CROFT

CHAPTER *One*

Hex was on the prowl.

The chill had shot up his spine earlier, gotten him out of bed and onto the mostly deserted streets of New Orleans at two A.M., searching for the something—or someone—who called to him.

At times, being a slave to his desires was exhausting, at others, exhilarating. Tonight, it was a combination of both as he stood in front of the old house, just waiting.

The vines withered, shrubbery was overgrown in spots and bare in others, a testament to what the combination of nearly two years of neglect and a force of nature could do to what was once a beautiful Victorian home.

Since Hurricane Katrina, the paranormal activity in the city and her outlying regions was off the charts. And the paranormal was Hex's bread and butter—as a member of the Agency for Covert Rare Operatives, he investigated hauntings and captured images of ghosts on film in a way very few before him had the ability to do.

He'd seen some pretty good fakes of ghost images, had exposed his share of the hoaxes and made a name for himself with his black-and-white stills of haunted houses, with or without ghosts. His career as a photographer was his cover, since both ACRO and his work for the agency were secret.

He hadn't been to his main office in upstate New York in months. ACRO set him up in a satellite office in one of the best hotel suites in New Orleans, and most people thought he was here compiling his newest photography book.

He'd been doing that too, but this was more about releasing spirits who'd been displaced, who needed guidance to get to where they needed to be than getting images for the new book. Hex wasn't the most powerful of mediums at ACRO, but he did attract a special breed—the loneliest of the ghosts, ones who desperately needed someone still living to help release them.

Alone was something Hex understood well. He never wanted for female company when his needs called, and his travels took him far and wide enough that worries of long-term entanglements weren't an issue. He was a kind of social worker for ghosts, and very few people understood his work enough, or at all, for him to begin to think he had the hope of a normal relationship.

The only time he actually felt the pull to settle in with someone was when he was here, in New Orleans.

This city had always intrigued him, stirred his cock with the scent of heat, steam and perfume, sugar and sex that even the stench of destruction couldn't overpower. The pull of the city's inherent sexuality was something even nature couldn't erase, and yes, he was getting restless.

There was a single light shining through a second-floor

window. As he watched, a shadow moved past the sheer curtains. Human, not ghostly.

Brenna St. James, the well-known supermodel, had called him earlier—the desperation in her voice clear even in the simple message she'd left for him on his cell phone. He hadn't bothered to call her back, but then he'd been summoned here to her house by something bigger than both of them.

Tonight, the moon was full, and he was more superstitious than most. As soon as the dusk had settled, the white orb called to him, made him want to take Brenna under it with a mournful howl that would shake his soul, which rattled him to the core, because as a rule, he never went anywhere during a full moon. He was too exposed, vulnerable.

His senses flared and he focused on the area of white mist to the right of the house. A ghost exiting the desolate house. Hex was once again in his element—the flood of emotions, both his own and the ghost's, nearly overwhelming. Luckily, he had control over that.

The whir of his camera cut through the night, the clicks echoing through the lonely darkness.

The click of a camera had once been Brenna St. James's drug of choice, the rush almost sexual, the high almost orgasmic. Now the sound brought dread to the pit of her stomach, because she knew what she'd see in the photos.

Still, she had to try.

Six cameras topped storklike tripods, all aimed at her as she posed on the 1920s Victorian-style chaise, one of the few pieces of furniture remaining in the nineteenth-century Queen Anne. She'd sold everything else, and in a few days an antiques dealer would come for the last of it.

Brenna smiled for a few shots, did the sexy pout thing

for a few more and then stuck out her tongue for a couple others.

Monthly ritual completed, she hurried to the two digital cameras. She'd have to sell the others when the film ran out, but until then, she wouldn't waste a single frame.

She plugged one of the cameras into her laptop balancing on the end of the chaise and waited until the images appeared.

When they did, cold sweat broke out on her forehead. Nothing had changed. The chaise, the hand-carved stairway railing behind it, the hallway to the kitchen on the left—everything in the formal sitting room stood out in sharp definition. Everything except her. Her body and features were so blurred that she could have been any blond blob.

Then again, she wasn't so sure she wanted to see what the camera would reveal. Her waist-length hair, no longer pampered by designer products and cared for by top stylists, hung like a wiry horse's tail. The dark circles under her eyes would probably never go away, and her skin had rebelled against the New Orleans humidity in the form of a dull, bumpy complexion. And she'd always been thin, but a combination of poor diet and irregular meals had taken even more weight off her—another couple of pounds and she'd meet the requirements for heroin-chic fashion.

Hands shaking, she plugged the second camera into the computer and came away with the same results.

"Dammit," she whispered, and then, louder, "*Dammit!*" Sinking to her knees, she screamed at the top of her lungs and then buried her face in her hands.

She was in so much trouble. A model who couldn't be captured on film was pretty screwed.

The sound of someone knocking on the door brought her head up. Knocking? At two in the morning?

Maybe one of her neighbors had heard her scream. Then again, the neighbors on either side couldn't care less about the down-and-out supermodel who had inherited a house they believed had been ill-gained by her mother in the first place. They'd made it clear that they didn't appreciate Brenna's charlatan mom tricking Foster Duncan, marrying him for his money, and they'd made it equally clear that the very sight of Brenna in the front yard was a disgrace.

The nosy jerks wouldn't have to worry about it for long. If she couldn't scrounge up a house payment by next month, the bank would foreclose, and it didn't look like she'd be coming into money anytime soon. She'd sold nearly everything of value and had already shut off the phone, cable and Internet, and this week she'd have to make a choice between paying the electricity or the water bill.

The knock at the door became more insistent. It was stupid to answer, she knew, but at this point, she had nothing left to lose. She didn't even care that she wore nothing but a tank top and a pair of men's Snoopy boxers that kept sliding down on her hips. No, she'd worn far less in swimsuit layouts.

She'd worn nothing at all in the men's magazine spread. Of course, that particular job had been unique, had taken place after her images had gone blurry and no one else would hire her. The magazine had printed the fuzzy pictures—on the cover, even. But the real draw had been the article itself, supposedly written by the photographer and describing her body to the male readers. The result had been a record number of sales for the magazine, and now, months later, men still told her how they'd jerked off to the article.

Flattering, but creepy.

Never in all my years as a photographer have I been turned on by a nude model. But as I shoot Brenna St. James, I'm required to jot down my observations, and that, my friends, is torture. I have to imagine what her full breasts would feel like beneath my palms, how her dusky pink nipples would pucker under the caress of my lips. Her pussy is clean-shaven, probably very lickable, and although she has said that she doesn't have sex with photographers, I think I'm going to test her ideas about that. Wish me luck.

She still cringed when she thought about that last paragraph. All the guys who admitted to getting off on her spread asked if she'd slept with the photographer, probably assuming that if she had, she'd sleep with them too.

"Hey! You okay in there?" A low, powerful voice boomed through the door.

"Who is it?" she called out, grasping the door handle but not turning the knob.

"I was out walking. Heard you scream. My name is Hex—"

She yanked open the door, welcoming the blast of sultry night air that stirred the staleness in the house. "Oh, my God. It's you. It's really you." Her prayers had been answered in the form of a blond god of a man who captured ghosts on film and captured the imaginations of women everywhere. "Come in. Please."

The shadows fell from his face as he entered the lit parlor, revealing the graceful, high cheekbones that would have made his face beautiful if not for the rugged line of his jaw and hard set of his mouth. Reportedly, he was a recluse, but as something of a celebrity in the Deep South thanks to his amazing photos, pictures of him could often be found accompanying newspaper interviews, and now she knew first-hand that he was even better-looking in person.

"You're Brenna, right?" He didn't look at her. Instead, he eyed the room while moving deeper inside, his booted feet clomping on the wood floor that squeaked with every step. And wow, he had a nice butt. Lean, but not flat, and perfectly shaped for a woman's hands. The man was a walking Levi's advertisement.

"That's right. Brenna St. James." She closed the door. "I don't understand. I left a message, and when you didn't call back, I assumed—"

"Like I said, I was taking a walk and heard you scream."

"It's called frustration," she muttered. "You're here to help me, right?"

He hooked his thumbs in his jeans pockets and stared up at the balcony on the second floor. Finally, just as she was about to ask what he was looking at, he shook his head and swung around. "You said the house wasn't haunted. So I'm not sure what you need me for."

Those eyes. So clear and piercing, the color of fine whiskey and just as intense. And when his gaze traveled leisurely down her body, she felt the burning path like a shot of Jack Daniel's down the throat.

"I don't want pictures of the house. I want pictures of me," she said hoarsely, and his eyes snapped back up, darker than they had been a moment ago.

"I don't shoot people. Sorry." Hex stalked toward the door, and panic rose up in her chest. "If everything is fine here, I'll be going."

"Wait!"

She grabbed him by one arm, and *oh, my.* Sleek, powerful muscles rippled beneath her palm, sending a current of awareness shooting through her body. It had been a long time since she'd looked at a man with interest—not since Nicky dumped her over a year ago—but this Hex guy... the strength, the sensuality that radiated from him, well, it called out to parts of her she'd thought had gone as blurry as her images.

"I said no."

"Please. I'll pay anything." A lie of sorts, since she was down to her last hundred dollars, but once he took care of her problem, she'd find work and could pay him. And this time, she wouldn't be so reckless with her money. She certainly wouldn't trust a boyfriend or manager with account information and investments again.

"What do you want from me?" he asked, and boy, she could think of a lot of ways to answer him, ways that involved his slim fingers on her suddenly inflamed skin. "I take stills of buildings, not people. I'm sure you could find dozens of local photographers who would jump at the opportunity to take your picture. Why me?"

Reluctantly, she let her hand drop and wished she had coffee or wine to offer him, but she'd been living off ramen noodles and Popsicles for weeks.

"Because I'm being haunted."

One tawny eyebrow shot up. "How do you know?"

"Can we sit down and talk about this?"

"I'm fine where I'm standing."

Near the exit. Yeah, she picked right up on that one. Now if she could just convince him not to use it.

"My mom used to own this place. After Hurricane Katrina, I came to help her repair the damage. A month later, I went to Milan for a photo shoot, and none of my pictures turned out. It's been that way ever since."

His gaze narrowed, focused, and she got the impression he was taking his own mental pictures. When he finally spoke, the appreciation in his voice said the images had turned out just fine.

"And you think a ghost is responsible?"

"I don't think. I know." She wrapped her arms around herself, a nervous habit born of a childhood where she'd often had to explain her mother's gift to skeptics. They never believed her. "I grew up here, and my mom was a medium, so I've been around the hocus pocus and supernatural all my life. I know ghosts exist, and I know a haunting when I see it."

"Have you been to a medium recently?"

A bitter laugh escaped her. Before Katrina, New Orleans had supported a thriving population of psychics, but it seemed like only the frauds had returned. Still, she'd tried them all in hopes that one might possess even a thread of talent.

"Several. It's always the same. They can't see him, but they go through the motions. Tell him to cross over and all that. Then I come home, take a picture and nothing has changed. I need you to capture him on film. Then maybe we can talk to him. Figure out what he wants. Who he is."

"And once that happens?"

"I can get out of this hellhole and move to New York or L.A., where I belong. So please, will you do it?"

He shoved his fingers through his hair, leaving it mussed and begging for her touch. "I told you, I don't shoot people. I'll contact some colleagues and see if they can help. Give it a couple of weeks—"

"I don't have that long!" She threw herself in front of the door. "Please. I know I have a reputation for being difficult, but I'll do anything you say. Anything you want. If you want me to stand on my head while you snap pictures, I'll do it. I'll do anything. Anything at all."

His gaze dropped to her breasts, which hardened beneath his stare until her nipples were pressing against the thin fabric, and one corner of his lush mouth twitched. "Somehow, I suspect that our ideas of what constitutes *anything* are very different." His voice was a low, rough challenge.

Sensation washed over her skin, and heat swam beneath it, all from nothing more than Hex's suggestive look. Desperation tore at her, hunger gnawed at her and urgent, erotic need had begun to build at her center.

Unlike her mother, Brenna had never used sex to get what she wanted, even though she'd been shown the casting couch on several occasions. Sex had always been about pleasure, about the sharing of bodies and minds after she'd gotten to know a man.

What she was about to do went against her nature—and against everything she used to spout for the "Love First" teen magazine campaigns for which she'd been a spokesperson.

An image of Nicky in bed with her former best friend flashed in her brain, and she shrugged.

Love was overrated anyway.

Before her pounding heart pumped some sense into her brain, she stepped away from Hex and peeled off her tank top, exposing her breasts to the steamy night and his glittering gaze. Encouraged by his response, she shifted slowly, subtly, to expose her best angle, and pushed down her boxers. His audible swallow echoed through the cavernous room as she took her time rolling her spine straight.

"Then again," he murmured, "I could be wrong."

"Anything," she repeated, and a gust of wind shrieked through the house. Somewhere upstairs, a door slammed and she jumped.

"Your ghost isn't happy."

"That's the first time he's done anything like that. He never makes noise."

He looked up at the ceiling. "He doesn't like it that I'm here."

The rise and fall of Hex's chest beneath his T-shirt grew irregular as he stood there, and for a humiliatingly long moment, she thought he'd refuse her. Then, in a blur of motion he moved, and she found herself pinned to the wall, her wrists shackled above her head by one of his hands, her flank being stroked by the other.

"I thought you don't screw photographers," he murmured into her ear, and she flushed from head to toe at the knowledge that he'd read the article accompanying the men's magazine spread. She'd sent him the photos, but not the magazine itself.

"You can't believe everything you read." Though in this case, it was true. She had a strange aversion to dating men with cameras. Pictures revealed what a person looked like on the outside, but when a photographer looked at her through a lens, it felt like he was seeing her on the inside as well.

And inside, she wasn't nearly as beautiful.

"I read that you're lickable. Was that bullshit too?" He rocked his hips into her so the hard ridge of his erection rubbed her bare mound. "Because I'm thinking maybe I should find out."

She went utterly wet between the legs at his words, her body firing up, preparing for him even as her mind shut down—not from fear or hesitation, but from the sudden, devastating knowledge that no matter how impersonal she would try to make this, Hex would turn it into something very good, and *very* personal.

CHAPTER Two

None of this was good.

Brenna St. James would let him take her, right here, against the wall—Hex could smell her arousal and it was hell on his. His head dipped down to her shoulder, his lips brushing her neck lightly, and the familiar ache ripped through his body like the dull paring of a knife through his aura.

Hers was calling out to him. Faint, like a shadow refusing to be caught. *Save my life, Hex.*

How goddamned familiar all of this seemed, as though he was coming home to something rather than just visiting. The feeling was still vague enough to make him uncomfortable and he wondered if there'd been some kind of spell cast over this house . . . over her.

He tried not to think about how her nipples were a perfect, dark rose color, how they rubbed taut against his T-shirted chest. How he could drive into her in a single stroke and watch the pleasure highlight the stark cheekbones and heavy lids, imagined how tight and wet and hot she'd be for him.

Instead, he pulled his hands away. "I don't want sex."

"Oh." She grabbed for her top, and he could see the burn of humiliation on her cheeks as she held it up in front of her. It didn't hide much, and the image of her naked body had already seared itself onto his brain.

"Not right now...I want to take pictures first," he amended, because he would have Brenna St. James before the night was over. Had to have her.

"I'm not just going to be your sex toy—available whenever you're ready," she challenged, her voice dark and smoky, with an inherent sexuality that couldn't be faked. There was nothing fake about the woman who stood in front of him—she was stripped as bare as she could be—and if there was really a ghost haunting her, she could be stripped far more than she ever thought possible. And she wouldn't like it.

"Really? What happened to the *anything* clause?" he asked.

"Do you always take advantage of desperate women?"

"I never take advantage of *any* women. You're the one who came up with the offer. Like I said, I'd be more than happy to find you another photographer."

She sighed and backed down. "They say you're the best. And I need the best."

Yes, he was the best at what he did. Always had been, which was why he was as haunted as the spirits he helped. "You haven't been eating. Or sleeping."

"Do you always state the obvious? I know I look like death warmed over. Nothing like I used to be in the magazines, right?" She gave a short laugh. "As if you don't know all of that is retouched."

"I told you, I don't work with people. Which means you'll have to do exactly what I say or I'm out of here."

"I can do that," she said, and he believed her, even as he wished at the same time that it wasn't true. There was a small spark there, and even though Hex only knew her from the before-and-after photos he'd studied, he sensed that Brenna was a shadow of her former self. He didn't like that, and he didn't want to think about why it bothered him so much.

He ran his hands through his hair and realized he'd have to actually move into this place if he wanted to help her. Bringing out a ghost and convincing it to leave for the Other Side wasn't a sideshow trick done in the course of an hour. No, there was a fine art to the deal, and one that Hex respected too much to try to rush through. "Before I came into the house, the only time you felt the activity was when a camera was trained on you?"

"Yes."

His eyes caught hers. "I'll stay through the morning. Then I'll go collect my things—I'm going to have to stay here until this job is done."

"Okay. But you should know . . . there might not be any electricity. Or hot water."

"Trying to scare me off?"

"No. *No,*" she emphasized, shaking her head hard.

"Don't worry—I've worked under worse circumstances."

"I wish I could say the same thing. How and where do you want me?"

"Are you always this agreeable?"

"When my entire career is on the line, yes."

He couldn't shake the feeling that there was so much more on the line, like his body and soul. This whole scene was far too reminiscent of that single haunting he tried so hard to forget.

There was too much here to pull his focus askew.

"On the couch. Keep your clothes off." He fiddled with the shutter speed, glanced up to check out the lighting she had available.

Right—candles. Only candles. When he glanced at them, she crossed her arms in front of her breasts and squared her shoulders proudly. He didn't make any comments about turning on the lights and started snapping pictures instead, camera at arm's length.

Almost instinctively, she put her hands up, as if she'd been photographed before without her consent and still harbored resentment.

"Relax, I'm just taking some test shots—I'm not even focused on you. And I'm not going to do anything with these pictures but use them to help you. All I ask is that you do the same and not use them for personal gain or public consumption. They stay between us and get destroyed when this is all solved."

She nodded. "Fair enough."

He continued snapping as she moved, off to the side and out of range of his shots. "You don't like spirits much, do you?"

"Not when they ruin my life."

"They don't mean to, you know. Most of them are just... lost. Kind of like you are right now."

She opened her mouth, as if she was going to reply to that, but she didn't. "Let's get this over with," she said instead.

He didn't bother to tell her that they'd barely begun.

The spirit hadn't come into the room yet, but the air had already started to change, as though it would crackle and snap any second. The heat became nearly unbearable. He fought an urge to strip down himself to catch any breeze that happened through the half-opened window and wondered if it was truly the heat, or the sight of Brenna naked. She was thinner than she'd been, but her body was a perfect model's hanger—and her face held the cross between innocence and seduction that enticed the camera.

What he did when photographing spirits came close to what photographers referred to as shadow play, the interaction of light and dark. Shadows were powerful to shoot—emphasizing form over detail.

Brenna's body was a perfect combination of shadow and light. The pictures would be startling, beautiful . . . just like Brenna herself.

His vision blurred as flashes of black and white, blues and purples, a dizzying array of images that popped like too many flashbulbs threatened to overwhelm him, even though he wasn't actually looking through the camera's lens yet.

This was too much—he'd taken on too much in this agreement. He'd known that from the moment he'd walked into Brenna's mansion, the moment he'd walked down the street that led to her house. The moment he'd gotten out of bed.

But still, he was here and she was stripped naked for him, as he'd asked, and his body began its familiar ache.

"Why don't you pose on the love seat?" he pointed to the small chaise in the middle of the room. Even in the half light, he spied the intricately carved wood that ran along the top and the legs and knew it must be an antique. The rest of the house was strangely bare, and he wondered why she'd hung on to that particular piece, one that could probably pay her electric and water bills for the next few months.

She complied, draped herself across the cushions so her lower body turned teasingly in a don't-you-wish-you-could-see-all-of-me position, while she hid her breasts seductively behind her arm.

It was a pose Hex was all too familiar with, the first one of the now-famous photo spread in the men's magazine.

Unaware that he owned the issue, Brenna had sent him the pictures with a note, told him that she believed something paranormal was going on that was affecting them. He'd been able to feel the desperation behind her letter, even though she'd attempted to cover her fear by signing her name like an autograph.

He'd studied the photo spread, tracing the blurred features of Brenna's body with a long index finger, as if he were actually caressing her curves.

The pictures were the least graphic that magazine had ever produced and yet there was something extremely sensual about them that drew men like crazy.

No one could stop talking about it. Hex couldn't stop thinking about it, dreaming about it.

He'd pore over those pictures, use magnifiers, and then he'd close his eyes and see the images of Brenna's gorgeous, blurred form and he'd break out in a sweat, his body shivering from near simultaneous heat and chill, his body roaring for release.

He'd felt as if he'd been the one to take those photos, even though that was ridiculous. But he swore that if he closed his eyes tight and rubbed his fingers on the pictures, he was with her, in that room, with the camera clicking away at full speed.

"Is this going to happen? Because the faster we do this, the faster I can salvage my career," she said.

"Right, I forgot—Hollywood's calling." He took a deep breath and brought the camera up to his eye, the way he'd done a million times before, less than an hour before, even, outside the house. But this was different—this was capturing a spirit who'd actually attached itself to a human being.

Rare, but it did happen.

As always, the vision of that haint from hell flashed in front of his eyes, the demonic image burned onto his brain, thanks to the single encounter with it when he was seventeen years old. Whenever he thought about it, he'd repeat the Scottish prayer his mother used to soothe him with like a mantra. She'd always told him that it would make everything bad go away.

From ghoulies and ghosties
And long-legged beasties
And things that go bump in the night,
Good Lord, deliver us!

He knew much, much better now, and yet he still said the prayer anyway.

"Have you ever sensed spirits or ghosts here before?" he asked, in hopes of quelling the panic that threatened to make him leave the room.

"Yes—when I was growing up, there were always hot and cold spots, strange noises. Nothing sinister. And nothing out of the ordinary for New Orleans."

"Your mom sensed them as well?"

"Yes. But it was stronger for her, obviously. I don't have the gifts she had," she said quietly, and he wondered when to reveal the fact that he had that gift himself or if he even should. He could do more than prove Brenna was being haunted—there was a very real possibility that he could help rid her of the spirit, if the bastard would just show his face.

He needed the spirit to come out and play. While simultaneously wishing it would just go away on its own.

Brenna was waiting for him to make his next move.

"Have you ever just asked it to leave?"

"I'm pretty sure it's a he... don't know why. And yes, I've asked. Begged. Pleaded. I've tried burning candles and sage, and smudging the ashes around the doorways. I've tried everything."

Hex would have to tempt the spirit out—and bruise his ego. And he was tired of wasting time. "Come on, Brenna baby, you know you want to show it all to me," he said, hiding his expression behind the safety of the camera's lens, shooting film all the while.

She tensed visibly at the change of his tone, and the spirit's anger shot through him fast and hard, seconds before he actually saw the vision of the man in the 1920's-style suit and hat standing behind the chaise. It was threatening to touch Brenna's bare shoulder.

Hex fought the urge to growl and stop shooting, but he didn't. Whether Brenna could sense the near touch or not, he couldn't tell, but she'd frozen up again, and the spirit's hand began to wander too close for Hex's comfort as it continued to stare at Hex and mouthed, *She's all mine... forever...*

"No!" Hex roared, yanked the camera away and stared at the space where he knew the man's spirit still stood. Brenna glanced between him and the area behind the couch in confusion. "Come here, Brenna," he said, in a tone that left no room for argument.

Dealing with the ramifications of Brenna's haunting tonight meant first showing the spirit who was in charge here. And that was most definitely Hex.

She'd have no way to handle the ghost's touch. He knew all too well what a touch would do and he even hesitated before he basically yanked her up and took the brunt of the touch.

Arlen Rousseau's emotions invaded Hex's senses—Hex felt intense elation, which soon gave way to the pain and torment Hex remembered feeling the first time a tortured spirit had touched him.

Knocked flat on his back as Arlen's emotions surged through his, Hex was vaguely aware of Brenna leaning over him, her hands gently stroking his face... Arlen's face.

Mattie...

Arlen was attempting to invade, trying to take over Hex's body. If Hex wouldn't let Arlen have and haunt Brenna—who Arlen believed was someone named Mattie—Arlen would try to find another, more effective way, and that would be through Hex.

She's beautiful... I don't want to share her with anyone, Arlen whispered, and Hex got it, understood why Arlen was smudging Brenna's images. It was a possessive respect that could easily border on the horrifying if Hex couldn't shake free of this possession.

She's not Mattie, you're disenfranchised... you're lost, Arlen...

Not lost... found, Arlen whispered back, and Hex found his own hand reaching out to stroke Brenna's cheek. She pulled back slightly, as though surprised by both the familiarity and sensuality of the touch, but he heard himself whispering, "*So beautiful,*" and she softened.

But for now, Hex was half possessed and still struggling to retain himself. And although his mind and body had responded easily to Brenna's beauty before, the need doubled, until he was propping himself on his elbows and pulling her already naked form toward his. He needed Brenna now as much as he wanted her—and joining with another body physically would strengthen his protective aura. Being locked together would save them both from the possession... at least for now.

"Take my clothes off, Brenna," he said in a voice that

didn't exactly sound like his. It didn't matter; it was as if they'd both been pulled into some kind of force field of EMGs—electromagnetic activity—supplied by Arlen. EMGs could be produced by many things other than ghosts—batteries, pipes, you name it—and they could cause everything from hallucinations to physical sickness.

The same reactions one could have when an actual ghost was attempting to invade, which was exactly what was happening to Hex now.

Brenna's hands fumbled along his shirt—she pulled it off, her palms ran along his chest in a way that made him shiver.

"I want to touch you . . . I'm going to touch you," he said as he warred for control over his own body and free will.

Brenna unzipped his pants, and she was already touching him, as if she couldn't stop.

When he kissed her, doors and windows began to slam open and shut as the spirit reacted. She tasted like dark, rich chocolate, sweet and bitter at the same time, and he knew for sure he was in too deep.

This was insane. Hex had collapsed for no apparent reason, had come to a few seconds later to make sensual demands, and now she was kissing him like he was her lifeline.

Which he was, and she'd played her hand so early in the game that she couldn't protest now. Not that she wanted to, because she'd never been kissed like this in her life.

Hex's tongue teased her lips, pushing at the seam like he wanted in, and then drawing back before she could decide how far she wanted to go. Of course, seeing how she had offered herself to him just an hour ago and now had his cock in her palm, how far she'd go wasn't exactly a mystery.

Especially since he kept telling her how beautiful, how

sexy she was, something she hadn't heard in a long time. She craved the compliments and adoration like a drug, one she'd been forced to quit cold turkey.

And here was a man who knew exactly the right things to say, the right way to look at her.

He tore his mouth away from hers and pushed her onto the floor. Male heat surrounded her, engulfed her, and his scent filled her as he stretched his long body alongside hers.

"You're perfect. So perfect." His worshipful gaze swept over her body, and when he dipped his head to gently kiss her on one shoulder, she melted into a puddle.

"Hex," she sighed, and he pressed two fingers to her lips.

"Shh . . . no names."

An odd request, but as long as he kept kissing his way across her shoulder and up her throat, he could ask for anything he wanted. He shucked out of his pants quickly, and spread her legs with one thick thigh. Like a prowling, big cat, he covered her, pressed his hard body against hers.

"I've waited so long, Mattie . . ." He trailed off, his hands easing along her hip and around to cup her ass.

Mattie? "What did you call me?"

Hex blinked, a battle of emotions playing out on his features. The candles cast flickering light and shadow on the sharp angles of his face, bright warmth, darker confusion. Even his eyes seemed to shine and wane, flashing between the seductiveness of aged bourbon to a murky, smoky color full of secrets.

"Brenna." His voice, raspy, like he'd been screaming for hours, sent shivers up her spine. "Shit. The ghost . . . he's talking about his lover—" He broke off with a growl, teeth bared, eyes closed as if he was in pain.

"Damn you," she shouted to the rafters. "Leave him alone." It wasn't enough that the bastard messed with her career, he had to mess with her love life too.

Not that love had anything to do with what was going on between her and Hex. This was about putting her life back together. About forgetting her troubles for a few precious moments.

She ran her hands down his back, stroking the smooth, hot skin that jumped beneath her fingers. Knotted muscles gave way only slightly as she kneaded his shoulders, coaxing him to relax and focus on pleasure. "Ignore him. Don't let him interrupt this."

"You don't understand." He swore, hissed, and then suddenly his expression softened and his eyes once again brimmed with a look of worship and blatant hunger that made her stomach flip-flop. "I'm going to make love to you, and he's not going to stop me."

"Good," she whispered. "God, I hate this paranormal crap."

"Don't say that."

Before she could argue, his hand slipped between her legs, his mouth tipping up in a satisfied smile when he encountered her swollen, dewy sex. Heat shot through her in a lashing whip as he parted her labia, allowing the sultry air to swirl across her aching flesh. She whimpered and squirmed, raked her nails over his hard biceps to let him know she wanted more.

His touch smoothed inward, and the feather-light strokes with two fingers on either side of her clit made her quiver in anticipation. When his thumb brushed her hypersensitive nub, just barely, she hummed in approval and impatience.

"That's it, my greedy little bear-cat." His voice was dark and rough and it rumbled through her like a sensual growl.

"You say the oddest things . . . oh! Oh, *yes*."

She arched into his hand, gasping at the sweet burn of friction as he pushed a couple of fingers inside her. Her pussy clenched and pulsed, and she felt a rush of moisture bloom around his knuckles. Spreading her legs wider, she writhed, chasing his thumb because she needed his hot touch in the right place.

He denied her, instead using his talented fingers to trace her feminine tissues, teasing and skimming but never hitting the sweet spot. Oh, he was devious, watching her reactions as he played, his gaze burning and so full of desire she wondered how he could endure the leisurely pace he'd set.

"More. Please." She dug her fingernails into his skin, her frustration roaring through her like a hurricane.

Nostrils flaring, he looked deeply into her eyes. "Anything for you."

Heat pooled low in her chest. Never had anyone focused on her so single-mindedly. It both excited and frightened her, because she could grow used to that kind of attention.

His thumb spread her cream upward, circled her throbbing clit as he thrust his fingers in and out. Her body gripped him, sucked him deeply inside as she grew wild with need. She couldn't control the way she rocked into him, rubbed against him like a sex-starved feline, and at this point, she didn't care.

"God, you're good at this," she breathed.

He didn't pause to respond. Instead, he stroked her, laved her breasts with his tongue and then blew cool air across her nipples. The little nubs stiffened and puckered, aching for attention. He seemed to know, suckling each in turn, drawing her flesh into the warm depths of his mouth.

He was gentle, more so than she'd have expected. Every velvet touch, every tender flick of his tongue on her flesh made her want to whimper with ecstasy.

The smooth slide of his fingers as he pulled them out of her felt good, but not nearly as good as the sensation of his cock slipping between her folds to rub her clit on each slow pass between her legs.

Exquisite tingling sensations shot through her, overloading at her core and streaking out to nerve endings all over her body.

"Condom." She gripped his shoulders, the broad expanse of muscle flexing as he rocked against her. "We need a condom. Do you have one in your pocket?" *Please let him have one.*

He reached for his pants without leaving her, and after a moment of fumbling, held up a foil packet.

Thank God. She was on the pill, and didn't keep condoms handy. She'd left those with Nicky, figuring the cheating son of a bitch needed them more than she did.

Going up on his knees above her, Hex settled the rubber over the blushing head of his cock.

"Let me."

She sat up and took his shaft in her palm. It jerked at her touch, pulsed and swelled as she rolled the condom down his hard length. His groan vibrated all the way to his cock. It was beautiful—a dusky rose column marbled with bulging veins, and so thick she couldn't close her entire fist around it no matter how hard she tried, how hard she squeezed. And stroked. And caressed his sac, which drew up tight as she gently scraped her nails along the seam between the heavy balls inside. When she cupped them, rolled them tenderly in her palm, he threw his head back and sucked in a harsh breath.

"Yes..."

She smoothed one hand down her belly and between her legs, where she coated a finger in her slick cream. The temptation to stay there and play, to give herself the relief she needed, was nearly overwhelming.

Instead, she used her finger to coat the base of his sac, creating a slick, hot friction as she stroked. His body strained, each individual muscle starkly outlined beneath his golden skin. At his sides, his hands clenched and unclenched, as though he wanted to touch her but was too distracted by what she was doing between his legs.

She worked her thighs against each other, trying to ease the ache at her center. Silky honey began to flow, and wow, she didn't think she'd ever been this turned on.

"You are exquisite, *mon trésor.*"

Heart fluttering at the words, she lay back on the cool hardwood floor and spread her legs in invitation. "I didn't think you'd been in New Orleans so long. You have an accent when you're worked up."

His body went taut, all the sinewy muscles freezing hard. "*Dammit.*" He tossed his head from side to side, his lips drawn back into a silent snarl. "Not . . . me." Panting, he fell forward, buried his face in her neck as though exhausted. "Do you want this? Do you want . . . me . . . to take you? Because I need it. Need you."

Emotion flooded her. The intimacy shattered her. She'd given him an open invitation, but he wasn't taking advantage. How long had it been since any man cared what she wanted?

Any doubts she'd had about having sex with him were dispelled with his whispered words.

"Yes. Oh, yes." She wrapped her legs around his waist so his weight settled fully on top of her. "Make me feel beautiful again."

He groaned, his body trembling. When he lifted his head, the strange shifts in color and emotion were back in his eyes, an internal war she didn't understand. "Thank you. I can't . . . hold on."

Taking his shaft in hand, she guided him inside her, feeling a sizzle as his finely textured cock stretched her silken walls. "I can't hold on either." Her orgasm hovered hot, close.

A raw curse fell from his lips, followed by a sigh, as though he'd accepted his fate. He sank fully into her.

"Oh, yeah," he murmured into her hair. "You feel so good."

She moaned in agreement as he pumped his hips, slowly, letting her savor the sensation of release as it coiled in her loins, waiting for just the right angle, just the right speed.

The floor bit into her back but she didn't care. Couldn't care. All that mattered was how Hex held her tenderly, whispered hot, sexy, naughty things in her ear.

Slipping one hand low, he caught her buttocks and lifted her into his thrusts. She strained to meet his rhythm, which grew faster, more frantic, matching his breathing.

He pounded into her, the slap of hot flesh on hot flesh such a raw, base sound, but one that reached deep inside to excite the female animal in her. She wanted more . . . she sensed the power in him, sensed that he was holding back.

"Harder."

A low growl rumbled in his chest. He hammered into her, obeying her command, but still, his body remained taut, his strength leashed. He lifted her hips higher, driving so deep her womb rippled as he ground against her, his balls rubbing the delicate skin behind her sex. Lightning bolts of pleasure streaked from her tailbone to the back of her skull.

"Hex, yes, oh, God, yes!" She came in an intense rush of pleasure, her hips bucking, her thighs trembling, her blood thundering in her ears.

His cock drove into her harder, faster. His fingers dug into her shoulders with bruising force, all trace of tenderness gone, replaced by raw, primal passion. "Say my name when you come again. *Say it now.*"

Unable to think, she responded with a scream, crying out his name as he swelled inside her. He kept pumping, long after it was over, catapulting her to yet another violent release. Waves of ecstasy slammed into her, turning her inside out and leaving her legs quivering in their scissor-lock around his waist.

Finally, as the last of the spasms melted away, he collapsed on top of her, his breathing ragged, matching hers. His hand shook as he stroked her hair. "I'm sorry. Shit, Brenna. I'm so sorry."

Sorry? He'd just given her the most—and best—orgasms she'd ever had in a single night, and he was sorry?

"There's nothing to be sorry about. That damned ghost is the one who should be sorry. Trying to talk to you—"

"He wasn't talking to me." He lifted his head, his eyes clear, sad and at the same time sparking with anger. "He was talking *through* me."

"You mean . . . while we were having sex?"

"Before that." He rolled off her, his sculpted body gleaming with sweat as he lay on his back. "He was trying to get into me, but I got rid of him when we . . . when we started."

Suddenly feeling exposed, she grabbed her tank top and held it to her breasts. "How did you get rid of him?"

He didn't look at her.

Oh, God. Chills shot up her spine. "The sex."

"Joining with someone strengthens—"

"The protective aura," she whispered. "When two people are joined, it's harder for an entity to break in." Her mom had taught her way more than she'd ever wanted to know, and right now she definitely wished she was ignorant about the paranormal world.

Something reached up from the hollow hole in her gut and cut off her breath. The battle she'd seen in his eyes . . . that had been real, not some emotional thing going on in his head. He'd truly been fighting for control of his body.

And he'd used hers to win the battle.

Her breath whooshed out of her lungs in a painful rush,

and she started to shake. "You weren't making love to me because you wanted me. You were fucking me to protect yourself."

Hex moved with the speed and grace of a predator, had her in his arms before she could resist, his mouth against her ear. "It wasn't like that."

"Yeah, right." She tore away from him. "I need a shower."

"Brenna?"

"Don't." She gathered her clothes and darted up the stairs, feeling like a complete idiot. Her mother had been able to feel a spirit's presence a mile away, but Brenna couldn't tell when one was trying to possess the man whose hands were all over her.

Tears stung her eyes as she ducked into the bathroom. The man who'd looked at her with adoration and hunger in his eyes, who had brought her to the most powerful, amazing orgasms of her life, had been screwing her to fend off a ghost.

Not because he wanted her.

CHAPTER Three

Hex lay on his back against the hard oak floor for a few minutes after Brenna left, catching his breath, coming down from the orgasm that had rocked through him as though it had been years since he'd taken a woman.

He'd known it would be like that with Brenna. From the first time he'd touched the naked picture of her, he had felt her right down in his soul.

Hands behind his head, he stared at the cracked ceiling and the way the flickering candlelight threw dancing shadows. He had no doubt Brenna would've already kicked him out on his ass if she didn't need his help so badly. And he'd be more than happy to go, right now, if he could lift his damn head off the floor.

He knew why he'd promised to help her in the first place—it was why he always agreed to help. This was his job, his calling, his livelihood... the thing he both feared and craved, the high he needed. He'd been studying her for months, had found himself unquestionably drawn to her pictures, and for a bigger reason than her beauty.

Helping Brenna meant taking himself to the edge, and while he didn't mind being there, he wasn't all that sure he'd be able to pull himself back this time.

The kitchen door swung open and Brenna emerged, dressed in a man's long-sleeved, button-down shirt and boxers, and approached him tentatively.

She still looked confused and angry, but she was also scared. "Are you all right? Do you need anything?"

"I'm okay, Brenna. What about you?" He kept his tone low and even, soothing.

She responded by coming closer and sitting on the floor next to him. "I've been better."

Something upstairs creaked and she jumped slightly. Unconsciously, he crossed his arms over his chest so he could touch the markings on his biceps. Immediately, his breathing calmed, and as much as he hated depending on them, he was grateful to have them there.

"What are those?" She was staring at his arms and the markings as if for the first time. She'd been touching his biceps earlier, digging her fingers into them as he'd pumped into her, but probably hadn't realized just what they were. Now she reached out gingerly to trace the waved lines with a fingertip, and it was as if her touch zinged straight to his groin. "They're not tattoos."

"They're tribal markings," he said through his teeth, hating feeling helpless—the way he always did after a physical encounter with a ghost. Helping one cross over was exhausting in its own way, but nothing like this.

And still, she continued to caress the markings, which stood out in sharp contrast to the unblemished skin. They encircled each biceps in an intricate and definite pattern.

"Where did you get these done?"

"They're courtesy of an indigenous people who live along the Amazon Basin." He paused, ran his tongue over his bottom lip slowly—he was growing aroused again by her touch, hadn't ever really come down after he'd taken her. Could've taken her over and over again, on the floor, the chaise—and the way things were going, he still might.

"How did they put them there?" Her finger brought a heat like lightning beneath the surface of his skin, much the same way he'd felt when the markings were first put there. He shifted as though that would make the sting disappear, but it only intensified.

"They were carved and burned."

"Didn't that hurt?"

They'd given him something to drink first, some potent mix of roots and God-knows-what-else that helped him to fly. When the burning ritual commenced, he'd been caught in that strange place where extreme pain cut off any feeling. "It was worth it."

"It's some kind of protection spell, isn't it?"

"The tribe called me the ghost king and gave me the markings so another possession couldn't happen—at least not fully."

"Another possession?" She stared at him, her eyes soft—understanding, the anger draining away. "You've been possessed before?"

He paused for a second before answering, realized he'd never told anyone outside of ACRO and the tribe this story. Never trusted anyone to see his vulnerability. But Brenna, she was as close to vulnerable as he'd been, and perhaps in as much danger. "Yes. It tries, but it can't get fully inside—the markings force it out. It can't take over unless I invite it in."

"But tonight, it nearly happened again—you told me that damned ghost got inside of you."

"It's a full moon," he said quietly. "That's the one time of month I'm vulnerable. The markings fail and it's up to me. The tribe feels that a man should be able to protect himself for twenty-four hours, to keep his mind strong." The full moon was one of the reasons he'd fought coming to Brenna's house, but he'd been dragged here anyway by a force bigger than both of them. Now he'd have to depend on the force of their joined auras for full protection until the morning.

"How do I know you're not possessed right now?"

"I guess you're going to have to take my word for it. And I told you before—I didn't do anything with you I wasn't planning on doing anyway. Been dreaming about that since I first got the pictures you sent me." He ran a hand over the soft blond hair, pushed some off her cheek.

"You couldn't even see anything in those pictures."

"I could see, Brenna."

She continued to trace the markings. "Will you tell me what happened? What happened with your ghost?"

"Are you sure you're ready to hear a ghost story?"

She laid down on the floor next to him, on her side. "I need to know."

He turned onto his side to face her as well. "I was just shy of six years old when I'd first tried to explain to my parents, both professors at the local university, that I'd been seeing ghosts and spirits for as long as I could remember."

"My mother would've loved it if I'd told her that," Brenna murmured.

"Mine weren't as understanding." At first, his parents thought he had a big imagination and a lot of invisible friends. When he stubbornly set about proving to them that he was really seeing things, he'd started with his father's old Polaroid camera, shooting at the images. "When

I realized that I'd captured the ghosts on film, my urge to share the findings faded. So I told my parents that I liked taking pictures, spent my days honing my photography skills and combining that with capturing ghosts."

"You really weren't scared of them?"

"Were you scared when your mom saw ghosts? When she talked to them?"

"No. But what you're describing is much different. If I could actually see the ghost that's haunting me... well, let's just say I'd rather not go there."

He didn't bother to remind her that she'd see Arlen soon enough, once he developed his pictures. "I grew up seeing ghosts. I was never scared of them—not until I was seventeen." He drew a deep breath and Brenna reached out, touched a flattened palm to his still-bare chest and held it there, and yeah, that was nice. Calming.

"I'd been able to see the spirits without the aid of the camera's lens until that point. Until the spirit that lived in my closet proved to be malevolent."

He could still hear the voice echoing in his head.

Hex, can you come let me out to play?

Once the sun went down, Hex refused to open his closet. The spirit named Malachi seemed friendly enough during the day, manifested as a boy around Hex's own age, but there was always a sense of unease around the spirit that Hex was sensitive to. It seemed as if the other spirits stayed away until Malachi was securely locked up.

But one night, Hex's mother had mistakenly opened the closet door while Hex slept. "She was probably snooping, looking for things that all mothers of teenage boys look for—sex, drugs and alcohol."

He'd awakened to Malachi standing over his bed.

Hex, I've come out to play...

"I remember screaming, but no sound came out. Malachi touched me, and then it was like I was completely out of control, or falling into the deepest pit and still not hitting bottom.

"And while I was frozen, I saw Malachi's life—he wasn't a young boy, but a fully grown man who'd killed himself in prison."

A man who wanted to take over Hex's body and mind and find a new life through him.

"From that day on, I've only been able to see ghosts through the lens of a camera."

From that day, no ghost had ever gotten all the way in and been able to stay there—partly because of his strength of mind. And then he'd taken additional steps, dangerous steps, to make sure it would truly never happen.

He'd heard a rumor about a tribe that lived in peace among ghosts that regularly made their presence known—a tribe that held its ancestors' spirits on the earthbound plane for the first year after their death, in order to make their passing transition easier for everyone. The tribe had discovered a way to live among the ghosts but not become possessed by them, which was something angry ghosts often tried.

"You went to the Amazon Basin all by yourself?" she asked.

"Fear and need can do strange things to a man. To a woman too, I'm guessing." But still, the nightmare of what had happened to him when he'd been unprotected was fresh, always just below the surface and far too easily scratched.

He'd left the tribe after six months, had refused college in favor of traveling the world with his camera. Within a year, he'd already made a name for himself in both the mainstream photography world and the underground paranormal one.

ACRO tapped him quickly. They'd trained him thoroughly and sent him off to wander the world.

"I still have to fight the ghosts myself," he explained. "It still takes a strong mind. But seeing ghosts is my job. My gift."

"Sounds more like a curse to me. If I need to, I'll go get those markings done. Can you take me?"

"You don't need them. Arlen wants you for different reasons."

"Arlen? That's the ghost's name?"

"Yes. And I've got to get those pictures developed." He started to sit up and she helped him. He was weak, drained from Arlen's touch, lucky he was functioning. He'd seen people who remained semi-comatose for hours after a touch, who'd been unable to explain what they were going through.

He needed some food, some sugar, anything to keep him up and running.

Soon it would be dawn and the natural light would filter in through the windows and then it would get even hotter in the old house. He was intensely aware that he was still naked, and nothing but a cold shower or being inside of her was going to help matters.

And she was staring, until he reached for his jeans, and yanked them on roughly.

He could see her blush in the dim light. "Having sex with me must have been a real nightmare for you," Brenna said. "Which is pretty typical of the way my life's going right now."

"It wasn't a nightmare, Brenna. Not even close."

Somewhere upstairs, a door slammed, as if Arlen was

telling them that neither of them had heard the last word on the matter.

Exhausted but unable to sleep on an empty stomach, Brenna sat in the kitchen, twirling her fork in a bowl full of ramen noodles. She'd loved the things since she was a kid, when her mom had barely been able to make ends meet and had fed them to Brenna for breakfast, lunch and dinner. She hadn't eaten them since she was nine, when her mom had figured out how to make money off her psychic gift, opening a shop where she'd read palms and tarot cards, scratching out a meager living as a fortune-teller and psychic medium.

Funny how hard times brought a person right back to the most vulnerable and familiar places in their life.

She sucked a single noodle into her mouth and wondered what was taking Hex so long. He was using her makeshift darkroom in one of the spare bedrooms to develop the photos he'd taken, and though she tried not to get her hopes up, she couldn't help but buzz with a tingle of optimism. If anyone could help her, it was him.

The tribe called me the ghost king.

She forced her brain to take her into that scenario, to a jungle full of mystical people and magic. He'd been young, probably frightened and desperate. She knew how that felt, and as he'd talked about it, she'd wanted to pull him into her arms and just hold him.

But she knew too well that hugs didn't erase the past, and besides, he hadn't seemed very receptive. Heck, she had no doubt he regretted telling her anything at all.

The bowl of carbs she never would have eaten just a few months ago grew cold as she listened for his footsteps upstairs, or for the ghost—Arlen—to slam something else around. The earthbound spirit, as her mom had called entities that hadn't crossed over, had been in a snit ever since Hex and Brenna had had sex.

Sex to keep Arlen away.

Yeah, some dark side of her was still bitter about that, but the reasonable, less selfish side of her knew Hex had done what he needed to do. The battle for the control of his body had been intense, and she could see that, now that she knew what had been happening.

How could he stand it? How could he stand to have another person inside him?

The memory of having Hex inside *her* twisted into a tight knot of pleasure. The sex had been good. Amazing. And despite Hex's denials, she couldn't help but think it had happened only because of Arlen.

"You bastard," she ground out.

"I guess you don't want to see the photos, then?"

Hex stood in the kitchen entrance, one big shoulder casually braced against the door frame, his expression unreadable, his eyes sharp, focused, unwavering as he looked at her. Working in a darkroom agreed with him, and a slow burn started in her belly at the utter masculinity he radiated.

"Sorry." She resisted the urge to play with her hair—another nervous habit she'd thought she'd left behind years ago. Mainly because it was hell on split ends and breakage. "I wasn't talking to you."

He nodded like he got that, and yeah, she supposed he did. He tossed the pics on the table, scattering them. "Got anything sweet? My blood sugar's bottomed out."

Great. As if seeing her house nearly bare of furnishings wasn't bad enough, now he would discover her lack of pretty much anything edible. "I have Popsicles. Help yourself. Just not the blue ones."

"Your favorite?"

Heat seared her cheeks. "Guess that sounds kinda selfish."

He shrugged. "You're an only child. It happens."

She watched him open the freezer door, amazed that he'd written off her behavior as something other than being a spoiled, famous party girl. "Sorry I don't have more to offer you. I haven't had time to shop," she lied, though he had to at least suspect the truth.

"No problem." Hex closed the freezer and plopped down at the table—with a blue Popsicle.

Pretending not to notice, she grabbed the nearest black-and-white photo. The air whooshed from her lungs and suddenly she didn't care if he ate every one of her favorite ice pops. "Oh, my God, you're a genius. I'm not blurry!"

"Neither is Arlen."

The milky, nearly transparent figure of a man lurked behind the chaise, peering into the camera, a smirk on his handsome face. "Well, at least he's good-looking."

"Yeah, that's the important part of all this. The ghost should look as great as you do in pictures." Hex tore off the Popsicle wrapper.

She huffed. "I only meant that if I had to be haunted, at least he isn't creepy and gross, with his skin falling off or some crap."

She shuffled through the rest of the photos, which were all the same. Clear. Blessedly clear. Sure, there was a ghost in every one of them, but she didn't care. Thanks to the wonderful world of technology, he could be easily removed.

"These make me look so thin. And since the camera adds ten pounds . . ."

"The camera doesn't lie, Brenna."

"Ever?"

"Ever."

"Well, that's what imaging technicians are for." She held one shot close, still amazed at the clarity. "I don't know how to thank you, Hex. I can't believe this. You've done it!"

He drew the ice pop out of his mouth and shook his head. "I haven't done anything. You won't show up in any other photographer's photos."

Her stomach bottomed out. "What? Why not? Are you sure?"

The way he combed his fingers through his hair told her he was almost as frustrated as she was. "Whatever Arlen is doing to blur your pictures doesn't allow him to show up on your average photographer's film, but since I can capture him, you're captured too."

If she hadn't been sitting, her knees would have buckled. This couldn't be happening. "Wait... I'm clear in *your* pictures. So you could come work for me. You can be my personal photographer. Arlen can be taken out of the photos. No problem."

"Do I have any say in this?"

"Of course you do. You can pretty much name your price with any company I model for. And, obviously, you'll have to move, but—"

"No."

She blinked. "No? No what?"

"All of it. What makes you think I'd want to leave New Orleans?"

That stumped her. Who would willingly live in the dank, hot bowels of Louisiana when they could live somewhere that teemed with life and sparkled with light twenty-four seven? "Well, I guess you could always just fly out for jobs..."

"Jesus Christ," he muttered. "Did it occur to you that

maybe, just maybe, I don't want to be your little camera-spank-boy? That maybe I don't want to drop everything and follow you around like a stray puppy just so you can have your glitzy life back?"

How dare he? How dare he . . . what? Want a life for himself that didn't orbit around her? Humiliation crawled up her spine. God, what a self-centered bitch she was. And it had nothing to do with being an only child. Her mother had once told her that Brenna had felt a sense of entitlement from the day she was born, and it had only grown worse once she was on her own and being fawned over by designers and photographers and everyone else around her.

"I'm sorry." She pushed aside her bowl of now-cold noodles, her stomach rebelling. "It's just that you're all I have right now." He was all that stood between her and the streets. She had no job skills, hadn't done well in high school and had never been able to act. There was a reason her thief of a manager had rarely sent her on movie casting calls. She was a pretty face, and that's all.

"It's okay." He bit the top off his Popsicle—the man must have no nerves in his teeth. As he drew the blue ice away, she noticed a slight tremor in his hand.

"Are you all right?"

"Takes a while to get rid of the shakes after a near possession."

"Does it happen often?"

"No."

He didn't offer any more in the way of explanation, and she didn't push, merely watched him bite off another inch of Popsicle as juice ran down the sides and onto his fingers. Long, sexy, tapered fingers. Male hands had always fascinated her . . . calloused, rough ones appealed to the female animal in her, made her see the male form hard at work, muscles flexing, sweat gleaming on tan skin. Smooth, soft ones brought to mind luxurious, pampered fantasies of those hands gliding like velvet over her body.

Hex's hands were a perfect combination of the two—smooth yet strong, lightly calloused, as though he had done his share of physical work when he wasn't holding a camera. And she knew very well how they felt on her skin.

"You're staring at me." His voice was gravelly, like he had heard her thoughts.

"Because you aren't eating that right."

He cocked a tawny eyebrow. "There's a wrong way and a right way?"

"Depends on where you are, sugar," she drawled in a sultry Southern accent she'd put away a long time ago. "You can take your sweet time if you're a Yank eating one in the frozen wastelands of Minnesota, but down here where it's hot, you have to hone your technique."

A cocky smile turned up one side of his mouth, just enough to make her libido flutter with new life. "Why don't you show me?" He held out the Popsicle, his voice thick with sensual challenge that surprised them both, if the way his eyes widened was any indication.

The air grew heavy, charged with sexual tension that had sprung up from nowhere. "Is the ghost—?"

"Arlen isn't here." He leaned closer. "This is between *us*."

Never had anyone affected her like Hex did, the way just looking at him made her blood run hot, her skin grow tight and her sex throb with need. She couldn't think of a single reason she should want him or why she should encourage him to want her—other than getting a good ego boost—and though this was, no doubt, a huge mistake, she grasped his hand in hers and brought the column of ice to her lips.

"The trick is, you don't concentrate on the tip, though you do need to get things started." She swirled her tongue around the top, keeping her gaze locked on his. "Then you lick the sides to catch the trickle of juice." When she drew her tongue down the cold length, blue raspberry flavor exploded on her taste buds, and she moaned with pleasure.

Hex's gaze darkened as he followed the motion of her tongue. "Okay," he breathed. "I get it."

She gave him a slow, teasing smile. "I'm not done. Not even close. See, once the sides are cleaned up, you slide the flat of your tongue up to the tip, suck and nibble just a little..." She did as she'd described, and she thought Hex's breath hitched. "Then drag your mouth back down, because see how the base is starting to drip? Must lick the base very carefully. That's the most important part."

He watched as she lapped the sticky sweet drops from the bottom of the Popsicle, taking each one onto her tongue and swallowing before taking the next. The cool liquid felt good sliding down her throat, but it did nothing to ease the burn that had started to build between her thighs.

"It seems that your way of eating an ice pop is a lot slower than mine." His voice was dark and deep and so rough it vibrated in all the right places.

"Maybe." She took one of his knuckles into her mouth to suck the sweet syrup off his skin, and his sexy-as-hell lips parted in a silent gasp. "But my way is all about making it last and taking the most pleasure. That's the way Southerners do everything, in case you hadn't noticed."

"I noticed." He sucked air between clenched teeth when she flicked her tongue over the sensitive webbing between his fingers. "Oh, yeah, I definitely noticed."

"There are times when fast is good, though."

"Yeah?"

Holding his gaze, she closed her entire mouth over what remained of the Popsicle. With firm suction, she pulled the ice free of the stick.

Hex made a funny strangled sound.

The cold numbed her mouth, slid down her throat and felt so damned good because she'd gone hotter than Jackson Square's iron fence in August. Sighing with pleasure, she wrenched the stick from Hex's tight grip and took it to the garbage can next to the sink.

She didn't hear him move, but she felt his hands on her hips and his body pressed against her back. The hard, thick length of his erection ground into her ass.

He put his mouth to her ear. "You didn't think you could tease me like that and walk off, did you?" he whispered.

"Yeah, I did," she whispered back.

He chuckled, low and rough, hooked his fingers in the waistband of her shorts and pushed them, and her panties, down. She stepped out of them, figuring he'd take her like that, from behind, with her palms on the counter, but abruptly she found herself spun around, lifted and placed next to the coffeemaker.

"You got me hot and bothered," he said, moving between her legs, "so it's only fair that I return the favor." His hand found her soaked core, and one eyebrow came up. "Or maybe it's too late for that."

She arched into his hand, forcing firmer pressure of his knuckles brushing her clit. "I'm very hot and bothered."

"Can't have that." He gripped her hips, and before she could figure out what he was up to, he'd plopped her into one side of the sink.

She yelped at the feel of the cold ceramic biting into her bare ass, but Hex swallowed the noise with his mouth. His fingers found her pussy again, delved between her labia and began a mind-blowing, feathering stroke.

"Could you come from this?" He bit her bottom lip and soothed it with his tongue. "Are you still hot?"

"God, yes," she moaned.

He reached behind her and turned on the water in the other side of the sink. A wicked smirk turned up his mouth as he pulled the sprayer hose forward.

"What are you doing—" She broke off with a gasp as cool water hit her between the legs.

"Cooling you off, sweetheart."

The spray tickled, made her giggle and squirm, until he spread the folds of her sex with one hand and brought the nozzle in close. A sudden stream of water struck her clit with erotic precision. Crying out, she clutched his shoulders, tilting her pelvis up to catch every last drop of spray.

The water licked her like a lover, and when he moved the nozzle lower, pushed the round head into her, she shuddered with the need to come. Streams of sensation stroked her walls, filled her with icy hot whips of ecstasy.

"Don't come, Brenna." He voice was gravelly, thick with lust. "Tell me how it feels."

A sob escaped her. "C-can't."

"You can." He slid the nozzle through her slit, catching her clit once more. "Tell me."

Moaning, she looked at him, at the hard angles of his face, his firm, lush lips, his eyes that held more mystery than she'd ever seen. "Feels like I'm being licked," she breathed. "While underwater, maybe... Oh, please..."

"Underwater? You ever had a guy go down on you like that?"

"No," she moaned, picturing Hex doing exactly that. She saw them in a tropical, moonlit pool, her legs spread, his blond head bobbing as he suckled her, his tongue plunging deep.

"You'd taste so sweet, Brenna. I know you would."

He moved the nozzle just a little, but enough to line up the stream and her sweet spot just right and suddenly she was shattering, seeing stars and lights and Hex's intense, handsome face as he talked her through it with sexy, naughty words.

She'd barely come down when he slammed the faucet off, pulled her up onto the counter again, and entered her with one smooth, hard thrust. She had no idea when he'd released himself from his jeans and sheathed himself in a condom, but it didn't matter.

Behind him three cupboards opened and slammed closed, rattling the dishes inside. *Arlen.*

"Ignore him," Hex said. "Concentrate on me."

Grasping her ass with both hands, he held her for his powerful, punishing thrusts. All thoughts of Arlen fled as she buried her face in the crook of his neck, panting against the hot skin there. He smelled like the best parts of New Orleans, the parts she'd forgotten about. Chicory, spicy honey, sultry night air.

She didn't want to like the way he smelled, didn't want to like what he was doing to her, but she locked her ankles at the small of his back and sank her teeth into his neck, because like it or not, she wasn't letting him go.

At least, not until he gave her another orgasm.

His groan told her he approved of the way she tightened around him, gripped his shoulders, waist and cock. He pumped harder, faster, the wet slap of their bodies growing more frenzied as their breathing became more irregular and harsh.

"Do you want me, Hex?" The pleasure coursing through her body prevented her from regretting her question. She needed to know that this wasn't a keep-the-ghost-away fuck. She needed to be desired again, even if only on a physical level.

"Hell, yeah," he growled, tucking her even closer, grinding his cock into her pussy so hard she felt fire ignite. His hands kneaded her butt cheeks, his fingers spreading her, stroking her crease.

His rhythm became erratic—deep, hard thrusts punctuated by short, shallow punches that sent lightning streaking outward from the ultrasensitive flesh of her entrance.

She cried out, gasping, hanging on the precipice. A groan shook his body, an erotic sound that hurtled her off the edge where her release had been balancing.

Arching into him, she let it take her, let him stretch her with his thick length that swelled as he peaked. He jerked, his body twitching like he'd touched a live wire. Her pussy pulsed around him, milking him, sucking him so deep she felt his broad head strike the entrance to her womb.

So... good.

He collapsed against her, one hand around her to hold her to him, the other bracing them on the counter. Her heels still dug into the hard globes of his ass, the soles of her feet tickled by his waistband that had slid lower as he'd pumped into her.

Sweat dampened her bangs, plastered them to her forehead, which she propped against his chest. Recovery was going to be slow and sweet, and even with the first morning sun rays streaming through the window, she knew she'd sleep well for the first time in months.

When their breathing had evened out, he slipped out of her wet sex but didn't back away. Instead, he caught a lock of her hair between his fingers. "It's as soft as I imagined," he murmured.

"Imagined? You've thought about touching my hair?"

He pulled his hand away. "I'll bet every guy in America has thought about touching you. Hell, after that men's mag spread, they've done a lot more than think."

"What about you?" She trailed a finger down his T-shirted

chest, which was damp from the humid air and sweat. "Have you done more?"

The image of him taking his cock in his fist and stroking himself to climax while fantasizing about her stirred her insides, which had no business being stirred again so soon.

"*You* might let it all out to the public, but most things are private for me. Like the answer to that question."

The heat that had been coursing through her veins like a river of lava suddenly chilled. She knew he hadn't meant to be a jerk. She *had* let it all out—she'd shared her body with millions of people. But he had no way of knowing how much she kept hidden, things no one had ever seen.

Feeling numb, she shoved him away and slid off the counter, tugging down her shirt to cover herself. "It's late. I need to get some sleep."

He reached for a paper towel and began to clean himself up. "I didn't mean to upset you. This is just . . . I need to keep some distance."

Sure, they'd had sex twice, but she got it. He needed emotional distance. She did too. She already liked Hex more than she should, was probably suffering from some hero-worship complex.

"My mom once said that distance is a lifesaver when you're psychic," she mused. "Especially if you're a medium."

Hex zipped up and propped a hip against the counter she'd never look at the same way again. Not when her body still hummed with the pleasure he'd given her. "Without it, you'd go crazy."

"Yeah, I know." She closed her eyes against the flashes in her brain, the memories she wished she didn't have. "There were so many times I'd find my mom sobbing in a corner or beneath the blankets on her bed. The spirits wouldn't leave her alone. She had a hard time keeping it together." The instances had mostly happened when Brenna was young, before her mom learned to truly shut out the voices when she didn't want to hear them. But every one of the occasions had stuck with her, had convinced Brenna that she wanted nothing to do with that particular *gift*.

Hex folded his arms over his chest, crossed his feet at the ankles. "She obviously kept it together well enough to provide a good home for you." He cast an appreciative gaze around the room. "This is a great place."

"It is. But I didn't grow up here. My mom didn't marry my stepdad until I was fifteen. He died six months later. He was eighty-two."

One blond brow shot up, and yeah, she'd let him chew on that one. Her mom hadn't been a gold digger, but she'd wanted more for Brenna than life in a car or in a rusted-out trailer.

"No one knows that about me, Hex. So see, I don't let *everything* hang out to the public." She shrugged. "I've just learned that the more I show them of my outside, the less they care about what's inside."

"Looks like you've perfected the distance thing too," he said quietly, and yeah, she supposed she had.

Smiling tiredly, she eased toward him as he watched her warily, like she might bite. When they were chest to chest, she went up on her toes and brushed a kiss across his rough-whiskered cheek. "Time for a little distance. Good night, Hex."

CHAPTER *Four*

While Brenna slept, Hex went to the hotel, his home away from home for the past months. He'd been staying here long enough to get rid of any lingering ghosts, and so far he'd been able to keep new ones from entering either the room when they shouldn't, by using the protection spell he'd learned from Creed, his buddy and fellow ghost hunter at ACRO.

He'd kept an old camera set up on a tripod in the corner, just in case he wanted to check and make sure. But up until now, the room had been the place he could relax and not worry about the monsters, in—or out—of the closet. And so he'd crawled into the familiar bed and slept until late afternoon, in an attempt to rid himself of any residual effects of Arlen's haunting, which hung on him like a silken spiderweb.

He woke up fisting his cock and longing for Brenna, the way he'd done countless times before actually meeting her.

But this was far more intense, a nearly uncontrollable urge that had him stroking himself the way she'd done earlier, with a slow, unrelenting rhythm. It was as close to an out-of-body experience as he'd ever gotten, and even as the tribal markings burned against his biceps, his lower body writhed in pleasure.

He could still feel her on him, could picture the way her lips wrapped around the Popsicle, and with very little effort he pictured her lips around him, her tongue teasing the sensitive flesh around the head of his cock. Taking her earlier, with his fingers, his cock pulsing inside of her had been sweet—amazing—but the way things had ended left him with a knot in his stomach.

As he stroked, he imagined her face before she'd gotten upset, the way her lips parted in pure pleasure. The way her pussy contracted around his cock, sweet and slick and hot.

That was all it took. His back arched off the bed and he cried out and didn't attempt to stop himself from coming.

For the next few moments, he lay immobilized, sweating and still trembling from the aftershocks.

Each orgasm was more intense than the last and none came close to erasing his longing for Brenna, didn't even ease the throbbing ache that had haunted Hex since he'd walked inside her house.

It had been that way from the first time he'd seen her picture, but he hadn't realized the intensity had built so fiercely.

You've never had this reaction from a picture before, Creed had reminded him a couple of weeks prior, when Hex had confessed his unnatural reaction to the pictures.

He'd wondered if he was being possessed through the pictures, if there was something happening to him that he'd be unable to control. Creed had urged him to speak with a stronger medium to get some answers, but Hex had refused.

Now that he'd touched her, had her, there was no turning back for him. He'd assumed that what he saw in ink and on paper was just a fantasy, that she'd never live up to it in real life.

Without the makeup and the airbrushing, she was even more beautiful. Real. The way she'd held him was real too—he was sure of it.

All of this was far too real.

It would be so easy to not go back to Brenna's house, to leave New Orleans and go on assignment in Ecuador or lose himself in the Amazon again. But they were entwined now. Until he could free Arlen, Hex himself would be linked to Arlen and Brenna both. There was no turning back.

He packed quickly, not wanting to leave her alone at the house for too long as the witching hours approached. Most haunting activity occurred between midnight and four in the morning, but Arlen was strong—he could hover over Brenna any time he wanted.

Brenna was strong too. She was also spoiled as hell, he mused as he walked through the sticky heat that lay on him like a curtain of steam, carrying his own bags and the bags of food he'd bought from a nearby restaurant to fortify them both. They were going to need energy if the plan he had in mind had a shot at working.

She was awake when Hex let himself into the house well after the sun went down, didn't say anything when he put the bags from the restaurant on the counter and unpacked them. She stared at the red beans and rice when he pushed a container of the still-warm food at her, but she opened it and began to eat without complaint.

He left her, to set up his equipment in the parlor room.

They'd use the old chaise again, he thought as he caressed the old jacquard fabric with one hand, where Brenna's back had pressed earlier.

A heaviness enveloped him, part outside heat, part internal warning system. He ran a hand through his hair and just tried to freakin' breathe.

Brenna came in from the kitchen—he could feel her standing there, watching him set up. She was still upset, and her aura vibrated through the small room, through him, and shot holes in his concentration.

Normally, he only had to worry about himself on a job, not another person as vulnerable as she was. But Arlen wasn't going to let her go that easily and Hex tried to shake the feeling that the ghost was already winning the battle.

"This room—my mom used to call it the soul of the house," Brenna said finally.

Soul of the house, the place where the spirit activity was strongest. That had been Hex's bedroom, unbeknownst to his parents.

Some nights, when the whirring EMG energy got to be too much, he'd sleep in the small darkroom he'd set up, sneak back into his own room at the first morning light. "Your mom was right. There's a strong energy here."

He still hadn't turned to face her, didn't want to until he was behind the relative safety of the camera's lens. "Was the food all right?"

"It was perfect. Thanks."

"I didn't mean to make you feel like shit before, I would never do that intentionally. It's just... I'm an intensely private person, Brenna. And I've already told you things that very few people know."

"I can understand that. I know you don't think I'm capable of keeping secrets, but I am. I told you, I'll do anything to get my career back."

"Yes, you mentioned that."

She shrugged as if it wasn't a big deal, but it was a very big deal. All of it was—her career, sleeping with him. Trusting him. "So what happens now?"

"I'm going to take some pictures of you. Just get comfortable on the chaise and relax. Arlen should make an appearance, and then I'm going to try to talk to him." Hex adjusted the shutter speed on his big camera and focused it on Brenna. She shifted nervously on the couch, but as soon as the camera began to whir she relaxed a little. Years of training, he supposed. Years of posing when she was tired or hungry or not in the mood. Except she wasn't really posing for him, she was just... sitting and giving him sort of a half smile. One that was for him alone.

He could do this all day—focus only on her. The problem was, after ten minutes and two rolls of film, there was no Arlen. Oh, he was around, but he wasn't showing himself. Hex could feel the ghost on his skin, but Arlen was deliberately staying out of the camera's range.

He sighed and dropped the camera from his face.

"It's not working, is it?" she asked.

He shook his head. "He's around. He just won't let me see him."

She fidgeted. "So what's the plan?"

"We're going to make him want to show himself," he told her, and checked his watch.

"How?"

"We're going to re-create the photo spread you did for the magazine," he said, and finally turned to look into her eyes. She'd lit more candles around the room than she had last night, and he could see the anger cross her face.

"You want me to take off my clothes again? Just because I *let it all out to the public*, you think I'll take off my clothes at a command?" She bristled, her eyes flashing, and he suspected that if she were in any other situation she'd throw one of the temper tantrums she was famous for, according to the magazines.

"I'm not screwing with you. But we need to screw with Arlen—together. We need to pretend..." He took a deep breath. "We need him to think we're together. He seems to not like it when you're naked with me."

Hex, of course, liked it just fine. More than fine.

"You want to piss him off again? How is that a good idea?"

"I need to get him back into the shots in order to see him. That's the only way I can reason with him."

"But if he touches me... can the same thing that happened to you happen to me?" she asked.

"I'm not going to lie to you, it could. But right now, I'm in more danger than you are."

She still looked unsure, but he was already behind the lens, snapping some test shots. Arlen still wasn't showing himself, but the room had gotten colder as Brenna shed her clothing.

She moved tentatively in front of the chaise, one arm wrapped across her breasts, almost shyly. Shyer than she'd been before they'd had sex.

Within seconds, Brenna wasn't the only one standing by the chaise. Arlen stood in his familiar position behind the furniture, gazing at the woman he thought to be his long lost lover.

"Kneel on the chaise, elbows on the armrest, baby." Hex kept his voice low, heard the desire in there he didn't have to fake. Brenna started, but then relaxed a little as she did what he asked.

Arlen glared at Hex as Brenna moved gracefully into position. A position that exposed her moist sex to Hex briefly, and he longed to get closer, to concentrate his camera there... to be followed by his mouth.

Lickable, the men's magazine photographer had written.

Warm, orange flickers of candlelight licked her skin, and when she stretched into a sensual, slinky pose with one leg forward and one back, he wanted to be licking her as well.

"Do you like this, Hex? When I pose for you?"

"You have no idea how much." The bulge in his jeans grew, the fabric tightening almost painfully, and he resisted the urge to reach down and stroke himself, but just barely.

Brenna knew, looked at him with liquid desire in her eyes.

He took a few shots, keeping an eye on Arlen, who still glared as he moved a little closer to the chaise.

As she kneels on the velvet sofa, her round ass begs for my hands to cover it. I'd continue down her slim thighs, massaging, tickling...

His mouth was dry, his throat tight. His words came out low and husky: "Now I want to see you up on your knees, facing me, like the second shot in the magazine."

He'd loved that one, even though the image was as blurred as the others. The photographer's description had filled in the blanks, making the page steam.

She's on her knees now, on the sofa and facing me, her hands cupping her breasts, her legs parted just enough to get a mouthwatering view of that perfect pussy. If I got down on my knees in front of her, my face would be right there in the sweet spot. My tongue would slip between—

Fuck. He longed to put the camera down, but he hadn't accomplished what he'd set out to do. Instead of being angry, Arlen merely grinned. The bastard.

"Hex, is everything all right?" Brenna asked, uncertainty evident in her voice as the shooting paused.

"I'm all right. Distracted—by you. I'm not used to shooting

people. People who are still breathing anyway." He directed the last comment at Arlen, who bared his teeth. "Okay, one more. The last pose in the magazine."

She hesitated, and he knew why. The pose, while not graphic, hinted at outright porn.

"Is this really necessary?"

Through his viewfinder, he saw Arlen smirk as he moved forward, hand outstretched.

"It is. God, you look so beautiful, Brenna. Just concentrate on me—I'm the only one who's going to see these pictures."

Don't touch her, don't touch her, he screamed in his head, but Arlen was moving around the couch, getting close.

She bit her bottom lip and then sank down to sit on the couch. Slowly, looking directly into his eyes in a way that made his breath catch, she slipped her hand between her thighs. With teasingly seductive timing, she spread her legs wide, leaving her hand in place to hide her sex . . . but just barely.

"Happy?" she asked, one brow cocked, and he couldn't answer because his imagination had just taken off.

Even Arlen had stopped his approach, stood back and admired the view.

Damn, it was hot in here.

"Very," he murmured.

She threw her head against the chaise and arched her back, keeping her hand over her sex, almost as though pleasuring herself. "The photographer loved this one," she murmured. "He wrote about how he could picture me touching myself, slipping my finger inside, where it would be tight and hot. Wet."

Hex dropped one hand to his crotch—the other shook and there was no way he was getting a decent photo now. Arlen shot forward and kneeled between her legs, and fuck no, if anyone was going to do that to Brenna, it was going to be Hex.

Practically tossing the camera to the small table next to him, he closed the distance between them in three strides, grasped her wrist and tugged her up against him. And suddenly, the anger, the possessiveness, reached the boiling point. "I don't want to hear about what the photographer liked. Or what any other man who's been with you likes. I only want to talk about what I like."

She was breathing hard as he held her pressed to him.

"Do those men do it for you, Brenna? With their fame, their power, all of them wanting you all the time . . . wanting what you represent?" He touched her, let a finger travel insolently across her cheek. "Do you like having everyone wanting you, living and dead?"

"I used to," she whispered.

"Did you know that some primitive tribes claim that when you let someone photograph you, they're taking away your soul?"

"Is that what you're doing to me, taking away my soul?"

"No, not taking . . . giving." He kissed the bare skin of her shoulder as his fingers traveled downward across the smooth expanse of her belly, toward the juncture of her thighs. He stroked her warm, wet heat with a single finger, felt her shudder against him as if she was going to come from just that single touch.

"We're doing it right this time," he murmured. "I'm not letting you get away, not leaving your side."

Somehow, he meant the words—but they meant far more to Arlen, who let out a low, mournful scream that pierced through both Hex and Brenna.

She pressed her head against Hex's chest. "Make it stop, Hex. Please, just make it stop."

Hex pushed her back, just a few inches, and stared down at her. "You heard him, didn't you?"

"No." She shook her head and lied to Hex as much as she lied to herself. She couldn't have heard Arlen. She refused to hear him. "I just want all of this to stop. I want him gone. I want my life back." A life where lights, glamour and parties keep everything paranormal away. Where outside noises drown out the voices from beyond.

Closing her eyes, she sank against Hex, using his hard body as a brace. "I'm sorry." For bringing him into this nightmare, for asking so much of him, for needing him.

His only response was to pull back once more, enough that he could slip his hand under her chin and lift her mouth to his. The moment their lips touched, drugging heat flowed through her veins. He pushed his tongue into her mouth and began a slow exploration of her teeth, her lips, the sensitive spot on her palette.

"You like this," he murmured against her mouth, and she realized she'd been moaning.

"No one has ever kissed me like you do."

His hand slid down her throat, leaving a path of heat in its wake. God, she was on fire. "How do I kiss you?"

Like you care about me.

"Like who I am doesn't matter."

"It doesn't."

Prickles of pleasure spread over her skin as his fingers found her nipple and squeezed gently. "Hex." His name came out as a sigh.

"Say it again." He dragged his lips along her jaw and nipped at the tendon in her neck.

Alarm made her gut clench. "To make Arlen jealous?"

"No." He shoved his jean-clad thigh between hers, putting the most delicious pressure right where she needed it. "I just like hearing my name on your lips."

She melted. Inside, outside, against him. "Hex," she breathed. "Don't let him have any part of this. Please."

"I won't," he growled. His hand dropped to cup her bottom and rock her against his leg. Sensation popped all over her body as she rode his thigh. She dropped her head back, giving him more access to her throat, and he took advantage, ravaged her with his mouth and tongue. Each stroke was like wet satin on her skin, and each one spun her lust up higher.

Light flashed behind her eyes. Clicks and whirs rent the air. Lost in passion, it took her a moment to realize that the cameras were taking pictures.

By themselves.

"Hex?"

"Shh. He's angry. Let him throw his tantrum. Keeps him from trying to get inside me. But no one is shooting you naked but me." He angled his body to shield her nudity from the cameras and pulled her as close as possible, the move so possessive and protective that she nearly cried.

He kept kissing her, though, kept moving with her, the hard ridge of his erection knocking against her belly, the firm muscle in his thigh rubbing her clit with the perfect amount of pressure. In moments she was panting, not caring about the cameras because all she wanted was to come.

"Please," she moaned.

Immediately, he spun her away from the cameras, around the corner into the foyer. Before she could catch her breath, he'd pressed her back against the wall and was kneeling in front of her. His big hands closed around her thighs and spread them, exposing her sex to the steamy air and his steamier gaze.

"Christ, you're gorgeous," he murmured so roughly she felt the vibration of his words travel a path from her pussy to her womb. "Tell me what you want, Brenna."

Heat flooded her cheeks.

"You've never asked a man for specific acts, have you?" He swept his thumb through her cleft, spreading moisture up to her swollen knot, and she had to bite her lip to keep from crying out. "You have a shy streak. You're so much more than what the world sees." He looked up at her, and she got lost in his slumberous eyes. "Open up to me. Tell me what you want."

Overcome by his seductive voice, she relented. "Make me come."

"How?" His thumb made lazy circles around her swollen nub, never hitting the right place but sending her up in flames nevertheless.

"Lick me. God, Hex, put your mouth on me before I scream."

But he didn't. He closed his mouth over her inner thigh and bit down, the pressure ending just short of pain. She couldn't fight the feeling that he was in some way marking her, though the idea was ridiculous, brutish.

And such a huge turn-on that she wanted him to bite her everywhere.

Instead, his tongue pierced her slit, a warm, wet stab that made her gasp in pleasure. Her legs nearly buckled, began to shake so badly she didn't know if they could support her without the brace of the wall at her back. Oh, he knew how to go down on a woman, how to suck delicately at the very tip of her clit, how to plunge deep into her core and wield his tongue like a cock.

Her body surged, arching into his mouth without her consent. Alight with sensation, she grasped his head, tunneled her fingers in his silky hair to guide him. Not that he needed any urging or instruction. His mouth was magic, firm yet soft, wet and hot, and dear God, she could feel every taste bud rasp over her sensitive flesh.

She looked down at him, her breath catching at the sight of his face buried between her legs, his tongue dancing in her cream, lashing at her with lush, punishing strokes. And when his glittering gaze lifted to capture hers, the sheer eroticism of it all sent her over the edge. Sharp and searing, her climax shot through her. Her nails dug into his scalp as she pumped her hips, lifted one leg up over his shoulder to force his tongue as deep as possible. The wet sucking noises as he finished her off nearly had her coming again.

But then he was on his feet, tearing at his fly with one hand and holding the back of her neck with the other, keeping her captive for the possession of his kiss. She whimpered at the taste of her orgasm on his lips.

"You like that," he panted, flicking his tongue along the ridge of her teeth. "So do I. You taste like sweet tea, dark and honeyed." He kept kissing her as he lifted her, and in one smooth motion sheathed himself deep inside her. "I could spend all day between your legs."

She shuddered with pleasure at his words, at the sense of fullness at her core, at the pounding he began to give her right there against the wall. His big body dwarfed her, his hands held her, his mouth loved her. *Yes.* This was what she'd wanted since she first saw him, since she first felt the unusually strong attraction.

This is what you've wanted all your life.

Shoving that thought away because it wasn't true, it couldn't be, she let herself drown in Hex and the savage thrusts that drove her toward another explosive peak.

"Fuck," he snarled. "No. *Fuck. No.*"

She opened her eyes, saw the battle in his. *Oh, please, not Arlen*... Framing Hex's face between her palms, she forced him to look at her. "Hex. Hex! Stay with me." She stroked the strong contour of his jaw with her thumbs and repeated his name over and over.

He groaned, pumped his hips as though trying to anchor himself to her. "She's mine," he whispered. "Damn you, Arlen, get the fuck away." He chanted something in another language, something she couldn't understand, even as his hips swiveled, and he hit that place inside that made her cry out.

Suddenly, the air went still and the temperature plummeted. Hex smiled. Hex. Not Arlen. He'd won. Relief swelled and her orgasm tackled her, ripped her wide open and left her sobbing as Hex released inside her, his hot splashes of semen filling her with a sense of rightness she hadn't felt in a long time.

If ever.

That they hadn't used a condom was only a passing thought, because right at that moment, all hell broke loose.

A roar like a freight train shook the house. Windows shattered. Every camera in the house, including Hex's, crunched into the wall beside them, exploding into tiny pieces. Hex lowered her feet to the floor and covered her with his body, sheltered her from the debris that bit into him and left bloody nicks on his skin. He didn't even flinch.

When it was over, he glanced down at the broken camera remains, his face pale and his expression haunted. "Fuck."

"What is it? Hex, tell me!"

He turned to her, his hand shaking, stroking her hair as it draped over her shoulder. "The son of a bitch declared war."

For the first time since the haunting began, Brenna was terrified.

CHAPTER *Five*

Hex didn't let Brenna out from under the shield of his body as he stared at the pile of broken camera equipment and weighed his options.

It didn't take long, as there weren't any.

"Hex, what are we going to do? Shouldn't we get out of here?"

He figured she wouldn't want to hear that there was no way Arlen would let either of them leave this house tonight. The doors and windows would be blocked until the witching hour came to an end. Even then, Hex wasn't sure if Arlen's power would diminish.

And no matter what, he wouldn't be able to see Arlen at all.

He could have new equipment overnighted to him, or he could go to town tomorrow and buy some, but it was a losing battle. Arlen knew exactly what he was doing. Hex could almost picture Arlen smashing each camera purposefully, could've sworn he heard the ghost whisper, *Your power here is gone,* into his ear.

The terrifying part was, Arlen could be anywhere now, even hovering above them. "You don't feel different, do you?" he asked Brenna, ignoring her earlier question about leaving.

"No, I feel all right. Scared, but all right. Hex, you're not going to be able to see Arlen anymore."

There was no use trying to sugarcoat it. "No, not with my equipment broken."

Her voice softened. "You're a medium... do you think—"

"I'm a medium through the lens only." He realized his teeth were clenched tightly and forced himself to remain calm. "I can only see the ghosts through the camera's lens. That's how I help them pass over; I guide them with the help of the camera. That's the way it's been since I was seventeen."

"Hex, you're going to have to do something. Maybe if you just tried—"

"Drop it, Brenna," he growled. He eased himself away from her. "Keep your back against the wall."

He began to rummage around in the darkness for her clothing and heard her move and stand behind him. His eyes had adjusted well enough in the dark so he could see her frame, silhouetted by the moonlight coming through the gauzy window coverings. There was no breeze, only heavy air.

"I'm so tired of this. Tired and confused. We fight and then we have sex and now the only chance I had at getting rid of this damned ghost and getting my life back is gone." Still naked, she moved to the middle of the room and held her hands up to the ceiling. "Come on out, Arlen! Come on out and play!"

Hex, can you come out to play?

"Don't," he yelled, tried to grab her, but she eluded him, stood on the chaise and continued to scream for Arlen.

Finally, he managed to get ahold of her around her waist. "Stop it, honey. Just stop...you're encouraging him. You're messing with something you know nothing about."

"If Arlen's going to play with me, you'd better believe I'm going to give it right back to him. I'm going to at least try, not just give up," she shot back.

"Is that what you think, that I'm giving up here?" he asked, and didn't have time to say anything further because Arlen had clearly heard Brenna's cries and was making his presence known again. The windows began to rattle in their frames and the old house creaked as if caught in another hurricane.

"Yeah, I think you're giving up. But I can't." She wrenched out of his grasp and stared at him, practically spitting fire. "You have the ability to see Arlen. I know you do. But you are too much of a goddamned coward to look beyond the camera lens."

"You don't know anything, Brenna. Just because I told you my ghost story doesn't mean you know me. So fuck you." Anger raged through him—he nearly picked up some furniture on his own to throw, the way Arlen was having his own ghost temper tantrum.

And fuck it all if he didn't know that being defensive about what Brenna said was akin to knowing she was entirely right.

Fuck. He picked up part of the destroyed camera and threw it hard against the wall—hard enough to leave a dent. And then he banged on the wall with his fist with enough force to make Arlen momentarily call a cease-fire.

"Hex, please..."

"Don't, Brenna. Just don't. Not now."

"I'm so sorry. I had no right to say that." Her voice was a whisper that wove its way through his seething temper, softened it somewhat. She stood with her arms wrapped around her and took a deep breath.

"I just . . . well, I used to have everything I wanted. Money. Clothes. Expensive cars. Now all I have is this house, which I'm going to lose any day now. I can't afford to pay my bills. I'm going to end up on the streets, Hex. I'm terrified." She looked down at her feet and said quietly, "I've never told anyone this, but when I was a kid, my mom and I had to live out of her car. There were times I was lucky to get one meal a day. I liked going to school, even though I had to wear the same dirty clothes every day, because at least I got a free lunch." She wrung her hands, swallowed audibly. "I can't live like that again."

He could still hear her calling him a coward in the back of his mind. "Arlen's coming for you. You told him what you wanted—you invited him back."

"It doesn't matter—he was going to come back anyway." Her voice was dull, uncaring, and he wanted her—needed her—to care. It was all the more apparent at that moment.

"Didn't your mother teach you not to invite trouble?"

Her head jerked up and she stared at him unsteadily. "I'm so tired of all of this. Please make it stop."

He caught her right before she collapsed, just as the windows began to blow in toward them, one by one.

He scooped her up into his arms and ran into the upstairs bathroom, the one with the claw-footed tub. He got them both inside and ran the water over them, icy cold and refreshing, despite the chaos happening around them.

"Brenna, honey, wake up." He gently patted her cheeks, and her eyes fluttered open.

Arlen would be here soon. It gave Hex limited time to get a plan together.

"Listen to me—are you listening?" he asked. She nodded through chattering teeth. "Baby, I'm sorry, I don't want to put you through anything more, but we've got to find a way to end this."

"I know, Hex." She caressed his cheek and suddenly it didn't matter that the water was freezing, because his blood ran hot for her, hotter than the hottest New Orleans summer.

His stomach knotted, his head swam. "I'm going to get Arlen's deal—and once I do that, you've got to be the one to convince him to leave my body."

"But that's what you're trained to do. I've never talked to a ghost." She paused. "Wait a minute. What did you just say?"

He was shaking all over, and it wasn't because of the chill in the water. "The only way I can try to figure out who Mattie was to Arlen, what actually happened to make him start latching on to you, is to let him inside of me. Invite him in."

"I can't let you do that."

"It's the only way."

"You're shaking." She rubbed his arms under the water.

He reached up and shut off the water before she had a chance to stop him. "If this works, I might be able to see him without the camera."

He didn't want that gift back. He'd been pretty damned happy with the light version of his gift all these years, but understanding just how fucking vulnerable he was by *not* being able to see the ghosts without the cameras made him realize how many times he'd probably escaped possessions by the skin of his teeth.

Just because he could only see the ghosts through his lens didn't mean they weren't always around him. The markings protected him, definitely, but he'd acted like if he couldn't see the ghosts, they didn't exist.

He was an idiot. And a coward, just like Brenna said.

He'd have to trust her to be strong enough to pull him out of this. Between her and the tribal protection bands, he'd been all right so far. But inviting a ghost inside was a very different thing. Once Arlen had an invitation, all bets were off—the tribal markings wouldn't work worth a damn and Hex would be possessed, for all intents and purposes. "It's up to you to join our protective auras if necessary, to bring me back when we learn what we need to about Arlen."

She nodded, leaned up to kiss him, and he noted that she was shivering badly. It was time to start the wheels in motion.

"I'm going to call out to him," he told her. "Just be prepared to talk to him. To tell him to go."

"Suppose you can't see him after you let him in?" she whispered. "Suppose he refuses to leave?"

"We'll never know if I don't try." He kissed her, a long, hard kiss that seemed as if it might go on forever, his tongue teasing hers, their wet bodies pressed together, steam rising as cold water hit hot air, and he yanked himself away from her with his last dose of willpower.

"Come on out to play, Arlen. I'm letting you in, all the way," he called out. The bands around his arms began to burn in protest, as if they knew what Hex was doing. As if they knew their power would soon be voided. "I'll be your vessel, Arlen," he continued. "Come tell your story to Brenna."

Not Brenna. Mattie. My Mattie.

Hex whirled around at the sound of the voice, but he couldn't see Arlen. Yet the voice was getting closer, whispering in his ear, until it started coming from inside his own head.

He didn't realize he'd fallen onto the bath mat, not until Brenna's body covered his and he heard her crying out, *"Hex, please, no..."*

Mattie, come home with me.

"She's not going anywhere with you," Hex told Arlen, even as consciousness seemed to whirl around him. Somehow, he rolled on top of Brenna. He was vaguely aware that her arms were around his back as he urged her legs to spread, and even the whisper of his own name didn't seem to change anything.

Brenna had never been so terrified in her entire life. Not even when she and her mom had been living in a shack on the outskirts of town and a drug-crazed burglar had broken in while they slept. He'd muttered incoherently, his words stringing together in a jumble, like what Hex was doing now.

Or maybe it was Arlen.

She pushed out from underneath him, escaping his roving hands, which felt so good, so warm, but until she knew who was in charge of them, those hands would have to wait.

"Hey, there," she said softly. "Who's running the show?"

His eyes opened and went half-lidded as a smile spread across his face. "Mattie, my love."

That she'd expected this didn't matter. She wanted to scream, to beg Hex to come back. But he'd given himself up so they could learn the truth about Arlen's connection to her, and she had to use what might be the only chance to fix all of this. Shaking with cold, she grasped Hex's hand.

"Tell me about Mattie, Arlen."

"It doesn't matter now. We're together. We will be always."

"I need to know." She leaned over him, smoothed her fingers over his cheek. "Please tell me."

Something like an electric current ran through her. Hex's

body bucked, stiffened, and she knew he was fighting, trying to come to the surface. Light flashed, and suddenly she was in another time, another place. A party. Somehow she knew the year: 1923. She was looking through Arlen's eyes at a woman who, with her blond hair and slim build, resembled Brenna, but who she knew was Mattie. And Mattie was angry. Very angry.

"You finally did it," Mattie snapped at Arlen. "You finally ended my career."

"Don't be so dramatic, doll. McKinney wants you to star in his new film. He'll cough up the dough." Arlen snared a flute of champagne from the man passing by with a tray laden with drinks. "He always does."

"I'm going after him."

"Oh, for heaven's sake, Mattie—"

She ran off, as well as she could in the tight dress and high heels. Arlen signaled a server to take his glass, but dropped it when a chill skittered up his spine from out of nowhere. Then the sound of a crash, and panicked shouts, reached his ears.

"Mattie," he screamed. He ran, stumbling into the darkness outside. "Oh, Mary, mother of God."

Mattie was lying in the road, her limbs splayed awkwardly, blood pooling around her broken body. The smashed front end of a Packard told the story.

Brenna gasped, the vision so real, so powerful she could feel Arlen's pain. She blinked. The bathroom. She was in the bathroom. And it wasn't 1923. Thank God, oh, thank God. Still, her heart pounded crazily, and tears streamed down her face. Finally, some of this was making sense.

Another image blasted through her, of Arlen in a graveyard,

staring at Mattie's monument. Then Arlen again, this time in a richly decorated study—in this very house—with a pistol. The sound of a single shot ricocheted off the inside of her skull.

He'd killed himself. After Mattie died, he'd been unable to carry on. She could feel his happiness when, immediately afterward, his spirit had found Mattie's on the earthly plane. They'd wandered New Orleans for decades, not realizing that a better place awaited them.

They had been happy until Katrina hit, and Arlen hadn't seen Mattie since.

Brenna continued to stroke Hex's cheek as something her mother said came back to her. *Reports of hauntings often peak after hurricanes. Their electromagnetic fields can confuse earthbound spirits, can shake up the ghost community like a beehive. Many of them cross over during that time. Others are more lost than ever.*

Mattie must have crossed over. Arlen had come back to the house where he'd killed himself, searching for Mattie... and had found Brenna here, helping her mom after the storm.

Confused and alone, he'd latched on to her, and when Brenna's mother had died of a fast-moving and undiagnosed cancer just weeks later, he'd identified with Brenna's grief and pain.

"Arlen, I'm so sorry for your loss."

He shook his head. Shook Hex's head anyway. "It doesn't matter. We're here now. Forever." He shot forward and grabbed her, tugging her against him with Hex's incredible strength. His mouth came forcefully down on hers.

"No! Hex!" She squirmed, turned her face away until he tangled his hand in her hair and wrenched her head back.

"Hex can't hear you, lover."

"I'm not Mattie, Arlen. She crossed over. You need to follow her, and you need to let go of Hex now."

Rage twisted Hex's handsome features. "*Never.*"

Chills swept over her flesh. Hex must have known there was a possibility that he wouldn't come back, but he'd risked it. For her.

The selflessness of the act sat like a lump in her stomach. Would she have done the same for a near stranger?

She didn't want to think about the answer to that. What she wanted was to get Hex back so he could send Arlen packing into the afterlife, and she could get on with her current life.

But where would that leave Hex? Because the truth was, they weren't strangers anymore. They were much more than that, and that distance he'd been talking about was closing with every minute they spent together.

Twisting, she tried to wrench free of Arlen's hold, but he brought her in closer, dropped one hand low on her hip as he flipped her onto her back on the fuzzy bath mat. "I won't lose you again."

"Hex, please." She pummeled his shoulders, ribs, everything she could reach, but he only settled his weight on top of her. "Fight him, Hex. Don't let him win. I need you."

"Shut up," Arlen ground out.

She was getting through. She could hear it in his voice. "Arlen, we can help you find Mattie, but you have to let Hex come back."

A low, rattling groan came from deep in Hex's chest, as though he was clawing his way back from the pits of hell. "Brenna..."

She grasped his face in both hands and held him so he couldn't rear back. The battle raged in his eyes once more, flashes of umber and fire. "Stay with me, Hex." Slowly, gradually, his expression softened, and whiskey eyes stared down at her. "Hex? Tell me it's you."

"It's me. Shit, it's me." He rolled off her, his breathing harsh and heavy.

She crawled to him, not caring that she was naked and he was wet and shivering, and climbed into his lap. Wrapping her arms around his neck, she buried her face in his shoulder. "Don't do that again. Never do that again."

"I won't." His arms came around her, pulling her close with precious care. "He's so hurt. Angry."

"He killed himself to be with her," she whispered.

"It makes sense now, why he attached himself to you."

"Besides looking a lot like her and sharing similar professions?"

He nodded. "This was his house. In all the confusion, he needed you."

"So what do we do?"

He pulled back and tipped up her chin to force her gaze to his. "You're going to call Mattie."

"What? No. I can't. My mom was the medium, not me."

"That's not true. You saw into the past with Arlen, didn't you?"

"That's because he made me—"

"Brenna, he couldn't have made you see anything if you didn't possess the ability to communicate with the dead."

Oh, God. She'd spent her entire life trying to avoid all this, to keep her feet firmly planted in the land of the living, and she did not want to open her mind to the bullshit that had made her youth miserable.

"There has to be another way."

"I can communicate with Arlen, but he's earthbound. I've never been able to channel those who have crossed over. You've got to give it a shot. We need Mattie, or you'll never be free of Arlen."

"What about him? Do you need your camera to see him?"

"No." He turned toward the door, his eyes haunted, his face pale, and at that moment, she realized what all this had cost him. "He's standing right there."

CHAPTER Six

For the first time in many years, there was no protective shield of the lens between Hex and the otherworld. No barriers.

One look into Arlen's lifeless eyes and Hex knew he'd never been safe anyway. The ghosts had always been there, surrounding him. It had been stupid to think otherwise.

He tried to calm his breathing, to forget that it was all happening again, just the way Creed had constantly warned him.

Hex, you'll have to try to see the ghosts without the aid of the camera lens—do it on your own, before you're forced to do it when you're not prepared, Creed would say. But Hex had refused to listen.

He'd told his friend that he would never willingly make that sacrifice—he didn't want to see dead people around him all the time, the way he had as a child and teenager.

And yet, there was nothing unwilling about what he'd just done for Brenna.

"Shit." He closed his eyes but he could still somehow see Arlen, as though the image had been seared into his brain. His wrist began to burn like the fires of hell, the way it had where Malachi had originally grabbed him. He had no doubt that there would be a raised, angry handprint on his skin within seconds.

"Hex . . . Oh, my God, what's happening to your wrist?" Brenna asked him, and he couldn't speak, could only will all the ghostly remains from his body with the last drops of energy he had.

"Leave him alone, Arlen. If you love me the way you say you do, you won't hurt Hex." Brenna held tight to his arm, protectively, and her voice was surprisingly calm. Firm, even.

I'll hurt anyone who gets in the way of you and me, Mattie. I promise you that. Arlen took a step forward, and Hex recoiled, and hated himself for that.

"Don't, Brenna," Hex heard himself whisper. "Don't antagonize him like that. He's already upset that we're close."

Hex had revealed things to Brenna, things that no woman had ever known about him.

Mattie, why don't you want to come back to me, Arlen asked.

"She's not Mattie," Hex said, hearing the hoarseness of his own voice. Getting Arlen and Mattie's story had been exhausting and Hex desperately needed a break. He would have to regroup quickly. "Go away, Arlen. You lost, and now you're too weak to fight me," he told the ghost.

This isn't over, Arlen told him. Like Hex didn't know that. He had to fight the urge to give the ghost the finger before Arlen dematerialized into a misty smoke and left the room.

"We're alone," Hex said. "He'll be back, but for now it's just us."

He ran his palms over his face and realized again how much this possession had taken from him. He brought his fingers around to the tribal markings, which seemed to burn more when he touched them, as though they were unleashing some of their anger on him for diluting their power.

They'd eventually forgive him, heal him, but it would be a slow process.

"I need..." he started, but he wasn't exactly sure what he needed.

"You need rest. Food. You need off this hard floor," Brenna said.

With her help, he peeled himself off the cold, tiled floor and let her lead him into the bedroom, where the shades were still pulled, keeping out the light...and some of the heat. It didn't matter—the feel of the soft mattress against his back was heaven. His muscles bore a heaviness, as though he'd run a marathon.

"Do you think he'll really leave us alone for a while?" Brenna asked him as she wiped his forehead with a cool washcloth.

"If we're lucky." He stared up into her eyes, still wide with worry. "I can see him if he comes back; I can warn you."

"So it worked—you've got your gift back, then?"

"Yeah, I guess I do." He managed to keep his voice calm, even as his heart hammered in his chest at the thought.

"What about getting rid of him for good?"

He shook his head. "He's not ready to go. That's why we need Mattie."

"Can't you cast a spell, a hex or something to keep him away until then?"

He managed a smile, because he'd been getting that request his entire life, based on his name. " 'Hex' doesn't mean what you think—it means six, which represents the universal number for sin. And sex."

"The Christians called it the number of sin," he reported to his mother when the nuns in the private school his parents had sent him to mentioned it to him. Mainly, when he wasn't following their rules. Which was practically all the time.

"Nonsense," his mother would sniff. "Pythagoreans know that six is considered the perfect number."

Brenna cocked one eyebrow. "Your parents named you after a sin?"

"My mother was a math professor; my dad, science. They had a love of numbers and practicality." He stretched, testing his muscles, the punch-drunk feeling lessening slightly. "But the sex part does come in handy, most of the time."

"Yes, I can see that." She smiled, and then it faded. "What was happening back there—the mark, on your wrist..." She trailed off as she picked up his arm and studied it, but the burn was already gone. At least on the surface. His nerve endings were still sensitive where the marking had appeared, a mark that was always going to be there, hovering beneath the skin, waiting for the right moment to resurface and try to push him over the edge.

Malachi's gone. You banished him for good. Anything else was merely left over, an imprint, something that couldn't hurt him beyond the physical pain.

"It's left over, from Malachi's possession. I told you that before Malachi, I did see ghosts everywhere, the whole I-see-dead-people thing. And I could always capture them on film as well, but I realized early on that it was easier not to tell people about that."

"They wouldn't have understood. They didn't understand my mother." She stroked his hair softly.

"People are always going to be scared of what they don't see, so they'll scoff at what others do see in order to ease their own fears. It's human nature. The only way most of us survive."

"How are you surviving, then? Because this has to take a terrible toll on you."

It would, more so now than ever. "No more than your job takes on you," he countered, and watched her recoil slightly.

"My mother always went out of her way to tell me I could be normal, that I would never have to be bothered by the visions and voices that woke her up at night from a sound sleep," she explained, and he got that. Passing on that particular set of gifts was a heavy burden to bear for both giver and receiver, a calling that could force a life of isolation and pain.

"You've suffered because of what you can see," she continued.

Had he? Or had he merely been surviving all these years instead of living, roaming from place to place like the ghosts who sought his help, ghosts who were constantly searching for something, someone, to make it all mean something?

Was Brenna that someone?

He pushed that thought from his mind as Brenna stroked his bare shoulders, first with the washcloth and then with her hands, massaging his sore muscles.

"Feels good." He shifted slightly, burrowing his cheek against the pillow as his skin tingled under her touch.

"I'm going to make you feel even better." And from the glint in her eye, he knew exactly what she was thinking.

Normally, he'd be all over that idea. Literally all over it. But he was still far too helpless for comfort.

"Brenna, I can barely move," he told her, but she wasn't listening, had moved her body on top of his. The way she watched him made his heart tug, and he realized he had no choice once again but to trust her.

"Let me help you," she was murmuring. Most of his body was still in recovery mode, but his cock came to life the instant Brenna's mouth suckled gently on his neck.

Now she seemed to be working on bringing the rest of him back around. His nipples hardened as she worked them with her tongue, alternately sucking and nipping, then blowing on them so the cool air mingled with the taut flesh, and fuck, yes, he didn't want her to stop. Ever.

"I won't," she said, even though he hadn't spoken the words aloud.

She was straddling his prone form, looking down at him. She was still naked, beautifully so, with the morning light leaking through the curtains throwing shadows on her form.

"I'd love to photograph you right now... like a tigress stretching out in the sun."

"Like a tigress about to take advantage of her mate," she murmured, and raised her arms to lift the hair from her neck, posing for him for a second. Her breasts tilted up slightly, her belly was already pulled taut and her sex was moist where it rested near his thighs. "But really, you'd stop me now to take a picture?"

"If I could lift a camera."

She moved off his thighs in order to pull down his already loosened jeans. "Maybe I'll take a picture of you like this—helpless and spread out and so devastatingly handsome."

He flushed, felt the heat spread from his cheeks to his neck, and yes, he'd been called handsome before, but none of those women had ever looked at him the way Brenna did now. "Go for it," he whispered.

His cock was fully erect, pointing up toward his belly, engorged and ready. Brenna ran a single finger around the head, smearing the moisture and causing his hips to raise slightly.

He wanted to grab her, flip her—take her. But her warm mouth circled his cock, worked him slowly with her tongue the way she had in his dreams last night, and this was it, the place he needed to be.

He hissed as she slid his shaft in and out of her mouth, working it slowly with her hand in the same rhythm.

"Fuck, Brenna," he groaned, even as she urged his legs farther apart—he could barely comply, but when he did, she worked her way down, licking his cock and then focusing her attention on his balls. She suckled one, then the other, until his hands fisted the sheets, his head rolling from side to side on the pillow as she worked the sensitive thin skin.

"Fuck me, Brenna—come up here and fuck me," he heard himself say.

Slowly, so slowly, she released his cock from her mouth. "You taste so good, Hex... I could taste you all day."

She moved up his body and hovered over his erection. He tried to lift his arms to yank her down, to impale her on his cock, but they still felt heavier than lead. "Don't tease, not now."

She lowered herself, her sex taking him in, inch by excruciatingly pleasurable inch, until she'd completely sheathed him.

His body trembled, the earlier shock combined with the intensity of his pleasure nearly too much for all his senses. He closed his eyes in an attempt to block out some of the stimuli, to just give his body the chance to integrate his senses as a whole again.

"So hot, Brenna," he murmured. "Hot and tight."

"I'm going to take you, Hex. Make you all mine."

Brenna was rocking against him, arcing her body and moaning as he throbbed inside her. She moved a hand up his chest, alternated pinching and caressing a nipple with one hand, while her other hand reached back to stroke his balls, and oh, man, this was good—made his nerve endings shock back to life, eased the ache in his muscles, even as the urge to come was fast overtaking him.

He opened his eyes and managed to prop himself first onto his elbows and then finally all the way to sitting. She settled back in, her feet locking behind him, her hands on his shoulders.

He braced himself with his arms behind him at first, but he was meeting her, thrust for thrust. And after a few minutes, he was able to throw one arm around her waist, to pull her tighter to him, so he could get deeper inside of her hot, slick sex, which contracted around him with each arch of her body.

She'd thrown back her head, rode him with her eyes closed and her mouth curved in an open bow of pleasure, until he came, his orgasm even more intense than it had been earlier. He cried out her name, and her entire body shook with the force from his.

He eased back slowly—she remained pressed to his chest as she uncurled her legs. For a few moments, they lay against each other in silence.

Brenna's next words hit him squarely between the eyes.

"You've done so much for me, Hex," she whispered. "I'll never forget you or what you're doing to help me get my career back. To help me finally be done with this paranormal crap."

I'll never forget you.

Her words brought home the enormity of what he'd just done, what he'd allowed to happen. He saw dead people, would be able to see them all the time, without barriers.

He would never rest.

He pushed back and away from her. "I'm so fucking tired of being everyone's pawn—living and dead."

"Hex, wait. Please. I know this has been a lot for you to deal with."

"You have no idea what I'm dealing with. You think you know, think you understand what it's like to live with ghosts. But you have no idea what it's like to see them, night and day. To have them begging for your help. To not be able to get any kind of relief. But don't worry, we'll get rid of Arlen, and then you can go back to forgetting all about this paranormal crap and get on with your life."

She recoiled as if he'd slapped her.

He struggled off the bed and into the bathroom, away from Brenna, and knew he wouldn't find relief anytime soon.

CHAPTER *Seven*

Brenna stared at the closed bathroom door, unsure what to say or do. A few months ago her first instinct would have been to throw a tantrum—and maybe a lamp—but something had changed since she'd been away from the world of glitz and glamour.

Something had definitely changed since meeting Hex, because strangely, she wanted to talk this out instead of stomping off in a huff.

She crossed the room and tapped on the bathroom door. "Hex?"

"Give me a minute."

Ignoring him, she reached for the doorknob. She hesitated when her hand closed around the antique handle.

I'm an intensely private person.

She had to respect that, no matter how badly she wanted to barge in and make him listen to her.

"Look," she began, propping her forehead against the door, "you're right. I don't know what it's like to have ghosts bugging me night and day. But I watched my mom go through it. She did it alone because she refused to bring a man into our lives until I was old enough to defend myself." She paused, unsure if she really wanted to go there, to the place where her father had been an abusive scumbag her mom left when Brenna was three.

No, she definitely didn't want to go there.

"What I'm trying to say is that I hated what she went through. I hate all of it. I didn't want to be around it, and I found a life that kept me as far away as possible."

Hex said nothing. She was making things worse, obviously.

"Okay, I'm tired of talking to a door. When you decide to quit hiding, I'll be here to talk."

Keeping a tight rein on her temper, she threw on a gauzy sundress, even though she was exhausted enough to fall into bed and stay there for days. But there was no way she could sleep, and something she'd seen in one of Arlen's flashbacks lingered in her mind, a puzzle that needed to be solved.

Downstairs, she snared a Popsicle from the freezer, grabbed her shoulder bag and slipped on her sandals.

"Where are you going?" Hex's voice startled her, nearly made her drop her purse.

"To find Mattie," she said, knowing that sounded insane. Then again, everything about the last couple of days had been insane.

Barefoot, and wearing only fresh, dry jeans, Hex sauntered into the kitchen, halting five feet from her, looking tired but gloriously fired up. "I don't think that's a good idea."

"I've got to do something. I can't just sit around here and do nothing but have sex." Not that having sex with him had been a hardship, but she wasn't about to hang around and wait for Arlen to try to possess him again.

He hooked his thumbs in his pockets and watched her with that intense, whiskey gaze. "Why have you been having sex with me, Brenna? Because you feel like you owe me? Because of the *anything* clause?"

Unbelievable. She crossed her arms over her chest, realizing too late she looked ridiculous with the Popsicle in her hand.

"Yes, Hex. There has to be a reason, because it's simply not possible that I like you." He snorted, and her tenuous hold on her temper finally snapped. "You'd think someone who can see ghosts wouldn't be so damned blind when it comes to the living."

"You said you hate the paranormal, that you want nothing to do with it." He closed the distance between them in two strides, filling her personal space with his rampant masculinity, stopping just short of touching her. "But, baby, I'm about as paranormal as it gets. It's part of me, and it ain't going away. So yeah, I have a hard time believing that you want anything to do with me."

"Believe what you want," she snapped. "I'm leaving."

"I'll go with you." He grasped her wrist as though to stop her, but his grip was gentle, soothing, and her anger melted like the ice pop in her hand.

"I can handle this by myself. You should stay and get some rest."

"Do you have a car?" he asked, ignoring everything she'd just said.

She hefted her purse onto her shoulder, avoiding his eyes. "I was going to take the bus." She'd had to sell her Mercedes a month ago.

Releasing her, he snagged his cell phone off the table. "We're taking a cab."

She huffed, but he merely dialed the taxi company, whose number he must have programmed into his directory. After he hung up, he silently took the stairs and left her to wait, but just as the cab pulled up to the front of the house, Hex came downstairs, freshly shaved and wearing a forest green short-sleeved button-down shirt that made his eyes glow.

"Where to?" the driver asked once they were inside the air-conditioned cab. The icy interior felt like heaven after so many weeks in a house cooled only by fans and nighttime breezes.

Brenna slipped on sunglasses as Hex did the same. "Metairie Cemetery."

"Have you been there before?" Hex asked.

"I've never been to any cemetery," she said quietly. Her mom had warned against it, saying that the spiritual energy could be too intense. It had been out of concern for Brenna that she'd been cremated instead of buried. "You?"

He nodded. "It's one of the city's most prestigious graveyards, and since Katrina, paranormal activity has been off the charts. I've gotten some great pictures there."

The drive was short, silent, and once they arrived, Hex paid the fare while Brenna wandered around the main entrance. The monuments were stained by Katrina floodlines, and many of the statues had been damaged, but the sense of familiarity couldn't be washed away by a storm surge. She'd seen all of this through Arlen's eyes.

The morning heat bore down on her, scorching her bare shoulders as she moved with purpose down Avenue Bell, ignoring Hex's curse far behind her.

Her heart began to thump with the force of a horse's hooves on pavement. Her blood pounded in her ears. She broke out in a cold sweat and even her vision started swimming. So many tombs, all aboveground because of the low water tables in New Orleans. A city of the dead.

Her mom had been right; the spiritual energy fairly vibrated in the air, bounced off her skin, closed in on her like a tunnel that grew smaller as she walked.

Statuettes of praying angels guided her way past plots surrounded by black ironwork fences, and giant effigies of weeping women pointed her in a direction she somehow knew well.

"Brenna!"

Hex's footsteps grew louder, spurring her faster. She was close. Her throat tightened, so much that her breath felt like it was being funneled through a straw.

There.

She stumbled to a stop in movie-slow-motion. In front of her, the tomb loomed, dull white stained by time and storms, chipped and worn by the elements. Four stone pillars rose out of the ground, lending a grand, mansionlike quality to the tomb, and between them, two names had been carved into a marble plaque.

MADELYN "MATTIE" ROUSSEAU, 1903–1923.
ARLEN ROUSSEAU, 1895–1923.

"Oh, God," she whispered. "It's all true."

Hex's hands came down on her shoulders, his comforting presence holding her steady. "You knew it was."

Yes, she had. But to be confronted with the evidence shook her. Literally, because she had to clench her fists to keep them from trembling.

"Hex . . ." Her legs gave out, but he caught her, hauled her up against him so she thought she'd never fall again.

"It's okay, Brenna."

She stood there for a moment, folded into Hex's strong arms. "I want this to be over."

"You know what to do."

She closed her eyes, hating the truth in his words. She remembered how her mom would contact the spirits of those who had crossed over, and she knew she had to open herself up the same way. But if she did that, there might be no turning back. She might be hounded day in and day out by spirits who wanted her to communicate with their loved ones.

"I'm afraid." Taking a deep breath, she took his male essence into her, as though his strength would transfer to her through his scent. "That probably sounds so lame to you, after all you've done." And after she'd called *him* a coward for not facing his own gift. God, she was the biggest coward of all.

He pushed back from her, just enough that he could look directly into her eyes. "Brenna, I've hid from the full power of my gift for a long time, so I'm the last person on earth to think less of you for being afraid to use yours." He feathered his fingers over her cheek in an unbelievably comforting gesture. "You're strong. You can do this. And when it's over, I won't leave you alone to deal with the fallout." His throat worked on a hard swallow. "I'll be there for you."

She didn't know what to say. He'd already done so much for her. How could she ask for more once this was over?

Stepping away from him, she closed her eyes again and concentrated. In her mind, she called out to Mattie. Over and over. Gradually, voices began to invade her thoughts... a jumble of them, hundreds, perhaps, but she couldn't pick out a single one. Wincing, she covered her ears, but that only made the noise inside her head grow louder.

She cursed. "I can't do this." She opened her eyes, to see Hex standing there.

And he was surrounded by people she didn't know, looking as solid as Hex, but she knew they didn't live on this plane.

They all started talking at once, asking her to find people, to send messages to parents and spouses and children.

"Hex?" She stumbled backward, reeling.

"What? What is it?"

"Can't you see them?" She swept her arm in an arc at the crowd. "They're everywhere."

He looked around, but shook his head. "I told you I can't see those who have crossed over. Only those who are earth-bound, like Arlen. But listen to me, okay?"

She nodded, clinging to every word because at least his made sense.

"Tell them to go away. That you'll speak with them later. You need to find Mattie."

"Okay." Taking a deep, calming breath, she addressed the crowd. "I can't talk to you now. Please respect that."

Disappointment filtered through the throng, but most of them faded away, back to what her mother had called the Other Side, what others called heaven. A few lingered, but she ground her teeth and did her best to ignore them as she called out again to Mattie.

"Mattie, come to me. I can help you find Arlen."

"Who are you?"

Brenna's breath left her in a rush. Slowly, she turned away from Hex. There she was: Mattie, dressed in the glittery gold gown in which she'd died. She looked just like she had in the vision Brenna had seen through Arlen.

"My name is Brenna," she said, thankful there was no one in this part of the cemetery—no one living anyway—because anyone watching her speak to what they thought was empty air would think she was nuts. "I'm a . . . friend of Arlen's."

Sorrow filled Mattie's eyes. "I can't find him anywhere."

Brenna swung around to Hex. "Can you summon Arlen?"

He gave a single, sharp nod. "He's never far from you." His hand went to her face, and he used his thumb to caress her cheekbone in long, sensuous strokes. "Arlen?" he said loudly enough that his voice echoed off the hundreds of mausoleums. "I've got Mattie. Here at your grave. I'll make her mine right here in front of you."

Brenna gasped, and so did Mattie. "You're going to make him so mad—"

"That's the point. The angrier he is, the more power he'll have during the daylight—power he'll need to see Mattie and cross over." A mournful wail shook the ground beneath them. "He's here."

Yes, Brenna could see him, next to the monument, lips drawn back in a snarl as he went for Hex.

"No!" She darted forward as Hex raised his arm, his markings practically sparking with energy. Arlen hissed like a vampire confronted with a crucifix and shrank back.

"The daylight is *my* realm, Arlen. *I* have the power," Hex growled.

"Arlen?" Mattie called his name softly, and Hex turned. He could see her now. And oh, thank God, so could Arlen.

Time seemed to stand still for the span of several heartbeats, and then Arlen and Mattie met in an embrace so powerful that Brenna felt it to her very soul. Tears stung her eyes, and she let them fall freely as Hex wrapped his arms around her. Love spiced the air, rolling off Mattie and Arlen in great waves. Light surrounded them in streaks of gold and silver so bright Brenna was glad she was still wearing her sunglasses.

"Go with her, Arlen," Hex said.

Arlen tore his gaze away from his beloved Mattie for just a moment. "I'm sorry, Brenna. So very sorry."

She had to swallow the lump in her throat in order to talk. "I know. Go. Be happy."

Before she'd finished speaking, they were gone in a flash of light. A sob finally escaped her as she turned to Hex. "You did it. You really did it. I'm free."

He tucked her head against his shoulder and tenderly stroked her hair. "Yeah, you're free."

CHAPTER Eight

Yes, Brenna was free—free of Arlen's hauntings, free to go back to her modeling career. He wouldn't have to report this one to ACRO at all, seeing as how Brenna was a GV, short for *garden variety,* which was what most psychics were. Low-level abilities, a dime a dozen. They'd be welcome at ACRO, but the agency wouldn't waste resources trying to recruit anyone with less-than-spectacular or unique powers.

So Brenna could remain free. But Hex felt as if he'd never be truly free again.

That thought made his throat tighten, for both of them, and still he refused to mourn this soon-to-be separation... there would be plenty of time for that. No, for now he'd make the most of the time he had left with Brenna, before they went their separate ways.

He paid the cabdriver and helped Brenna up the walk

and back inside the house. She was drained—he could see it in her eyes, as if she wasn't sure what to focus on. She was obviously still seeing spirits, lining up all around her.

She had so much to learn. "They go away for a little while, and then they come back." She waved her hand at them. "I need some time. You all need to go away now."

He paused for a second. "Did they listen?"

"I think they did."

"You could attempt to shut it all off again," he told her. "There are ways." He imagined her in the Amazon with him—her body naked in the tropical rain forest, head thrown back in pleasure.

But Brenna was shaking her head. "I can see how living like this can be hard, but my God, Hex, it was so beautiful to watch them find each other, to watch them cross over. Is it always like that?"

"Yeah, it is. Even if they fight it until the end, that feeling of peace when they finally give up the ghost and move on is amazing." It was why he continued to do what he did, why he didn't just chuck it all and only do his adventure photography.

"What happens now?" she asked, and he had an idea what *he* wanted to happen now.

He took the black bag off his shoulder, knelt on the floor and unzipped it. He'd had the cab stop at his hotel, had gone up to retrieve the last camera he had, an old Nikon he'd taken into the Amazon with him and kept for obvious sentimental reasons. He'd kept it in good condition, ready to go, and now as Brenna cocked her head quizzically at him, he smiled.

"Pose for me. Only me," he said.

"Like the pictures in the magazine."

"Like any way you want. I just want to get you on film."

She walked over to the chaise, where it all began, and she

began to pose for him—slow, sensuous poses with her long-limbed body, the sundress swirling around her legs as she shifted on the chaise.

But her poses were different from the other pictures he'd seen of her; the come-hither look was replaced by something softer, something just for him. These poses were fun, and she looked happy.

"You're so pretty, Brenna," he heard himself murmur. "You don't understand how badly I want you all the time. Especially right now."

In response, she tugged her bottom lip between her teeth, and then she smiled and held out her hands to him.

He couldn't refuse an invite like that. He set the camera down on its tripod and went to her. "I want to make love to you. Not because of ghosts or possessions or anything else. Just because I want to."

"Please . . . yes," she said as he lowered himself on top of her and kissed her, long and slow, taking his time the way he hadn't been able to before, when their couplings had been frantic, full of passion and danger.

She tasted like sweet wine, and he could get happily lost here, with her, in her. Her tongue moved against his and she made soft noises in her throat as his mouth took hers.

His hands moved along her shoulders—pushing one strap and then the other off her shoulders, pausing to nip and suck at the smooth, soft skin as the dress fluttered to the floor in a puddle at her feet.

"I like this dress," he murmured, as he palmed a breast and mouthed a nipple, teasing it until it was a deep rose color and impossibly hard. She sucked in a breath as he did so, was teasing the other nipple herself while she watched him, so incredibly sexy, and yet, somehow, she still looked almost shy.

"It's just us, Brenna," he reassured her.

"I know. I didn't think I'd be nervous with you like this. It's just that . . ."

It means so much now—more than it did before. "I'll be right back. Don't move. Please." He went to the kitchen, and returned with the last blue Popsicle, already unwrapped. She remained in place and daylight streamed in through the windows, casting a glow on her creamy skin.

"Your favorite, right?"

"What are you planning to do with that?"

"How about I just show rather than tell." He let the blue ice trail lightly first across one nipple and then the other. She gasped and smiled as he bent down to tug a nipple in his mouth. The hot and cold sensations mingled on his tongue, along with the taste of Brenna and of blue raspberry mixing together.

He let her slide the Popsicle into her mouth, and she teased him, the way she'd done yesterday, working it between her lips, swirling her tongue around the tip. His shaft hardened to the point of pain at the memory of the way she'd worked him over just that morning.

She smiled around the blue ice and shifted so her hands could work the button and zipper on his jeans. He let a moan escape as she freed his shaft and stroked it with a warm palm. He felt the slide of smooth skin over hard muscle, took the ice out of her mouth and kissed her, her cold mouth against his warm one.

She fondled his balls as he let the ice travel down her belly. He moved between her legs as well, let the ice brush her clit. She gasped, shifted, and he took that opportunity to free himself of her grasp and sink to his knees. He flicked his tongue where the ice pop had been, tasting the sticky mixture of sugar and woman before he sucked, bringing the nub between his teeth gently.

She arched up and cried out, her fingers digging into his

hair, and he did it again and again, until she was begging him, her words incoherent.

Finally, he threw down the melting ice, because he couldn't wait anymore. She spread her legs for him, actually yanked on his shoulders to bring him in closer, and they ended up with his heavy weight on top of her.

"Hurry, Hex. Please," she begged, and he entered her, one long stroke that was slower than before. He kissed her again, his tongue sweeping her mouth, her hands kneading the muscles in his ass, forcing him to pump inside of her deeper with each stroke.

Together, they rocked back and forth, her body pinned against the cushions, her flesh hot and willing beneath his. Her ankles locked around his back, pulling him into her, deeper and deeper until she started to come, her body going taut, a surprised cry escaping her throat.

He came just from watching her, a soul-shattering, mind-fucking-blowing orgasm that rivaled any he'd ever had.

He'd hungered for her for so long and in a way he'd never be able to forget. Right now she was safe and in his arms and he chose to only think about the present.

Brenna woke to the smell of bacon and eggs. Yawning, she glanced at the bedside clock. Seven A.M. She and Hex had spent the last sixteen hours alternately sleeping and making love—the most incredible sixteen hours of her life.

Her newly opened psychic eye had attracted spirits all night long, but Hex had taught her some simple techniques to ensure her privacy. He'd reminded her that there were ways to turn off her psychic abilities permanently, but she'd need professional help to do so, and after the experience at the cemetery, she wasn't sure she wanted to go that route.

She'd finally understood what her mother had known all along: Those who had crossed over were as alive as those who hadn't, and they desired contact with loved ones with the same intensity. They just needed people like Brenna's mom to help. To listen.

Brenna wasn't about to make a career of listening, but she wasn't ready to shut out anyone who needed help either.

Feeling better than she had in years, she threw on a short silk robe and padded barefoot down to the kitchen, where Hex was loading plates with food. Sunlight streaked through the three kitchen windows, to cast dappled shadows on his bare back, where his muscles flexed with every sure, efficient motion he made.

"Look at you and your domesticity. I'm impressed."

He laughed, a deep rumble that tripped her heart. "If I hadn't learned to cook a long time ago, I'd have starved."

"You've been alone for a long time, haven't you?"

His smile faded. "Yeah." He gestured to the table. "Have a seat."

The food was wonderful. So much so that she had to stop herself from reaching for a second helping of bacon.

"Have more," he said.

"Thanks, but I can't."

He shifted toward her, his eyes darkening seductively. "If I offer to feed you, will you reconsider?"

"That's a pretty tempting offer." Drawn by the low, rough edge of his voice and the full, lush line of his mouth, she leaned forward, until their lips nearly touched. "A lot about you is tempting."

He brushed his lips over hers, and instantly her nipples hardened and her sex tingled, as though they hadn't gone a dozen rounds last night. Or maybe because of it. Her body remembered every lick, kiss, suck . . . it remembered how he'd fetched another Popsicle and used it in such wicked ways that she would never look at one the same way again.

"So that's a yes?"

She sighed. "You're so bad. But I can't. Too fattening."

Frowning, he drew back. "Sweetheart, a couple or twenty pounds is not going to hurt you."

"It'll hurt my career. Which I have back, thanks to you."

There was a distinct shift in the atmosphere of the kitchen, one that had nothing to do with ghosts. "When do you leave?"

She dragged her fork through the bits of egg on her plate. "The sooner the better, I think."

He pushed away from the table and started to gather the dishes. "Right. Rip the bandage off quickly. Less painful that way."

Silence settled like a shroud. Even the sound of the dishes clanking in the sink seemed muted. She stood, took a step toward him. "You could come with me."

He shut off the water but didn't look at her. "I can't."

"You won't."

"I'd never fit into your world, Brenna." His tone said he didn't think she'd fit in anymore either, but he was wrong. New Orleans was not where she belonged, and nothing that had happened over the last couple of days could change that.

"So this is it? We go our separate ways and pretend this was nothing but a nightmare?"

He swung around and pinned her with a heated stare. "We go our separate ways," he gritted out. "But I won't think on any of this as a nightmare."

Her heart hurt so much she had to force herself to breathe. "Me either."

"Then don't go. You'll need help with your new gift. I told you I'd be there for you. I'll take care of you."

God, it was so tempting to take him up on his offer. But right now, she was too close to him, to the situation. That distance they'd talked about was more important than ever, and the desire to run far and fast made her temples throb.

"I can't, Hex. Not now. I need time. I need the normal world."

"A world where the men in your life don't see ghosts?" Ice formed a glaze over his eyes. "I thought we were through hiding, but I guess I was wrong."

An onslaught of emotion made her chest ache. "I'm not hiding from my ability. You saw me in the cemetery—"

"You're hiding from me, Brenna. From what you feel for me. And you're using the paranormal as an excuse."

She jerked like she'd been slapped. "You're so far off base."

"Am I? You ever been serious with anyone? Ever talked marriage and kids?"

"Have you?" she challenged, and his gaze narrowed.

"No. But for the first time, I want to remedy that."

Oh, God. She pushed out an agonizingly slow breath through a suddenly narrow passage, and now she knew what toothpaste must feel like when it came out of the tube.

"I can't do this," she whispered, frantically looking around for a distraction. Anything to put an end to this conversation. "I—I have so much to do. I have to contact my agency. Sell the house—"

"I'll buy it."

"What?"

He looked as surprised as she was, but he quickly recovered, his expression shuttering. "I can write you a check right now. I'll take good care of her."

She hadn't truly wanted to sell the house, but she needed the money to survive until her first modeling job, and if he could write her a check right now...

"Yes. Fine." Her voice sounded distant. Hollow. "It'll take me a couple of days to pack and make arrangements to move."

"No problem."

She swallowed at the abruptness in his voice. Their relationship couldn't end this way. The thought of losing him so quickly was like a hot poker through the gut, and she spoke before she could think things through. "I'd like it if you could stay until I go."

Hex cursed. "How can you ask that of me?"

"I just thought—"

"What, that I'm a masochist? That I'd be happy to sit around and beg for whatever pity-scraps the great Brenna St. James deigns to dole out to the lowly photographer, until she leaves without a backward glance?"

She stopped breathing. "That's not what I want."

He shook his head and grabbed his camera, which had been sitting on the counter. "I don't think you know what you want. No, that's not true. You know. You just won't admit it. So who's the coward now?" He turned on his heel and headed for the front door.

"Hex..."

He paused, hand on the knob. "Unless you're going to tell me you aren't leaving, don't say anything."

She swallowed, the lump in her throat blocking whatever she might have said.

"That's what I thought," he said gruffly. "I'll have a check delivered to you in the morning."

And with that, he was gone.

CHAPTER Nine

There was no way Hex could go with her. Especially with his gift back in full force—he'd be even more of a recluse now, wouldn't be able to deal with Brenna and her celebrity and the invasion of press and people that came with that.

God, he'd been stupid to think she'd stay with him, to even hold out a small bit of hope. She'd told him so just twenty-four hours ago, had been honest from the start about what her goal was, and still it hit him like a fresh evisceration of his heart.

But even so, he couldn't let Brenna sell the house to strangers. Sentimentality had never been his thing, but the connection to her, to New Orleans . . . to the gift he'd allowed to return, was too much to ignore.

He'd never really had a home once he'd left his parents' house. ACRO didn't count—when he went there, he either crashed at Creed's house or stayed in one of the guest billets on the main compound. Several times, he'd been offered his own land, but he'd refused. It hadn't felt right—no place felt right for very long. The longest he'd ever stayed anyplace was in New Orleans.

He let himself into the quiet of his hotel room, threw his camera equipment on the bed and ran his hands through his hair as he paced. Yes, he'd buy the house from Brenna, make it his home away from home while he continued to wander around the world doing what he did best.

It was what he was built for, and trying to change that was almost as ridiculous as thinking Brenna would settle down with him instead of going back to her old job.

He dialed the familiar ACRO number and got Henry Stockton, the Paranormal Division director, on the line. "Hey, it's Hex."

"How's ghost hunting going in New Orleans?" Henry asked.

"For now, I think my work here is done. I've helped a lot of the spirits who were causing trouble in the hotels and inns cross over. I'm ready to head to Ecuador and take care of that haunting issue we keep hearing about, if the job's still open."

There were rumors of ghosts in a small South American town who invaded humans and turned them zombielike, a mission he'd nearly accepted before Brenna St. James had contacted him. Hex had told Henry he still had unfinished work and Henry, who'd never been the type to micromanage, hadn't pushed the issue.

"The job's still open. You'll need to be briefed—I'll send you the files. When do you think you can leave?" The director's tone was clipped. No nonsense. No games. Which was the way Hex liked his life.

He'd have to give himself time to close on the house—

something the ACRO lawyers could push through quickly. "Give me a week and I'm out of here," he said firmly.

The jungles of Ecuador were as good a place as any to lose himself.

It was funny, really, how once word got out that someone was once again a marketable commodity, people flocked to them as though nothing had ever happened. As though they hadn't turned their backs on Brenna when she'd needed them the most.

Now she sat in her "good friend" Jacqueline's L.A. apartment, where she'd be staying until she could find a place of her own. Thanks to Hex and the check that had arrived as promised, she had the money to do so.

Jacqueline sifted through the file of photos Brenna had set out on the coffee table but had been reluctant to look at. She hadn't seen them since the day she'd developed them in her darkroom—the day Hex had walked out, leaving behind all cameras but one. The cameras had been smashed, but some of the film had, thankfully, been salvageable. She hadn't been able to destroy them as Hex had asked. These shot were all that remained of their relationship.

"These are amazing, Brenna. The ghost looks so real."

She didn't bother to say the ghost *was* real.

"The photographer's very talented." In more ways than one. Ways she wasn't about to share with Jackie.

"You slept with him, didn't you?" Jackie sighed. "Oh, honey, you never, ever sleep with a photographer, unless he can give you something."

Brenna wanted to throw up. Hex had given her something—something much more than just her career. And the thing was, she'd approached him for the exact reason Jackie had mentioned. She'd offered to sleep with him in exchange for his services.

And she'd been okay with it, had been so desperate that she hadn't cared who got hurt in the process.

"There's a party at Jojo's tonight," Jackie said. "I know he always has that fancy buffet, but we'll pop some dexies before we go."

Taking diet pills and socializing up a storm didn't sound nearly as appealing as it had mere weeks ago. No, too much had happened.

Hex had happened.

You're hiding from me, Brenna. From what you feel for me. And you're using the paranormal as an excuse.

She could hear his voice, the deep rasp that touched her like a caress even in her memories. Even when he was talking about things he didn't know jack about. Like that she was hiding behind the paranormal thing in order to avoid her feelings for him.

Jackie tossed the file of photos onto the couch beside Brenna and sauntered to her bedroom. The top photo slid out, a picture of Hex holding Brenna, shielding her from the camera as Arlen snapped a barrage of photos. Her gaze fixed on how his arms were wrapped around her protectively, how his eyes were closed and his expression was one of pure bliss. She remembered how she'd felt, safe and wanted.

A glutton for punishment, she pulled another snapshot from the file. In the new one, Hex was still holding her, his big body angled to hide her nudity from the camera. But his eyes were open and he was gazing at her with such intensity of emotion.

Heart aching, she put her fingers to his face. "Oh, Hex..." She trailed off, drawn by the clarity in his eyes.

The camera doesn't lie, Brenna.

She slapped a trembling hand over her mouth. The look he was giving her... no man had ever looked at her like that. She hadn't noticed it at the time, but now... well, the camera didn't lie. Was it really possible?

"He loves you."

Brenna jumped, startled by the sound of Mattie's voice. "That," she said, turning to see the other woman sitting next to her on the couch, "was not cool. You scared me half to death. And you're supposed to be gone."

"Surely you know by now how this works? We are just as alive, if not more so, than you are. We can come and go as we please."

Brenna rolled her eyes. Yes, she knew that. Her mother had explained how the afterlife worked, and she'd learned even more since opening herself up to the spirit world back in Metairie Cemetery.

"Why are you here? No offense, but I was really hoping all of this was behind me."

"It will never be behind you until you confront the truth." Mattie took her hand. "Hex was right. This isn't about your mother's ability or yours, or what Hex does for a living. It's about your inability to allow yourself to feel."

"That's ridiculous."

"Is it? Did you not tell Hex that you show your outside to the world so people won't look too deeply into your insides?"

Brenna gasped as images swirled through her head, running from frame to frame like a video set on fast-forward.

Brenna, at three years old, one eye swollen shut and her nose bleeding as her mom carried her from their house. Brenna had watched, with dry eyes, as her father followed, begging forgiveness.

Brenna, eight years old, sitting on the school playground and ignoring kids who were making fun of her secondhand clothes.

Brenna, mere months ago, standing in her bedroom doorway and watching with detached interest as her boyfriend screwed her friend.

"You were always strong," Mattie whispered, bringing Brenna back to the present, and how the hell did spirits queue up home movies like that?

She should have been hurt by what Nicky had done. Destroyed. But, like everyone else who'd come into her life since the day her mom left her dad, she'd never allowed Nicky inside enough to be capable of hurting her. Oh, she'd been angry at the betrayal, but hurt? Only mildly.

"I had to be."

"You did. But it's time to stop pretending that your goal in life was to be normal and get as far away from your gift as possible. You didn't want to open yourself up to it because doing so would mean you'd feel the need to help lost souls. You'd have to care. You'd have to let other voices into your head. And doing so might result in you getting hurt."

Brenna squeezed her eyes closed tight, wanting to call Mattie a liar, but God, she was so on the money.

"Let go, Brenna. You shared your mother's burden. Let someone else share yours."

Brenna opened her eyes, realized she still had the photo of her and Hex in her lap. He was so handsome, so gentle with her. And he'd been so willing to stand by her side when she'd needed him. "It's a big step," she finally said.

"The biggest."

Brenna chewed on that for a moment, feeling the strong, steady cadence of her heartbeat thudding against her rib cage, as though her heart was trying to weigh in on the whole let-someone-in debate. Her ticker was definitely on the side of *yes*. It wanted Hex, and she was running out of arguments.

"Can I ask you something?" When Mattie nodded, Brenna said, "Why you? Why not my mom?"

"She'll be in touch," Mattie assured her. "But I am so grateful for what you did for me and Arlen that I wanted to do this. Besides, I know what it's like to run away from someone to pursue a career. I died when I ran from Arlen and was struck by the car. I don't want the same thing to happen to you."

Brenna wasn't in immediate danger of being run over by a car, but yeah, she got it. She'd run from Hex, and the price could be more than she was willing to pay.

A nearly crippling stab of fear cut her like a knife. "What if it's too late? What if he doesn't want me anymore? What if I totally blew it?"

"A man like him? He won't let you get away again."

"Brenna? Who are you talking to?" Jackie stood in the living room entrance, dressed in a designer miniskirt and halter top that covered less than a bathing suit would. They were Brenna's clothes. "You aren't still muttering about that photographer, are you?"

"Yeah, I guess I am." Mattie was gone, and now it was time for Brenna to go too. "I don't belong here. I belong with him." She just had to hope she wasn't too late.

CHAPTER *Ten*

Brenna hurried up the familiar porch steps of the house she'd sold to Hex, but before she reached the landing, the front door opened. Hex stepped out, freezing in place when he saw her.

He was carrying a suitcase. And he looked shocked as hell to see her.

"Hi," she said, lamely.

"Brenna. Ah . . . hi."

They stood there staring at each other, the tension in the sultry air between them practically shimmering. Finally, Brenna hugged herself, shifted her weight in her strappy pink sandals and blurted out, "I know you're leaving, but do you have a minute?"

Please, please, say yes.

God, he looked good. It had only been a few days since she'd left, but it felt like months, and the sight of his hard body and long limbs nearly had her tongue-tied. The sinful fit of his Levi's and his Brennan's T-shirt definitely had her drooling.

"Yeah. Come on in."

She followed him inside, and wow, the house looked great. He'd bought furniture and decorated—haunting black-and-white photos of landscapes and houses, but not a ghost to be seen. And in the great room, in the very center, her antique chaise took center stage. Her gut clenched at the memory of everything she and Hex had done on the small lounge.

"Want something to drink? I think I have some sodas—"

She grabbed his arm to stop him from moving into the kitchen, and to stop the polite, neutral small talk. "I'm not here for a Coke."

"Did you forget something?"

"I remembered something." Her voice vibrated with emotion, but she didn't care. This was too important. "I remembered what being with you felt like." She cleared her throat, because the vibration had become a downright tremor she could barely speak through. "I remembered how much I liked it."

"Sex wasn't exactly a problem for us, Brenna." His voice was low and gravelly, as full of emotion as his expression was lacking.

"I wasn't talking about sex," she whispered. "I was talking about everything. The way you talked to me. Looked at me. God, I'm making a fool of myself, aren't I?" Tears stung her eyes, but thankfully didn't fall.

"No, you're not." Hex pulled her into his arms, but the embrace was stiff, like he was afraid to comfort her because any moment she might stick a knife in his back. "But I don't understand—"

"Please, let me finish." Before she lost her nerve. Before

he kicked her out of his life. "I'm an idiot. I should never have left you, and if you'll take me back, I promise not to leave you again."

He dragged in a harsh breath. "But what about New York and L.A. and your career?"

She drew him closer, holding so tight he'd never get away. "All I ever wanted was to be normal. I know that sounds crazy, because nothing about modeling is normal, but at least I didn't have to worry about ghosts and psychics and crystal balls."

"And now?" He sounded so wary, like he expected her to say this was all a big joke, that she'd come back to hurt him again, and it broke her heart.

"I finally realized all of that *is* normal. For people like us anyway. The rest of the world might think we're freaks, but as long as we have each other, we'll be fine." She stroked his back as she took a deep breath, ready to finish what she'd started. "And you were right. I was hiding behind the whole normal thing. I mean, yes, I wanted to be normal because I watched my mom suffer. But more than that, I didn't want to let anyone in. As long as I filled my days with parties and cameras, I didn't have to get close to anyone—living or dead."

"And now?"

"Now I want to get close to you. So wherever you go, I'll go too."

He relaxed against her, dipping his head to nuzzle her neck. Instantly, she broke out in goose bumps, her body responding to him like they'd never been apart.

"Are you sure?" he asked, his hot breath feathering over her sensitive skin. "I was just leaving. And I don't exactly go to places where five-star hotels are the norm."

She pulled back so she could look directly into his eyes. "I've lived in shacks with no indoor plumbing. I've slept in cars and tents. So I can handle whatever you throw at me. Maybe I can even help."

"Brenna." Her name on his lips was a seductive whisper that made her heart flutter. "You really mean it." When she nodded, he teased her lips with the softest of kisses. "God, I want you."

Relief flooded her, and love filled her until her chest felt tight. "I want you too. So much." She took his face in her hands and kissed him, a slow, deep kiss that joined them together in a way not even the great sex had.

Desire sparked quickly, heating her blood, but Hex kept his hands in PG-rated territory, even though hers roamed into much more adult areas.

With a soft groan, he broke off the kiss. "I want to make love to you, but I have something to tell you first."

"Does this have anything to do with the fact that you were leaving when I arrived?"

He nodded. "The world thinks I'm a photographer. I am, but the photography is mainly a side business." He paused. "I work for an agency that employs people with unusual skills and talents."

He went on to tell her about the type of missions ACRO engaged in, the secret nature of the agency, the sinister threat posed by other, similar agencies. When he finished, Brenna shook her head, feeling in a daze. Stunned, she stepped away from him, needing to process what he'd said.

"All I ever wanted was to be normal, to be as far removed from what my mother could do as possible, and now you're saying you're even more deeply involved in that life than she was?"

"Yes, but everything there *is* normal. We're normal. In fact, most people at ACRO make us look tame by comparison." His expression fell. "You've changed your mind."

"No!" God, she'd nearly shouted that. But he couldn't

think she'd change her mind about being together. Never again. "It sounds... it sounds wonderful. Like maybe my new ability could be useful."

"They would make room for you if you wanted a job, or just wanted people to talk to who understand."

She grinned. "Then what are we waiting for?"

A slow, wicked smile spread across his face as he reached for her, drawing her into his arms once more. "We're waiting until we've gotten enough of each other, over and over."

Joy and lust and everything in between shot through her. "Then we'll be here a long time," she whispered. "Because I don't think I'll ever get enough of you."

"Somehow," he said, his gaze bursting with heat and possession, "I think we have an eternity ahead of us to find out."

She trailed a finger down his chest, over his cut abs and down the hard ridge of his erection, smiling when he hissed in pleasure. "And somehow, I still think eternity isn't going to be long enough."

He swept her up and headed toward the stairs. "Then we'd better get started."

As far as she was concerned, they couldn't get started soon enough.

NIGHT VISION

STEPHANIE TYLER

It doesn't work to leap a twenty-foot chasm
in two ten-foot jumps.
(American Proverb)

There came a time when the risk to remain tight
in the bud was more painful
than the risk it took to blossom.
—Anaïs Nin

CHAPTER *One*

Bayou Rouge, Louisiana, was a six-hour ride from Houston, an hour outside of New Orleans and home of a once well-known bar called the Bon Temps, which was now known as trouble personified.

Bat Kelly had seen—and caused—enough trouble to recognize the calling card.

He arrived at the bar's door just before midnight on a Friday, looked up at the burnt-out neon sign that hung crookedly above the doorway and thought about all the places he'd been before this bar, this town, this type of life. They all strung together in one big blur.

"Owner's got a big problem," Dominick, the man who'd always managed to find Bat enough work to keep money in his pockets, had warned him hours earlier. "Place is a mess. You'll only get half the money on arrival, half if you finish the job, as usual. There's a bonus offered if you finish early."

Gete toi.

"It won't be a problem," he'd told Dominick as he set out on his Harley from his last job in Texas.

It never was. For the past six years, Bat had built himself a reputation up the East Coast as one of the better coolers in the business. A crazier, willing-to-do-anything one, which put him at premium demand.

The scar that ran from just below the outer corner of his left eye toward the curve of his mouth proved the extremes to which his job pushed him, a reminder of an unfortunate incident involving an empty tequila bottle and a customer who refused to leave the bar.

Still, that scar, and the other war wounds along his body, didn't stop the women from throwing themselves at him. For a while he'd considered that the biggest benefit of the job. Lately, it had grown old, and he'd begun to realize that growing up wasn't nearly as much fun as running wild.

From where he stood, he could hear the music begin to play inside—jukebox rather than live band, and still the crowd began to cheer.

It was always the same sounds. Always the same.

Bat could still hear Big Red explaining the job to him, all those years ago. Bat had just turned twenty-two, was fresh out of the military after spending four years as a Marine sniper, on his belly in any and all godforsaken jungles the military needed him to be in—and going nowhere fast with his particular skill set, except maybe jail. He'd gotten tired of following orders.

The cooler's in charge of everything, dig? The bouncers, bartenders, the entire tone of the bar. Keep a cool head and stay in control. That is, if you can get control in the first place.

Big Red died three years ago in a nasty barroom brawl over in Chattanooga. Bat had been called in a week later to continue Big Red's work, by cleaning up a bar that had been on its way to closing. He'd almost refused, but did it in his friend's honor, and used the money to give Big Red a proper burial. Once Bat had taken care of the local riffraff, business turned right around.

Not, of course, without significant risk to his own life, which was why the money was always so good. And he'd never planned on living very long anyhow. Probably what made him such a success. Either way, it left him unable to be caught in any one place by any one person for long, which was the way he wanted it.

"It's the nature of the job, sugar," he'd say, gazing soulfully into Gina or Jenny or whatever the fuck her name was this month or week or night, and she would nod back in understanding, because somehow he always managed to pick a woman who expected to be left.

Made him feel more like shit than if they'd just hauled off and slugged him.

Good thing he had pain management perfected. The freedom of town-to-town and the open road kept him sane, especially because he no longer had his friend to turn to. A man who was the closest thing to a father Bat had ever had.

It was why he still carried the letter Big Red had written to him, just weeks before he'd been killed. Kept it, but didn't plan on listening to the instructions—the ones that told him to find a good woman to love before it was too late.

He was dead certain he wasn't going to find that woman here.

He yanked the door of the Bon Temps open, stood one foot in and one foot out and surveyed the scene. The mix of smoky seduction—part danger and part sex—and that element of the unexpected when the lights dimmed and the music got louder always got his blood humming, aroused him like a woman's touch.

"You coming inside all the way, baby? I'll let you buy me a drink." The woman who motioned to him from one of the tables near the door had already had a few too many.

"I'm sure you will," he said, and maybe last month he would've taken her up on that offer, but not now. Instead, his eyes went to another woman—slim, tall, with a tray tucked under her right arm. Most of the eyes in the bar had turned to survey him, something he was used to, but not hers. She remained focused on her own thoughts. She leaned, elbow on the corner of the bar, surveying the scene with a serious face, but her body betrayed her by swaying to the music.

He moved closer to the bar to get a better look, and ordered a beer. The crowd was picking up steam fast—there were women climbing up to dance on tables and men who were ready to fight over them. And all of this was his problem now.

He leaned on the old bar, with its cracked wood that hadn't seen loving care in a long while, and took a long swig from the bottle before glancing at the woman with the tray again. She was still moving to the music, watching the women on the tables, and he wondered if she'd ever allowed herself to lose that much control.

She was pretty, in a very regal, too-good-for-him way, with neat blond hair pulled back into a short, low ponytail, and startlingly dark brown eyes, the color of a cool, sweet glass of Coca-Cola on a damned hot day.

His first urge was to pick her up and get her out of there, but he'd been around long enough to know that if she was working here it was for one of two reasons: either she liked the attention or she needed the money, badly.

An argument between two guys in the far corner of the bar pulled his attention reluctantly. Their voices were loud, but no one could really hear them well over the jukebox, the drunken bragging, the tinkling giggles of the women—and no, this scene never changed, north or south, from state to state and county to county. The mating dance was still the same, even in a run-down old place like this, where the patrons tipped the scales more on the wrong side of the law than the right one.

Midnight was both the witching and the mating hour whenever alcohol was involved. He'd forgotten how badly the heat affected things around here, forgotten how easily it made his blood boil and his body ease, until he was loose and languid enough to do some table dancing of his own.

The pretty blond woman moved to a table near the men—began to pick up empty bottles and balance them on her tray. He found himself taking a step in her general direction as the men grew louder, glass shattered in the form of beer bottles knocked off a tabletop and everyone quieted to watch the fight.

Things could—and usually did—go downhill fast, from good times to bad times in seconds; it took as little as one punch or the flash of a knife, and it was all over. With the music fueling the backdrop, the men began swinging and threatening to involve others in their brawl.

And somehow, the pretty blond woman thought she could break up the fight all by herself. She stepped nearly in between the men, tray up to protect herself, and she was yelling something—probably *Stop* or *Please stop*—and she was going to get herself knocked out, at the very least.

He saw the flash of the knife's blade before anyone else, was over between the two men in seconds, cracked the wrist of the man who held the knife and broke the blade. But the entire thing had gone to shit—and so Bat took the blond woman by the waist, picked her up and set her down on the bar.

"Get behind it and stay down," he growled in her ear. She smelled sweet, like gardenias, and fuck that he'd notice that now.

He watched the bouncers rush to the rescue and took a step back in that general direction. The two guys, who until this point had been spending the better part of their night mixing with the crowd instead of working it, did their best to stop the fast-growing melee. Until one of them decided it was a good idea to pick up one of the fighting men and hurl him toward the plate-glass window at the front of the bar.

Yeah, good thing Bat had been promised a bonus for this one.

It had only taken the big blond man one arm to effortlessly save Catie from the melee and place her gently on the bar. The voice that told her to *stay down* was not nearly as gentle, but it strummed her insides as surely as if he'd touched her intimately.

She didn't duck down the way he'd told her; instead, she continued to watch the man cut through the brawlers with a near effortless grace, hair falling over his forehead, and his hands—she could spend hours, days even, sketching them and still not get them right. Large, graceful and strong, they flexed and fisted, capable and rough, scarred and elegant. Hands meant to cover a woman's body.

After one of the bouncers threw a patron in the direction of the new plate-glass, last-of-her-savings front window, the next few moments happened in slow motion.

The man who'd saved her caught the other man midflight without seeming particularly concerned, set him down right in front of the window and called out, *Laisse les bon temps rouler,* in perfect Cajun cadence.

The crowd went wild, the fight immediately dissipated and suddenly everyone was ready to simply continue the party again.

She'd been in town for two weeks, that phrase was repeated at least fifty times a night—and still, no one had ever said it in a way that shot heat straight through her like his rendition just had. Maybe because he'd been staring directly at her as he'd drawled the words. He had a long scar bisecting his right cheek and a way of looking at her that made her blush.

"Bat's back," the bartender named Henri said as Catie watched the crowd.

"That man's name is Bat?" she asked.

"Yes. He grew up around here. I didn't think he'd ever come back to town," Henri said. "He was a wild one."

"Looks like he still is."

"Tigers never do change their stripes."

Despite the heat, Bat wore a black leather jacket, along with boots and faded jeans. She pictured him riding a Harley, fast and hard, and then she tried to catch her own breath.

She slid through the throngs of people—mostly women—angling themselves to get a better look at the man who had to be the cooler she'd hired earlier that week.

She went through the supply room and pushed out the door that led to the small alleyway behind the building. The air was a pungent slap, hot and thick, and her vain hope of catching any sort of breeze vanished immediately. She put her palms to her face, which was still flushed, and drew in a deep breath.

The alley led to the main road on one end and the back lot on the other, and she turned to face the parking lot, leaning a shoulder against the rough wall. A big, black motorcycle was parked so it nearly blocked the entrance to the alleyway, and she fought the urge to move closer to it. The bike had to be Bat's.

Bat.

Dominick, the man she'd dealt with on the phone, had refused to give her a name. Then again, she'd refused to wire him any money, so she supposed they were even.

You'll know him when you see him, Dominick had said, and yes, apparently so.

She'd thought she could handle anything after working in New York. One look around and she knew she'd been really wrong. She was definitely out of her element here. Severe culture shock.

Her mom had grown up here, right in Bayou Rouge, and up until her death six years ago, Mama still had the slight twinge of a Louisiana accent and the weakness for bad boys she'd never been able to shake.

Catie had stayed clear of that path, even though this kind of life at the bar was what she knew—late nights, big crowds, hard work.

There was a lot more of that waiting for her inside. As she turned to head back, an unfamiliar hand gripped her tightly around her throat. She scratched at that hand, unable to scream or breathe, as his free hand went roughly from one breast to the other.

"You don't belong here, bitch," a voice menaced in her ear, and she started to panic in earnest as the grip grew tighter, flailed her arms uselessly as the man used the element of surprise against her and put one hand between her legs.

As quickly as she'd been grabbed, she was released. She stumbled forward a few steps, drew gulps of precious air into her lungs and turned back in time to see Bat reaching out for her, and the attacker taking off toward the street and not looking back.

Suddenly she was sure her own legs weren't going to hold her up any longer.

"What the hell's going on here?" Bat demanded, grabbing her before she slid to the ground.

"Nothing," she managed, buried her face against his chest and stayed that way for a few moments. He smelled like leather and soap and the freedom of the open road, and her hands clutched the supple material of his jacket until she finally lifted her head to meet his gaze. Being in his arms was comforting and she didn't want him to let go.

He didn't. Instead, his eyes searched hers. They were light green, like a smooth piece of sea glass she'd found at the beach years earlier on a rare weekend off.

He didn't seem angry anymore. He kept one arm around her waist while he took his free hand to caress the tender, bruised skin around her throat, then put two fingers to the right of her collarbone.

"Your pulse is racing," he said. "Do you need a doctor?"

His accent was thicker now, as though being inside this bar had brought it out. She was aware of the too-close proximity of every part of his body to hers, the scare from the near attack fast becoming a distant memory thanks to Bat's touch.

"No. He scared me more than he hurt me."

"Good. That's good." Concern—and something else—flashed in his eyes for a brief moment. His thumb traced her jawline and rested finally on her chin. And then he leaned in, close enough to kiss her. "You were dancing back there, before the fight."

"I was standing by the bar, not dancing." She had moved away from the crowds, took temporary refuge behind the bar while dropping the empties in the garbage as the jukebox started up. And even though the crowd was more than rowdy, she'd felt a hit of jealousy as she watched the women dance and smile.

"I asked inside about the owner—they pointed me in your direction," he said, and here, in his arms, desire was back. It was an odd feeling, like the heat, only worse, as if her skin was pulled too tight and was too sensitive for even the softest fabric.

"You're the cooler I hired."

"Yes. I'm Bat Kelly."

"Bat? What's that short for?"

"It's just Bat—not short for anything. And normally, I don't find the owner taking orders and bussing tables."

"I can't just sit around."

His next words were a growl, the way his very first words to her had been. "Do you always get into this much trouble in one night?"

She pulled back. "It's not my fault I was nearly attacked."

"You got in the middle of something inside the bar you shouldn't have. And you fired the manager, Catie *chere*."

The employees and patrons must be only too happy to talk about it—the woman named Catie Jane who the regulars nicknamed Catie *chere*—the woman who'd arrived in town to threaten their good time. "I thought they'd stop if they saw a woman. And yes, I fired Darren, two days ago. He was skimming." She put a hand to her throat. "You don't think . . ."

"I don't put anything past a man whose livelihood went up in a puff of smoke. That wasn't a smart move. What made you think you could waltz in here—"

"I didn't waltz in—"

"And clean up this place single-handedly," he finished.

"You were supposed to wait for me before you made any changes."

"I didn't know when you'd be arriving."

"Impatient," he muttered. "Stubborn too."

"If you've got a problem working for a woman—"

"I've never had a problem working for a woman—under them, on them, whatever gives them the most bang for their—"

She held up a hand in protest. "That's not what I meant."

"Don't worry, sugar. Fine city girls like you aren't my style. But you've alienated the staff and the regulars. This isn't New York City and you're doing a shitty job. You've got to step away from this place and let me handle it."

"I have to keep working—my tips are the only money I've got coming in now that I'm here."

"What's your deal, *chere*?"

"My deal? My deal is that my uncle left me this place in his will and all I'm trying to do is sell it." But the Bon Temps, with its post–Hurricane Katrina crowd, was tougher than she'd thought. The crime in the area and the insurance premiums were both up, and the heat was enough to drive anyone insane. She'd tried to shake it by standing under an ice cold shower—even though her skin went numb from the freeze, her insides still ran hot and she itched for something that she was apparently unable to scratch.

The locals didn't seem bothered by the heat at all.

"You've got no one to help you?" he asked.

"If I did, I wouldn't have hired you."

"The bartender told me about your uncle. I'm sorry," Bat said, his drawl sincere.

She'd refused to concern herself that this particular establishment had been in her family for generations or that it was her uncle's dream to restore the place to its previous reputation, before drugs and lowlifes had taken hold. The hurricane hadn't helped. The college draw was minimal, even though the location was perfect for that type of crowd.

"You should see the place during bike week," the lawyer who was in charge of her uncle's estate had told her. "It's a pit stop for the Hells Angels on their way to Florida."

Yeah, she'd be so far gone by then. "I didn't know him. Didn't know he existed, or that he knew anything about me, until after he died."

Bat nodded and she wondered why she was telling him all of this. She blamed the scare, the fact that no one here talked to her, the fact that being in his arms eased an ache of loneliness she hadn't realized ran so deep.

"Why didn't you just leave all of this for lawyers to handle? Why pick up and drive halfway across the country?"

"You want something done right, you've got to do it yourself." Less disappointments that way.

"Sounds like you don't need me at all," he said, and he let go of her, too suddenly. She immediately missed his touch, the warmth from his body.

"None of them trust me—not the employees or the town. Half of them tell me to not give up the bar and the other half just want me gone. *City girl doesn't understand.*"

"People are loyal."

"Loyal to a dump."

"Wasn't always a dump. Doesn't always have to be," he said. "But you're too young to understand that, just a baby."

"I'm twenty-four, and I've seen plenty."

"Yeah, you're all grown up." He reached out to caress her cheek with his hand, and she pushed it away.

"I just want out of here—out of this bar, out of this town," she said firmly.

"That's pretty clear, considering you offered a bonus if I

could get the job done in half the time. You really want to dump this place, don't you?"

"Is that a problem?"

"No. It's just that most people don't bother fixing something up that they plan to let go of. Makes things that much harder," he reasoned.

"Is it hard for you to go after you've cleaned up a place?"

"I wasn't talking about me."

"No, Bat, I'm not going to have a problem walking away," she told him as she pushed past him to go back inside the bar.

"Makes two of us, then," he drawled.

"So since you're so much older and wiser, let's see you put your mouth where my money is, old man."

He laughed softly as he held the door open for her. "You're on, Catie *chere*. Let's go close up for the night."

Bat knew he'd come to the Bon Temps once or twice as a teen, but the bartender ringing the ancient bell above the bar to signal last call confirmed it. The feeling of déjà vu made sense, even though the concept of coming home after ten years still left him uneasy.

Home was three towns over. Not more than twenty miles, but a comfortable enough distance for now. He shrugged out of his jacket and laid it across one of the few unbroken tables. "Come on, Catie, dance with me."

"I don't dance," she protested, even as he tugged her toward the middle of the room, which served as the dance floor. She didn't resist as hard as she could, mainly because most of the patrons were watching them now.

He drew her into his arms and they began to sway to the slow, steady beat of the zydeco music. Truth be told, he wanted her back in his arms. She fit there well, even as she continued to protest.

"What are you doing?"

"I'm marking you. Letting them know you're mine." His mouth tugged to one side as her eyes widened. He wanted to take her hair down, run his hands through it, get her down and dirty naked on the bar.

"Why would you do that?"

"So they'll leave you alone. That's what you want, right, to be left alone?"

"Yes, Bat, that's what I want."

"I like the way you say my name. You sigh it, almost like you're rolling it around in your mouth."

"I don't say it any special way," she told him, but he knew she was lying. Wanted her to be anyway. "And I thought you said fine city girls weren't your type."

"Don't you know a liar when you meet one?" He released her from his arms as the music ended, and together they watched the patrons file out of the bar, some stumbling, others paired up for the evening. The bouncers would follow them out to the parking lot, where, no doubt, more fights would ensue. Bat had known he'd have to bring in a couple of his own people, had called Keith and Jase—men he'd counted on for help in bars in the past—before he'd left Houston for Louisiana. They'd be here tomorrow, in time for Bat to meet with the staff.

"Who told you I fired Darren?" she asked as the last of the revelers left, the bar suddenly completely quiet.

"Bartender. Waitresses. Bouncers. They couldn't wait to fill me in on the new girl in town."

"What else did they say about me?"

"That you're unfriendly. Uptight. That you don't know how to have a good time."

"You call this mess a good time?"

He walked across the now empty floor, toward the bar, spoke over his shoulder, "Some people do—or they did, until things got out of hand."

"I believe in work, Bat. Business and pleasure just don't mix."

"That's where you're dead wrong," he said as he ran his hands along the length of natural grain of one section of the bar, where it was still pretty smooth. Yes, it would clean up nicely.

"This is the worst I've ever seen this place," she muttered as she began to right chairs.

"I've seen worse. Your staff should be here to help clean up."

"I can't afford to pay them to do that," she said, refusing to look in his direction. "What made you want to clean up bars for a living anyway?"

"Money's good," he said. "Locations change. It's an honest living."

"Do you really think you can turn the Bon Temps around?"

"I wouldn't take your money if I didn't," he told her. "I'm going to grab my bag from my bike, then you can show me where I'm staying."

"I know I promised that you could stay in the upstairs apartment, but it's not exactly ready yet. I was going to spend the day tomorrow cleaning it."

"Then where do you sleep?" he asked, and she lifted her chin in a proud gesture she couldn't stop.

"I've been staying on a cot in the back office."

"Then I'll stay on the floor."

"I can't stay in the office with you."

"I'm supposed to get free room and board in exchange for this job. I know Dominick told you that."

"Yes, he did."

He strolled over to the front door of the bar to check the lock, found it woefully insufficient. "I'm not leaving you here alone with a door lock that a three-year-old can pick. It's not safe. Not after what happened. We're going to have to work together. You willing to do that, Catie *chere*? Work with me?"

She blurted out, "I don't have the money to pay you."

He stopped from where he'd been shoving a chair under the doorknob and turned slowly to stare at her. And then he took two strides with his long legs and stood in front of her, eyes locking her in place, strong hands on her shoulders. "What the hell is going on here, Catie Jane?"

Her eyes were ringed dark and mysterious, a startle of contrasts against the cool, pale blond of her hair which would feel like silk between his fingers, he was sure, and far too fine for him. And he was even more pissed that he'd think about that now, when she'd just told him that she'd screwed him.

"I'll have the money for you in a few weeks," she said. "As soon as business starts to turn around."

"That's not the way this works. It's not a gentleman's agreement and I'm no gentleman." It was the truth. Even though the Marines had instilled a moral code in him and Big Red had done more of the same, he still had the Kelly blood to contend with. Drink and deviance running on both sides of his lineage left him with desires he couldn't contain, and he'd never tried all that hard.

No promises to anyone, including himself. Other people lived by their own rules. He did the same.

They were the only rules he could handle.

But his hands stayed on Catie Jane's shoulders, and like before, she felt both fragile and strong at the same time, and something was happening here.

And she didn't have shit to pay him with. "I don't do something for nothing—that's a good way to get screwed."

"These people, they know you."

He let go of her and shrugged. "Some of them know me. Others by reputation."

"But you used to live around here. The locals will listen to you, right? You can really help."

"I help clean up bars for a living. I don't do it for damsels in distress, and I sure as hell don't do it for people who lie to me."

"I knew you wouldn't come any other way. I didn't have any choice."

"We all have choices, Catie. You made yours. And I'm not happy with it."

"This place isn't my past, it's my family's. I don't belong here. Don't you understand, I want to put it behind me."

He wanted to tell her that trying to outrun her past was futile, that she would just chase her tail and end up in the same spot, the same place everything had started. But there was something in those deep brown eyes that tugged him in a way he'd never been tugged before and he couldn't tell her anything of the sort. "Yeah, well, this is my past too. I guess I'm trying to make peace with my ghosts as well."

"Then you understand. Bat, I need the money from the sale of this bar. I can't do this without . . ." It was as if she couldn't bring herself to say the word *help*. He suspected that had been the case for her for some time.

"You don't want to give up control. But sometimes it's the only way to get things done. The only way to let yourself go."

"Who said anything about wanting to let go?"

"Everything about you screams *let go,* Catie *chere*. Every time you move your body to the jukebox and then stop, like you've done something wrong. Every time I catch you looking at me."

"It's not your job to fix me, Bat. It's the bar you're supposed to be breathing life into."

"I'm not talking about fixing you. I'm talking about sharing your bed." He saw the flash of something behind her deep brown eyes—amazement, desire, maybe even a hint of fear as well.

It took her a moment before she found her voice again. "You want me to sleep with you because I don't have the money to pay you?"

In two strides, Bat was in front of her and she was pressed against him again, his voice fierce and low and touching all the right buttons. "I'd share your bed for free. You want my other services, you'll have to pay up front, just like everyone else."

Catie was glad to know that Bat had responded to her in kind, that she hadn't imagined the tension between them, hot and unmistakable. His arousal jutted against her belly, her throat tightened as her hands played along his shoulders. His mouth—that fine, lush mouth—could play with her body in ways she'd only imagined, and all she had to say was *yes*.

And still, she couldn't let herself go. "I don't think...I don't think I can do that, Bat," she heard herself whisper, even though everything in her body was pulling her to say yes. Her nipples hardened as though she'd entered a freezing cold room, and she was painfully aware of their swell.

Bat was too; his gaze raked her up and down, a possessive gesture that she liked. "I'll stay tonight, Catie. And I'll install a few new locks tomorrow before I go."

She crossed her arms in front of her, feeling horribly vulnerable and completely, utterly turned on at the same time, wished that he hadn't left the decision up to her. Wished he'd just grabbed her and kissed her, so she could acquiesce that way.

Wishing now she could beg him to stay, offer him something—anything—in return.

The fact that he'd agreed to stay the night meant something—that he had a heart hidden under that layer of badass, tough-guy persona—but if she wanted to keep him around longer, she needed to find cash, fast.

God, she was in such trouble.

He'd walked past her, toward the office, and now she hurriedly followed him to the back.

Her sketch pads were strewn around the floor and on the desk, some opened to the useless pieces of crap she'd drawn over the past weeks, and one opened to the series she'd begun a few months earlier—her only drawings worth anything over the past year, and they were only for her private collection. She'd been inspired by a book she'd been reading—and when she'd come across a particularly graphic scene, she'd found herself reading... imagining... fantasizing. And then she'd blocked the scene on paper the way she'd imagined it happening.

The pictures she'd drawn were all done with soft charcoal—shaded, black and white and grayscale... and in the one Bat was looking at intently, the hero's head was between her spread legs.

The sketches were beautiful—graphic and sensual—and she was proud of them. But she was also sad at how much longing they represented on her part.

Her face flushed hotter than she thought possible, but Bat didn't say a word, just finished his perusal and walked out the back door, presumably to grab his things.

She wondered if Bat would've turned the pages if she hadn't walked in so soon, if he would've liked the pictures of her on her knees in front of a man, a man whose face was always shaded in the shadows, since she couldn't quite picture him.

Her knees went weak as she realized she'd just put Bat's face to the man, and she knew she'd never be able to look at those pictures in the same way again.

She closed the sketchbook hurriedly and put it to the side of the desk. There was no good place to hide it, and it wasn't as if she was ashamed of the work at all.

But God, he'd seen that she'd drawn her own face.

She could barely recognize the woman in that drawing, no matter how hard she stared.

Before she could clean up further, the lights sputtered off with a heavy thump and she was plunged into darkness. The door creaked open, but it didn't do anything to alleviate the pitch black that filled the office. "Bat, please tell me that's you."

"It's me," he drawled.

She couldn't see her hand in front of her face, much less Bat, and the frustration rose in her throat. "I paid the last electric bill. I know I did."

"Relax. These miniblackouts happen all the time. The county can't handle the heat."

She backed up a step, reached out a hand to find the cot before she tripped over it. The old mattress sagged as she lowered herself onto it, and finally she was able to see the darker shadow that was Bat looming in front of her. She missed seeing the detail of his face and she held the picture of him in her mind.

"Why don't you lie down and get some rest?" he suggested. She heard the thump of what she assumed to be his bag hitting the floor and she wondered why her eyes weren't adjusting to the heavy blanket of darkness.

"I can't sleep when I'm too hot," she admitted.

"Then you're in the wrong town."

"Tell me about it." She heard the groan of protesting wood as the small window across from the desk was opened. A light breeze fluttered through the room, but she knew it wouldn't be enough.

"I'll be right back," he told her.

She heard his footsteps echo out into the hallway that separated the bar and the office, and then things got quiet.

She was still spooked from the mugging, was glad she'd never considered how stupid it was for her to stay in the office all alone for the past two weeks. She'd been lucky.

The footsteps returned. "Bat?"

She heard the flick of a lighter and saw his form outlined by the small glow. She fought an urge to ask him to stand there while she did a quick sketch, with the combination of the dark and light tones dancing in a mesmerizing pattern around his face.

"Were you expecting someone else?"

"No, I . . ." She stopped, feeling foolish.

"Hey, it's okay. That's why I stayed. And I brought some ice to cool you off." He held up the bucket, then walked over to the cot and put it down next to her.

Then he snapped the lighter shut and darkness surrounded them again. "You might want to think about stripping down to sleep. More comfortable that way," he said casually.

"Yeah, right."

"I'm planning on it." She heard the sound of a zipper and then the light scraping sounds of jeans being pulled off a body.

She lay down and tried not to think about the naked man on the floor, and quickly discovered she couldn't think of anything but him. A thin trickle of sweat worked its way between her breasts and she reached for the ice.

She took a cube and brought it to her neck. She ran it along her throat for a few seconds of blessed relief, and the water dripped along her skin as ice melted on contact. And she wanted more.

Bat couldn't see anything if she couldn't. She couldn't even make out his shadow anymore, though she knew he was only a few feet away from her, stretched out on the floor below the cot.

Tentatively, she lifted up her T-shirt, almost sighing in relief as the slight breeze touched her bare stomach and breasts. After a few minutes, she grew bolder and left the T-shirt hiked up completely, enjoying the way the air brushed her bare skin and wishing the tickling came from Bat's fingers instead.

"I wouldn't have pegged you for an artist." His drawl floated up around her in the darkness, thick and comforting, and she trailed the ice along her belly, traced a figure eight around her breasts and smiled.

"How come?" Her voice sounded lazy and far away even to her own ears.

"You're too tightly wound."

Bat didn't know the half of it. But that lazy, decidedly unwound feeling was beginning to take over as she ran another ice cube along each breast and shivered in silence as hot and cold converged to tighten her nipples.

"Yeah, well, you would be too if your entire future was riding on the Bon Temps." She would just keep him talking, let his voice take her to the place she wanted. He'd be gone tomorrow and she'd have nothing left but a memory.

"What are you going to do with the money?"

"I'm returning to art school."

"But you already know how to draw, Catie *chere.* So what did you learn in school, except someone else's way of doing things?"

Another ice cube, another pass over her breasts, and then she brushed one nipple lightly with her thumb and bit her lip to keep from gasping. She pressed it between her fingers, the warmth and the cool mixing together to shoot sensation straight to her groin. She knew if she touched herself, she'd already be wet.

"How did you learn your job? Didn't someone teach you?" she whispered, afraid her voice would give everything away.

"Someone showed me the ropes, but I developed my own style. And from the look of your sketches, you did the same thing."

She knew her face was flushed and was grateful for the darkness. "I want to finish school. And I plan to, just as soon as I'm done here."

She put a palm on her bare stomach, wondering if she had the nerve to slide it downward and stroke herself to the gentle caress of his drawl. "How long have you been a cooler?"

"Long enough to be good at it."

Very good at it. She was more than sure of that. Her hand dipped lower, and she reminded herself to keep him talking.

"The work you do . . . it's very dangerous."

"Yes. But that's a big part of the attraction."

She grew bolder, slid her hand across the silky fabric of her thong and forced her breathing to stay even. "You like the danger."

"Everyone likes danger. And that's how I built my name."

Danger—yes, she could see that. Her finger slipped in between her folds, wet and hot; the flesh contracted and she nearly jumped off the mattress. She slid the finger up and down, stroked her clit as her hips rocked gently, slowly, silently, and thinking along a straight line was next to impossible as she imagined Bat's fingers working her. "Your name . . . where did it come from?"

"You really want to know?"

"Yes." She really, really wanted . . .

A pause, and for a second she thought he wasn't going to answer. Then he gave a low chuckle, and when he spoke, his voice was husky and full of want. "I got the nickname Bat because I can see in the dark."

The breath caught in her throat, her hand froze in place, between her legs, and she tried to picture what exactly he saw, pictured the way she looked with her T-shirt pulled up over her breasts and her thong pushed to the side to reveal her own hand working her sex.

"Don't stop on my account," he drawled, and no, as embarrassed as she was, she didn't want to stop, had never felt this sexually powerful in her entire life. It was still dark enough for her to feel cloaked, even though she could actually feel his eyes on her; her nipples throbbed in time with her sex.

She wondered if he'd been stroking himself in time with her own caresses, wondered if his naked body looked as good as she'd imagined.

"Are you thinking about me?" he asked. "Wondering if I'm down here doing the same thing while I watch you?"

"Yes," she managed, let her finger stroke her labia gently.

"How often do you do that, Catie *chere*? Do you touch yourself every night, spread your lips wide and work your clit until you want to scream? Or was this all for me?"

For you . . . all for you.

Her hands remained on her own sex until he drawled, "Let go, Catie *chere*—let go and come to me."

That was all it took. She swung her legs as he rose off the floor to meet her—her legs ended up on his shoulders and his head moved forward, between her legs, and *oh,* she hadn't even kissed him yet, but he was kissing her in a far more intimate place.

The first touch of his tongue was to the silk of her underwear. His breath was hot as his mouth locked there, his hands running along the sensitive skin of her inner thighs.

She attempted to squirm away but it was too late, had been since Bat walked into her bar, and within seconds the scrap of fabric was pushed impatiently to the side and his tongue stroked her far more effectively than her own hand. The first probe left her breathless and aching for more as the tension flared in her belly.

She'd dreamed of this, of a man's head between her legs, taking her until she lost all control... dreamed of a man who knew exactly what she wanted, needed, even before she did.

Bat was that man.

"Bat, oh God, I can't." But she could, and she was, spreading her legs and twisting her hands through his hair while his tongue explored her folds, rubbed the tight bud of her clit with a patient rhythm that had her rocking her hips and making the flimsy cot shake and squeak, and she didn't care if they both tumbled to the ground, as long as he didn't stop.

Her releases had always been tight, hot bursts she'd only been able to accomplish with her own hand. With the few men she'd been intimate with, orgasms had eluded her. She had written it off and allowed her sexuality to show in lush ripeness in all of her paintings and sketches, big and bold and full of passionate energy.

That sexuality was unmistakable on paper, and obviously in Bat's arms. An orgasm wasn't going to be a problem with him, not the way his tongue rasped and probed over her most sensitive areas.

She was going to explode, right against his mouth, and all she could do was let it happen. The climax was strong enough to make her moan his name, over and over into the still of the darkness.

Her legs trembled from being held open, her head felt heavy and she was so drowsy.

"You taste sweet, so good." Bat's voice was low and soothing and she let out another small moan as his head dipped down to take her again with his mouth.

Hot and sweet, and this was all so obviously for her pleasure . . . only for her pleasure.

"Bat, I can't . . . I won't be able to, not again." She'd never been able to come twice in a night. But this, being spread in the dark, her sex pressed to a near stranger's mouth—oh, what a mouth—tongue working the sensitive knot of nerve endings with a hard pressure that caused her ass to nearly rise off the mattress . . . or would have if his hands weren't firmly anchored to her thighs. He was holding her legs apart so he could remain with full access to the most intimate part of her.

Her hands were braced on the mattress behind her, holding her body upright, and she glanced down at the dark blond head moving between her legs, and that was all it took. Her body stiffened, so taut, as if she'd break in two, and then yes, she went over the edge again, his tongue filling her as she climaxed even harder than the first time.

He licked her through the crest, as if he couldn't get enough, his touch lighter now as she trembled. And then he kissed along her inner thighs and the relief coursed through her like a sharp blast of air, and finally—finally—her body felt cool.

She whimpered as he released her legs, fell back against the mattress, drained and sleepy.

"How's the heat?" he murmured in her ear.

"Who cares."

He pulled the sheet over her breasts and stroked her shoulder. "Now you're beginning to understand the bayou, Catie *chere*."

The heat was worse already and it was still before noon. The power had come back on while Catie slept and the air conditioner built into the wall sputtered worthlessly, but it didn't matter. The first thing she did was reach for her sketchbook.

Those sketchbooks and art school had mocked her for the better part of two years. Ironic that she was planning to use part of the money from the sale of the Bon Temps to finish art school, and she hadn't been able to bring herself to draw anything more than a rudimentary, unsatisfying sketch in months.

She broke open the tin container that held her soft charcoal sticks and turned to a fresh page in the brand-new sketch pad filled with charcoal paper.

Her strokes were tentative at first, grew to sweeping marks that colored the paper, her hands black with dust.

She sketched furiously with bold, dark lines, line work first, then the shading details after, afraid that if she didn't capture Bat's face she might never see him again.

Foolish, yes, because she'd never be able to forget him, not the way his eyes flashed or the hard planes of his cheekbones or the way his hands and mouth had touched her.

It was as if something invaded her that she couldn't control. She balanced the values effortlessly—the shadows, the contours filled the page . . . the scar on his face, shaded slightly by the cheekbone, the way Bat looked in front of her in living, breathing color.

She finished, breathless, wanted to crumple on the floor in a heap, the way she had last night onto the cot after she'd let Bat . . .

Oh, God, she'd *let* Bat.

A quick glance out the window, and she spotted the big, black Harley, parked in a different spot than it had been last night.

She could still feel his mouth between her legs. Remembered wanting more from him but being too satiated to do anything more than fall asleep as he'd stroked her back. He hadn't pushed for anything more, and she wondered why.

She took a quick, cool shower in the tiny bathroom off the office and then tucked her hair up into a ponytail and threw on some clothes before she walked out to the main area to find Bat.

He was standing by the front entrance of the bar, installing a heavy-duty lock on the door, just as he'd promised. One large hand held the big brass lock steady while the other worked the old power drill she'd seen lying around the storeroom.

"Morning," he called over his shoulder to her, and she started, hadn't realized he'd sensed her standing there. His greeting was friendly enough, although he looked even more intimidating this morning. A blue bandanna was wrapped around his head; his T-shirt had the sleeves ripped off, exposing rock-hard arms, with a tattoo on his left biceps.

It looked like a military emblem, served to remind her that she didn't know this man very well at all. He had to be as dangerous as he looked in order to survive in this business, and he'd told her as much last night.

God, she didn't want him to leave.

"I need to talk to you," she heard herself call over the sound of the drill. He nodded, his back still facing her as he finished up and tried the lock, clicking the heavy bolt back and forth.

"This should hold well. I'll put another one on the back door," he said. "What did you want to talk about?"

"I don't want you to leave. This morning was the first time I've drawn anything decent—no, better than decent—in nearly a year," she told him, and then drew in a deep breath. "Please, I know I'm asking a lot..."

"Why couldn't you draw?"

"I don't know. Everything just seemed to dry up. It's hard to explain." She rubbed her fingertips together; they were still faintly smudged with charcoal. "You don't have to listen to my problems."

"I'm still here, aren't I?"

Yes, he was.

And she was normally so full of pent-up frustration that the want and need spilled over into her work, which was usually enough to take the edge off. She could lose herself in the work, let the broad strokes of hard pastels or paint on the canvas soothe her, until she was so sure that everything she felt was on the page.

And then, one day last year, she couldn't bring herself to pick up a brush or chalk or anything more than a pencil to make a grocery list. The only thing that saved her was drawing those pictures he'd seen last night. But she wanted more.

And she stood there and told Bat all of that, as if she had nothing left to lose but her pride. But he didn't look at her with anything that resembled pity.

"I sold everything. My brother has his new life—he's making his own fresh start. And I knew that if I didn't do that, didn't sell everything and buy a car to get me cross-country, I'd have a safety net. That way, I had no choice but to come here and see this sale through."

"So this bar is your way out?"

"I took it as a sign when I got the notice from my uncle's lawyer. I didn't stop to think it through. For the first time in my life I did something impulsive. Normally, I'm only like that in my art—the only place I'm never afraid to fail. Well, until lately. I like drawing you. I like the way you made me feel last night." She heard the passion in her own voice as she made her case.

"I liked it too, Catie." He turned around and looked at the lock. "This will help, but it's not enough. I can't have it on my conscience, leaving you alone like this."

"You were planning on staying anyway," she said, and wondered why she wasn't angry that he'd let her spill her guts. But she felt strangely free. "I'll never be able to repay you for this, for staying on."

"I don't remember asking you for repayment. Just what I'm owed at the end of the job." He paused, stuck his hands in his pockets and looked out the window, as if a memory had caught him by surprise. "Sometimes it's easier to ask a stranger for help."

"But you don't feel like a stranger. Last night was—"

"Last night was a promise of what's to come." His drawl grew thick and his gaze settled back on her, the way it had last night that sent a hot thrill straight to her belly and outward. He closed the distance between them until they were separated by mere inches. "Don't fight it now—don't fight me. It's going to happen no matter what."

It was—and it actually made her swell with a strange pride that she could give in so easily to her desires. That she could make him want her in that way.

For most of her life, at least on the outside, she was Catie, the reasonable one. Here, she was Catie *chere,* and Catie *chere* was ready to give herself to Bat.

He put a hand under her chin and tilted her face to look up at him. "Last night, that was the first time a man did that to you. Put his mouth on you, made you come like that."

"Yes." There was no reason to lie.

He tilted her face toward his with a finger under her chin. "Are you a virgin?"

"No. Not technically." Not if she counted a few unsatisfying, silent encounters in her bedroom when her brother was out with friends, and the one time in the back of a car that happened so quickly it was over before she'd even begun.

No, she'd learned to pleasure herself. And with her drawing, she was free, could explore her needs as she poured out her dreams and her frustrations, sexual and otherwise. Between last night and this morning, she'd finally been able to combine the two. "I'm not good at this."

"At sex?"

"Sex. Asking for help. Giving up control," she admitted, and she saw a flash of compassion in his eyes.

"I kind of caught that."

"I've managed to hide it from everyone for most of my life."

"I may be a stranger, but I'm not just everyone. And I'm good at the first thing I mentioned—lucky for you." He pulled her tight to him and she took careful note of his admission of what he wasn't good at either. "I can't stop thinking about the way you looked when I walked into the bar—swaying to the music, wishing you could climb on the tables and dance. I can't stop thinking about the way you tasted last night, the way you moaned my name."

His erection was rock hard against her belly and she'd never felt so protected, so turned on, and she sighed softly against his broad chest. "I want to sketch you."

"Sketch me?"

"Yes. For my portfolio."

"You didn't ask my permission before," he said, and yes, he might've come into the office earlier when she'd been drawing—she'd been so engrossed in her work that walls could've fallen and she wouldn't have noticed.

Her sex grew moist at the thought of him watching her again, and she wondered what he'd done last night, after she'd fallen asleep, if he'd lain there in the dark on the floor and stroked himself to completion, wondered if he'd thought about her while he did so.

"This time I want you to pose for me. I want to sketch all of you," she explained.

He stuck his tongue in his cheek as he considered her words. "What's so special about me? There are plenty of people around this place."

"I don't want anyone else," she said. "You're the perfect subject."

"What were you drawing this morning?" he asked.

"You." She reached up to slide a finger down the long scar on his cheek.

"You like my scar, Catie *chere*?" he asked, as his hand moved under her T-shirt to caress the bare skin on her lower back. Slowly, his hand traveled upward to rest near the swell of one breast, and she shivered.

"Yes, I like your scar."

"Why? Because it makes me look dangerous?"

"I know how dangerous you are, Bat." His name came out as a moan when a calloused palm brushed her nipple. At the same time, two fingers slid inside her shorts and between her thighs—she was already wet, and she should've been embarrassed by how quickly she spread her legs for him, but she wasn't. Mainly because the way Bat looked at her, his own lids heavy with desire, told her that he liked it that way, liked it when she opened herself to him.

They'd only been together once, in the most intimate of ways a woman could let a man touch her, and her body was already responding as if it couldn't get enough.

"I wanted to take you last night. Wanted to strip you down right on that old cot and whisper dirty Cajun magic in your ear." His breath was warm on her neck. "I'm going to do that tonight. With my fingers, and then my tongue, lick you until you're so wet you can't stand it. Just like last night."

He brought his mouth down on hers, inhaling another long moan with a kiss that took her up on her tiptoes, a kiss meant to claim, to conquer. And she let it, let him take her mouth with a brutal, satisfying kiss as she breathed him in, and yes, he was staying with her, and she was going to stay in his arms as much as humanly possible.

Her hands clutched his shoulders as his tongue teased hers and his fingers worked the hot flesh between her legs until she went dizzy, until he was pulling his mouth off hers for moments at a time because he liked *hearing you moan, chere.*

"Hey, I've got a liquor delivery here for you!" a voice called from outside, through the open window in the storeroom.

Bat put his mouth back down on hers and worked her clit with his thumb faster now, pinning her against the wall and letting her know he wasn't letting her go until she came. And when she did, it was hard and fast, and her grip on him no doubt left marks on his arms. But he wasn't complaining, and neither was she, as she let the delicious feeling travel down to her toes.

Bat broke their kiss slowly, reluctantly, and when he pulled away he stared at her for a second. She licked her bottom lip and stared up at him, feeling wild and wanton and completely desirable.

"I'll be right there," he called over his shoulder, never taking his eyes off her. "Work before play, Catie. I've got to deal with the staff and you've got to make this place comfortable for both of us. For later."

Yes, for later. She touched her fingers to her lips and tried to hide her smile beneath them.

His low chuckle vibrated through her the same way his hands and her orgasms had, and she had no doubt she'd made the right decision asking him to stay on.

CHAPTER *Four*

Bat could almost hear Big Red's voice in his ear all day long, as he cleaned up the bar and signed for the liquor deliveries and tried his best to keep his mind off of Catie and the way she'd tasted, like woman and richly sugared tea and promises, the way she whimpered when she came against his hand less than an hour ago.

So kid, you're finally sticking around.

"Only until the job's done," he muttered under his breath as he hauled the boxes off the truck in exchange for the driver waiting until the end of the week to get paid.

"Easy to pick up and go. Much harder to stick around," Big Red used to comment as he'd watch Bat do the same kind of heavy work in order to get the bar out of the red quickly.

"Not my fault if they let things get messy after I leave."

Big Red laughed. "That's not what I'm talking about, boy. All life is messy."

"You leave all the time," Bat pointed out.

"I go home to my wife," Big Red told him.

Bat hadn't had a permanent home since he was sixteen. Repo work kept him busy for a while until he joined the military at eighteen.

His mom and dad had had permanent, they'd stayed married until his father died. His mother died six months later. Bat had always seen them as going nowhere fast—they'd always been nothing but miserable together. But for his sister's sake—his only family—he'd have to start settling down.

Tonight it was all about settling into the new job. It was after two in the morning, the fog was still thick and there was a ring around the bayou moon he watched through the front window of the Bon Temps.

Trouble, he could hear Big Red whisper in his ear.

"Trouble," Jase said from behind him. Jase and his older brother, Keith, were friends from his early post-military days. The brothers had grown up like drifters, pulled around the country by a father who'd worked repo and bounty anywhere and everywhere, and now neither brother could sit still for longer than six months at a time. These days, the brothers worked repo and bounty, as well as bouncing in bars up and down the coast, and they were always happy to respond to Bat's calls to come work with him.

Bat looked toward the door, to where Jase motioned, and recognized the guy the minute he walked in the door. Last night, in the alley, he'd worn a mask, but he'd had a distinctive tattoo on the back of his hand. "That's the old manager."

"I'll handle it," Jase said, but Bat held out a hand.

"I've got this one." He walked toward Darren slowly, and the crowd stopped to watch the show.

Up until that point, the night had been brutal—just about every asshole had come out to prove they could challenge the big bad cooler and win. None of them had, of course, but none of them had his training either.

Except for Darren.

Bat could recognize height and weight and walking patterns, but the Eagle/Globe/Anchor tattoo on the man's hand—the Marine symbol—was the dead giveaway, and it was on the same hand that had been across Catie's throat. Bat had known Darren would be back.

He was also glad he'd convinced Catie that her time working the bar at night was over until he could get things under control. He hadn't seen much of her for the rest of the day—she'd been cleaning the large loftlike apartment above the bar, and he'd been busy meeting with the staff, firing a few leftovers from Darren's posse and, yeah, he'd known there would be trouble tonight.

He'd put a heavy-duty lock on the door leading to the loft, told Catie to stay upstairs and not come down unless he called for her. And now, as he approached Darren, an emotion suspiciously close to anger stirred deep within him. Anger was never good in these situations, and still he felt it, hot and deep.

"Hey. Bat, is it?" Darren extended a hand, which Bat ignored. "I thought maybe you and I could talk."

"Nothing to talk about."

"Yeah, well, see, I've worked at this bar for a long time. That new owner bitch doesn't realize how much her uncle needed me."

"Her uncle was probably too nice and too sick to realize

you were pushing drugs out of here and stealing his profits. Catie's a little sharper than that. And firing you was her decision. I'm just here to enforce it."

"I've heard all about you, Bat Kelly."

"Then you know that you should leave right now, before you get hurt," Bat drawled.

"You're sleeping with her, aren't you? She'll do that—sleep with you and then fire you. She's a real bitch, that one."

Bat tamped it down hard and tried to push Catie from his mind, the way she'd clung to him last night when he'd pulled Darren off her . . . the way she'd clung to him today. Two different feelings entirely—there was no way Catie had been involved with this guy. She'd been too honest about everything else to hold that bit of information back.

"You touch her again, ever, and that will be your last day on this earth. Are you hearing what I'm laying down, brother?" He stared at Darren's tattoo as he spoke.

"Yeah, I'm hearing it, *brother.* I'm just not real good at listening anymore. That's why I left the service. I suspect you felt the same way . . . I thought maybe you and I could come to some sort of arrangement."

"The only arrangement we're going to make is, you're leaving this bar and I'm staying."

"I want my job back—and I'm going to make sure that happens."

"Why don't we step outside and finish this discussion?" Bat brushed past Darren and pushed the door open. He knew Darren followed him, didn't bother to turn around until they were fully on the red dirt that covered the side area of the building.

Darren's fist came at him fast. Bat blocked it and Darren slugged him in the gut before Bat got in a crack at Darren's nose. Blood spurted everywhere, and within seconds Bat drop-kicked the big man to the ground and held him there, hand on Darren's throat.

"Big guy hasn't been practicing his moves. Too much time building muscle, not enough time actually using it," Bat whispered in Darren's ear. "Touch Catie again and you'll be one sorry motherfucker."

He pushed off Darren roughly, left him lying on the ground and walked back into the bar, past the crowds who'd come outside to watch.

"Show's over, people," Jase called. "Come on back in for last call!"

Bat was done. He gave Keith a wave and knew the brothers would take care of closing up the place for the night—cleaning it too. And so he walked up the long, narrow flight of stairs and down the hallway and used the key to let himself inside.

Catie was waiting for him, had been sitting in the center of the bed in the loft she'd cleaned today. The space needed some work, just like everything else around this place, but it was nice—open and airy, and it would let in plenty of light during the day.

The bar came with enough property to build a house on. Why he thought about that now, with Catie sitting there in just a tank top and light pink underwear, was anyone's guess.

She'd put the sheets he'd bought earlier that afternoon on the bed. He'd taken the mattress outside earlier in the day and beat the dust out of it, and now it smelled like fresh air and sunshine. It was dark now, the fog still thick around the bayou moon.

The knuckles on one of his hands were raw, his shirt was ripped at the collar, his cheek bruised and throbbing. All in all, not a bad night pain-wise, but Catie was staring at him.

"You're hurt."

"I'm fine."

"I don't call this fine—you're bleeding."

He glanced at his shoulder and the rip in his shirt, which showed fresh blood from when one of the patrons decided that a broken bottle was a good weapon. "Flesh wound. Won't need stitches, just a Band-Aid." He strolled over to the large, stand-up mirror in the corner as he peeled off his shirt and discarded it on the floor.

But Catie was already off the bed and headed to the bathroom. He watched her cute ass shake in the reflection when she walked, and he waited for her to return.

She did—with cotton and peroxide and bandages.

"Let me," she told him. He remained in front of the mirror, watched her stand on tiptoes to reach his shoulder. When she was finished, she took each of his hands in hers and dabbed the ointment on the raw spots, rubbing it in gently.

"That's enough," he said, and pulled her against him so she was directly in front of him, both of them facing the mirror.

"Did you draw tonight?" he asked as he began to skim her tank top off her body, losing the contact between them for only a second before the soft skin of her bare back was pressed to his bare chest.

She was flushed and her nipples were already taut as he cupped a hand under each breast. "Yes. And don't forget that you promised I could draw you."

"Why people? Why not sunsets and bowls of fruit?" he asked, let his thumbs move to her nipples, his tanned fingers a contrast to her creamy skin. She leaned her head against his chest and smiled as she watched.

"I like drawing the body, the human form," she explained, her tone breathy as he played. He loved the way she jumped at each caress and then pushed her breasts into his palms, searching for more contact. "It's more fluid. There's always movement—flesh and blood and beating heart, all showing on the skin and the face . . . It's exciting. Always changing."

He dipped his head to kiss along her neck. "So why did you stop? You said you didn't draw for a long time."

"I don't know. It just became hard, almost rote." She ran a hand down one of his arms. "I was probably lonely. Needing contact."

He didn't say anything more, merely drew her in tighter as his fingers continued to play on the taut nipples. Contact.

Yes, this was what she needed. He was sure of it. "I want to see you naked, totally naked, Catie *chere*."

She complied, slid out of the thong, and he murmured, "So pretty," against her ear. And she was, from the swell of her breasts to the smooth, taut stomach and the curve of hips he pictured himself grabbing as he drove into her later.

"Now you." She tugged at him so he was the one standing in front of her, and she slowly unzipped his jeans, pulled them and his boxer briefs down at the same time, to reveal his arousal jutting out toward the mirror.

"I didn't have the chance to do this last night—just look at you," she breathed. "I could study you all night. With my hands, my mouth . . ."

"Nothing stopping you."

Her hands moved across his abs, down toward his cock, her mouth pressed to his biceps. When her hands encircled him, he groaned.

At first, her touch was tentative, an exploration, and he let her know that she was doing everything right, by the way his body jerked with every caress. She grew bolder, stroked his shaft slowly up and down, watched his reactions reflected in the glass, and what a picture it was, her naked body pressed to his side.

He wondered for a brief second if Catie would mimic one of the other pictures he'd seen in her sketchbook. He'd paged through it that morning, while she slept, his cock growing impossibly hard at the sketch of her on her knees in front of a man, the man's head thrown back in complete pleasure.

She smiled at him, as if she knew what he was thinking, and within seconds, she was on her knees, facing him. She still held him in one hand, the other moved to cup his balls, while her tongue brushed the tip of his cock. He didn't know where to look, at her face or the sight of her between his legs in the mirror. Instead, he closed his eyes and let the sensation take him over for just a second.

She took his cock inside her mouth, studying him with her lips and tongue, and fuck, she might be new at this, but he loved it. He ran his fingers through her hair, along her shoulders, all the while repeating her name and struggling to stay on his feet.

When her tongue began to dance on the sensitive strip of flesh behind his balls, he barely stopped himself from coming. He steeled himself, because he wanted to come inside of her—he'd waited for nearly twenty-four excruciating hours—he could wait a little longer.

"Catie, please." He urged her to her feet, and then he carried her over to the bed, and even the thought of her spread out beneath him was almost too much to handle.

He wanted her fast and furious, wanted to leave himself no time to think about anything but sinking inside her and getting his rocks off. But something about Catie *chere* begged for a long, leisurely fuck.

He lowered her to the bed, covered her body with his

even as she wrapped herself around him—arms around his neck and legs around his waist. His cock brushed her wet pussy and sent a jolt through his body, as if hers was made of pure electricity.

He dropped his head and took a nipple in his mouth, fondled it between his teeth and tongue until it was taut and hot.

She jerked upward as he sucked hard and began to enter her at the same time.

She was tight—so tight. Even as her body welcomed his first intrusion, her nails dug into his back and she arched against him to pull him more deeply inside of her. "Bat—oh, Bat —yes!"

Using small strokes, he opened her until she relaxed. He pulled his cock out of her almost completely, leaned back slightly on his haunches to watch his cock begin to fill her again.

Her hips had been rocking with his until this full entrance inside her hot, slick sex. She paused, her mouth a soft O as he took her fully—a long, low moan that sounded like a combination of his name and *oh, my god* escaped from her throat. He forced himself to remain still, kissed her as he reached between her legs to caress her clit, his finger sliding along the tight bundle of nerve endings until she started to squirm underneath him in an almost uncontrollable rhythm.

"You like this, *chere*?"

"Oh, Bat—yes . . ."

"Tell me you like it," he told her, even as he drove deeper.

"Like it . . . like everything," she managed, but he was fucking her hard, so hard, even as the needy sounds escaped her throat and her words were incoherent.

He tried to ground himself by holding onto the sides of the mattress, and in minutes it was *oh* and *Bat* and *don't stop now* as her ankles pressed the small of his back in time with the rock of his hips.

The bed moved and creaked in protest and he ignored it, found a rhythm to drive them both wild. She was slick, hot—so fucking hot—and he wanted to take her over and over again, to watch her back arch and her eyes close in complete abandon.

He didn't want it to end, wanted to stay locked into her, but the way she clenched around him like a wet vise forced the orgasm to rock through him, shutting down coherent thought for a few amazing minutes. The way she held him when he came, with such a hunger and need and want, like she was holding him as if both their lives depended on it, made the aftershocks shoot through him with a vengeance. And when he collapsed on her, she still didn't let go.

The fan whirred lazily above them, the flutter of air cooling their damp skin, and gradually his breathing returned to normal. Catie's eyes were closed, her mouth curved in a small smile, and there was no mistaking the peace on her face.

There was a time for control, and that would be later, when the insistent desire spilled from them and he could take his time going over every inch of her body. Normally, he'd be out of there long before that, unwilling to wake up next to a stranger who expected more.

Catie already expected more from him, and that was something he wasn't sure he was ready to deal with. But she was tracing his tattoo with her finger and he had hours left until morning light. He wasn't going to waste it on thinking.

CHAPTER *Five*

Hours later, Catie was lying spread out along Bat, her head on his chest, an arm and a leg flung over his body. She caressed the ridges of his abs and the sharply contrasted hip bones that led down to the large, still partially firm cock, a column of veined dusky skin and steel that she hadn't known could be so beautiful and masculine at once.

There was a long scar that ran across one hip. Her fingers trailed that lightly, her own body still humming from the rough tips of Bat's fingers on her. Now they played with her hair.

Finger at the bottom of the scar, she said, "It sounded bad down there tonight. Was it?"

"Nothing we couldn't handle," he said, and then he paused, as if weighing something heavily in his mind. When he spoke again, his tone was guarded, as though bracing for her reaction. "Darren came around looking for you tonight."

She shivered as she recalled Darren's hard, cold eyes, the almost violent bearing that seemed to be his norm. He'd been so angry when she'd fired him, so much so that she'd been sure he was going to hit her. But he'd clenched his fists and walked out of the office and the bar instead, and she'd breathed a shaky sigh of relief. She'd thought that was the end of it, but she now knew she couldn't have been more wrong.

If Bat was right and that had been Darren in the alley, that meant he'd taken the time to plan his revenge. What would she have done if Bat hadn't come along?

"What are you thinking, Catie *chere*?" Bat asked quietly. "Because you're safe."

She hadn't realized that she'd frozen, was reliving the attack again in her mind, until Bat wrapped his arms around her and held her with a fierce protectiveness she'd never known. "I know. How do you know it was him last night?"

"His tattoo. It's better that you don't go anywhere alone."

"Tell me what he said."

"It's not important."

She saw the clench of his jaw and reached out to touch the bruise on his cheek. "You fought him."

"Yes. I told him that if he came near you, he'd regret the day he was born."

"What do I do now?"

"You need to stick close to me. He won't touch you, he knows better. And then you'll leave this town and he'll forget about you."

He'll forget about you. She wondered if the same would hold true for Bat. And then she wondered why she cared, because she'd known the man less than two days.

"It'll be all right. That's why I'm here. This is a tough

enough business for anyone, but especially for a woman with no protection—a woman in a strange place."

"Don't get me wrong, I'm grateful you're here, but it's frustrating. I'm used to doing things on my own, getting them done. Here, I can't make a move without something going wrong."

"You've been on your own for a while now, haven't you?"

"Since I was eighteen," she admitted. But really, it seemed longer. Her mother had never been a responsible one—she'd always left that up to Catie. It was something Catie hadn't minded at the time, but now, looking back, she got a tightness in her throat when she thought about what she'd missed out on all those years, when she was cooking and cleaning and caring for her brother, years she should've been having fun.

"After my mom died, things got really intense," she said.

Art had always been her escape. At times, after her mom died, it had been her only salvation, something to carry her through when she wasn't sure if she was going to make enough money that month to keep her brother with her, or when she wasn't sure she was going to be able to make it a second longer working what she knew were dead-end jobs that left her too tired to work on her own art.

"Sounds like you stayed busy," he said, and she noted he hadn't let her out of his arms.

"I probably never took the time to grieve properly," she admitted. "I had to take care of my fourteen-year-old brother. Which wasn't new, but without the safety net of my mother, I was really on my own."

She'd worked her ass off to make sure that he'd be able to stay with her and that they weren't separated. She'd had to meet with social workers and judges, and after a year they'd deemed her responsible and she'd been given continued support from the state.

"Where's your brother now?"

"College—thanks to scholarships—and on the road to law school." He was actually her half brother but she never considered him so. He was brilliant. Funny. He'd told her, with all his twenty years of wisdom, that she needed a new beginning.

Before she'd driven out here she'd bought all new art supplies in hopes that would be the case.

It was a step in the right direction. She knew that being in Bat's arms was another—he was the kind of man mothers warned their daughters about. Every mother except hers, she supposed, because she couldn't shake the feeling that her own momma would've urged her to get as close to Bat as possible, and stay there as long as she could.

For the moment, that's exactly what Catie would do.

Using the early morning light as her guide, Catie sketched Bat, replicated the shadows along the muscles in his chest and arms and thighs onto the paper, created his form with charcoal smudges and fast strokes.

She took some time to study the various scars on his body—the ones she'd noted in the mirror last night and explored with her fingers and mouth in the moonlight, assumed they were tokens from his work. If they were an indication, he had gotten off easily with the Bon Temps crowd last night.

He cradled the pillow against his face the same way he'd held her when they'd finally both settled to sleep after he'd taken her with his hands and mouth and long, thick cock, filling her up until she was sated and sleepy and strangely pulled even tighter, wanting more. The man was addictive, even while asleep, his breathing deep and comfortable, his body splayed across the bed and tangled in the sheets.

She put down the sketchbook and stretched, went to put on some water for tea in the kitchenette off the smaller sitting room. When she came back into the bedroom, the bed was empty and her sketchbook had been paged through.

She wondered if he had a favorite drawing—if he liked the shadowed sketches of the two of them together in front of the mirror or the ones of him alone, one large arm curled around the pillow.

And then she followed the sound of the shower and waited in the doorway for a second, just watching him.

There was no shower curtain and Bat faced the tile, head under the steady spray, water rippling off his body.

"You slept well, Catie *chere*." He didn't turn around and she wondered how he did that, knew she was there behind him despite the noise of the shower.

"Before you came, I was having a tough time sleeping around here," she said. "I'm used to a lot more noise. Different noise."

"Sounds of the night Bayou coming alive," he said as he continued to let the water pour down over him. "You ever really been out on the Bayou Teche, *bebe*?"

"I haven't had time for the grand tour. It is beautiful country, from what I caught on the drive in."

"I don't see a car in the parking lot."

"I had to sell it once I got here, to start in on the bar's repairs." The roof had been badly damaged. Now, she'd been assured, it was hurricane proof and she had no mode of transportation except her own two feet.

She wouldn't need a car once she got back to the city anyway. "Wait, how did you know I slept?" she asked.

"Because I don't," he answered, and she wasn't sure what it meant that he'd lain there in bed holding her while she slept, and then for a couple of hours pretended to be asleep so she could draw him.

"Are you coming in?" He finally turned to face her, his hard body slick with soap and water, and yes, she was coming in. Anything to stay close to the strength of his body.

She stripped out of the shirt and underwear she'd pulled on this morning for working, and climbed into the old claw-footed tub with him. He held her steady, turned so she was under the spray of the shower with him, his arousal hard against her belly.

But he didn't do what she expected—instead, he turned the bar of soap in his large hands and lathered her back and shoulders, massaging her as he did so. His hands were strong and sure, left soapy trails as they kneaded and probed away tension she hadn't even been aware of carrying.

"God, that feels good," she murmured.

"You need more nights like last night." He'd squirted shampoo onto his palms and now his fingers moved to her scalp, rubbing and pressing. "Good thing I'm available."

"What did you think of the sketches?"

He smiled, a slow, lazy tug that began at the left corner of his mouth and spread. And he took her hand and wrapped it around his erection. "I thought they were hot. Turned me on almost as much as seeing you naked, under me."

She'd gotten turned on drawing them, and now she let her hand travel up his shaft to the heavy sac. "Why don't you sleep?"

"Military trained it out of me. I was a Marine sniper."

"Where did you get this done?" She traced the outline of the tattoo of the skull and crossbones surrounded by stars on his biceps with a soapy finger, letting her other fingers trail underneath his balls.

"A guy I used to know did it for me, down in Chattanooga. Told me to never forget my past."

"Swift. Silent. Deadly." She repeated each word that was inked around the symbol, as his hands moved over her hips to travel lower, between their bodies, nestling between her legs.

"Does that describe you?" she breathed as his first stroke threatened to undo her. How was that possible?

"What do you think?"

She thought yes. *Definitely yes.* And she didn't want him to stop what he was doing with his hand. "So that's what being a sniper is all about?"

"Yeah. It's all about precision. One shot, one kill," he murmured as his finger found the precise spot that nearly made her leap out of his arms. If he hadn't had her pinned against him, her knees would've given out from the quick, sharp orgasm.

She dug her fingers into his shoulders, leaving marks and not caring. He didn't seem to mind, continued to watch her face carefully as he shifted her, picked her up by her hips so she was forced to wrap her legs around him.

"Let me take you back to bed, Catie *chere.*" He didn't wait for her answer before he was carrying her out of the bathroom and placing them both, still damp from the shower, on the rumpled sheets. The cool morning breeze was replaced by a hot, steamy breath of air that escaped from behind the half-drawn shades and the old window screens, but it was still quiet outside.

She pushed his chest and he grinned and complied, lying on his back. This time, she covered his body with hers, and she began to make her way down his body with her mouth. Her hands caressed what her lips left behind, tracing the smooth skin over all that hard muscle, committing it to memory.

She sucked a nipple, hard, until it tightened in her mouth and he groaned, tugged his hand through her hair. "You're killing me, Catie."

He shifted under her, his hips rocking into her persistently—he was hard against her and she liked the idea that he was trapped that way, waiting for her. Needing her.

She inhaled the scent of the damp, crisp hairs that trailed down from his abs, let her mouth drag down lower, toward the thick head of his cock.

There was a drop of moisture at the tip, and when she squeezed the shaft, the moisture lengthened, beaded like pearls against the plum-colored head.

"I can't even get my hand around you, Bat, that's how big you are," she murmured before she licked the drops of pre-cum, suckling lightly along the slit, then pulled back to watch her palm move up and down, her fingers unable to encircle him fully.

When he'd first entered her last night, she'd felt stretched to the hilt. Her body was pleasantly sore today, but judging by how wet she was between her legs, she was more than ready to take him inside of her again. Her sex ached for that, contracted at the mere thought, but she wanted more of the heavy sex between his legs first, wanted to explore that unmistakably male part of him that her body craved.

"You were so tight." His voice was rough, his breathing faster than normal, a flush on his cheeks that wasn't from the shower or the sun. "Want to be inside you again—want you to come, over and over."

In response, she moved down to take his balls, one by one, into her mouth, until he writhed up, nearly off the bed. She still had him in her hand, worked him up and down as she felt his restraint in the tense muscles of his thighs.

He shifted, reached down and tugged at her shoulder. "Catie, I want to taste you at the same time. Turn yourself around."

Her cheeks flushed even as she moved her body so his face could reach between her legs, until his tongue made contact with her already swollen clit. When it did, she gasped around his cock and then hummed in pleasure, which made him jerk in response.

He spread her thighs, pulled her closer so she was actually sitting on his face and he was buried, mouth and tongue, inside of her, his tongue invading her core until she writhed against him helplessly.

He was just as helpless, a prisoner to her mouth—every suck and lick made her do the same to him in kind, every muscle in his body tensed so hard that he shook, but he stopped himself from coming.

She couldn't; she came on his face with a blinding intensity that shook her entire body, her sex fisting around his tongue. She didn't even realize that Bat had eased her away from his cock, was taking her from behind before she recovered from her orgasm.

His weight was heavy on her, his chest pressed to her back as they moved in tandem. His hands held her hips fast and she writhed back against him, wanting him deeper, letting his relentless driving bring her over the edge again.

He came quickly as well, pulsed inside of her, and she didn't know how he'd gotten the condom on as quickly as he had. They collapsed together, his heavy weight pinning her to the bed, and oh, yes, this was the right way to spend a morning.

CHAPTER Six

Normally, Catie would make the three-block walk to Flo's—the cheapest and best place she'd found to eat in town—alone. This morning, Bat walked her there and told her to stay put until he returned from the hardware store.

She didn't argue. Besides, the diner had become her second home, and the namesake of the place was a tall, bleached blonde in her sixties who spoke in a heavy Louisiana drawl and had become a mother hen to Catie.

It made sense, since Flo and Catie's momma had been best friends growing up, their friendship breaking off completely when Catie's mom left town. The first time Catie walked into the diner, Flo had paled as if she'd seen a ghost and called Catie *Marie*.

"You didn't have dinner last night, did you?" Flo chided Catie as soon as she walked in the door.

The breakfast crowd was large and noisy, thanks to the

weekend. Catie moved to sit at the counter on one of the comfortably worn stools, and Flo pushed an iced coffee toward her and called for a special over her shoulder, toward the cook at the grill.

"I need one special to go this morning too."

"Heard there's been quite a show over at the Bon Temps these past two nights."

"Just the usual fights."

"Uh-huh. And a mystery man who just happened to roll into town at the right time, on a vintage Harley, no less." Flo winked.

"He's the new cooler I hired. His name is—"

"Bat Kelly. Yes, I know. He grew up two towns over," Flo said. "A real wild child, that boy. Drove his momma and daddy crazy until he left to join the Marines. Hasn't been back since, until now. Heard he's made quite a name for himself."

"I heard the same thing," Catie murmured, flashing back to the morning spent in bed and the delicious soreness between her legs.

"Catie Jane, where'd you go?" Flo was saying as she put a huge plate in front of her on the counter. "Dreaming about your new cooler?"

"No," she protested, felt her cheeks grow warm and shoveled a forkful of eggs into her mouth so she didn't have to speak for a few seconds.

"I would. The man is beautiful. And it's about time Bayou Rouge got some new life to it—it could only help my business. So many people left after Katrina. I can't blame them, but I feel like the history of this place is going to be lost to that damned bitch of a storm." Flo sighed, propped her elbows on the counter and rested her chin in her hands. "I remember when the Bon Temps first opened. Your uncle Carl was just a kid himself when he bought the place. Barely nineteen, fresh out of the service and handsome as the devil."

"Sounds like you knew him pretty well."

"He was a heartbreaker, but then again, so was I." Flo smiled.

"So why didn't you and Carl end up together?"

"Fate just didn't line us up right. And then my Jimmy roared into town on his motorcycle and I never looked back." Flo smiled and pointed to a picture that hung on the wall closest to the counter. It showed a much younger version of her sitting on the back of a bike, a tall, handsome man next to her. "I've always been a sucker for the bad boy, I guess."

"Just like my mom." It was the first time Catie had brought up that subject in front of Flo, and it made her stomach ache. She pushed the plate of half-eaten food slightly away from her.

Flo pushed it right back. "Your mother always told me that she felt as though she loved your father too much. She always was a romantic, although too dramatic at times to suit people's tastes. She used to tell me, *Flo, I know Ed will break my heart—shatter it into a thousand pieces, and I'll never get them pieced back together just right.*"

"Is . . ." Catie couldn't bring herself to call him her father. "Is Ed still around?"

Flo's face changed, her eyes darkening a little. "Oh, honey, your momma never knew . . . Ed was killed riding his hog up to New Orleans about two weeks after your momma left town."

"Would Ed have . . . I mean, do you think he would've stuck around . . . raised me?" Catie asked.

Flo shook her head sadly. "I think Ed would've done just what your momma said he'd do. Maybe that's why she left—maybe her heart was only broken in five hundred pieces, a little easier to put together."

"No, it wasn't easier."

"It's a good lesson."

"Of what?"

"Not to waste time on what might have been. To let what's supposed to happen just be." Flo waved her hand. "People these days spend too much time thinking and not enough time just doing."

Flo's words hit a little too close to home for comfort and Catie played with a piece of toast so she wouldn't have to respond.

"Did your momma ever get over him?" Flo asked finally.

Catie's mom was always running from one place—and one man—to another. Still, she'd been a strong woman, never let anyone hurt Catie or her half brother, but when it came to giving men her heart, her mother seemed completely hopeless.

"You know what, Flo, I don't think she ever did."

The thing was, Momma always got her heart broken, but she always seemed . . . happy.

I've lived, honey—lived and loved. If you can't say that, then what's the point?

Lived and loved.

"Your momma, she ran. Too far . . . too far from her family." Flo shook her head.

"The way I heard it, her family would've disowned her for having me." Catie tried not to let the bitterness creep into her tone, was glad the diner was mostly cleared out so no one could hear the story of her life and times.

From the start, she'd dreaded getting into this with Flo.

"Marie's family would've forgiven her. Your momma should've stayed here. You should stay here. Come back, help us rebuild—don't spend a lifetime repeating her mistakes."

"That's great, now you're accusing me of running?"

"Your family's history is here. Your brother's across the country in school. You told me you moved from town to town growing up—you have no home base. You need roots."

Flo was right—all her life, Catie had been floating along with her momma. Now that she was on her own, Catie was simply looking for a place to settle in, a place to belong. And as much as Catie wanted to see the sale of the Bon Temps as a means to an end for her future, she'd still wanted to feel something when she'd first arrived in Bayou Rouge, an instant connection that let her know she belonged, that she was meant to come here to her mother's hometown. Instead, the people who worked at the Bon Temps made her feel unwanted, and she'd been easily overwhelmed. After meeting Flo, she had some inkling of what life might've been like growing up here, but it wasn't enough.

Still, since Bat had arrived, the feeling of ease had grown, almost enough to make her forget about the incident with Darren.

Right now, she could only chalk that up to lust and Bat's protective nature. Imagining it was something else would only serve to confuse her more, and she was tired of being confused. She wanted a clear path for herself.

"I've got everything I need, Flo," she said. "After the Bon Temps sells, I'll have even more."

Coming back here—to a past, a family that could've been hers but wasn't—made every resentment rise up in Catie's mind, until her head hurt.

Her past was going to pave the way for her future and then she was out of here. She'd find her own roots someplace.

Bat had known something was wrong the second he'd picked Catie up from the diner—she'd been waiting at the door, looking agitated, and damn, he didn't like seeing her upset. His body had hummed the whole time he was in the hardware store and he'd wanted to find her as relaxed as she'd been when he'd dropped her off.

The owner, Flo, who he remembered from when he was a boy, had stared between him and Catie Jane and he could just imagine the stories Flo told her. But Catie refused to talk about it, told him that nothing was wrong, and he was smart enough not to press the issue. Yet.

He barely took the time to eat the take-out breakfast from Flo's before he was dealing with deliveries and payroll, all things Catie had handled over the past few weeks. He'd been doing this kind of thing for so long, he streamlined the process quickly. Now that the Bon Temps was no longer taking its liquor deliveries POD, it could begin a slow climb out of the red.

And Catie was still absently staring out the window.

"Time to stop brooding—tell me what's wrong, Catie *chere*." He pulled the stool she sat on toward him so that he was between her legs.

She paused for a minute as if weighing telling him the truth, and then he saw the tears in her eyes. "Flo grew up with my mom. They were best friends when they were younger. Best friends up until the time my mom left town."

"You're upset. She upset you."

"I'm okay. Really."

"Do you always pretend you're okay when you're not?"

"Do you always pick up on everything?"

He slid closer, pressed his body to hers and waited for her to answer, would wait there all day if he had to, even as he wondered when the hell he'd grown a patience gene.

"My mom got pregnant with me young. Left this town because she was ashamed and scared, and she never came back," she said finally, with a hitch in her voice. "The break she had with her family was because of me."

"No," he told her fiercely. "It wasn't you. Nothing to do with you at all."

"Flo asked me if I was going to keep running, like my mom."

"What did you tell her?"

"I told her that I didn't think I was running, that I came here to sell the bar and then go on to school."

"Do you feel like you're running?"

"Do you?" she shot back.

"It's the nature of my job to move from town to town." That was the truth, but he still felt like a goddamned liar when the words came out of his mouth.

"Flo said that I should stay. Get in touch with my family's history."

"And that's not what you want."

"Maybe if my mother had come back here at all—if she'd stayed in touch with her family, even, I'd feel something for this bar or this town. I wanted to feel something when I got here. But there's nothing here for me—it's just a run-down bar and a family that's gone."

"But you wanted there to be, and you're scared that you're making the wrong decision by selling the bar."

There was that jut of the chin she probably didn't even realize she did when she was trying to prove something to him—and to herself. "I'm not scared."

No, *terrified* would be a more accurate description, if the tight fists she made were any indication. And still, he couldn't help but feel she was a hell of a lot tougher than he was. "Putting down roots doesn't happen overnight. What is it you want, Catie? What do you really want?"

"I want things to have turned out differently. Flo told me about my father, how he was killed before I was born. How he never even knew about me. And I wonder so many things. Would my momma have been happy if she'd stayed here and married Ed? Would he have reformed?"

"Why are you looking at me like that when you ask that last question?"

"Because you're the man every momma warns her daughter about. Every mom except mine." She gave a short laugh, ran a hand through her hair. She'd let it loose from the ponytail and it was messy and sexy. "They never would've been happy. Things like that never do work out."

"And you're never going to know the answer to that one, Catie. Why bother going over it again and again? The ending's not going to change, no matter how badly you want it to."

"I've got work to do." She suddenly pushed at his chest and he moved away from her so she could slide off the stool.

"You're mad now."

"What do you care? You've got no investment in what I do—beyond your money." The words shot out and straight into him, and he noted that she couldn't even bring herself to look at him, had already turned her back and was walking away.

His gut twisted—was that really what she thought of him? "Yeah, I guess you're right, Catie *chere,* no investment at all," he drawled quietly.

Catie spent the better part of the afternoon in the storeroom and felt as if she'd made no progress beyond working off some of her anger. She'd had to splash her face a few times—when she looked into the old mirror and saw tears streaking her cheeks, along with smudges of dust and dirt from the cleaning she'd done.

What was she doing, letting a past she'd never known or cared about rise up to bite her like this? And why was she taking it out on the one person in this entire town who'd helped her? The only person she'd really connected with in a way she'd never connected with anyone, and in such a brief span of time.

When she finally emerged, Bat was nowhere to be found in the main area of the bar. She went to grab herself a soda, and heard a sharp knock on the front door.

Hesitantly, she moved toward it and looked out the peephole, to see the local policeman who'd come to the bar several times on her first nights here, to break up fights.

Terrell Johnson was in his early thirties, also a town local boy made good, and he'd been nice enough, but he'd told her that she couldn't keep calling him to break up bar fights. It was after one such night that she'd called her old boss in New York who she'd bartended for, gotten Dominick's name and hired Bat.

She opened the door and Terrell nodded at her. "Afternoon, Catie Jane. I'm looking for Bat Kelly." His tone was formal—this was no social call.

She stuck her hands in the pockets of her jeans. "I'm not sure where he is, but he should be back soon."

"I'll just wait for him here, then. I have some questions for you too—might as well get those over with."

She stepped aside as Terrell walked past her into the bar, asked, "Is everything all right?"

"You haven't heard?" His eyes were dark and serious as he flipped open a small notepad. Her stomach tightened.

"I've been in the storeroom all day. Cleaning. And I'm not exactly in on the gossip loop in this town." Besides Flo, no one really talked with her. After this morning and the way she'd been almost rude to Flo when she'd left the diner abruptly, Catie wasn't even sure Flo would talk to her anymore.

He looked up from the notepad. "Darren White is dead."

Her hand flew to her mouth.

"Time of death was sometime after three this morning. After the Bon Temps closed," Terrell continued.

"What do you want with me and Bat? Do you think he had something to do with this?"

"Darren was found with a bullet between his eyes. A sniper shot. Bat has the kind of experience it would take to kill a man like that."

"So do a lot of other people."

"Not with the kind of motive Bat has. So you two are dating?" Terrell asked without looking up from writing.

Dating? She didn't think they were even speaking after her outburst. "No, he works for me."

That was the simplest of truths.

"Everyone at the bar heard him threaten Darren," Terrell pointed out.

"That's because Darren tried to hurt me two nights ago in the alleyway," she protested.

"Why didn't you report that?"

"I don't know. I didn't realize it was Darren until last night, when he told Bat that he wouldn't stop coming after me. Bat's a smart man—do you think he'd challenge Darren so everyone could hear him and then kill the man?" she asked.

"Bat Kelly is a smart man, ma'am. So yes, that's something I'd expect from him."

"It sounds like you know him."

"I used to know him."

"We used to be best friends." Bat's drawl was deep and unhurried and she turned to find him leaning against the door frame, smoking a freshly rolled cigarette. His eyes held hers for a second, the translucent green dark with anger, hurt, maybe even some shame. But there was no guilt there. She'd never been more sure of anything in her life. "How's it going, Terrell?"

"Heard you were back in town, Bat."

"Yes, I'll bet you did."

"A man can't outrun his past, no matter how hard he tries."

"It's a good thing I wasn't trying all that hard, then." Bat hadn't moved away from the door. "Are you still holding a grudge about me dating your sister?"

"You broke her heart, left town without saying goodbye. To anyone. But I'm not here for a walk down memory lane. You need to come with me for questioning."

"Am I under arrest?"

"No."

"Then I'm staying right here. I didn't have anything to do with Darren White's death."

"But you did threaten him."

"I did. He attacked Catie in the alleyway and he made threatening statements in front of me and the entire bar. Did your sources conveniently forget to mention that? Because I've got witnesses of my own."

"Can you tell me your whereabouts between the closing of the Bon Temps last night and five this morning?" Terrell asked.

She knew Bat was going to tell Terrell no, and so she piped in. "He was with me."

"Ma'am..."

"He was in bed with me." She stared at Terrell, daring him to say another word about it.

Terrell stared between her and Bat for a long second. "This nice lady here just gave you an alibi for the murder. But I don't want you leaving town until I've done a complete investigation."

Bat took a long drag from his cigarette and didn't answer.

"He's working for me—he's not going anywhere," she said.

"Nice to see things haven't changed for you, Bat. Still got the ladies sticking up for you," Terrell said.

"Things have changed, my friend," was all Bat said.

"He has no loyalty, to anyone or anything," Terrell told Catie. "I'd be real careful if I were you, miss. Real careful."

"I always am," she told Terrell, and yes, until she'd met Bat, she always had been. Now she wasn't sure of anything except Bat's innocence.

"Why would you do that?" he demanded once she'd closed and locked the door behind Terrell.

"Wait a minute—you're pissed that I stuck up for you?"

"You didn't have to do that, put your reputation on the line. You're having enough trouble around here without that." He stubbed the cigarette out in an ashtray on a table. "I'm moving downstairs, into the office."

"Oh." The heavy weight bore down on her chest again. "Did I do something wrong?"

"Catie, I'm not going to have you be with a man under suspicion of murder."

"You haven't forced me into doing anything so far, and you're not forcing me now."

"Don't you get it? I'm capable of killing Darren, of killing any man, exactly the way Terrell said."

"You were serving your country. That's completely different."

"Look at the line of work I'm in. Everything I've done can make a violent man more violent."

"You're not violent," she told him fiercely. "Your work might require you to use force, but you're not a violent man, Bat Kelly. A woman knows these things. I know this about you."

He wasn't sure why it was so important that she believed that. "No, I'm not."

"You're not sleeping in the office. You're sleeping with

me, in the loft." She pulled him into her arms and he didn't bother to protest or pull away, because it felt damned good to be in them, to have someone who believed in him.

"I'm sorry about before, what I said about trying not to think about the way things might've been if your mom had stayed . . . or if your dad hadn't been killed. I try not to think in the past or think in what-ifs. You can drive yourself crazy that way."

"No, you were right about that." She pressed a cheek against his chest, against his heart, and just kept it there for a few moments. "But you also said that you can't outrun your past, and I don't know if that's what I'm trying to do. I wish I thought that it would be easier to stay, but to stay here—to know what I'd missed, to know what's not here anymore . . ."

"I know what that's like. Coming back here, to a place I never thought I'd be again . . ." He didn't finish, didn't tell her that something just felt right about being back here, a feeling he hadn't expected at all. How much Catie had to do with that feeling was something he'd been avoiding thinking much about.

"Why did you leave?"

He shrugged. "My parents drank too much. Fought too much. Pretty much ignored me and my sister. She got pregnant and left when she was eighteen. I kept getting into trouble. I guess I thought getting out of here would solve everything."

"Did it?"

"It made me grow up. Made me realize that things in my childhood could've been a lot worse."

"Sometimes I do feel like I'm running by selling the bar, just like my mom did, and I feel so weak that I can't stand it." She whispered the words as if she could barely bring herself to speak them in the first place.

"You're not weak—you're a survivor, Catie."

"I always hoped that there'd be more to life than surviving," she said, her voice still soft and full of threatening tears.

That was something he'd never considered, not until she spoke the words earnestly, until he laid in bed with her, her body twined around his, limbs tangled until there was no beginning or end. A continuous press of flesh to flesh. She was undoing him at every turn, every time she drew him, every time she captured him with her charcoal. Stripping him down on the outside the way she had before, when she told him that he wasn't violent. And she was threatening to do so again as she just held him, stroked her hand down his back.

He'd never been very good at comfort, had never wanted or needed any. Until now.

"I've been thinking about slowing down, retiring from this line of work," he admitted into the quiet of the bar, his words feeling a bit like sacrilege, but they were also a relief.

"Why's that?"

"Because it is dangerous. And I have family to think of. My sister and her little girl—they're down in Florida." He paused. "Her daughter needed an operation that insurance didn't cover. Would've wiped out her business—she owns a bakery."

"So you lent her the money."

"I gave her the money," he corrected. "It's what you do for family. I guess it took me a long time to realize that I still did have family."

"That's why you didn't leave me here that first night."

"Part of it. The unselfish part."

She smiled. "So what will you do when you retire?"

"I don't know. I'm not like you—I don't have this burning passion for one particular thing."

"Well, what do you like to do?"

There was the question that hit him right between the eyes. He tried to think as he stared out the front window, into the breezeless late afternoon.

What *did* he like to do? It had been so long since he just sat back and enjoyed. Hopping from place to place stopped him from getting caught, for sure, but it also stopped a lot of other things as well, stopped him from getting close to anyone or anything. Allowed him to keep a safe and reliable distance from everyone and everything.

"It shouldn't be this hard to answer you," he said finally.

"I know," she whispered against his neck. "But it's okay that it is. It sounds like we're a lot alike in some ways—sounds like you've never taken any time for yourself."

"I guess I haven't."

He leaned against the bar and took it all in, wondered if this area could ever rebuild itself the way it had been, even though he knew the answer.

Nothing ever stayed the same—that was the way things were supposed to work, which was why he changed and left before things did.

But there was no reason to say he couldn't stay in one place and weather the changes from there. Once he cleared his name with Terrell and the rest of the town against the charges of Darren's murder, Bat was going to do some serious planning for his future—for himself and his sister and his niece. He needed to be around to keep his promise to always be there for them. He needed to keep his promise to Big Red.

He needed to do more than merely survive.

CHAPTER *Seven*

The town appeared divided by what had happened to Darren, although Flo seemed to come down hard on Bat's side, and told both Catie and Bat that when she came to the bar with a big bag of her homemade food for them both.

Catie guessed that, for now, any bad blood that had passed between herself and Flo was gone, especially judging from the way Flo hugged her before leaving the bar to get back to the diner.

"I think it's cool that you stuck up for Bat like that," Jase told Catie as she helped restock the bar before it opened.

She took that as a major compliment, since the large man with the handsome scowl hadn't said more than two words to her since arriving in Bayou Rouge. She wasn't sure if he knew Bat wasn't getting paid in his usual way, but Bat had assured her that all the staff was being paid in full and on time.

"I know he didn't do it. Even if I hadn't been with him, I'd believe that," she said, and Jase shook his head.

"He's not an angel, Catie."

"I think that's one of the things I like most about him."

Jase mumbled something under his breath as he hauled a case of beer onto the bar and pushed it in her direction.

"Don't mind him," Keith told her. "He doesn't understand why anyone has a relationship that lasts more than one night."

She jerked her head toward him in surprise. "Relationship?"

"You guys are together most of the time. Eat together, sleep together, work here during the day together. I just assumed it was more than a one-night stand."

She didn't say anything else for a few minutes as Keith helped her shift the bottles around in the cooler to make room.

"Did you know Bat when he was in the Marines?" she asked finally, a safer subject than relationships.

Keith shook his head. "After he got out—we all worked a job together down in Georgia. Wild time. Bat was still new to the game—still bouncing, like we were. We didn't know what the hell we were doing."

"I always knew," Jase interrupted as he hauled over another two cases.

"Yeah, that's why Bat and I were always saving your ass." Keith shook his head. "Look, Bat's sniper days are behind him—and that was a job. Like working here is a job. He doesn't carry a weapon. Not even a knife. Has used nothing but his bare hands for as long as I've known him."

"Do you think he'll be cleared soon?"

"Word from a buddy who works for the city is he's the only suspect right now. No fingerprints on the weapon, and the police are working hard to place him at the scene of the crime." Keith gave her a hard look. "You know that some people say you lied to protect him."

"I know. But I wouldn't do that. And Bat doesn't need my protection—he was with me." No, she needed his protection. And because of that, he was in big trouble.

"He can take care of himself—he's been doing it for long enough. Jase and I, we're a lot like Bat, we don't like to stick around in any one place for very long," he said. "We grew up that way—followed in our father's footsteps."

"And you like it that way?"

Keith shrugged. "That's the way it's always been. Hey, customers are starting to come in. You shouldn't be down here."

"I know. I'm going," she said, casting her eyes across the room to Bat, who was near the front entrance, leaning against the wall. She caught his eye and he didn't smile, but he nodded once at her.

He probably knew she'd been discussing him, the way he seemed to know everything. But when she turned back slightly on her way up the stairs, she noted that he was still watching her.

That night, it was noisier than Catie had ever heard it in the bar. She looked out to the back lot, saw it was overflowing with cars and motorcycles, and she wondered if the investigation was the reason for all the people. Or maybe it was merely Bat's reputation that was ramping things up—Flo had mentioned that the Bon Temps had become the talk of several towns since he'd arrived.

By two in the morning, things had quieted down completely, and she'd been drawing nearly nonstop. Rubbing her wrist, she unlocked the door and went downstairs. The bar was quiet, most of the tables were still in their upright position and the floor had already been swept.

Bat came out of the storeroom, his shirt torn but otherwise looking intact. He stopped when he caught sight of her, stared at her legs. She still wore the loose denim shirt she'd been working in—it came down to mid-thigh, and beyond a small thong, she wore nothing else.

Being around Bat all the time made her want to walk around naked; this was as close as she'd risk it when coming down to the bar, in case Keith or Jase were still around.

"Rough night?" she asked.

"No different than the last couple of nights."

"Is there any news from Terrell?"

Bat snorted and shook his head. "He's been questioning everyone who was in the bar last night—asking about me, about you. About us."

About us. She liked the sound of that, if not the circumstances. "Let them talk."

"I don't like people talking about you, Catie. Not like that. Me, they can say anything they want. But you've got nothing to do with this . . . with my past."

She bit her bottom lip, fought the urge to go to him. Maybe he needed time alone. Or maybe . . . "You're always helping me—what can I do to help you?"

He stared at her, hair falling across his forehead. He shoved a hand ruthlessly through his hair, pushing it off his face. And then he rubbed the scar on his cheek with one broad knuckle. "You really want to help?"

She nodded.

"All right, then. You can help." He ambled over to start the jukebox, let the familiar zydeco music fill the empty space, and as long as she lived, she wouldn't forget the familiar strains of "Jole Blon," the wailing voice of the singer . . .

The way Bat looked as he went behind the bar, grabbed a bottle of tequila and several shot glasses and laid them all out on the cracked wood top. "Drinks are up, Catie *chere*. Come join me."

He poured several shots, put the lemon wedges out and slid the salt shaker to where she'd settled onto a stool across from him. The vinyl of the seat was cool under her nearly bare thighs.

"What did you draw tonight?" he asked as he pushed one of the shots toward her.

She played with the short, thick glass, stuck a pinky tip into the amber liquid and ran it across the tip of her tongue before she answered him. "Don't you want to be surprised?"

The newest sketch detailed their sixty-nine position—it was all shadows and light, half-hidden bodies and very abstract... sophisticated.

"You've been surprising me from the second I walked into this bar." He ran a hand through his hair again, shoving it away from his face, which served to emphasize his sharp cheekbones, and his scar, even more. And then he yanked a bandanna out of his pocket and tied it around his head so it kept his hair out of his eyes, and God, she loved when he did that.

She licked the outside of her thumb so the salt would stick, but he shook his head. "That's not the fun way to do that, Catie *chere*. And here I thought you wanted us to have a good time."

"Then I'll follow your lead."

He came out from behind the bar, toward her, a slow, almost predatory swagger that made her pulse quicken. And as he came close, she automatically spread her legs so he could nestle between her thighs.

He undid the first two buttons of her shirt and tugged it

down so one shoulder was bare, while she wrapped a calf around him, as if that alone could keep him close. She shivered when he put his mouth against the sensitive skin of her neck, rubbed it with the day's worth of rough on his cheeks to tickle her.

"You like that?"

"I like that." She twined her fingers through his hair while he ran his tongue in a long, slow lick across the bared skin of her shoulder.

She shivered as she felt the light sprinkle of salt dust on her shoulder and realized what he was doing. With the shot glass in his hand, he suckled the salt slowly off her skin in a way that shot straight to her sex, made her nipples tighten and the breath catch in her throat.

He lifted his head and downed the shot. She took a lime wedge, brought it up to his lips and watched him suck the juice out.

He licked his lips after she took the lime away. "That was nice. Best shot I ever had. Your turn, Catie."

Holding fast to his shoulders, she pulled him down to her so she could lick along his collarbone to the hollow spot at the base of his throat. He arched his neck back when she sprinkled the salt and licked it off, and then she did the remaining two shots in a row before he put the lime between her lips.

"Now, that's what I call having fun," he murmured as the tequila did a long, slow burn all the way to her stomach. "You know, this is where I first saw you. You were standing there, staring out the way you just were. What were you thinking about that night, Catie *chere*?"

"I was thinking about you."

"Nice try, but you didn't even notice me walk into the room."

She grinned as the pleasant, buzzed feeling kicked in. "I

was probably the only woman who didn't. But yes, I was thinking about you. A man like you. I wasn't even sure a man like you existed."

"A man like me who would watch you dance on tables?"

"How did you know that's what I was thinking about?" she asked.

"Am I wrong?"

No, he wasn't wrong. Nothing about the way she felt when she was with him was wrong. "No. I was thinking about what having fun would be like. I never had much time for fun—until recently."

"Tables are looking pretty lonely to me."

She laughed, until she realized he was serious. That's when she realized that she was serious too, although he was still smiling at her, and she brushed her hand lightly against his growing arousal. God, she loved being able to do that to him, to make him hard with a word or a stroke, the way he made her wet just by saying her name that certain way... hell, saying her name any way. "You've been stopping people from dancing on the tables. New house rules."

"You've been spying on me?" he asked. She wondered if he'd known she'd been sneaking down to watch what he was doing—not because she didn't trust him, but because she liked watching him. "For you, I'll make an exception."

He changed the song on the jukebox and a slow, sensual beat wafted through the room. "Go ahead... live it up."

She walked over to one of the front tables, where Bat helped her up on a chair, and from there to the tabletop, and stood near her, watching.

She worked the buttons on her shirt, one by one, until it swung loosely around her torso, separating slightly with each of her movements.

Bat shook his head and she noted the hard bulge in his jeans, thought about all the ways she'd let him take her over the past days and nearly lost all control of herself. He could undo her with a single glance, a low drawl of her name... with the simplest of touches.

Still dancing, she eased the shirt off her shoulders and then she let it drop from her body and float to the table, and there she was, on the table, nearly naked in front of him in the middle of the empty bar.

"Are you having fun?" His voice rumbled through her like a red-hot orgasm, and oh yes, she was.

The cool air from the ceiling fans hit her skin, and her nipples tightened. She put her arms over her head and ran her hands through her hair, turned so her back was to Bat and let the beat of the zydeco music guide her.

She felt the way she did that first night, when she was on the cot—completely uninhibited. Free.

God, she loved this.

She turned to face him and he slid her thong down slowly. She kicked it away impatiently, and he bent in and kissed the small blond triangle between her legs.

"Bat, I can't here..."

But it was too late—his kiss moved down, his tongue found her, began with small, stroking licks as his strong arms wrapped around her waist. Those were the only things holding her steady and upright as he sucked and probed and tasted. Her hands wound in his hair, and sensation shot through her like a rocket, and her core was melting like molten lava.

"You need to take a picture—draw your pretty little pussy. You're so beautiful down here, Catie *chere*. I could take up residence between your legs and live happily."

He separated her labia, blew on it softly and then tickled it with his tongue until she cried out, pressed her hand to the back of his head, forcing a hard touch. "Bat, please, I can't stay upright much longer. Not if you're going to keep doing that."

He obliged by bringing her down so she was sitting on the edge of the table. Then his face went right back between her legs. And when his tongue pressed her clit and circled it with a slow, rhythmic motion, she finally lost all control, called his name over and over as she came against his mouth.

Again, he didn't stop there, continued his assault of pleasure on her sex, but this time he slowly inserted a finger inside her. And when she groaned he added another and then a third, and began to rotate his hand in time with his tongue.

"Bat, please, I can't..." But he didn't stop, and she could, and did—was breaking apart, shattering into a thousand pieces against his mouth and hand as a long, keening cry left her throat and floated through the Bon Temps.

In seconds, he had them both down on the floor—he'd spread out his T-shirt and grabbed a condom from his jeans pocket. She ripped the packet out of his hand and sheathed him, moving on a mixture of adrenaline and lust as she straddled his thighs.

Her legs wrapped around his body while he remained upright, arms behind him. She held his shoulder fast with one hand as the other reached between his legs.

His erection was thick and long and impossibly hard. She began to ease him inside of her, her sex rippling as it opened to take him, inch by inch.

"That's it, Catie. Take all of me," he murmured.

She sheathed him fully inside of her, gasping his name out loud.

"Oh God, Bat, I..." She lost the train of thought completely as he drove his hips off the floor and into her. She lowered her face against his shoulder, bit down hard on his skin.

"Fuck, yeah, that's . . ." He groaned as she kissed the spot she'd bitten and began to grind against him. "Come on, *chere,* ride me just like that, make us both come."

Their bodies were sweat-slicked. The tequila and the sex made her bold as she moved, up and down on his cock. His mouth found her nipple, tugged it between his teeth, and she wound her hands in his hair as the orgasm shot through her. Her pussy contracted hard around him and his groan was muffled against her breast as she felt him come in pulsing waves deep inside her body, just as surely as if there were no barriers between them.

"Are you all right, Bat?"

Catie stroked his hair as they lay together on the bed, the dawn just outside the window. A small breeze caught the window shade. He'd forgotten what growing up around here had been like—the way the high grass smelled after a rain, the sounds of the swamplands at night, the way his skin tingled from the heat.

He'd carried her up the stairs after their wild tussle on the floor of the bar, and she was still warm and slightly drunk and completely loose after spending the last few hours in his arms. He'd buried himself inside her for what seemed like hours, took her over and over, while she made those beautiful noises for him. When she'd ridden him, he'd come hard enough to see stars, and still he felt his cock grow hard.

But even so, he was coming close to brooding, and there was no way to lie to her. "I'll live, Catie *chere*."

"They'll investigate, find out you didn't do anything," she assured him.

"The accusations are nothing new." He rolled onto his back, stared up at the ceiling fan as if that could give him all the answers before he continued his explanation. "Wherever I go, I'm the new guy. The dangerous one. The one who's capable of doing anything and everything. And yeah, it comes in handy most of the time. But times like this..."

He didn't finish, couldn't, shook his head and turned on his side away from her. He knew she wasn't going to let him get away with that, though—not anymore.

Nearly three days together felt a hell of a lot longer—and in a better way than he'd thought possible.

"Hey." She pressed her body along his back, spooned him as she leaned up on her elbow. "This time, you're not alone. This time, you've got me."

This time, you've got me.

Catie's breasts brushed his back, her breath fanned the back of his neck, and shit, he wanted to believe that. With other women, he could pretend he was the bad-boy loner with no past and no future, but here with Catie, she knew. Knew where he'd grown up and what he'd done when he left, and yes, some things were much easier to reveal to a stranger.

Except Catie, well, she wasn't a stranger anymore. He knew things about her no one else did, the places to touch that made her shiver, those that made her cry out unexpectedly. He knew that she sketched with her left hand, that she smiled as she worked and didn't realize it, and he knew with a certainty that nearly took him down to the knees that she could shatter his heart if he let this continue.

When Catie next woke, she was alone. She stretched discontentedly on the cool sheets and wondered how long Bat had remained in bed after she'd fallen asleep. And then she went to find him—padded downstairs toward where the music was blasting.

The bar was empty, save for Bat. He wore a T-shirt with the sleeves ripped out, the familiar bandanna around his head, and he was working on the bar itself, restoring it.

He used long, hard strokes with the sandpaper along the top of the bar to take off the old varnish, revealing a lighter, smooth wood with a rich grain running through it like a swirling river. Despite the loud music, he was in his own place, that space inside your head where your body went on autopilot, that thing that happened when you were doing something you loved.

She'd been there many times, especially over the past few days.

"Hey," she called out to him over the song when he stopped to check his work. "That looks great."

He ran his hand over the finished area. "I'll be able to put a varnish on it today. It'll dry in time for when we open again tomorrow night."

The bar was always closed on Monday nights. "You didn't have to do this—you're already doing so much around here," she said, moving closer to run her own hand over the wood.

"Careful—I don't want you to get a splinter."

"Have you always done this?"

He shrugged. "My daddy was a builder and a woodworker. He used to say that there was something about working with your hands and really feeling like you've created something." He paused, then laughed a little. "Look who I'm talking to about this."

"Can you show me how to do that?"

"It's rough work," he said with a shake of his head. "I don't want anything to happen to those hands."

Her hands were typically coated with charcoal and graphic pencil lead by now—but this morning, they were clean.

"No work for you this morning?" he asked.

"My subject snuck away."

"You're going to have to find a new subject soon enough, Catie. I'd think you'd be sick of drawing me by now," he told her, turning back to the sandpaper and the bar top.

She crossed her arms and tried not to let the hurt come across in her voice. "I was actually going to ask you for a ride into town."

"What do you need?"

"I think I'm ready to work in color." She'd been prepared to start using the hard pastels that afternoon, actually had been planning to ask him to pose for her in a very specific manner, but she didn't think he'd appreciate hearing that now.

"Did you fill out the application for the school yet?" he asked as he smoothed the sandpaper down a new section of the damaged wood.

He'd found the packet she'd received last week and she'd heard herself telling him that she needed to pick the sketches for her application to be completed.

But she'd been lying. Ever since Bat got here, both he and her art were in the forefront of her mind, and everything else, including New York, had faded away. Even with the suspicion hanging over Bat's head, she was more comfortable in this town now, more comfortable in her skin.

Three days. She didn't think it was possible for her life to change so dramatically in such a short time span, but it had. Things were different . . . she was different.

No matter what happens, Bat's planning on leaving once the Bon Temps is cleaned up and sold.

And then what? "I filled it out," she said.

"Good. That's good."

"I still have to sell this place first." She scanned the bar—even with Bat making repairs, because he told her that he enjoyed doing it, it was still going to take longer than expected. The crowds were bigger than ever, mainly because the word was spreading about Bat. Add to that his alleged role in Darren's murder and the fact that the owner of the Bon Temps was his alibi—well, the bar had become a sideshow.

Money was coming in, but the crowds were still rowdy and hard to control.

"It'll work out, Catie. Don't worry about the rowdiness. You knew it would take at least a month to see results. Concentrate on drawing, on getting into school."

"Is this something you could see yourself doing?" she asked, pointing to the refinishing project.

"I never really thought about it. It was always just a hobby; I'd end up helping out in whatever bar I was working or whatever apartment I was living."

"What's the longest you ever spent in one place, once you left home?"

"Six months, probably. When I was in the military. But most of the time, it's a three-months-or-less thing. Own only what you can carry and all that."

"We moved around a lot too. I didn't stay in one place until after Mom died—it was the first time my brother was in the same school for over a year," she admitted.

"Why did she move you guys around so much?"

"I've thought a lot about that, especially over the past few days," she said. "I think . . . I think she really wanted to come home—to Bayou Rouge. And all that time spent moving was because nothing satisfied her the way this place did. There's something about this town."

"You hated it here three days ago," he pointed out. "What changed?"

You came along. "A lot of things changed." She shrugged, as if it didn't matter. Not that he'd notice—he'd gone back to his work. "I've got some more stuff to do in the storeroom."

He nodded, still not looking at her, and she wondered if she'd dreamed last night . . . if she'd dreamed the entire thing.

She walked into the storeroom—it was nearly cleared out. There were only four more boxes to go through, what looked like her uncle's personal possessions. She'd almost put them out by the Dumpster instead of looking through them, but she hadn't.

Now she opened the boxes and began to rummage through the contents. There were some old newspaper clippings with her uncle's name in them—all sports related. It appeared he had been a star athlete in high school. A few articles focused on the Bon Temps itself—a piece on the bar's opening and then another on the celebration of twenty-five years open and going strong.

When she dug a little deeper, she found pictures, many in black-and-white and still framed, all of which showed the history of the bar. Carefully, not wanting to damage the old paper, she began to free the photographs from their prisons, turning them over to read the careful, fading inscriptions.

A history of the bar, chronicled painstakingly in what must be her uncle's handwriting.

Her family's history. One her mother had never gotten to see, one that Catie hadn't even known existed.

You did just fine on your own.

But didn't she want more than *just fine*?

"Find something worth keeping?" Bat was at the doorway, watching her. She couldn't tell if he'd been there long, but with his words her eyes filled and the pressure that had been building for weeks by being surrounded by memories that should've been hers, memories that could be if she decided to stay put, welled and couldn't be stopped. She bit her lip and shut her eyes tight to try to stop the tears, but a sob choked her throat. "I wish I had known my uncle. I wish so many things."

Bat had her gathered in his arms within seconds, and she put her face against his chest. "It's okay, Catie. I know you've had a tough time of it."

She rested against him for a few minutes, then pulled

away fiercely, angry with herself for letting go. He seemed to understand, took a step back and gave her space.

She wiped her tears with the back of her hand, and when she spoke again she was calm. "I was able to keep my brother with me. That's the most important thing. And he'll be able to realize his dreams, do anything he wants to do. He won't have to work nearly as hard as I did, and that's what I wanted."

"And now, thanks to your uncle, you both get to do what you want with your lives. Some people never have that."

"No, some people never do," she said quietly.

She walked out of the storeroom and into the bar. Her gaze caught on the way the light hit the bar, revealing the rich grained wood that Bat had refinished, and she couldn't help but run her palm across it. "This place must've been beautiful back in the day, when it was all brand-new."

"Might not have measured up to any of those fancy big city places you're used to, but it looked just fine."

"I'm picturing dark, mahogany wood–paneled walls, brass rails, pictures of the old-timers on that back wall..." She pointed to each object as she named it, lost in a dream of the way things were and the way things could be.

A dangerous line to straddle, and he was on the rope right next to her.

He nodded, and shit, she was beautiful even with dirt smeared on her cheek and red eyes and her hair tumbling all over the place as if she'd been running her hands through it. She was strong. If he hadn't intervened, she would've found another way to get the Bon Temps in order.

She didn't need him.

But his sister did. When she'd called him, the desperation plain in her voice, he understood, stepped up to the plate. He could've told Catie that he understood, for the first time in his life, about the importance of family—the importance of loving someone else. But she was already pulled in too many different directions. "I can take you into town now, if you still want to go," he told her instead.

"I still want to go," she said. "Just give me a minute to get cleaned up."

He nodded, washed his own hands and scrubbed some water over his face in the bathroom off the office, then waited for her. She joined him a few minutes later.

"It's a beautiful bike." She ran her hands over the red lines painted along the black frame. It was vintage Harley and it *was* fucking beautiful... just like Catie.

"Yeah, she's hot and she's fast," he said. "We better go, before the store closes."

He handed her his helmet, and she didn't argue about putting it on. She climbed on behind him, wrapped her arms around his waist and pushed against him so he fit snugly between her spread legs.

He guided them down the windy side roads, past the swamps, and let it loose down the stretch of straight highway.

Wind in his hair, speed between his legs and a beautiful woman holding him. Suddenly, he couldn't think of any reason this wasn't right.

He'd already told her that his life was about survival, about not looking past the next job or even, sometimes, the next hour, because it was easier. Safer. Which was a joke, coming from him, from someone who prided himself on the fact that *safe* was not a word in his vocabulary. Danger bred him young, whether he was escaping his father's wrath or joining the military or getting out and picking another job that threatened to end his life.

And the love of a good woman was supposed to take care of all of that, help him settle down? Save his soul, give him a clean slate and all that shit?

Big Red had thought so, had told him so, even though Bat always responded that he didn't want to hear it.

Bat wanted Catie to stay...so badly he could taste it. And he knew that with a few words of encouragement, she probably would. But then he'd never know if she stayed because she was too scared to try to live her dream. And if things didn't work out, would she blame him for holding her back, for making her stay in a town where she was haunted by memories? Would she eventually drift away?

It was the ultimate paradox: He'd finally found a woman he could see himself settling down with, and he had to let her go, let her fulfill her own dreams.

He heard her laugh, the sound floating over him in a rush of air, and then he pushed the bike faster. A light rain started, slicking down the roads and causing steam to rise around them in the late-afternoon heat.

Find a good woman to love you, boy. And then take it a step further and fall in love yourself.

Every time she looked at him, every time she let him inside her, another layer stripped off, until he was closer to that unburdened guy he'd always wanted to be, the one Big Red had always joked was hiding deep inside Bat's gruff exterior.

When you fall, you're gonna fall hard, boy.

Who you callin' boy, old man?

I'll call you man when you earn the title.

That conversation had happened the same night Bat's face was slashed open, because he'd stepped in front of an angry patron who was threatening to cut Big Red. Big Red had taken him to the ER to get him stitched up, all the while calling him a damned fool for stepping into someplace he didn't belong. And then he'd given Bat the bike, refused to take any money from him and headed up to Chattanooga to what was supposed to have been his final job.

Yeah, Bat was still working on becoming the man Big Red knew he could be.

"I need you," Catie had said when they'd gotten back from the store with her supplies. And now Bat was lying in the center of the bed, pillows arranged around him so he was leaning back comfortably. The light rain had turned steady and hard and it slammed the new roof of the Bon Temps, where they were dry and cool under the fans in the bedroom.

He'd shucked all his clothes at her request, save for the bandanna, which she'd told him to keep wrapped around his hair.

He'd protested that he had work to do, but she'd insisted. "The bar's closed tonight. It's the perfect time."

And he'd given in, because he'd hated seeing her sad earlier, hated that he'd had a part in it. Now the light in her eyes was back, and he wasn't going to be the one to put it out.

She told him that the work would be a little slower, that she wanted to get the skin textures, that she needed him to be in the room with her for that.

She told him that it was for her final piece in the collection.

He didn't know why the word *final* made his gut twist, but he quickly pushed it out of his mind. He'd been aroused the entire ride to and from the store—the vibration from the bike tended to do that, and now that's what he focused on.

It was what Catie focused on as well. It was as if she didn't know where to look—his face or between his legs, and she spent time gazing at both, the way she had in the mirror that night. It made his cock harden even more.

There was something completely decadent about lying in

bed in the early evening, with a woman staring at you, posing you . . . wanting you.

Damn, he liked it.

"I thought we were both going to work, Catie *chere*?" He heard the huskiness in his own voice, his skin prickling from the cool air of the overhead fan

"We are. You're already so hard. Touch yourself for me, Bat."

He slid a hand down his stomach, didn't take his eyes off her as he made contact with his cock. He stroked his palm slowly up and down his shaft. As much as he wanted her mouth on him, the look on her face was reason enough to keep going at it alone. At least for now.

Her eyes moved between him and the sketch pad, the pastels barely making any sound on the page, her bottom lip held lightly between her teeth. Her nipples were hard underneath the shirt she wore, her cheeks flushed and her body practically vibrated while she stood in place.

Barely keeping it together himself, he let his own rough fingers brush the head of his cock, rubbed his thumb over the leaking slit and spread it around as Catie sucked in a sharp breath.

Yeah, she liked that, liked watching as he fisted himself, hard and fast for a few seconds, until his body was covered with a thin sheen of sweat and the pre-cum oozed. He spread it on his palm, used it as a lubricant and let the friction of his hand move the thin, soft layer of skin that covered what felt like a fucking steel rod between his legs.

"I want to put this inside you, Catie. In your mouth, your pussy . . . You're wet, aren't you?"

She inhaled a sharp breath, nodded as he bucked against his own palm, his hips rocking off the mattress.

"Christ, I'm not going to be able to hold out for you if you keep looking at me like that."

"Please . . . you look so amazing. I want you to make it last." Her words washed over him like a hot breeze, and his hips pumped with a mind of their own.

He squeezed the base of his cock, tried to hold the impending orgasm at bay even as his balls tightened and pulled close to his body. "What do I get in return, *chere*?"

Catie was definitely going to give him something in return, but for right now, watching Bat grind against his palm was the most sensual thing she'd ever seen.

He was so big—when he was fully aroused, he seemed massive, his cock swelling well beyond his large fist, the head red, engorged, and she squeezed her thighs together as her sex throbbed in time with his long strokes.

She knew what he'd feel like if she dropped everything, went to the bed and took him inside of her. It would be a long, slow stretch of the ring of muscle, a pinch and a burn as she settled in on his shaft.

One hand continued to draw, furiously now, while the other drifted up to her breast. She drew the shirt away from one breast and touched her nipple, taking it between her fingers, heard Bat moan, *Oh fuck,* and knew—just knew that it was because of her.

She stroked a thumb over her nipple, flicked it lightly with a nail, the way Bat did when he wanted to start things up again, usually after an intense session that left them breathless. And she tried to concentrate on the paper in front of her, watching the way the dark blond hair dusted a pattern over his strong forearms and spread across his chest lightly between his nipples.

He continued to slow his strokes down, had thrown his head back and bared his teeth. His breathing was quick—

short, ragged breaths—and he didn't bother to try to hold back his moans.

She hadn't known it would be like this, look like this. The scent of sex and man filled the room, invaded her senses, until she was sure she could actually feel the arousal surround her, could reach out and touch it in the air. It was intoxicating, more so than the tequila she'd drunk with him last night. Every time she was with him, it grew even more so.

"Spread your legs wider," she instructed softly and he did it, though he seemed to be barely listening, on another plane, where only his pleasure existed.

It was exactly what she'd wanted. He even reached down with his free hand, began to fondle his own balls, as she watched, mouth open.

He finally picked his head up off the pillow to stare at her, his light green eyes darker than she'd ever seen them, like this was bringing out some kind of wildness inside him, stripping him down to another layer of raw, animal lust.

She gave up on the drawing, studied him instead, the textures, the way the light played off his skin, emphasizing the golden-hued, rich tones. One knee was bent up and lazily falling to the side, the other straight and relaxed; his whole body was relaxed and tense at the same time, and she watched the hard muscles of his abs contract with each stroke of his cock.

"Catie, *bebe,* you want me to come like this?" he asked, his drawl thick like hot syrup, and no, she didn't want that—she wanted to taste him, the way she hadn't been able to the other morning when Bat was so intent on her orgasm.

She moved quickly, was between his legs in seconds, her mouth covering the head of his penis, her fingers digging into his hips as though she could control his movements. But he was beyond reason now, rocking into her mouth as she swirled her tongue around and then took him in as deeply as she could.

He was trying to hold out—his hands twisting in her hair, which had fallen loose around his thighs—but he couldn't. He came, a salty, warm mixture that tasted just the way she thought it would. And after she milked him, held him in her mouth while his hips stopped moving, she realized he was still hard.

She climbed onto him without thinking, moving from pure instinct and lust, sheathing him inside her. She vaguely heard him mention a condom, but she was too far gone to care.

Her sex made greedy, sucking noises as she put her palms flat to his chest in order to give herself the leverage to take him, hard and fast, using short movements at first. Gradually, she deepened her own thrusts and pushed back so his cock hit her clit at just the right angle, his shaft so deeply inside her womb, it ached.

He watched her, his hands lightly on her hips, his mouth wet. Both their bodies were slicked with sweat and she was out of control, wild, the way he'd been.

He looked at her as if he loved it—as if, maybe, he could actually love her. Whether or not it was a trick of light didn't matter now. Here, on top of him, anything was possible, even Bat loving her.

The tightening spiral of her orgasm started in her belly, spread outward like a fever until she was clamping down on him, feeling him spill inside of her as she collapsed on his chest.

His strong arms wrapped around her within seconds, and he was murmuring sweet things in her ear, all the things she needed to hear from him, wanted to hear.

Bat was in the storeroom later that night, hauling out the final boxes, when he heard the knocking at the main door of the closed bar.

His body still felt loose, even now, after he and Catie had finally uncurled from each other, and he couldn't keep the stupid smile off his face.

One look toward the front of the bar helped with that immediately.

Terrell Johnson was at the front door of the bar. Catie stood in the doorway, arms crossed as if she could block him from entering.

"I'd like to speak with Bat," he said.

"It's all right, Catie." Bat was already behind her, urging her to move aside so Terrell could enter. "What can I do for you, *Officer*?"

"Evening, Bat." Terrell strolled inside, put a hand on the refinished bar and ran it over the smooth wood. "Things are looking good around here."

"I know you didn't come here to talk about the Bon Temps." Bat's gut tightened, the way it always had before his father started an argument with his ma, the way it had gotten when his Marine unit was called into combat, the way it got when he'd first seen Catie Jane—the element of fear combined with adrenaline, mixing until he wasn't sure which end was up. "I'm listening."

"Your name's been cleared in the murder of Darren White."

"You sound less than happy, Terrell."

The man ignored him, and Bat knew how much this grated on the police officer who'd once run as wild as Bat himself had. "Seems Darren owed a lot of money to a guy named Billy Thompson. Thompson was in the bar that night, heard the threats, did a little investigating on you and found the perfect scapegoat."

Bat's first thought, beyond the relief of being cleared, was how much work there still was to do around the Bon Temps. Drug dealers and loan sharks were nothing new around bars, but this place was overrun, and they could be worse than the outright brawlers. They worked from a place of intimidation and they were often harder to weed out of an environment.

Catie couldn't afford to be here for that long; he couldn't afford to be with her for that long. Because once that happened, he had a sinking feeling he wasn't going to be able to let her go.

"Bat, didn't you hear what Terrell said? That's great news." Catie tugged at his arm and smiled up at him, and yeah, it was great news.

Great.

He would make it great news for her, however that had to happen.

CHAPTER Nine

Three days had passed since Bat's name had been cleared: the Bon Temps was back to business as usual and Bat came up to bed at the end of the night looking worse than ever—the fights had seemed to escalate, and even though he'd assured her that this was normal, she still worried.

But since that evening when he'd lain alone in the bed, stroking himself for both her pleasure and her art, in a session that turned molten and caused her to blush every time she thought about it or worked on the picture, he hadn't waited in bed in the morning.

She'd been painting from memory, from the sketches, had even branched out from just drawing Bat and also worked from the pictures she'd found in her uncle's personal effects.

It still bothered her that Bat was no longer willing to

pretend to sleep in the mornings, to pose for her in the early sunlight that came through the shades.

She had to talk to him. About everything. About the fact that her feelings were something she'd always been able to control . . . until now.

He was sitting in the office, going over the books. He did things like that effortlessly. It took her all day to reconcile the columns and handle payroll; he handled everything with ease, including her.

He looked up when she walked in. "Hey, I've got some news."

"What's that?" For some reason, her heart thudded in what felt like an irregular pattern, and a strange sense of foreboding washed over her.

"It looks like you'll be getting out of here sooner than you think, and on your way to art school—once you agree to this offer," he said.

"I don't understand—" Before she finished her sentence, he handed her an envelope. She opened it and looked at the check inside, a check that she could only assume was for a bid on the Bon Temps. "That's more than I thought it would go for. But I haven't even put this place on the market yet. How would anyone know?"

"This guy approached Keith about the sale, and Keith pointed him in my direction. Figured you wouldn't mind. So, if you say yes and get in touch with the lawyer for the estate, we can start the transfer of the sale papers."

She nodded, still clutching the paper. "I was just thinking . . . Well, everything's not running smoothly . . . You said yourself it's going to take a while."

"New owner wants to keep me on. So I'll be staying until the job's done."

"So the new owner wants the Bon Temps restored."

"Yes, he does."

"I still have to pay you."

He was shaking his head. "No, you don't. It's all right, Catie *chere*. Take the offer and you can move on, back to art school. You can do what you need to do."

Her stomach clenched, when really she should've been ecstatic. "Bat, I think... I think I want to stay." The words came out more softly than she intended, and she almost couldn't look him in the eye.

His response was quick. And not what she was hoping for. "You're scared, Catie *chere*. But you need to leave this place and do what you originally planned. You'll never forgive yourself if you don't."

Wouldn't she? Hadn't she already forgiven herself, and maybe her family too?

She faced him, prepared to push harder, to fight, although she wasn't sure exactly what she was fighting for. She'd never thought she'd be one of those women to fall this hard, this fast. She wanted to blame it on the stress of the situation, but she couldn't dismiss her feelings that easily. "It's just that... I'm feeling things, Bat. Things I didn't expect to feel. For you. For us."

A look crossed his face, one she couldn't quite place. "I think it's just the heat." He pointed to the check in her hands. "Call the lawyer."

She pushed back the anger that threatened like the hot, fat tears she wasn't going to be able to hide. She headed up the stairs, but Bat was quicker, caught her arm as she was halfway up.

She refused to turn completely, even though the stairway was well shadowed.

"Catie, wait."

"For what?" She hated the pain in her voice, hated the fact that she'd let herself get pulled in over her head. The need refueled itself daily—every time she looked at him or he touched her or spoke, every time she pictured herself straddling his lap on one of the bar stools, running her fingers through his hair while he played with her breasts and whispered, *Just let go,* chere, and *Don't forget to call my name, I love it when you yell my name when you come.*

"Please, Catie. Wait."

She closed her eyes; the tears leaked out anyway. The only thing she could stop was the sob—she swallowed hard and it was gone. "Leave me alone, Bat. You're getting just what you wanted."

"You have no idea what I want. Turn around and look at me."

"I don't have to follow your orders." She jerked her arm out of his grasp, and he let her, even walked down a few steps to put distance between them.

He stood in the shadows at the bottom of the stairs, unmoving. She could've sworn his Adam's apple bobbed with a hard swallow of his own. But maybe, just maybe, like everything else, it was simply a trick of light.

She wiped the tears from her cheeks impatiently.

"I thought the sale was what you wanted. I thought it would make you happy. Why are you crying?"

She shook her head, not willing to tell him now that she'd never expected to feel like this, and she hated herself for wanting more, for not letting what Bat was offering be enough.

"I made you a promise, Catie, and that was to turn this bar around," he said, his drawl softer than normal.

"Right, I forgot—no other promises. No commitments. No strings. Freedom of the open road." Her chest actually hurt from holding back. "But you make me feel things. Things I didn't want or expect to feel. You gave me back my art. You've given me back *me*."

"That's good, isn't it?"

"I thought so. But it's not enough."

"I've known you for less than a week."

"And you already know that things can never go further than this?" she asked. "Because I don't know that. No, more, I don't believe that. I know there have been a lot of other women in your past. But I also don't see any of them here with you. You don't talk about them."

"No, you're right, I don't."

"Would you talk about me, Bat? Think about me after you've left this place? Will I linger in your memories when you're riding your Harley to the next job, and the next? Will you think about me when you've got another woman lying in your arms?"

"Yeah, I think I will, Catie *chere*. I think I'll never be able to forget you."

His answer made her throat tighten, her belly ache. "But you're going to try."

"But I'm going to try," he agreed. "You've got a big future ahead of you. You've got dreams to fulfill."

"What about you? What about your dreams?"

"You've got to stop worrying about my dreams. You've got to stop looking back, and keep moving forward. You can always come back, Bayou Rouge will always be here, but your other opportunities may not be."

"You won't be," she whispered, and he didn't correct her.

"Hey, Bat, we're ready to open the doors!" Jase's voice floated over from the front door. She'd completely lost track of the time, the way she'd tended to the past week. She'd forgotten other people were here besides her and Bat. Forgot about the real world and responsibilities.

"I've got to go. For now. I'll see you at the end of the night, if you still want that," he said.

Yes, she still wanted that, couldn't stop wanting that.

"I'll be waiting for you," she told him, then turned and

walked up the stairs. She went into the loft and locked the door, stared down at the check she still held in her hands and wished she had the will to rip it up.

Even if you stay, Bat's eventually going to leave.

When she studied the sketches she'd made every morning without fail, she noticed the progression. He was opening up to her, little by little. She noted it in the way his face wasn't stark black on white, but rather shades of gray, thanks to the smudged charcoal. He was telling her things despite himself.

Maybe telling her the only way he could.

Catie had left her sketchbook in the office. She must've come down unnoticed during the height of the craziness in the bar, and had left it on the desk.

He'd forced himself to page through it, barely recognized himself on the stark, white pages, his body sprawled in various stages of sleep. She'd captured the newer bumps and bruises, care of the Bon Temps, and the old scars that he could categorize by date, year and weapon.

He looked peaceful, even though they didn't spend much time sleeping. But the hours he did spend in REM were the best he'd known.

She'd captured him content.

There were other pictures too, him in various stages of get-the-fuck-out mode over the past few nights during the Bon Temps cleanup. She'd been sneaking into the bar, when she'd promised him she wouldn't.

Yeah, there were things she knew, but there was one thing she didn't—and couldn't—know. He had a promise to keep; he had to let Catie do what she needed to do.

It was after two in the morning before he walked up the

stairs and quietly opened the door. Catie was still awake—wide awake, and working on her art.

"Hey, do you feel like taking a ride?" he asked her.

She looked up from her canvas, and she smiled, the smile that could easily break his heart, and she nodded.

There was no mention of what had transpired that afternoon, as if she'd accepted that she was leaving. Just like he'd wanted.

And once they were on the bike and he pushed faster, harder along the old roads that surrounded the bayou swamps, he could forget how big the ache really was.

He pulled off the road, slightly into the swamplands, where they'd be hidden from any passing cars. When he cut the engine and put the kickstand down, he shifted his weight and got off the bike. She eased one leg around so she sat facing him. Waiting.

Yeah, the next move was up to him.

"I want you to know—need you to know—there's never been anyone special for me, Catie. Never."

"For me either. Until now." She held a hand over his heart, the flat of her palm warm against his chest, like it could burn a hole through his T-shirt.

"Don't. Please. You have to go, Catie. If this week has meant anything at all to you, you have to leave this place. I don't want to be the one who holds you back from anything." He didn't wait for an answer, kissed her, his tongue sweeping her mouth. She responded in kind, her mouth hot and wet, ready for him, even as she yanked his shirt up in a frantic motion.

He pulled back and let her pull it off him, though she wouldn't risk taking hers off here. Instead, he slid a hand under her shirt and caressed her breasts, loving the way her body arced toward him as she responded to his touch.

He tugged her shorts down, eased her back against the seat, making sure to keep his hands on the bike and her.

She gripped his biceps to keep her balance, and he lost all sense of his, vaguely aware that his feet were still somehow on the ground. He'd unzipped his jeans, readied a condom and rolled it on himself, quickly.

He took her in a single stroke. Her legs spread around him, ankles locked around his waist. Her moans echoed in the still air, mingled with the sounds of life on the bayou, and he breathed her in.

The bike began to shake as he took her, an urgency building, the way it had all week.

Steam rose off their bodies at the effort—fast and furious. When Catie let go first, her orgasm tightened around him, sending him to spiral down after her in a rush of blinding pleasure in her wet heat.

Later, lying in bed, Catie wrapped around him still, her hand caressing his chest, he felt both content and restless.

He'd taken them for a long ride on the bike after they'd recovered and gotten dressed, just her body clinging to his, the heavy vibrations between his legs drowning out any thoughts.

She hadn't mentioned anything at all—not yet. But when she sighed and turned her face to look at him, his gut tightened.

"I need to tell you something."

"Okay."

"When I first got here, I felt trapped. I was trapped. And now..."

"I thought you were serious about heading back to the city and to art school."

"I thought you said I didn't need school."

"Sometimes I talk too goddamned much." He thought about the way she looked in the early morning, standing at the easel she'd bought, clutching the palette close to her chest like she was embracing the colors. One brush between her teeth, the other working across the canvas, she'd stretch up and he'd watch the stretch of muscle along her calf and thigh, the peek of her bare bottom from under the T-shirt she'd pulled on hurriedly before she missed what she called the best light. "You're not backing out on the sale, are you?" he asked.

She shut her eyes tightly for a second, and he held his breath, because *fuck,* there was no good answer.

"I'm going to leave, Bat," she said finally. "If you're staying on to work, I'll trust you here until the transfer of the title goes through."

I'll trust you here.

There was nothing left to say now.

CHAPTER *Ten*

It took another full week before Catie felt strong enough to leave. She'd called the lawyer the morning after the offer and had him get the transfer of papers ready. And she'd continued to share Bat's bed, as if she was staying put—clinging to him every night and neither of them saying a thing about her leaving.

"I'll take care of everything. All you have to do is sign the papers and FedEx them back to me when they're ready," the lawyer told her now on the phone. She gripped the receiver so hard, she was sure she'd leave dents. She had dreaded this day.

"So I don't need to stay and wait for the papers, then?"

"No, you can do the final signing from New York, if you trust the guy who's taking care of the bar now."

Catie trusted Bat with everything, except maybe her heart. And it was too late now. She had to get out of here before she dug herself in impossibly deep. Before she had a chance to beg, to embarrass herself even more.

She'd come into town with two bags, and that's all she left with. She even left behind the pictures of her uncle and his friends. All but one, the one she handed to Flo over the counter at the diner.

"Sit down, honey. Let me get you something to eat," Flo said.

Catie shook her head. "I've got a cab waiting to take me to the bus station."

"The sale couldn't have happened this quickly."

"The new owner's paying cash. My uncle's lawyer's taking care of the paperwork, and Bat's agreed to stay on to oversee things until the bar is under control. The Bon Temps is in good hands with him."

"So were you—or so it seemed," Flo mused.

"Yeah, so it seemed."

"Honey, why don't you stay—"

"He doesn't want me to stay. He doesn't want me at all." To her horror, she felt the tears rise up. Flo came out from behind the counter and hugged her, and it was so nice to have someone care about her. Worry about her.

"He might've told you what to do, but that doesn't change the way you feel inside, Catie," Flo said.

"What can I do, Flo? He's right, I'd be giving up something I've always wanted to do . . . and it's only been a month. Less than two weeks with Bat. But . . ."

"Feels like a lifetime," Flo finished.

"I didn't even say good-bye to him. Couldn't. I snuck out when he went to the lumberyard," Catie admitted, although she wasn't sure why she'd left the way she had. She hadn't left anything behind—not a sketch, not a phone number or an address. Just memories.

"I'm grabbing your bags and sending the cab away. You

and I, we need to talk, sugar. And then you can make up your mind about what you're going to do," Flo told her firmly.

The woman wasn't going to take no for an answer, so Catie sat down at the counter and wiped her face and let Flo drag her bags into the diner and put them in the back room.

"Come with me, Catie."

Catie sighed, followed Flo out the back door of the diner. There was a man there working on a vintage Harley.

"This is my nephew, Joey," Flo explained, as Joey continued to wipe the rims with polish, pausing only to nod hello.

Bat's vintage Harley. "Why is Bat's bike here? Is it being fixed?"

"It's my hog now," Joey said with a smile of pride.

"He'd never sell his bike," Catie said.

The guy shrugged. "I've got the title. She's a real beauty. I told him that it was a shame he had to let it go, but he said he needed some fast money."

Her mouth dropped, and she knew in that moment exactly what he'd done. And why. "I'll be back for my things, Flo."

"Where are you going, honey?" Flo asked with a smile, even though she knew exactly which direction Catie's feet were headed.

"I'm going home," Catie called over her shoulder as she walked slowly down the street to the bar.

She was done running.

Bat hadn't thought Catie would leave so soon, and without saying good-bye. That was *his* patented move, and the weight of her decision hung heavily on him.

The pillows and the sheets still smelled like her, the scent of sweet gardenias that he'd noted their first night together.

She hadn't even left him a single sketch. Although part of him knew it was better that way, better to make a clean break of things, he couldn't help but hang his head and just stare at the floor for a few minutes.

When he looked up, Catie was standing in the doorway.

"What are you doing here? You're going to miss your bus."

She walked slowly toward him, not saying anything. It was only when she ended up in his lap, straddling him, that she finally said, "I'm done running. What about you?"

He opened his mouth, ready to tell her that he was out of here soon, that she needed to get back to New York, go to school. What came out instead was, "Louisiana's got some good art schools."

She smiled. "I know. But I can't take your money, Bat. Not that way."

"I want the bar, Catie *chere*. Want you too."

"But your bike..."

"The guy who sold it to me would've understood. Trust me on that."

"I couldn't think of anyone better to own my uncle's bar."

He felt his mouth tug into a smile. "We're right back where we both started."

"No, not right back. We're farther along than that. I'm falling hard for you, Bat. Falling in love with you."

"Catie, I've never...never told anyone that I've fallen for them. Because I never have."

"Me neither." She smiled, didn't push to hear the words from him. They were there, lurking just under the surface, and she seemed content with that. Seemed to know that they were in his grasp.

"So what do we do now?"

"We take it slow. See where the road leads us. Because I've got a whole lot more paper to fill," she mused. "If you're up for it."

Yeah, he was up for it, up for wherever this new chapter of his life took him, and his Catie *chere*.

He was finally home.

ABOUT THE AUTHORS

EDEN BRADLEY has been writing since she could hold a pen in her hand. When not writing, you'll find her wandering museums, cooking, eating, shopping, and reading everything she can get her hands on. Eden lives in Southern California with a small menagerie and the love of her life.

SYDNEY CROFT is the alter ego of two published authors who came together to blend their very different writing interests into adventurous tales of erotic paranormal fiction. The authors behind Sydney Croft live in different states and communicate almost entirely through e-mail, though they often get together for conferences and book signings. Both Sydneys share a passion for chocolate, coffee, and writing, and when not working on Croft novels, they are working on their own personal projects. You can learn more about Sydney Croft at www.SydneyCroft.com.

STEPHANIE TYLER has long since given up trying to control her characters, especially the Navy SEAL alpha males, and today she writes military romance. She also writes paranormal erotic romance with a military twist with coauthor Larissa Ione under the pen name Sydney Croft. Stephanie lives in New York with her husband and daughter.

Read on for a sneak peek of
Eden Bradley's seductive new novel

FORBIDDEN FRUIT

Coming from Delta
in November 2008

FORBIDDEN FRUIT

on sale November 2008

Chapter One

Mia Rose Curry looked up at the crowded classroom, at the rows of seats, full of expectant faces, at the others crowding in the door.

"This class is full," she told them. "If you're not already registered and you'd like to fill out a card to be put on the waiting list, please go to the registration office."

"This class is always full," a voice muttered from somewhere in the vicinity of the door.

Mia smiled. It was true. The Alternative Sexuality class she taught at San Francisco State was in high demand each semester. The students mostly came in looking for a cheap thrill and an easy grade, but she made them work for it. Made them do research, write papers. Tried to teach them something about the sociological effects of culture on sexuality. A few of them even learned something. And she always learned from watching them. From watching how they responded to the things they talked about in class, to the demonstrations, to the films she showed them. She studied her students as much as they studied the class assignments. She couldn't help it. As a sociology professor, people were endlessly fascinating to her. Her whole life was about studying people. Trying to understand them. Especially herself.

She looked over her classroom, making a quick assessment of each new student. She could usually tell which of them would work hard, participate in discussions. Who would hide in the back of the room and sneer. Who would leave as soon as any really controversial material came up.

Her eyes moved across the front row, drifting from face to face, and stopped cold.

God, he was too beautiful, this young man. Her student, she had to remind herself. A bit older than most of the others, maybe, but still...

Tawny skin the color of coffee with plenty of cream, dark, curling hair tipped with gold, as though he'd been in the sun. A close-cropped goatee framing a full, lush mouth. And the most startling eyes, a clear, crystal gray that contrasted with his dusky skin. Oh, yes, too beautiful to be believed. And he was looking right at her, those clear gray eyes intense, focused. She shivered.

Your student.

She tore her gaze away, but not before she caught his quick smile. Every bit as shockingly beautiful as the rest of him.

Pulling in a deep breath, she forced herself to concentrate on her job: evaluating her classroom, putting her notes in order. She had to command herself not to look at him so she could begin her opening lecture, but even knowing he was there, at the edge of her vision, made the back of her neck heat up.

She took a sip from her water bottle and began. "Welcome, everyone, to Alternative Sexuality. In this class we'll study the various avenues of sexuality which differ from what many might consider to be 'the norm.' We will be covering some controversial material. Some of you may even find it offensive. Here is a short list of some of the subjects we'll address."

She moved to the front of her desk and leaned back against it, watching the students as she spoke. "We'll discuss a variety of fetishes and alternative practices including foot fetishes, cross-dressing, bondage and mummification, domination and submission, pain and sensation play, leather, rubber and latex fetishes, food fetishes, sploshing, which is a fetish involving various kinds of liquids, bestiality, amputee fetish, exhibitionism, voyeurism, infantilism, and perhaps a few more."

There were a few requisite snickers from the back of the room. Certainly nothing she hadn't dealt with before. And she was entirely comfortable with her subject.

"Many of you might think of the people who practice these forms of sexuality as freaks, and I'll admit I find some of these practices repulsive, even harmful, and we'll discuss that as well. But I'm going to ask you to keep an open mind. To put aside any revulsion you may feel and consider these subjects with an objective, scientific perspective. To view these practices as a response to the person's environment." She put her notes down and looked at her students, trying to catch an eye here and there. "This is what we're going to really focus on. What causes people to have these yearnings? And are fetishes a healthy response to certain stimuli? Or are they a psychological defect?"

"What do you think, Professor Curry?"

Ah, God, it was him. The beautiful one. And he was watching her again, so intently. Was it possible she was imagining it? She had to draw in a breath, pretend he was just any other student. She would question why he had such an effect on her later.

"I think... what's your name?"

"Jagger. Jagger James."

"I think, Jagger, that it depends on the person, the fetish, and what it was in their lives that caused this response. Each situation must be evaluated on an individual basis."

"So you don't assume fetishes are a neurotic or even psychosocial tendency, necessarily?"

If they were, she was in very deep trouble.

"Not necessarily, no."

He smiled, and her legs felt as though they were suffused with a warm liquid. Melting. Yes, like melted chocolate. Milk chocolate. The shade of his skin.

Stop it!

She tucked a strand of her dark hair behind her ear. "This is exactly the kind of idea I want you to throw out the window until we explore the subject in detail. Here, we're going to learn to stop making the usual snap judgments, rid ourselves of preconceived notions, and learn what truly goes on in a person's mind." She pushed off her desk and strolled across the front of the room, avoiding his gaze. Still, a small shiver raced over her skin when she walked past him. "We'll do research, assess data, witness certain events here in class, discuss others. And we'll have an opportunity to talk with some of the people who practice these things in their everyday lives. Please take a look at the class syllabus now to review the in-class activities. Then think about whether or not this is something you can handle. But I want you all to push yourselves a bit. To see these things, talk to these people, ask questions, and try to stretch your boundaries. To explore your own response to whatever the subject might be. To make yourself the subject of your own sociological study."

"Is that what you do, Professor Curry?"

Him again. Jagger. This time she looked him right in the eye. "Every day of my life."

Read on for a sneak peek of
Sydney Croft's dangerously hot

SEDUCED BY THE STORM

Coming from Delta
in August 2008

SEDUCED BY THE STORM

on sale August 2008

Chapter One

Faith Black had been beaten, drugged and imprisoned, but none of that scared her. No, what frightened her to the core was the man confined with her. Chained to an improvised medieval rack and bare from the waist up, he lay on his back, arms over his head, his incredible chest marred by bruises and a deep laceration that extended from his left pec to his right hip.

He might have been rendered immobile, but he was in no way helpless.

His weapon, far more dangerous than the telekinesis—to her, at least—was his overpowering sexuality, a force that tugged her toward him, made her burn with need despite their grave situation.

Head pounding from the brutal blow to the cheek, she pushed to her feet and padded close, her nudity barely registering. She'd been stripped naked while unconscious, her clothes tossed into one corner of the windowless, steel-walled room. The weak yellow light from the single bulb emphasized the deep amber of Wyatt's eyes, no longer green, as he settled into the transitional period many telekinetics experienced when their powers flared up. The air in the room stilled, and the chain around his right ankle began to rattle.

"Don't," she said quietly.

He shifted his head to look at her as though he hadn't realized she'd regained consciousness. "Faith." His voice was rough, as haunted as his gaze. "I didn't tell him. I swear."

"Tell who what?"

"Your boyfriend. I didn't tell him about us. He knew."

"Sean's not my boyfriend," she said, and Wyatt cocked a dark eyebrow like he didn't believe her. "And I know you didn't say anything."

She knew, because she'd been the one to spill the beans that she and Wyatt had been sleeping together.

Wyatt's head lolled back so he was staring up at the steel beams crisscrossing the ceiling. The corded tendons in his neck strained and tightened as he swallowed. "I'm sorry I got you into this."

"You didn't."

A growl rumbled in his throat. "I seduced you. I shouldn't have. Not here. Not on the platform where he could find out."

She inhaled him into her, the masculine scent that threw her off balance whenever he came near. No, she couldn't blame him for anything, least of all her out-of-control desire for him. He was here to do a job, just like she was, which meant getting the assignment done by any means necessary.

"I'm not here because Sean is jealous." Though Sean was, furiously so, but Wyatt didn't need to know that.

"Then why?"

Dragging her gaze from the strong, ruggedly handsome features of his face, she let her mind focus on a realm of existence most people never saw. Instantly, Wyatt's aura became visible, a shifting, undulating layer of light around his body. And God, something was wrong, so wrong she nearly gasped.

Wyatt radiated power, so his aura should reflect the same. Instead, it stretched thin around his body like an ill-fitting secondhand coat, ridden with weak spots and holes, like he'd suffered repeated supernatural attacks. She could repair the damage, but her efforts would amount to little more than a patch job on his psychic garment. Replenishing his aura, renewing it . . . that only he could do, through healthy living and mental wholeness.

For now, she concentrated on the cut on his chest, worked her power into a psi needle and thread that knit the wound together. The muscles in his abs rippled, carved so deeply that they cast shadows on one another. She knew how they felt beneath her touch, how they flexed when they rubbed against her belly, and she had to clench her hands to keep from reaching for him.

The wound closed in a whisper of sound, and Wyatt sucked in a harsh breath. "Jesus. You're a fucking agent."

His eyes glowed amber again, and the chains binding him rattled.

"Please don't," she said, letting her psychic fingers slide south on his body. "Let me. Follow my lead."

He moaned and then grit his teeth against the sensations she sent streaming into his groin.

"I'm going to need you to scream, Wyatt. Scream like I'm killing you."

His shaft began to swell with each of her virtual caresses deep inside his body, and his eyes flashed green fire. "You are, Faith." His voice rumbled, dark, dangerous. "I've been through the gates of hell and survived, but somehow, I think you're going to be the devil who takes me down."

Chapter Two

TWO DAYS EARLIER

Wyatt Kennedy was a dead man, and other than a few problems, like being unable to use his credit cards, it hadn't been so bad.

Of course, he'd already been declared dead once before, a long time ago, so he knew the drill. Lay low, use cash, watch your back.

When he'd dropped off the face of the earth years earlier, he'd had ACRO—the Agency for Covert Rare Operatives, of which he was one—on his side. ACRO had recruited him, changed his name and killed him off so he wouldn't face a murder rap for the death of his half brother.

Which, for the record, he still wasn't sure whether or not he was responsible for, thanks to a memory lapse that had lasted for the last five years, despite ACRO's best efforts otherwise.

This time around at playing dead, he got to keep the same first name, at least. The most important part of being dead this go-around was letting everyone at ACRO think he'd been killed—for reasons he didn't quite understand, but when orders were given, orders were followed. The rest of the world, and Itor Corp—ACRO's major rival—had never known Wyatt had existed anyway, and he knew the mission he was dealing with—finding the weather machine that Itor Corp had built and hidden on an offshore oil platform, was some serious, *we plan on destroying the world* shit.

Read on for a sneak peek of

HARD TO HOLD

the first novel in
Stephanie Tyler's sexy new series
Coming from Bantam in 2009

HARD TO HOLD

on sale in 2009

"We want to be in a situation under maximum pressure, maximum intensity, and maximum danger. When it's shared with others, it provides a bond which is stronger than any tie that can exist." —SEAL TEAM SIX OFFICER

Prologue

Lieutenant Junior Grade Jake Hansen had already muttered the word *motherfucker* as many times as he possibly could in under a minute's time. He'd used it as a noun and then a verb, planned on continuing to think of new and inventive ways to utilize it in his vocabulary until his Navy SEAL teammate and best friend finally told him to shut up so he could *motherfucking* bandage Jake's bleeding biceps.

It was a flesh wound, but it still hurt—and bled—like hell. Not that he'd ever admit that first part. And there was no way he was stopping, although Nick hadn't bothered to suggest that. Probably because Nick had been running with a stress fracture along his shin for the better part of the afternoon, at the tail end of a mission that had gone totally to shit after the first five minutes.

Those first five minutes happened three days ago. Now, they were intent on getting the hell out of Djibouti, Africa, and the water—and the point of convergence with their team sharpshooter, Senior Chief and CO—was only five miles away.

"Just Rebel fire—not aimed at us." Nick spoke quietly into the mic attached to his headset as the gunfire continued to pop, lighting the backdrop of the night sky to their west.

"Could've fooled me," Jake muttered, his anger aimed more at himself for letting the bullet catch him than at the random firefight. This country was full of small skirmishes and all-out wars, but none of that had been SEAL Team Twelve's concern this trip. They'd been forced to scatter to complete their mission to secure the missing equipment and the intel it contained. Now they were headed home.

Nick was still listening to the voice on the other end of his headset, intently enough to make Jake switch on his own earpiece.

"... hostage reported ... one klick North ... seen and left for dead by the Rebels," the Team's Senior Chief was saying, although the line was breaking up fast.

"Who reported the hostage?" Jake asked.

"Source was verified reliable. Red Cross relief workers heard it from the refugees moving north. They were scared to stop and take her—didn't want to draw attention to the fact that she'd survived. She's American. Can you get there?"

"Confirmed. We can get there," Nick said.

Jake mentally traced the route—one mile back the way they came. Toward the line of fire. He and Nick began to hump it, weapons drawn and still listening to the report.

"... Senator Cresswell's daughter ... a doctor ... first name Isabelle, last name Markham ... thirty-one ... missing and believed kidnapped for seventy-two hours ..."

This way. Jake motioned as they cut through some thick underbrush and headed up a path off the main road. It was easy to see how they'd missed the small hut in the first place—it was completely camouflaged by brush and entirely invisible in the dark.

Trap? Nick motioned.

Jake walked the perimeter slowly while Nick followed, weapon drawn. No wires were apparent, and when they walked around the front, he saw the structure had no door.

Seen and left for dead. Jake's stomach had turned on hearing that atrocity, but the reality hit him like a punch to the gut when they actually found Dr. Isabelle Markham. All his doubts about the veracity of the report fell away as he and Nick moved forward into the darkened room. Nick took the sweep, speaking quietly into the mic, and Jake turned his off and dropped to his knees beside the prone body.

"Jesus," he whispered.

She lay on her stomach, hands tied behind her back, cheek to the dusty floor, her mouth gagged so she couldn't yell. Eyes closed. Pale. Naked. Gingerly, he brushed a hand down the back of her neck. She didn't stir, and he was frozen.

Nick knelt opposite him, his fingers on Isabelle's wrist. "There's a strong pulse," he said, before he turned to work on freeing her hands.

Jake untied the filthy gag and pulled it out of her mouth. She made a quick gasping sound but didn't wake up.

"Doesn't look like there's head trauma. We need to turn her, make sure she's not bleeding anywhere," Nick said. He threw the filthy ropes that had once bound her behind him as Jake unbuttoned his jacket, trying to ignore the fact that his fingers felt as if they were made of lead, and placed it over her where she lay. There was no way to put it on her fully without actually turning her and exposing her more.

He'd been in the military for eleven years—since he was fifteen—had seen shit both before and after his enlistment that would turn a man ugly or crazy or unemotional.

He'd gone none of those ways, no matter how hard others might argue, but nothing he'd ever seen or done had prepared him for this. Because, even though she was down, Isabelle Markham was not out. He could tell by the set of her shoulders, defiant, even in sleep or unconsciousness, could tell by the way her hands were bruised and her nails broken, because she'd fought back. She was still fighting, and he wasn't sure why that affected him so badly, but it did.

"Can she make the trip?" he asked Nick, who was assessing her facial area with a penlight, and at the sound of his voice, Isabelle stirred and finally opened her eyes. They were a dark hazel, her pupils dilated from fear and pain, and they locked onto his with a force he felt physically.

"Dr. Markham, you're safe. We're with the United States Navy, and we're going to get you out of here," he said, placed his hand lightly on her shoulder.

"Can't move me," she whispered, her voice breathless, as if it hurt to speak. "Not far."

"What's wrong?"

"Ribs... broken. Too close... to my lung," she managed. "Not safe."

"We need a vehicle to take her out of here."

Nick nodded his assent, then asked, "Ma'am, can we turn you?" even though she was staring up at Jake.

"Yes. Onto... right side," she whispered after a long moment, as though she realized they'd see her completely exposed.

She'd been through so much already, neither man could stand that she'd have to bear more humiliation. But the firefight was drawing closer, and Jake forced his emotions to lose to logic.

"Let's do it then. On my count," he said. "One, two, three."

He rolled Isabelle to her back as one unit by pushing simultaneously on her hip and shoulder, avoiding her side completely. Nick had already laid the jacket out underneath her, and Jake noted a dark bruise by her temple from a blow just hard enough to knock her out. Tears streaked her face, fresh ones, and her breathing was labored and still she held it together.